THE SECRET OF SANTA

Shiloh Ridge Ranch in Three Rivers, Book 4

LIZ ISAACSON

The Glover Family

Welcome to Shiloh Ridge Ranch! The Glover family is BIG, and sometimes it can be hard to keep track of everyone.

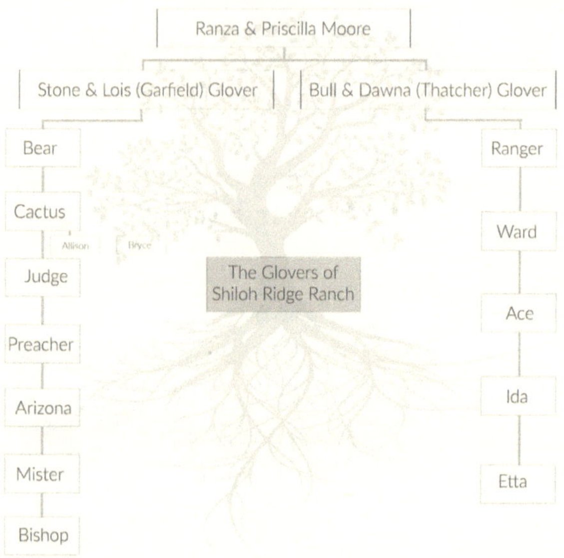

THERE IS A MORE DETAILED GRAPHIC HERE, ON MY website. (But it has spoilers! I made it as the family started to get really big, which happens fairly quickly, actually. It has all the couples (some you won't see for many more books), as well as a lot of the children they have or will have, through about Book 6. It might be easier for you to visualize, though.)

HERE'S HOW THINGS ARE RIGHT NOW:

Lois & Stone (deceased) Glover, 7 children, in age-order:

1. Bear (Sammy, wife / Lincoln (9), step-son, Stetson (new-born), son)

2. Cactus (Allison, ex-wife / Bryce, son (deceased))

3. Judge

4. Preacher

5. Arizona (dating Duke Rhinehart)

6. Mister

7. Bishop (Montana, fiancée / Aurora (16), step-daughter once they marry)

DAWNA & BULL (DECEASED) GLOVER, 5 CHILDREN, IN age-order:
1. Ranger (Oakley, wife)
2. Ward
3. Ace
4. Etta
5. Ida (dating Brady Burton)

BULL AND STONE GLOVER WERE BROTHERS, SO THEIR children are cousins. Ranger and Bear, for example, are cousins, and each the oldest sibling in their families.

THE GLOVERS KNOW AND INTERACT WITH THE WALKERS of Seven Sons Ranch. There's a lot of them too! Here's a little cheat sheet for you for the Walkers.

MOMMA & DADDY: PENNY AND GIDEON WALKER
    1. RHETT & EVELYN WALKER
    Son: Conrad
    Triplets: Austin, Elaine, and Easton

    2. JEREMIAH & WHITNEY WALKER
    Son: Jonah Jeremiah (JJ)
    Daughter: Clara Jean
    Son: Jason

    3. LIAM & CALLIE WALKER
    Daughter: Denise
    Daughter: Ginger

    4. TRIPP & IVORY WALKER
    Son: Oliver
    Son: Isaac

    5. WYATT & MARCY WALKER
    Son: Warren
    Son: Cole

Son: Harrison

6. SKYLER & MALLERY WALKER
Daughter: Camila

7. MICAH & SIMONE WALKER
Son: Travis (Trap)

THE GLOVERS KNOW AND INTERACT WITH THE SEVERAL OF the cowboys and their families at Three Rivers Ranch too... There's a lot going on in Three Rivers!

You'll see:

1. Squire and Kelly Ackerman

Mother / Father: Heidi (owns Ackermans bakery) / Frank

Son: Finn

Daughter: Libby

Son: Michael

Son: Samuel

2. PETE AND CHELSEA MARSHALL (CHELSEA IS SQUIRE'S sister)

4 sons:

Chapter One

A ce Glover ignored the knock on the front door of his house, though he sat in the office only a few paces away. He knew who it was, and he didn't want to talk to Bishop. Besides his brothers, his cousin was his best friend, but Ace didn't want to explain anything.

"I'm not going away," Bishop called through the front door. "I know this thing isn't locked, and I'm coming in if you don't come open the door."

Ace sighed and pressed pause on the video he'd watched four times already. He should've known he couldn't just leave the family party without someone noticing. Truth be told, there were a ton of people at the homestead, and he'd hoped and prayed that maybe, just maybe, he would be overlooked this one time.

"Just another prayer the Lord didn't answer," he muttered to himself. Louder, he called, "Come in then," and Bishop wasted no time entering the house. Three steps later, he appeared in the doorway of the office.

"What's going on?"

"Nothing," Ace said. "I just don't want to be there."

"You missed dinner."

That was saying something too, as Ace could barely boil water. His brother, whom he lived with, was a good cook, though, and there was always something to eat next door anyway.

Ace swiveled in the office chair he'd spent entirely too much money on. But he needed it for the computer gaming he participated in with Preacher, though they hadn't played in a couple of weeks now.

He smashed his cowboy hat further onto his head and avoided Bishop's eye. "I don't want to talk about it."

"Holly Ann didn't show up." Bishop entered the office and sat in the chair across from Ace. "Why not?"

"Did you not hear what I just said?" Ace growled. The more time he spent with Cactus, the more he thought the man had the right idea about everything. Live far away from the epicenter of the ranch. Give short, curt answers. Never smile. Eventually, everyone would leave him alone.

The problem was, Ace loved to laugh, and he loved living right at the heart of Shiloh Ridge Ranch. He usually liked talking, and he definitely enjoyed big family meals, movie and game nights, and horseback riding on Sunday afternoons with anyone who wanted to saddle up and go.

"It's just me," Bishop said. "You tell me everything."

"Not everything," Ace said, though Bishop was ninety-nine percent right. He sighed, his stomach growling loudly.

"Just come eat," Bishop said. "Or I'll bring you something."

He was missing the angel tree decorating too, and Ace loved that family tradition more than any other. "Bring me something," Ace said, and Bishop got to his feet without hesitation.

"Be right back." His cousin walked out, and Ace frowned at the laptop in front of him. Part of him wanted to pick it up and hurl it through the front windows. The other part wanted to watch the video again.

He leaned forward and pressed play, the image of his beautiful Holly Ann coming up on the screen. "She's not yours," he practically growled as a smile lit her face and she surveyed the crowd he couldn't see.

She spoke into the microphone about how "delighted" she was to be named this year's Christmas Festival chairperson, and that she pledged to do her best to make this holiday season the best one Three Rivers had ever seen.

She'd texted him an hour ago, when she should've almost been to the ranch. They'd held a family meeting before dinner, and while he was serious about Holly Ann, he didn't think they were quite to the point where he involved her in the business decisions of the ranch.

Bishop had had his girlfriend there, and of course, Bear and Ranger had their wives. Cactus had not invited his girlfriend, but Ida had her boyfriend there with her.

Ace picked up his phone, which he'd silenced after Holly Ann's first text, and found at least a dozen more.

Ida had sent the most messages, and that didn't surprise him one bit. He was close with the twins, and while they were identical, Ida was far more approachable than Etta. She was also worried about him.

I'm okay, he typed out. *Bishop is getting me something to eat, and I'm just going to hole up here for a while. I'm really fine. Hang one of the cowboy boots for Daddy for me, okay?*

If Ace was a betting man, he'd put ten bucks down that Ida had already hung the boot, and that she'd call within the hour.

Got the boot for you already, her next text said. *I'll call you on the way home, okay?*

Ace grinned at the predictability of his sister. His heart expanded too, because he knew she cared about him. Genuinely cared about him.

Just like Bishop did. He walked right into the house, no knocking or doorbell ringing, only a few minutes later, a plate laden with more food than both of them could eat.

"Here you go," he said, putting the plate in front of Ace. "What's playing?"

Ace hastened to pause the video again, but Bishop had already come around the desk to see.

"Holly Ann," he said. "She's the new chairperson. No wonder she couldn't come." He looked at Ace, their eyes meeting for a long moment. A lot was said there, and Ace should've known he wouldn't have to explain. He'd just have to look at Bishop, show him the video, and sigh.

Ace picked up the fork Bishop had brought. "She texted to say she'd been nominated and voted in as this year's chairperson, and I should go watch the press release." He looked at the plate of food, noticing the extra tall pile of shredded brisket. Bishop knew him so well.

"So I ducked out to the porch to do that, and there she was, live. *Live*. Not on her way here. Not pulling in." He stabbed his fork into a roll and split it open, then stacked meat onto that. "What's so important in Three Rivers that we need a *live* press release?" He shook his head and swiped his utensil through the barbecue sauce Ida spent hours perfecting. With that slathered on his meat, he folded his roll over and took a bite of his sandwich.

Ace liked nothing more than smoked meat sandwiches. Fine, maybe Holly Ann. Maybe even Christmas. She loved the holidays as much as he did, and they both volunteered at the town's six-week Christmas Festival. Ace had been looking forward to it with everything inside him.

"Can I see it?" Bishop asked.

Ace pulled the indicator back to the beginning of the video and hit play. He turned the laptop around, because he'd seen it enough to have some of it memorized already.

"This is Winn Clark with Channel Three in Three Rivers. We're live outside the City Council chambers, where we're expecting to hear who the chairperson for this year's Christmas Festival will be."

Ace rolled his eyes at the exuberance in the man's voice. Did he honestly think this was news? Was he seriously *so excited* about this announcement?

"Here we go," he said a few seconds later. "It looks like Mayor Hall is going to make the announcement."

Pause, shuffle, mic feedback.

Ace added a fork full of pea salad to his next bite of brisket sandwich, the bright pop of the peas and the addition of mayo to the meat and barbecue sauce was a match made in heaven.

"I'm pleased to announce that long-time volunteer and small-business owner, Holly Ann Broadbent, has been appointed as this year's Christmas Festival chairperson," the mayor said, his voice deep and rich and rolling with plenty of Southern accent. "She recently started Three Cakes Catering, which quickly shot to the top of the review charts online, as well as our own Three Rivers Two Cents app."

"That's not what it's called," Bishop said, which was exactly Ace's reaction. Ace had yelled some different choice words about how *he* had been the one to recommend Holly Ann and Three Cakes to literally everyone, in every online forum, on Two Cents itself, and to anyone who even got close to mentioning a party or get-together.

He'd gotten her all that business. *He'd* put her at the top of those charts, where organic visibility took over after that.

Ace wasn't an idiot. He'd earned a business degree with an emphasis in marketing, thank you very much. He knew what it took to get a business off the ground, and the power of word-of-mouth should never be overlooked.

He'd been that mouth.

She'd still be baking in her momma's kitchen without him.

Surprised at his bitterness, he shoved the rest of his sandwich in his mouth, already looking at the plate for the next thing to soothe his bruised ego. His heart had already been cracked by this woman, and he felt it starting to flake off piece by piece.

"She specializes in desserts, I've heard," the mayor

continued, chuckling. "And she comes with the greatest endorsement of all—that of long-time chairperson and founder of the Christmas Festival, Ruth Deerfield. Ruth?"

"This part is stupid," Ace said. "She drones on and on about the festival, as if we don't know what it is, and then says Holly Ann is literally the only person she trusts the festival to."

"So I can skip ahead?"

"Yeah."

Bishop did that while Ace loaded a ridged potato chip with his mother's famous frog eye salad. The salty chip only added to the cool salad, which also had a fruity tang to it.

"Oh, she's on now." Bishop sat back down. "She looks good, Ace."

"She always looks good," Ace said. That was true. Holly Ann knew how to put on the exact right shade of eye shadow to convey a message. She never wore too much lipstick, and her eyelashes always looked a mile long.

Her nearly black hair fell in soft waves over her shoulders, and Ace knew exactly what it felt like between his fingers as he kissed her. He shoved another potato chip in his mouth so he wouldn't grind his teeth together.

She wore professional clothes tonight, almost like she'd known—she'd *known*—she'd get selected as chairperson. He scoffed but ignored Bishop's curious look.

"Hello, Three Rivers," she said, her voice bright. It wasn't the same one she used when she was alone with Ace. When she wanted him to kiss her, she spoke in a low, throaty tone that made his blood burn like fire. When she was excited to see him, her voice pitched up as she laughed and squealed.

This was such a fake, fake voice, and Ace hated it. He kept his head ducked as he shook it, hating the sound of her presentation voice.

"Who's ready for an amazing holiday season?" he asked with her, waving his fork as the crowd cheered.

"Wow, you're really bitter," Bishop said.

"Yes," Ace said, deciding to own the feeling. "Read this." He used his fork to push his phone closer to Bishop.

His cousin picked it up, and it didn't take long to read Holly Ann's few texts. The one where she said she'd been appointed as the chairperson.

The one that said she wouldn't make it for dinner and the angel tree decorating.

The last one where she'd said she was so, so sorry, but she'd be so busy for the next few months, and maybe they should take a break.

"Take a break?" Bishop asked. "Why?"

"Did you read my mind?" Ace asked.

"You didn't ask her."

"I don't need to ask her," Ace said. "She gave me this exact same excuse when she started Three Cakes. It's like, she's...I don't know. She can't walk and chew gum at the same time. She can't have a boyfriend and do anything else, it seems."

"That's just ridiculous," Bishop said.

"You're telling me."

"What are you going to do?"

"Eat another brisket sandwich," he said, looking over the lid of the laptop. "What can I do?"

Bishop closed the laptop, and he hadn't even gotten to

the part where she laughed like a hyena about the addition of a children's bike parade this year. A fake hyena.

"You like this woman, right?"

"Of course I like this woman." Ace glared at Bishop. "She's dominated my life for almost a year now. Even when I want to walk away, I can't. She's...." He shook his head. For him, Holly Ann was who he wanted. When they were together, she sure did act like he was who she wanted.

She'd said those words right out loud. To his face.

Then she sent texts about "taking a break."

"You don't need to explain," Bishop said quietly. "I understand." He took a long, deep breath. "Here's what I think, and it's going to go against what we always do."

"Honestly, what I always do isn't working for me," Ace said.

"You stop stuffing your face," Bishop said. "You go brush your teeth real good. Get your hair all fixed up under that cowboy hat. Make sure your clothes are clean."

"I was going to see her at dinner," Ace said. "I'm ready." Maybe he should brush his teeth, though.

"You know where she lives. You know she's still dealing with press or City Council members. You go wait in her driveway, and when she gets home, there you are. You hold up your phone, and you say, 'I don't want to take a break. Life is busy, Holly Ann. Are we going to break up every time you get a little busy? Heck, I'm busy all the dang time. I work overnight during birthing season. I ride for twenty hours during round-up. I go out at three a.m. to start planting, which takes over a month. I—"

"I get it," Ace said, holding up his hand so Bishop would stop.

He did, and the two of them looked at one another. Hope started to collect in Ace's chest, and it pressed against his heart, which banged like a drum.

"I go tell her no, I don't want to take a break," Ace mused. "I don't just let her dictate to me how things are going to be."

"That's right," Bishop said. "You go fight for her. For the two of you. For your relationship." He grinned at Ace. "Women like that. And we—" He gestured between the two of them, and then around the room, likely indicating every man on this ranch. "We never do that. We never just say, 'no, that won't work for me.'"

"Ranger did," Ace said quietly. "When Oakley wanted to date him and other men...he said no. That won't work for me." He looked at Bishop, his eyes wide.

"And now she's his wife."

"This might work."

Bishop chuckled and leaned back in his chair, folding his arms across his chest. The moment sobered, and then he asked, "Why are you still here? Go. Go already!"

Ace got to his feet, his heart racing. He didn't do things like this. He wasn't even sure where to start.

"Teeth," Bishop said. "Just in case there's any kissing, you don't need that frog eye breath."

"Teeth," Ace said, striding out of the office and taking the steps up to his room.

Bishop followed him, saying, "Then you need to wipe your face. Spray some of that sexy cologne on your collar.

Drive down to her house, and wait. That's it, Ace. You can do that."

Ace brushed his teeth and washed his face. He let Bishop spray the cologne, and then he was ready to go.

"Drive, wait, talk to her," Ace said, his fear diving through him. He *really* didn't do things like this.

"You look great," Bishop said, looking down to Ace's boots and back to his hat. "Everything is on-point. You've got this."

"Thanks." Ace drew in a lung full of air and held it. "Okay, well, will you tell Mister and Ward where I am?"

Bishop started to say yes, and then said, "Mister?"

"He lives here," Ace said.

"No, he doesn't," Bishop said. "He lives up in a cabin by my mother."

Ace shook his head. "He told everyone that, but there aren't even dishes in that cabin. Or toilet paper. He sleeps in one of the bedrooms in the basement." Ace started downstairs to the kitchen to get the keys to his truck. "We keep tellin' him to go get his clothes and just bring it all down here. He doesn't want anyone to know he lives here."

"Of course we're going to know. We'll see him go in and out."

"You live right next door and didn't know." Ace cocked his eyebrow at Bishop. "He's been here for months."

"Huh."

"He just needs to be left alone," Ace said. "We all feel like that from time to time."

"Yes, we do," Bishop said.

"Okay." Ace opened the drawer and took out his keys. "Here I go."

"Good luck," Bishop called after him, and Ace leaned on his luck all the way to Holly Ann's.

Her windows were dark, but she had outside lights on. He pulled right into her driveway, leaving only half for her, adjusted the radio so it wasn't quite so loud, and unbuckled his seatbelt so he could settle in to wait.

He didn't have to wait long, actually. Only about twenty minutes went by before a pair of headlights carved their way through the darkness and her SUV eased to a stop next to his truck.

"Now or never," he whispered to himself. He'd steadfastly refused to pray, because he felt like he jinxed himself every time he did. The Lord seemed to think it would be funny to do the exact opposite of what Ace prayed for anyway. He didn't see the point anymore.

He got out of the truck and rounded the back of it so he was approaching Holly Ann as she got out of her SUV. She carried an oversized purse, a forty-four-ounce soda cup, and a bag of take-out.

"Ace," she said, her voice full of shock. "What are you doing here?"

He hadn't memorized Bishop's speech, but Ace had never really had a problem speaking his mind. He held up his phone. "I don't want to take a break." He cleared his throat. "Life is busy, Holly Ann. We can't break up every single time you have something going on in your life. That's not how real relationships work."

She stared at him, her eyes wide. She was stunning, even

with only the light from her car spilling onto her, and the house lights haloing her from behind. She wasn't wearing a jacket over her nearly sheer blouse, as it was the same one she'd worn on-camera.

He'd been able to see the outline of her black camisole underneath the blouse, which was cream-colored and covered with multi-colored stars. She'd paired it with a black pencil skirt and a sexy pair of ankle boots that gave her an extra three inches.

He did not want to break up with her. He was not going to let her break up with him. He wished she'd say something.

The tension in her shoulders broke, and she eased out of the way of her door, using her foot to close it. "Do you want to come in?"

"Yes," he said instantly. "Let me help you with all of that." He stepped forward and took her drink and her food. She smiled at him, and it wasn't the horrible, fake smile he'd seen on TV. His hope rebounded and shot into the sky, because maybe—just maybe—doing something he'd never done before would get him something he'd never gotten before.

Chapter Two

Holly Ann Broadbent put her heavy purse down on the built-in desk in her kitchen while Ace Glover set her food and drink on the counter. Her little brown and white dog, Snickers, yipped at her, jumping up on her legs in excitement.

"Yes, I see you," she said, grinning at the dog. "I left you home for so long, didn't I?" She scooped him into her arms and took him to the sliding glass door. "Go out and go potty." The little dog ran into the darkness, and she flipped the switch to turn on the lights in the back yard.

Turning around, she faced Ace. She couldn't believe he was here. He had a lot of nerve to be sitting in her driveway this late at night. She could've called the cops on him for loitering and scaring her half to death. If she hadn't recognized that half-ton truck in an unusual matte gray the color of river mud, she would have.

At the same time, every cell in her body vibrated with a new kind of energy, all of it screaming, *Ace Glover is here!*

Ace Glover didn't just give up this time!

"Did you eat?" she asked, reaching for the white paper bag her Chinese food had come in. "I have plenty." She glanced at him, but she'd never been able to just take a casual look. Ace demanded that she really soak him in, even when she tried not to.

Tonight, he wore a sexy pair of dark wash jeans that made his legs look impossibly long. He always had the cowboy boots, the cowboy hat, and the belt buckle. Always. They were three of her favorite things about Ace.

His gray shirt peeked through his jacket at his throat, only a triangle of light against the dark brown leather. He lit her up every time he walked in the room. Every single time.

"I ate," he said, and she wondered how much time had gone by while she drank him in. She hadn't even taken one container out of the bag yet, so probably not much.

"Did you hear what I said outside?" he asked.

"Yes," she said, opening the box and getting a nose full of orange mixed with fried food. Her stomach growled, and her mouth watered. "That's why I invited you in."

"So...we're not breaking up?"

"You said you didn't want to."

"I don't."

"I'm going to be incredibly busy." Not only that, but Holly Ann didn't deal well with stress or exhaustion. She would be both stressed and exhausted, constantly, from now until New Year's Day. "And Ace, you thought I was bad when I was taking care of Snickers after his surgery, *and* catering events, and no one was sleeping. This is going to be ten times worse."

"I'll come sit with you while you sleep," he said quietly.

Holly Ann saw no point in dirtying a plate she'd have to wash later, so she took the whole bag and a fork to the table and sat down. A groan came out of her mouth, because while these boots were adorable, they also pinched her toes and reminded her that she carried fifty extra pounds and doing that on a heel no wider than a penny was hard work for her feet and calves. Really hard work.

"I'll come rub your feet after a long day of baking and then Christmassing." He stepped over to the door and opened it for Snickers, who hopped inside and trotted right over to her side, clearly wanting some Chinese food too.

She grinned at Ace, and he took that to mean he could sit at the table with her, which he did. He didn't touch her, though Holly Ann wouldn't have objected to that either.

She didn't want to break up with him, especially now that he'd shown up to fight for their relationship.

"I can support you while you're busy," he said while she opened her ham fried rice. "When I'm busy, and you're not, you can support me."

"Sounds romantic," Holly Ann said, tossing him a dry look. She *loved* the romantic things of the world, but she was practical too.

"It's called real life," Ace said, his voice somewhat sour. "You don't see marriages breaking up when someone gets too busy."

"Actually," Holly Ann said, spearing a piece of orange chicken and rolling it around in her ham fried rice. "You do see that." She put the food in her mouth, at least a dozen things getting satisfied with just that simple action.

"Holly Ann," he said. "Not every marriage is going to end the way your parents' did."

She sucked in a breath and glared at him. "I know that."

"Okay." He backed right down, and Holly Ann wasn't sure if she liked that or not. No one usually spoke to her like that. They let her wallow in her reasons why she didn't date too seriously—or at least why she hadn't until Ace Glover.

They said things like, "You're right, Holly Ann," and "It's hard to maintain a relationship with someone who's so busy all the time."

Ace might have even said those things in the past. He hadn't tonight.

"Sorry," she murmured, pinching a tiny piece of chicken between her thumb and forefinger and feeding it to Snickers. "It's just, I...I don't know how to keep everyone happy."

"That's not your job," he said. "I know how to make myself happy, and Holly Ann, you're a big part of that. I'm very *un*happy without you, and I'd rather bring you dinner so you can keep working, or volunteer to pick up the popcorn for an event so you don't have to, or coordinate with the pastor to make your life easier, than not talk to you. Than not see you at all. Than think about you all dang day and all night, wondering why I'm not good enough for you."

He pulled in a breath, which inflated his chest, widening it the same way Holly Ann's eyes had widened with every word he'd spoken.

He thought about her all day and all night?

He'd rather bring her dinner and call that a relationship?

He thought he wasn't good enough for her?

Holly swallowed and dropped her gaze to her gooey orange chicken. "I apologize if I've ever given you the feeling that you are not good enough for me," she said. "That is simply not true, nor has it ever been true, and whatever I did to give you that impression, I'm sorry."

Ace said nothing while she rolled around another piece of chicken, popped it into her mouth, and ate it.

She fed Snickers another chicken snack and finally looked up at Ace, and he seemed to be warring with himself.

"You made me feel like that when you chose Three Cakes over me," he said. "And you did it again tonight, by suggesting we end things between us so you can run the Christmas Festival."

Holly Ann opened her mouth to deny such a thing, but her mind thankfully worked faster than her voice. She snapped her mouth closed when she realized he was right.

"You're right," she said. "I didn't realize it."

"You didn't realize it?"

"I—" She stabbed another piece of chicken, wishing it was her own eyeball. "I sometimes get caught up in things, is all," she said. "I have a hard time focusing on more than one thing at a time."

"You can use your ADD or your dyslexia all you want," he said. "I understand they're real, and they're hard for you. But I'm sitting right here, telling you that I'm not going anywhere. In fact, *I* can help you focus on us when it's the right time, and the Christmas Festival when it's time for that."

Holly Ann nodded and doctored up her next bite of chicken. "You're the one who's too good for me, Ace."

"That's nonsense," he said. "We really should stop thinking that about ourselves."

"I will if you will."

"Deal," he said, and she loved this back-and-forth between them. They'd always gotten along so well, and Ace was one of the easiest men for Holly Ann to talk to.

"I don't want to break up," she said.

"Good," he said. "Neither do I."

She ate another bite of chicken, and then asked, "So where do we go from here?"

He grinned at her and reached over to take her fork-less hand between both of his. "You open your calendar, sweetheart, and you tell me when you're available for breakfast, lunch, or dinner. I'll take you out or bring the food to you. Whatever you want. If it's twenty minutes, it's twenty minutes."

He looked at her with those beautiful, sky-blue eyes, so full of hope and desire, and Holly Ann loved being looked at by Ace. "I just want to be with you. Deal?"

"Deal," she said, a yawn immediately following. "Will you stay while I change into something that's not squeezing me like a python?"

He chuckled and slid his hands away from hers. "Sure."

"Will you stay with me until I fall asleep?" she whispered. "I'm so tired."

"Yes," he said, his voice quiet too. "Go change and come lay with me on the couch."

Holly Ann took one more bite of chicken and rice and

went to do exactly what Ace had suggested. She could admit that coming home alone added to her burden, and when she'd realized it was Ace waiting for her in the driveway, she'd been almost giddy.

"Come on, Snickers," she said to the little dog, who trotted into her bedroom after her.

After closing the door, she stripped out of her confining clothes and tossed them toward the closet. The red Santa suit hanging there caught her attention, and she pulled in a tight breath. Crossing the room quickly, she closed the closet door so the suit couldn't be seen from the doorway.

Not that Ace would be there. She'd closed the door besides.

Still. "He can't know about that," she whispered to Snickers. "That's why I needed to take a break." She looked from closed door to closed door, her heart battling with her brain.

We can do it, her heart said. *He'll never know. He works up at that ranch a lot. It's fine.*

This is too risky, her brain said. *We don't care how handsome he is, or how many times he says such perfect things. He can never know you wear the suit.*

"He won't," she vowed, going with her heart for maybe the first time in her life. She could only add a prayer to her internal debate that following her heart wasn't going to be the biggest mistake of her life.

Chapter Three

Ace entered the kitchen the next morning, a whistle coming from his mouth. "Morning, all," he said to his brother and his cousin, who both sat at the table opposite the island.

Ward looked up from his bowl of oatmeal, his eyebrows raised high over those dark blue eyes. "What's with you?"

"Nothing," Ace said with a grin, though he had plenty going on with him. "What's with you?"

Ward looked at Mister, who bit into a piece of toast as if nothing was different with Ace. Ace appreciated that about Mister. He didn't enjoy drama, that much was certain. Ward didn't either, and Ace always found himself in the middle of something the others didn't. He put himself out there more than almost any other Glover too, and that definitely made his life more interesting than the other cowboys at Shiloh Ridge Ranch.

"He went to town last night," Mister finally said, after

chewing and swallowing his toast. "He didn't bring back any milk, though, so I don't think it was to get groceries."

"Groceries is today," Ace said, opening the fridge and daring to turn his back on Ward and Mister. "So tell me what you want. Cactus and I will get it all."

"Cream," Ward said. "We never have enough cream. You need to buy twice as much."

"If you'd make oatmeal with water, we wouldn't need gallons of cream," Ace said without turning from the fridge. Leftovers from last night's meal at the homestead sat on the top shelf, and Ace normally liked any type of food for breakfast.

Today, though, he felt like pancakes. He pulled the eggs out of the fridge and asked, "Do we not have any milk, then?"

"There's a swallow or two," Mister said. "Not enough for cereal."

"I'm going to make pancakes," Ace said. "Do you guys want some?"

"I can't wait," Ward said. "Ranger and I have a conference call in twenty minutes."

Ace pulled a bowl out of the cupboard in the island and walked over to the pantry in the corner of the kitchen. If he went next door, Bishop would probably have something on the counter for breakfast already. He fed Lincoln bacon and eggs, French toast with whipped cream and strawberries, and creamed wheat with raisins and brown sugar.

Ace *loved* Bishop's creamed wheat—which was supposed to be made with cream—far better than his brother's oatmeal, which currently sat in a pot on the stove.

Bishop hadn't texted though, so Ace got out the pancake mix and took it back to the counter. He measured the powder and the milk, adding water to make up the difference, and cracked in two eggs. His mother had taught him that trick to make the pancakes a little bit more filling. They also cooked up cakier, and Ace really liked that.

He set a pan on the stove next to Ward's oatmeal and turned the flame on underneath it. "No grocery requests? You guys can't text me while I'm at the store. It makes everything too hard."

"I'm sending my list right now," Ward said, and Ace glanced at him to find him typing furiously on his phone. "I'll send you some money."

"I will too," Mister said, though his phone wasn't anywhere in sight. "I emailed you my list last night."

Of course he had. Mister liked schedules and routines. He liked having a list of things to do, and checking them off one-by-one. He disliked anyone who didn't fit into his schedule or who didn't operate quite the same way he did.

He'd come to live with Ward and Ace over the summer, because he really didn't get along with Judge, one of his older brothers. Ace understood having problems with a family member, as there were nine Glover cowboys at the ranch. They each had their own opinions about things, and sometimes personalities and ideas clashed.

The best part about Ace's family, though, was that they always came back together. They forgave one another, even if it took a long time to do.

Ace added butter to the pan, smiling at it as it sizzled against the heat. As it continued to melt, he found the syrup in the fridge and squeezed some into bowl to put in the microwave. There was nothing worse than hot pancakes and cold syrup.

"Sent," Ward said as he stood and brought his bowl into the kitchen. He set it in the sink with the other dirty dishes and added, "I'll clean up tonight."

"Okay," Ace said. They didn't have assigned chores in their house, though Mister had freaked out a little when he'd moved in. He was a lot like Bishop in that he wanted things clean and orderly. But the three of them managed to keep their clothes clean, their fridge full of food, and the dishes done. One of them took the trash out every morning, and today, Ward did the job while Ace turned back to his batter.

"That pan is going to be too hot," Ward warned, tying the bag. "When are you leaving for the store?"

Ace whipped back to the stove, taking the bowl of batter with him. The butter lay in a pool in the pan, and he poured some batter over the edge of the bowl. The batter hissed, and the butter spit, and dang it. Ward was right. The pan was too hot.

Ace wasn't a great cook, and he wasn't sure why he'd thought he could make himself pancakes for breakfast. He should've grabbed one of those pastry pockets with ham and eggs from the freezer and flipped on the toaster oven.

He reached to turn down the flame under the burner, hoping that would help keep the blackness on the bottom of the pancake to a minimum.

Just another reason he liked Holly Ann so much. She could take any number of ingredients and turn them into something delicious. He honestly didn't know how she did it. Probably magic.

Ace smiled to himself, jumping when Ward barked, "What time?"

"Oh, uh." Ace turned away from the pancake that filled the entire bottom of the pan. "Probably right after lunch." Cactus had a therapy appointment at one-thirty, and that gave Ace an hour of free time in town.

He needed to text Holly Ann and ask about a late lunch with her. He wouldn't last from seven-thirty to one-thirty, but Ace had no problem eating more than one lunch. One could be an early lunch and one a late lunch.

"Okay," Ward said. "You'll be back for dinner?"

"Yes," Ace said. "Do you need some of the groceries to cook?"

"Yep." Ward lifted the bag. "I invited Ida and Brady, remember? And Etta is bringing her new boyfriend." Ward glanced at Mister. "Ranger and Oakley are coming. Dinner is at six. I need the stuff back here by...say, four-thirty."

"We'll be back by then," Ace said, though they'd have to really race through the grocery store. Cactus would be in therapy until two-thirty, and with a half-hour drive back to the ranch, that only left them a little over an hour to shop for all the groceries seven grown men—two of whom were married—needed for the next week.

His phone chimed again, and Ace pulled it out of his pocket. He'd ignored Ward's text, so he saw that one, and then he'd gotten one from Sammy. Bear's wife had sent him a link to her grocery list, and a moment later, his SendCents app *cha-chinged*, indicating that he'd been paid.

Sammy's name sat on that too, along with a note that read, *Thank you, Ace. If it's not enough, let me know, okay?*

He tapped on the link to see her list, and Ace's thoughts scattered for a moment. The list was huge, but at least Ace knew where all the kid-friendly foods were now. When Lincoln had joined the family upon Bear and Sammy's marriage, the grocery list had changed quite a bit. Ace had literally walked up and down every aisle, trying to find the fruit roll-ups, the perfect flavor of Pop-Tarts, and creamy peanut butter mixed with grape jelly in the same jar.

He didn't understand creamy peanut butter on a fundamental level, but he wanted Lincoln to be happy, so he took the time to get the right things on the list.

He sent her a thumbs-up and started to navigate back to his main list.

"That's burning," Ward called over his shoulder. The back door slammed a moment later, and Ace jerked his head up.

"Dang it," he hissed, tossing his phone onto the counter and yanking open the drawer to find a spatula. Steam poured from the pan, and he obviously hadn't turned down the flame enough. He slid the spatula under the pancake and flipped it.

Pure blackness stared back at him.

A sigh leaked out of his mouth, and Ace reached to turn off the burner completely.

Mister stepped next to him, his chuckle low and growing with every passing moment. Soon, he laughed fully, and Ace raised the spatula as if he'd hit Mister with it. His cousin danced away, still laughing a little bit. He didn't like getting his clothes dirty, that was for sure, and today, his jeans looked brand-new and he'd paired them with a light blue, long-sleeved shirt with a dark blue paisley pattern on it.

Ace had never seen such a shirt in his life, but he did like it. Mister had shown him where he'd been buying his shirts, and Ace could admit he'd bought a couple of the "men's western fashion wear" items from Modern Cowboy.

He should wear one to town today, in fact. Especially if he was going to see Holly Ann for even a few minutes.

While his stomach grumbled, Ace sent a quick text to her, asking about her availability between say, 1:40 and 2:20 p.m. Then he removed the pan from the burner and left it next to Ward's pot of cold oatmeal. He wasn't about to eat that, and he went to the freezer for that breakfast pocket with ham and egg.

"THANKS," CACTUS SAID AS HE OPENED HIS DOOR. ACE simply nodded and watched his cousin walk into the office building. The first time he'd brought Cactus to begin his therapy, Ace had gone all the way inside with him. He'd waited in the waiting room and everything. He didn't need to do that now, though, and he usually played games on his phone or left comments on Ranger's app, Two Cents.

Today, though, Cactus had barely disappeared through the door before Ace pulled away from the curb. Holly Ann had said she was in "testing mode" that day, and he could definitely come over for a late lunch at 1:40. She'd even feed him, though she'd told him at least three times that it could be disgusting.

I'm trying new recipes, she'd told him. *They might not be good.*

Ace didn't care. He'd be her taste-tester any day of the week, and if she made something that didn't taste good, he'd eat his own boot. After all, someone didn't open a catering company if they couldn't cook.

He'd eaten Holly Ann's food before, and she was very good in the kitchen. He also admired that she continually tried new things, stretching herself and growing, getting better at her craft.

Ace could admit that sometimes he felt stagnant. He knew how to fix tractors, balers, or harvesters. He knew how to plant a field, and how to tell if it was growing well and correctly. He knew how to fix the crops if they were suffering. He knew how to prep dirt, and how to test it for acidity, and how to care for it so it would produce for him over decades.

He loved his agricultural work on the ranch, but even he could admit he was bored sometimes. That was why Ace volunteered to do all the grocery shopping for anyone who wanted him to. It was why he'd been volunteering through the church for anything and everything over the years— including the Christmas Festival. It was why he was the Glover who signed up for the painting classes, the paper-making workshops, and the publishing seminars offered through the Three Rivers community outreach program.

He'd never actually painted a picture, made any paper, or published anything. But he sure liked learning how to do different things.

His heart beat a little faster as he turned onto Holly Ann's street, and he glanced at the clock. About one-forty, just like he'd predicted. He pulled into her driveway and started to ease off the brake as he was hardly moving anyway.

Behind him, someone leaned on their horn, and Ace yelped and flinched, his foot slamming onto the gas pedal.

The truck lurched forward before he could stop it, and a horrible, deafening, crunching sound filled the air while he jammed his foot on the brake.

When he came to a stop, he blinked, his adrenaline surging through him, sharpening his awareness and his eyesight.

The silence hurt his ears, and he groaned as he realized he'd driven right into Holly Ann's closed garage door. Not a bump. Not a little dent or ding. The whole thing bowled in, the front of his truck bending the metal door inward in a terribly unnatural way.

He got out of the truck, noting that his door didn't open very far before it met the garage door, and he surveyed the damage.

"This is bad," he said to himself.

"I'll say," Holly Ann said in her sexy, low, twang.

Ace whipped around to find her walking toward him, a definite frown between her eyes.

Chapter Four

Holly Ann put her hands on her hips, feeling the grainy flour on her apron. "You ran right into my house." She looked at Ace, fighting a smile. "What happened?"

"I'm so sorry," he said, pure worry in his eyes. "Someone honked, and I got startled, and...." He turned back to the garage. "I hit the gas instead of the brake."

He seemed to be doing that a lot lately, and not just when he sat behind the wheel. Holly Ann had no idea how to fix something like this. She knew she needed to get her car out of her garage for a meeting at four o'clock, but she didn't think the door would be moving.

"Let me back up, and we'll see how bad it is," Ace said. "I'll fix it."

Of course he would, and not only because the man had more money than most professional athletes. Anyone who drove their truck into someone else's garage door would pay to fix it.

Ace jumped behind the wheel and backed up, leaving his door open as he did.

Holly Ann stood in front of his truck now, staring at the garage door. It looked like a giant had taken his fist and jammed it right into the house.

Ace came to her side and sighed. "I'm such an idiot."

"It was an accident," Holly Ann said. "Everyone has accidents."

Ace's fingers fumbled over hers, finally aligning a moment later. She blinked as a rush of heat flowed up her arm and into her face. Her vision turned white, and she couldn't believe the way her body reacted to his. She smiled at him and everything.

"I do need to get my car out of the garage for a meeting at four," she said.

"There's no way that's happening," he said miserably. "That door has to come off. It's not going up or down." He sighed and looked at her.

She met his eyes, and it suddenly didn't matter that she couldn't go to her meeting at four. *Yes, it does*, she told herself as she swam around in the dark, oceanic depths of his eyes. She closed hers, and her brain gained control over her hormones.

She couldn't miss the first planning meeting for the festival. Their calendar of events would be scheduled, and they had to get that to the printer today, so it would go out in the mid-month utility bills, as well as up on the website for those looking to schedule all of their family activities for late November and all of December.

"I'll get you a rental," he said. "I'm starving. Can you feed me while I get you a car?"

"When aren't you starving?" she teased.

His mouth curved up into a slow smile, and she watched it lift centimeter by centimeter. She jerked her attention away from that mouth that had kissed hers many times and took a step around him.

"I'll make a few calls while we eat." He dialed someone before they even reached her front door, and he said, "Yes, I need a rental car delivered by three-thirty. Is that possible?"

Holly Ann didn't know anyone who would tell Ace Glover no. He spoke in an eloquent tone, and there wasn't anything money couldn't buy. Was there?

She continued into her house and kitchen, getting down a couple of bowls and two small plates. Ace's voice filled the house, but she couldn't make out the words as he stayed in the lobby, which had a two-story-tall ceiling and made everything echo.

She stirred the beef and kale stew, the scent of salt and cumin rising up to meet her nose. She hoped this new recipe would make the cut for her winter menus, because she really loved making it, and it could feed a large crowd.

She'd ladled one bowl of soup and picked up the second dish when Ace entered the kitchen. "They'll have a car here for you by three-thirty." He sighed as he sat at the bar. "I'm so sorry. I'll call someone to come replace that door."

Holly Ann filled his bowl and turned back to him. "It's okay, Ace." She smiled at him. "I know you'll take care of it."

He returned her smile and looked at the soup. "What is this? It smells great."

"This is a beef, carrot, and kale stew," she said. "With a hint of heat, and a little cumin." Nutmeg too, but that was a super-secret pinch of spice she didn't tell people about. Not even Ace.

Holly Ann kept her smile fixed on her face, because she actually had a few things she hadn't told anyone—not even Ace. She bent to pull the sweet buns from the oven. "It's a rich dish, so I made these sweet potato buns to go with it. The idea is to eat them together, if you'd like." She dipped her pastry brush in the bowl of melted butter and brushed the buns. A gorgeous, peachy color bloomed under the butter, and Holly Ann smiled at the bread.

"I love bread," she said, using a pair of tongs to serve Ace a sweet potato bun. She pushed the small plate toward him, noticing how his eyes widened. "What?"

"Sweet potato buns? I've never heard of such a thing."

Holly Ann grinned, because that was such a great compliment. He probably didn't even realize it. "That's the idea," she said. "People hire me because my food is unique, but familiar. Something they haven't thought of but would really like to try. And always delicious."

She put a bun on a plate for herself and nodded to him. "Go ahead."

"Come sit by me," he said, and Holly Ann pushed her bowl and plate across the counter to the spot next to him.

"I want to see your reaction," she said, edging toward the corner of the countertop.

He picked up his spoon and focused on the stew. He stirred it around for a second, and then scooped up a bite. He put it in his mouth, a hint of steam rising from the spoon a moment before he did. His eyes drifted closed and a groan emanated from his throat at the same time.

Pleasure filled Holly Ann. She loved feeding people, and she loved watching them enjoy her food.

"It's amazing," Ace said, his eyes opening again as he dug into his bowl for a second bite. "Fantastic. It's perfect for fall and winter."

"Thank you," Holly Ann said, finally moving to sit beside him. She ripped off a piece of her sweet potato bun and dipped it in the stew for her first bite, and a new dimension came to the stew. She'd been tasting it while she made it, so she knew what the stew alone tasted like. "The bun takes it to a new level," she said.

Ace pulled off a chunk of his bun and ate a bite of soup with it. "Oh, yeah," he said. "It's like that sweet potato is now in the soup."

"It doesn't have a starch," she said. "The bun is supposed to be the starch." She wasn't sure she could call it a stew if there were no potatoes, but sometimes people counted carrots as a starchy element. In her book, though, carrots would never be potatoes. But a sweet potato bun certainly counted.

"I love this with my whole soul," Ace said.

Holly Ann giggled. "I'm glad." They ate for a few minutes, and when Ace finished, he picked up his phone and started tapping and swiping. "Oh, Two Cents says The Door Dude is a good choice for garage doors. How does that sound?"

"It sounds like a guy who dropped out of college," Holly Ann said.

Ace chuckled and lifted his phone to his ear. Their eyes met again, the air crackling between them. Holly Ann ducked her head and dipped her spoon into her bowl again. She had so much to tell her dad at dinner that night, and she couldn't wait to get his opinion on everything.

"Yes, I need a brand-new garage door," Ace said. "The other one is all bent, and there might be some other repairs to the tracking system or something." He paused, cocked his head, and added, "Yes, I said bent. It's super bent." He looked at Holly Ann. "Like, I drove my truck right into it bent, and I need it done fast." He grinned at her, and it should be illegal for a man to have such a great smile, complete with straight, white teeth and that dimple in his right cheek.

Utterly and perfectly illegal.

"Who's car is that?" Dad asked the moment Holly Ann stood from behind the wheel of the rental.

"Hello, Dad," she called, stepping to the back door to get out the extra cookies she'd brought from her meeting.

Her dad came down the front steps. She'd never arrived at her childhood home and not found him lurking in the screen door or, if it was really cold, the front windows. He said he liked to know precisely when his girls arrived, but she and Bethany Rose suspected he stood there a lot, keeping tabs on the neighborhood.

If the police ever needed to know who'd driven up and down this street, the sisters knew their dad would have a record of it, complete with make, model, year, color, and the license plate of every vehicle.

He'd been a detective for thirty-five years, so it was something they all laughed about. Holly Ann had never actually seen a notebook or record like that, but she didn't doubt for a second that it existed.

"It's a rental," Dad said, peering at the windshield where the sticker sat. "Why are you driving a rental?"

Holly Ann handed him the cookies and closed the back door. "Ace ran into my garage," she said. "I couldn't get my car out, so I'm driving this until the door gets fixed."

"Ace Glover?" Dad asked, his eyes narrowing.

"Yes, Dad. The same man I've been seeing for a while now." She rolled her eyes and nodded to the cookies. "Eat one of those on the way in. I've got a lot to talk about tonight."

"So much that I need a cookie before dinner?"

"That's right," she singsonged. "Is Bethany Rose coming tonight?"

"They'll be here in a few minutes." Dad led the way up the walk to the steps. "Anything I need to know you don't want them to know?"

Holly Ann thought as she followed him inside, scowling at the horrible shag carpet he refused to replace. It kept coming clean, so he saw no reason to spend money on it. Holly Ann had considered spilling something really greasy or oily on it just so he'd dig into his savings account and step into the twenty-first century.

"Just about the suit," she said, her voice automatically hushing. "I tried to break up with Ace, because I don't know how I can keep it a secret from him. It's going to be hard enough to run the festival and sit on the throne without anyone finding out, and I don't know." She sighed and tossed her purse on the counter in the kitchen where everything piled up.

"Tried to break up with him?"

"He wouldn't let me this time." Holly Ann smiled, gazing out the window at the pastures her father used for his horses.

"You seem happy about that."

"I am," Holly Ann turned and faced her father fully. "How are you?" She stepped into him and hugged him tight. Her dad gave the best hugs, and Holly Ann had never doubted for a second that he loved her. She loved him with the fierceness of the sun, and she tried to hold him as tightly as he embraced her.

In the end, she just giggled and said, "You're squeezing me to death, Daddy," something she'd been saying since age five. He laughed too and released her.

"Holly Ann, the suit will take care of itself."

"I don't even know what that means," she said, rolling her eyes. He always said something cryptic about it, and Holly Ann had given up trying to get a straight answer from him.

"Just remember to wear the contacts," he said. "They help a lot."

"Okay," she said, facing the array of bowls on the counter. "What are you doing here? What can I help with?"

"Omelet bar," he said, and all the chopped vegetables and shredded cheeses made sudden sense. "I've got some of that buffalo sausage in the oven too, so try to control yourself."

"It'll be hard," Holly Ann said dryly, as she really didn't like game meat at all, even when it was made into a sausage. She cooked with it from time to time, but it wasn't her go-to protein.

Something sounded on her dad's phone, and he said, "Bethany Rose and Kevin are here." He left the kitchen and strode past the couches in the open-concept living room. He'd torn down the wall separating the two rooms himself, and he'd had some of his police buddies come help him install the massive, load-bearing beam he'd left exposed in the ceiling.

He lurked at the screen door, and then opened it, calling, "Don't worry. That's Holly Ann's rental. She has a great story for us tonight," as he stepped out.

Holly Ann looked down at his phone, which he'd left on the counter. She saw a notification from something she didn't recognize, and she took a closer look. She started to laugh when she realized how he'd known Bethany Rose and her husband had arrived. He had security cameras on the house—she knew that. One of them had been installed on the power pole next to the front driveway, and it pointed toward the garage, so he'd know when someone pulled into the driveway.

"No wonder he always knows when we get here," she said, still giggling. She couldn't wait to tell Bethany Rose about this particular quirk of her father's. Right now, though, she put on her game face, because she was going to be talking about Ace tonight.

Chapter Five

Ace pulled into the parking lot at the post office, scanning for a spot. It seemed like everyone in Three Rivers had decided this Tuesday would be the opportune time to mail something, because every space held a vehicle already.

"Ward owes me big-time for this," Ace grumbled as he came to a stop at the exit and checked to see if he could turn right to go back to the entrance. Maybe he'd catch someone coming out after mailing their packages.

It was far too early to be getting Christmas gifts off, as November had just started last week. He supposed some people had loved ones overseas, but certainly not the whole dang town. Ace reminded himself that he'd wanted to come to town. When Ward had asked if he'd be going today, Ace had said, "I can. Why?"

Winter at Shiloh Ridge Ranch wasn't nearly as busy for him as for some others. Since he primarily worked on their crops and agriculture, he wasn't monitoring growth, soil pH, or constantly checking the sprinkling system. He frowned as he thought about that, though, because the ranch needed some serious upgrades when it came to their sprinklers.

He'd already spoken with Bear, his eldest cousin, and Ranger, his oldest brother, about it. Together, the two of them made the majority of the decisions for the ranch, though anything that required a major purchase would be given to the whole family to discuss.

The sprinkling system would definitely be one of those items, and Ranger had suggested that Ace put together an official proposal for what was damaged or outdated, what he needed or wanted to improve or fix it, and then come present at one of their weekly meetings.

Ace had said he would, but the concept still existed out in the ether somewhere. It took him a while to get his thoughts and ideas down on paper, and as he turned back into the post office parking lot, he caught sight of a couple of men he knew walking into the restaurant next door.

Liam and Tripp Walker. The brothers lived just down the road from Shiloh Ridge, and Ace knew all the Walkers, as well as their ranch, Seven Sons. His mouth watered, and he did love Chinese food....

"Get the package mailed," he told himself as a blue sedan up ahead started to back out of spot. "Call Holly Ann." Maybe they could share some Sesame chicken and chat for more than twenty minutes.

After he'd hit her garage yesterday, he'd enjoyed his soup before calling The Door Dude to get it fixed. He'd just gotten off that call when Cactus had rang, asking where he was. Apparently, his appointment was only thirty minutes, not an hour, and Ace had jumped to his feet and practically run out.

He'd gone back to kiss Holly Ann quickly, but only on the cheek, and his lips wanted more. A lot more. Not only that, but he'd had to admit to Cactus that he'd gone to Holly Ann's, and his cousin hadn't seemed too thrilled. Ace wasn't sure why, as Cactus kept his mouth shut about a lot of things, including how he felt about certain things.

Other things, he had no problem getting in anyone's face about. The tricky part was knowing what would cause Cactus to erupt and what wouldn't. The more time Ace spent with him, the more he learned about the man. He admired Cactus on a variety of levels, and he'd apologized for mixing up the times.

Ace pulled into the now-available space and reached for Ward's package on the passenger seat. His brother had been participating in the Cowboys Provide Christmas program for at least a decade. Cowboys from ranches all over Texas came together to help families in their communities, and Ward spent a lot of time in the dedicated forum for the program.

One year, about half a decade ago, Ward had been the chairperson of the entire organization. He'd coordinated over five hundred Christmases for families sprinkled across the entire state—and Texas was huge.

The amount of work he'd put in had actually caused him to become physically ill, and Ward had vowed to never take on something that big again. He'd told all of his concerns to others in the program, and now Cowboys Provide Christmas employed a full-time manager, and had two volunteer chairpeople to avoid burn-out and exhaustion.

This first package was simply his application for this year's program. He had to volunteer each year, and he had to send in ranch paperwork to show he could actually afford to help someone. Ace could still hear him talking about a family who'd been a sponsor one year—and a recipient. When the chairperson had found out, things had gotten ugly.

Rules got changed. New regulations put in place.

Either way, Ward could certainly afford to provide Christmas for a family somewhere. Heck, Ace could too. All of the Glovers too. And not just one family.

Ace flipped up the collar on his jacket and hurried inside the post office. The weather had started to bluster today, and he hoped Mother Nature would get her frustrations out and let the sun return to the Texas Panhandle.

Once he'd waited in the insanely long line to get Ward's thick envelope of papers off to the home office for Cowboys Provide Christmas in Lubbock, Ace left the post office parking lot and pulled back in to China Isle, right next door.

Chinese for lunch? he asked Holly Ann. She'd brought Chinese food home the other night, after her meeting—and the dinner and family celebration up at Shiloh Ridge she'd missed as she became the Christmas Festival chairperson— so he knew what she liked.

Can't, she said. *Sorry, Ace. I'm in a meeting with the hospital administrator and about ten other people. You wouldn't believe what I'm hearing right now.*

His curiosity piqued, he waited for her to go on. When

she didn't, he got out of his truck and went inside China Isle. He could order to-go and take it back to the house for dinner. While he waited behind another customer in the to-go ordering line, he texted Ward and Mister for what they'd like.

Their orders came flying in, and his SendCents app chinged as Mister paid him for dinner with a, *Thanks, Ace.*

He frowned and tapped to get to the transaction. He refunded it and added a note. *You don't have to pay for dinner. I'm here, and I offered.*

He half-expected Mister to send the money again, but he didn't. A text came in from him instead, and Ace tapped to move back over to that app.

"Sir?"

He looked up and realized it was his turn. "Sorry," he said, shoving his phone in his pocket. "I want two orders of the chicken and snow peas. Sesame chicken with the ham fried rice." He looked up at the menu, so ravenous. He could eat Chinese food now *and* later. "Give me one order of the crab Rangoons, and I want the orange chicken too. White rice with that."

He paid for the food, and the man said, "Fifteen minutes or so."

Ace nodded and moved out of the way. No one waited behind him, so he leaned against a pole facing the rest of the restaurant and pulled out his phone. Mister had said, *You don't have to buy my dinner, but thank you.*

Something seethed beneath the words, and Ace wanted to unearth them. *Why did you think you needed to pay for it? Ward didn't.*

If you were Judge or Preacher, they would've expected me to pay them back, Mister said.

Ace frowned, but he didn't ask his cousin anything else. Mister's relationship with his brothers was complicated—and utterly fascinating to Ace. He got along really well with Ranger and Ward, both older than him, as well as his two younger sisters. Ace sat right in the middle, and he felt like he was crucial to his family. He wondered what it would feel like to not feel like that, and his heart hurt for Mister.

I'm only making you pay for those disgusting PopTarts, he tapped out with a smile. *But Chinese food, especially when I offered to get it for you, is no big deal.*

Preacher and Judge had plenty of money too. Why did it matter if one of them bought a ten-dollar meal at China Isle for Mister?

His mind working hard now, he glanced up from his device and out into the restaurant. It wasn't hard to spot the Walker twins eating at a table near the middle of the room. Neither of them looked at Ace, and he wasn't going to go interrupt them for no reason.

He let his eyes drift to the booths lining the windows, and his heart stuttered. His eyes widened, and he even took a step into the dining room, sure what he was looking at wasn't happening.

But it so was.

"Aunt Lois?" he whispered just as his seventy-eight-year-old aunt tipped her head back and laughed at something the distinguished gentleman across the table had said. He smiled too and looked like he was laughing as well.

Aunt Lois was on a date.

Ace narrowed his eyes at the man, finding him familiar. His heartbeat ricocheted around in his chest, and horror filled him as the two of them stood. The man put some money on the table and reached for Aunt Lois's hand. She actually slipped her fingers into his, and they started to walk toward Ace.

Leave! his mind screamed at him. *Go! Get out of here!*

Bishop was going to freak out when Ace told him about this date. And Bear....

Ace could hear the growling all the way from the ranch already.

As Aunt Lois drew closer, Ace wondered if they knew. If any of her sons knew she was dating...the fire chief.

Donald Parker.

Ace sucked in a breath, his eyes going wide again.

In that moment, Aunt Lois looked away from the dark-haired fire chief—and right into Ace's eyes.

Her expression changed from joy to horror in less time than it took to blink. She continued forward fluidly, though, pausing in front of him, a fierce look entering her eyes.

Ace knew this look well, because his own mother could pierce a person's soul in the exact same way. He swallowed, his voice hidden somewhere deep down in his throat.

"Andrew," Aunt Lois said, using his real name.

This is bad, he thought. *You should've run when you had the chance.*

"Hello, Aunt Lois," he managed to say. His eyes flew to Donald's, who wore a pleasant smile. He had to be in his late sixties or early seventies, and Ace's mind fired half-formed memories at him about an article he'd read about the need for the fire chief to retire.

He honestly didn't keep up with the small-town politics in Three Rivers, but he knew the reason the article had cited was because of Chief Parker's age.

"Do you know Donald Parker?" Aunt Lois asked, glancing at him and then back to Ace.

"Sure," he said, extending his hand toward the older man. "Nice to meet you."

"And you." He looked at Aunt Lois too.

"My nephew," she said. "My husband's brother's son. He lives and works the ranch, along with his brothers and all of my sons."

"Of course," Donald said, his smile only growing wider. "Lois says you boys don't get off the ranch much. What a funny thing to run into you here."

"Oh, yeah," Ace said, nodding for a reason he couldn't name. "I was just down here mailing something for my brother, and Chinese food sounded good." He didn't dare look at Aunt Lois again, but somehow his eyes gravitated toward hers anyway.

"Ace," a man behind him called, and he spun that way.

"My food is ready."

"We'll let you go," Aunt Lois said briskly.

With his attention divided between the couple and his bags of Chinese food, Ace didn't notice that Aunt Lois had sent Donald out the door by himself until he turned around and found her singly blocking his escape.

"Andrew," she said very quietly, but with plenty of power

in the two syllables. "This is not your news to tell. Do you understand?"

"Yes, ma'am," he said instantly.

"My sons do not know about this," she added. "Neither does Arizona. I am not ready to tell them. I expect your...discretion."

"Yep," he said, hoping she'd simply nod and leave.

When she did, he sagged against the counter behind him in pure relief. A bell dinged, and he jumped away from it. "Sorry," he said. "Sorry, that was just me." He waved to the man who'd started to come toward the register where Ace stood.

He needed to get out of this restaurant before something else got blown up. Back in the safety of his truck, he managed to exhale. "Holy cow," he murmured. "Aunt Lois is secretly dating Donald Parker...and you can't tell anyone."

Bishop's face blipped behind Ace's eyelids when he blinked. How was he supposed to keep this a secret from his best friend?

"Lord," he said, pressing his eyes closed as he gripped the steering wheel tighter. "What do I do here?"

A question popped into his mind. *Is she hurting anyone?*

"No," Ace answered himself aloud, his answer clear. *Leave it alone, then.* She was a grown woman, and her husband had died fifteen years ago. She was allowed to date.

Ace was also very, very good at keeping secrets, so he drew in a deep breath, exhaled, and opened his eyes. "Aunt Lois and the fire chief," he said, his voice full of wonder. He started to chuckle, because love was an amazing thing, and he wanted his aunt to be happy.

He thought of his own mother, widowed now for coming up on six years. She lived in an assisted-living facility, because she had a few health problems. Could she have a boyfriend there?

She could, and Ace wouldn't even know it.

When he should've turned left to get on the highway that led south of Three Rivers and up to the ranch, he kept going straight instead. He needed to go see his mother and ask a couple of questions.

Chapter Six

❧❀❧

Holly Ann burst out laughing, which earned her a disgruntled look from Snickers. She kept giggling as she stroked the little dog, then quickly started typing a response to Ace. The man was a brilliant flirt, and she'd been telling him about her meeting with the hospital administrator over the children's wing.

Seriously, Ace, she said no sexy elves, Holly Ann had sent to him. *Like she made a strong point of it, so we'd know for sure. Who's dressing up as a sexy elf to deliver presents to terminally ill children?*

He'd said, *Someone confused about their holidays, obviously. Sexy elves on Halloween? Fine. For Christmas? Scandalous!*

Holly Ann sighed as she leaned back against her pillows and nestled down into her comforter. She hadn't seen Ace that day, but he'd sent her a couple of pictures of his Chinese food, claiming he missed her. He'd then sent her a picture of him and his mother, and Holly Ann scrolled up to look at it again.

His mother had bright blue eyes that shone like stars. She radiated beauty, and with Ace's face right next to hers, both of them smiling for all they were worth, Holly Ann experienced true joy. She smiled back at his picture, swiping away the text that came in from April Thorne.

Her smile faded quickly, despite Ace's handsome face still grinning at her. He made her feel so amazing about herself. He loved everything she cooked. He shared himself and his life with her. He asked about her meetings and her life, as if he really wanted to know.

Her eyes automatically moved to her closet, but Holly Ann had shut the door a few days ago, and the suit couldn't be seen. Her father's cryptic messages hadn't helped her at all, but Holly Ann told herself she still had a few weeks before it would be an issue anyway.

Santa didn't show up in Three Rivers until the day following Thanksgiving, and she ignored April for another few minutes while she messaged Bethany Rose about the meal her sister was hosting at her farm that year.

Can I invite Ace? she asked.

I thought you already had, her sister said.

Not yet.

Ace's family put hers to shame simply by sheer size. He'd surely be busy with them over the Thanksgiving holiday, but she wondered if he'd be able to carve any room into his schedule for her.

Another giggle spilled from her mouth as she thought about her pun. She put it in a text and sent it. *What are you doing for Thanksgiving? Can you carve my family dinner into your plans?* She'd added a turkey emoji and everything.

Her phone rang, Ace's name right there on the screen with his profile picture. "Hey," she drawled, and Snickers got up and moved to the end of the bed like her voice really bothered him.

"Thanksgiving dinner with your dad and sister?" Ace asked instead of saying hello.

"And Bethany Rose's husband," Holly Ann added. "They have two dogs too, and let me tell you, Boomer and Boxer have the names they do for a reason." She grinned up at the ceiling, the stress of the day melting from her. As long as she didn't look at April's text, the busyness of tomorrow couldn't touch her either.

Ace chuckled and said, "They must be bigger than Snickers."

"And not as well-behaved," she said, looking down to her little dog. "Beth's a decent cook, and her husband is fantastic with smoked meats. When she hosts, they always do a whole buffet. Smoked brisket. Smoked turkey. Smoked ribs."

"I think I'm in love with her husband," Ace teased, eliciting another giggle from Holly Ann.

"What's your schedule like on Thanksgiving?"

"We have lunch about one," he said. "My sisters and my cousin do most of the cooking. We eat all together at the homestead next door." He hesitated for a moment, and then added, "What time do you guys eat?"

"I don't know," she said. "Beth's pretty flexible."

"Maybe we could do both," Ace said. "Lunch out here. Dinner there."

Holly Ann didn't even really like turkey that much, but she could eat a vat of mashed potatoes any day of the week.

"Let me find out. She'd want to do like four o'clock or something, which isn't really dinner...."

"You just tell me," he said. "I'll handle my family."

"Does anyone else not eat with the family?"

"Uh."

That was a no. She marveled at that, though she supposed Ace's brother and cousin had just gotten married last spring. They hadn't had to try to mesh together two families or their holiday schedules and traditions yet.

Not only that, but the Glovers put up their Christmas decorations and trees really early. She was supposed to attend a family dinner and tree decorating celebration a few days ago that she'd had to miss because of the festival announcement.

She took a long breath, because Holly Ann didn't have time to be snuggling into blankets while she chitchatted with her boyfriend. Another meeting had been scheduled for tomorrow afternoon, and she needed to make at least five phone calls before then.

And perfect a cherry pie recipe that had refused to cooperate with her.

"I'm sure Sammy and Bear will go to her parents'," Ace said. "Though they usually do come up here...."

"If it doesn't work, it doesn't work," Holly Ann said. "It's fine."

"If she does it at four or so, it should be fine."

"I'll talk to her."

"Okay," Ace said. "Hey, while I have you, what's your schedule the rest of this week? I'm thinking maybe we should schedule things instead of me texting you ten minutes beforehand."

"I'm fine either way," Holly Ann said.

"Yes, but it's a thirty-minute drive from the ranch for me," he said. "And if I don't need to—if I can't see you, the only other reason I'm comin' that far is for pumpkin pie."

"Gross," Holly Ann said with another laugh. Warmth and a comfy feeling soared through her though, and her smile felt made of gold on her face. "Glad to know I'm up there with the most disgusting dessert on the planet."

"The most disgusting dessert on the planet?" Ace asked indignantly. "The whole planet, Holly Ann? Seriously, come on."

"I do not like pumpkin pie, Mister Glover."

He laughed, the sound delicious in her ears. "I thought chefs liked everything."

"Chefs are normal people too," Holly Ann said, shaking her head as she continued to grin. Snickers got up and came to snuggle into her hip again, and she reached over to pat him. "There are things I like and things I dislike. Now, I can *make* the best pumpkin pie on the planet, but that doesn't mean I want to eat it."

"What if you had to drive thirty minutes to get to town?" Ace asked. "What would you do it for no matter what? Rain, snow, wind, fire, you'd do it."

"Dessert-wise?"

"Anything-wise," Ace said, his voice somewhat serious now.

Holly Ann knew what she wanted to say. He'd probably

like to hear it too. "I do absolutely love with my whole Texan soul a pecan pie," she said, plenty of coyness in her voice. "I'd drive any distance to see a movie with Orlando Bloom in it."

"Oh, boy," Ace said dryly.

"And there's this man that always wears this sexy cowboy hat. Always black. He's got these dark brown boots that make my heart thump a little harder." Holly Ann grinned to herself. "He also wears these plaid shirts that I'd drive thirty minutes just to see. In fact, I'd like to get inside this man's closet and see if he organizes them by color."

Ace remained silent, and Holly Ann wondered if she'd gone a little too far. Her feelings for Ace weren't secret; they never had been. She just had so many other secrets that she didn't want to embarrass herself in front of him.

You've already done that, she thought. *With what you just said.*

"And oh, my, his belt buckles light up my life," she continued anyway. "I think his brother rode in the rodeo for a bit, and he lets him borrow some of the nicer ones."

"It was my cousin, actually," Ace said very quietly.

Holly Ann stroked Snickers, wondering why Ace wasn't laughing. Didn't he want her to be willing to drive through snow, sleet, fire, and flood to see him? At least he knew she was talking about him.

"Right," she said. "Cousin. That's what I meant."

"You have the Thorne reception tomorrow night, right?"

"Yes," she said, surprised he remembered that. She'd told him about the momzilla that had been fairly difficult to work with over a month ago, and she remembered that April had texted several minutes ago. Honestly, Holly Ann was surprised she hadn't called yet.

"Lunch?" he asked.

"I wish I could, Ace," she said, regret pulling through her. "I have a meeting at two-thirty, and I need to have all of the food for the reception done before then." Including those pesky cherry pies. "I've rented the kitchen at Sullivan's, because they don't open until five, and I can get three times as much done in an industrial kitchen."

"I suppose you'll be there pretty early," he said. "I should let you go."

"Eight's not too early," she said, though a yawn pulled through her throat. "But yes, I better get to bed."

"'Bye, Holly-berry," he said, and she smiled as she said good-bye to him too. She'd barely had time to sigh and set her phone on her nightstand before it rang again. She swung it up to her ear, expecting it to be Ace. He'd probably just forgotten to tell her something.

Thankfully, she caught the name before she answered, and her heart plummeted to her feet when she saw April Thorne's name there. "April," Holly Ann said. "I am looking at your one-sheet right now and was about to call."

She pushed back her blanket and got out of bed to go do what she'd just said. That way, she couldn't be called a liar, and she could dispute anything April tried to get her to do that she hadn't agreed to in writing.

THE FOLLOWING MORNING, HOLLY ANN DROVE AROUND Sullivan's and into a narrow alley that ran behind the restaurant and the cement wall behind it. She parked next to a sporty, yellow coupe, and she stood from her rental car at the same time Alta Barber rose from hers.

"Morning, Al." Holly Ann gave the other brunette a smile over the top of her car and pressed the button on her key fob to get the trunk to pop open.

"Need some help?" Alta asked. She had the personality of fire, and she could be warm and inviting or spitting and cruel. Holly Ann had always liked her, and since they both worked in the food business now, they'd become close over the past year.

"I'd love it." Holly Ann lifted one plastic tote from her trunk while Alta unlocked the door. She held it for Holly Ann as she walked inside, and then Alta went to get something from the trunk too.

Holly Ann had just plunked her bin on a stainless steel counter when Alta came in carrying the basket full of spices. "How's the baby?" She took the lightweight basket from Alta and hugged her.

She felt like a giant next to trim, petite Alta. Despite her being seven months pregnant and basically having a basketball protruding from her midsection, Alta grinned at Holly Ann. "He's doin' great." She looked down at her belly and put one hand there. "The doctor says I'll be lucky if I make it the full nine months."

"Is that right?" Holly Ann started for the back door, her friend coming with her. "How are you feeling about that?"

"I'm four-foot-eleven," Alta said dryly. "I told him to take the baby out right now." She trilled out a laugh and Holly Ann handed her a lidded tote with only large cooking utensils and her knives in it. She lifted out a second huge bin with the rest of the ingredients she needed to make the refreshments for April Thorne's daughter's wedding reception.

She was doing a three-slot hot dessert bar, with an assortment of room-temperature mini pies. Holly Ann's excitement grew as she thought about the raspberry bread pudding with almond-vanilla icing on tonight's menu. She and April had also agreed on a warm brownie batter cake with caramel swirls, and one of Holly Ann's signature desserts for this quarter: apple, pear, and white peach crisp with honey oat topping and brown butter maple drizzle. Her mouth watered just thinking about it.

She returned to her car to get another load of ingredients from the back seat, and then she started unpacking everything while Alta talked about the nursery she and her husband had been setting up for the past six months.

Holly Ann listened, because she genuinely liked Alta. She'd married Trevor almost a decade ago, but this was their first baby. Her family owned Sullivan's, and Alta was set to take over the restaurant once her father retired.

With the menu and checklist in front of her, Holly Ann started marking off the items on the counter to make sure she had everything.

"Oh, I have to run," Alta said. "You're okay here?"

"Yes." Holly Ann glanced up and caught Alta looking at her phone and typing something in. "I'll be out by one, as promised. I just lock up?"

"Yes," Alta said. "I'll lock it now, and when you go out,

it'll just stay that way. So don't go out until you're ready." She kicked at something on the floor. "There's a doorstop here, if you need to make a couple of trips to load up."

"Perfect." Holly Ann consulted her list again, noting several missing items. The vanilla extract. Very important. Cocoa powder. Essential. Wild rose honey. A must-have.

A frown pulled at her eyebrows, and then, all at once, she remembered she'd put these things in a bin together, and it still sat on her front passenger seat. She turned toward the door, hoping to catch Alta.

Thankfully, she still stood at the door, fiddling with the lock.

"I forgot something in my car," Holly Ann said just as Alta rounded the door. She looked over her shoulder, her eyes wide. "What?" Holly Ann had much longer legs than Alta, and she strode forward at the aghast look on her friend's face.

"You better get out here," Alta said, her expression melting into a charmed smile.

"Why?" Holly Ann reached the door and put her hand on it to pull it open further. She peered over Alta's head and found someone else had arrived in the back alley. A gasp flew from her throat, and she covered her now-pounding pulse with one palm.

"There's a cowboy here with breakfast," Alta said. "That's why."

Not just a cowboy, Holly Ann thought as she drank in the glorious sight of Ace Glover in that black cowboy hat, the biggest belt buckle she'd seen yet, and those dark brown boots. Not only that, but he wore a loud plaid shirt today in bright pink, blinding turquoise, and bleached white that strained across his chest and upper arms as he held a tray in front of him with breakfast balanced on it.

He's a man among men.

Chapter Seven

❧

Ace swallowed, glancing from Holly Ann to Alta. He knew Alta Sullivan—Barber now—just fine. He knew she and Holly Ann were friends. He hadn't anticipated her being here, but the yellow sports car had given it away.

She looked one breath away from popping, and he wasn't sure how she walked as pregnant as she was. She grinned at him, and said, "Good morning, Ace."

"Morning, Alta," he said, the tray starting to get heavy. He'd spent far too long organizing it to stand there in the parking lot and let his hard work get ruined should the tray start to slip. "Can I come in?"

"Absolutely," Alta said, and Ace watched Holly Ann nod too.

He approached, the vase with the flowers definitely trembling too much. He'd obsessed over where to put them, and it might not even matter. If the glass shattered on the floor, he'd get in his truck and never leave Shiloh Ridge again. He'd be unable due to death by humiliation.

You've already rammed the woman's garage, he thought as he slid the tray with French toast, scrambled eggs, and an assortment of breakfast meats onto the closest horizontal surface.

He heard female voices behind him, and only Holly Ann returned to the kitchen. The huge, heavy door slammed behind her, and she cringed, her shoulders hunching up for a moment.

Her eyes met his when they opened again, and a smile bloomed on that beautiful face.

"My shirts aren't organized by color," he said.

Holly Ann laughed and practically danced over to him. She took his face in her hands, her eyes wide and filled with so much happiness. Her happiness made him happy, and Ace slid his hands along her waist. "I thought you might need breakfast to start off your busy day right. They say it's the most important meal, you know."

"Mm." She let her eyes drift closed. "I didn't eat breakfast."

He gazed at her, and with her eyes closed, she was a softer version of the sexy woman he'd started to fall for. He liked the strong version of Holly Ann too. And the sweet one. The woman who'd performed at his aunt's birthday party last summer. The woman who'd flirted with him shamelessly last night.

He simply liked her, and he leaned down and matched his mouth to hers, a fire rising within him that knew no limit...

and that could really burn his entire life to the ground with one errant spark.

———————

"Banana bread," he said to Bishop as he tossed the loaf in front of his cousin. He sighed as he sat at the table. "I had to wait in line for twenty minutes to get that."

"Thanks," Bishop said with a grin. He nudged the box of pizza toward Ace, who reached for a slice. The cardboard bore heat and char marks, which meant Bishop had put the whole thing in the oven to warm up the leftovers.

"What's that?" Bishop asked, nodding to the paper bag Ace had left on the counter.

"Ward's sprouted wheat bread." Ace made a face, and the two of them laughed. Just then, Ward walked into the homestead using the side door, and he didn't look happy.

"…not your decision to make," he finished saying, and Ranger followed him. Cactus came last, and he glanced at Ace and Bishop sitting at the table. He rolled his eyes, which meant Ranger and Ward were just having a brotherly spat. They did from time to time, because they worked closely on the ranch's finances *and* Ranger's app. Sometimes his oldest brother would think he was right simply because he was older. He did have a brilliant mind, especially with complicated things like coding and sending out messages to thousands of people. But Ward thought outside of any box Ace had ever seen, that was for sure.

"What are they arguing about this time?" Bishop asked,

reaching down and feeding a bit of sausage to The General, Oakley's black and white cat.

"Ranger ran into Sabrina Hendrick," Cactus said. "He told her that Ward would call her, and well, Ward doesn't want to call her." Cactus reached for a piece of pizza as Ranger and Ward continued into the kitchen and poured themselves cups of coffee. "At least they're not ganging upon me to sing in the blasted Christmas program again."

He spoke with a measure of darkness only Cactus could achieve, and Ace watched as he exchanged a glance with Bishop. Ah, so there was something there.

"What was that?" Ace asked, because he could. He knew Cactus too. Maybe he didn't get invited out to the man's cabin as often as Bishop—or ever—but he'd been driving him to therapy for months now.

"Nothing," Bishop said, moving his attention back to the cat.

Cactus pulled out a chair and sat. "There's this woman at church." That was all he had to say, and Ace got it.

"She must sing."

"She leads the choir," Bishop said, and Cactus growled. "What? You started it."

"You just told him exactly who it is." Cactus shook his head and took off his cowboy hat. He ran his fingers through his getting-long-again hair and sighed. "I don't know why I care. *She* knows I like her. Why does it matter if the rest of the world does too?"

Ace didn't say anything, though he knew who Cactus was talking about. Willa Knowlton led the choir. She'd come to town several months ago with her brother, who'd come to stand in for Pastor Summers. He'd fallen and hurt himself, and though Pastor Summers was healed up now, both Willa and her brother had stayed in Three Rivers.

"She knows?" Ace asked, his voice pitching up a little in his attempt to seem nonchalant.

"I asked her out once," Cactus said.

"I thought you were going out with Violet Hamshire," Bishop said. "Are we not doing that?"

"*We* never were doing anything with Violet Hamshire," Cactus said, rolling his eyes again. "Listen, will you ask Montana if she'll come look at my roof? I swear I felt the wind blowing in my face all night."

"Sure." Bishop stood up. "Let's go right now."

"Where is she?"

"She's out in True Blue," Bishop said. "She had a meeting with a client, and she's using the big room there because the homestead is a little crazy."

"I'll say." Cactus didn't move to get up. Bishop looked at him for an extra moment and then walked away.

"He worships you, you know," Ace said, reaching for another piece of pizza. "It wouldn't kill you to throw him a bone every now and then."

Cactus turned his hooded, ultra-dark blue eyes on Ace. "Bishop knows how I feel about him." He really could be scary when he wanted to be.

"Okay," Ace said, refusing to let himself be intimidated. It was all an act anyway. A way for Cactus to cover up the extreme pain he dealt with on a daily basis. "How are the new hires doing with the fences?"

"They're eighteen-year-old kids," Cactus growled. "I'm pretty sure half of them will quit before the weekend."

Ace chuckled, because he wouldn't blame them. The pay sounded really good—and it was for cowboys in the area—but when it came right down to it, the work was hard and never-ending.

But they only re-fenced the ranch once every five or six years. In addition to his veterinary work, Cactus oversaw a handful of big projects, and he had to work with a variety of people. Ace found it odd that he could do that, but he couldn't come to a family party or live closer to the core of Glovers.

At the same time, when Holly Ann hadn't come to the party last week, Ace had immediately left. His brothers and cousins asked so many questions. And the twins were far worse, and since they'd been there, Ace had figured anywhere else he could go, he should.

Ranger and Ward sat down at the table, each with something leftover from the fridge in front of them. The General meowed to make sure everyone with food knew how terribly hungry he was. "How'd breakfast go?" Ranger asked, pushing the cat away. "No. Stop it."

"Yeah," Ward said. "Tell us about it."

Ace thought of the scorching kiss with Holly Ann, his internal temperature blasting off like a rocket.

"Turns out, she doesn't like sausage links," he said. "Only the patties. But the candied bacon was a big hit, so remind me to tell Bishop." He grinned at his brothers, knowing that wasn't the kind of update they wanted.

Ace wasn't sure he could give them the emotional update.

Or the one where he confessed how strong his feelings already were, and that he was actually terrified that Holly Ann wouldn't reciprocate them.

She sure had kissed him back, though, so maybe he was worried about nothing.

Thankfully, everyone seemed distracted today, and no one pushed him for her reaction, what she'd said, or anything past the candied bacon.

Eventually, Ranger got up with the words, "I have to go run an update for a minute," and Cactus left without saying anything to anyone.

Ace looked at The General, who closed his eyes almost all the way as if telling Ace he was a nice, docile cat. Hungry, but docile. "I should probably go find something to do in the equipment shed," he said. There was always something that needed to be repaired, as he'd been helping with the fences here and there and then finishing up the plowing under of the fields they'd leave dormant next year.

"Can I tell you something first?" Ward asked, glancing around to make sure they were alone.

Ace's heart seized. "I guess," he said, though he and Ward had shared many things with each other over the years. "Is it a secret?"

"Yep."

Ace swallowed. The number of things he was storing for people kept climbing, and he wasn't sure if he could keep all the secrets straight.

He hadn't dared to breathe a word about Aunt Lois's boyfriend, not even to Ward, who wouldn't say anything to anyone. Aunt Lois would never know Ace had even told him.

He hadn't told anyone he was driving Cactus to therapy, though a few people knew Cactus was seeing a counselor.

He hadn't told anyone that Mister lived with him and Ward. Well, just Bishop, who wouldn't have told anyone else.

"Ida's fairly sure Brady's going to propose soon," Ward said, leaning away from his empty plate and clearing his throat.

"That's it?" Ace asked. "That's not a secret."

"She asked me if I'd walk her down the aisle." He glanced over his shoulder again, and when his eyes came back to Ace's, they were dark and filled with something dangerous. "I don't want Ranger to feel bad. Ida's worried about it too, and well, neither of us know what to do."

Ace blinked, his mind blurring as he tried to think multiple thoughts at the same time. "Well," he said slowly. "Surely Ranger will understand that you and Ida have always had a special relationship."

Ward nodded, but he folded his arms, which indicated he hadn't heard Ace at all. "She's worried about Etta's reaction too."

"That's actually legitimate," Ace said, sighing. "Etta's going to feel left-out, no matter what. Ida and Brady can't help that."

"I know." Ward sat stoic and still, but Ace knew that mind was working overtime. Sometimes, when Ward really needed to work through a problem, he took his guitar out to the back porch and plucked away on the strings for hours.

Night after night, and then one day, he'd come inside and sit at the writing desk he'd inherited from their father. An hour later, he'd have a brand-new song. Ace had encouraged him to bind them all together and make a book, but Ward had never done it.

He groaned as he stood up. "Okay, well, I have to go get some stuff done for the Cowboys Provide Christmas thing."

"Did you get approved already?"

"Not officially," he said. "But I will, and I want to check-in with everyone."

Ace nodded and flipped his phone over and over while Ward left the homestead.

Ace stood and headed for the front door, as it provided a more direct path to the equipment shed. He left the house and closed the door behind him quietly, because Ranger had been complaining about how everyone came and went at the homestead at all hours of the night, and they weren't even quiet about it. A family memo had been sent on their group text about respecting the privacy of those who actually lived at the homestead and trying to be quiet when entering and exiting.

Sammy was pregnant now and due in the next few months, and Ace wanted to be respectful.

He found Benny lying on the front porch, and he stopped to scratch the black and white dog that had come to Shiloh Ridge when Sammy had married Bear. Benny belonged to her, but the dog was really Lincoln's, her son's. Since they both left during the day, the pup usually hung out with Bear, who'd trained him up real nicely to work with horses, as well as the other cattle dogs.

"Hey, bud," he said, smiling at the canine. "Where's Bear?" He glanced around, but he didn't see his big, broad-shouldered cousin.

He did, however, hear his voice.

"What's going on, Duke?"

Ace straightened, but he still didn't see Bear. He cocked his head to the side as another voice joined the conversation.

"I'd like to marry Arizona," Duke Rhinehart said, his voice steady and strong. "I'd like to ask her knowing I already have your blessing. You're like a father figure to her, and it'll be important to her."

The voices came from down the porch, and Ace turned that way. The deck wrapped around the house on both sides, and the two men must have retreated to the side verandah to talk in private.

"I don't know, Duke," Bear said with a heavy sigh.

Ace's muscles tensed. His curiosity shot toward the sky while his brain beat at him to get out of there before he heard something he wasn't supposed to hear.

"Is this because of what happened almost twenty years ago?" Duke asked.

"I suppose so," Bear said. "You've been welcome around here, Duke, but she deserves to know the truth."

Ace could just imagine Bear's pointed look as he asked, "Have you told her about it?"

"No," Duke said, his voice hard and almost a bark. "Like you said, it's in the past. I'm surprised you know about it."

"I worked with my daddy long before he died," Bear said. "Here's the deal, Duke. You tell her the truth. If she doesn't break up with you, that's my blessing."

"Bear," Duke said, but footsteps met Ace's ears. To his horror, he realized he'd actually been edging closer and closer to the corner of the house, and he had zero time to move before Bear arrived.

Duke came right behind him, and they both stalled as they met Ace's eyes.

"I was just heading out to the equipment shed," Ace said, gesturing in some random direction out onto the ranch. "I heard you, Bear, and remembered I needed to ask you something."

Bear settled his weight on one leg and cocked his eyebrows at Ace as if to say, *Well, go on then.*

Ace swallowed and looked at Duke. Big mistake. The man wore a storm on his face, and he knew Ace hadn't just happened by.

"I didn't mean to overhear," he blurted out. "Honestly. I really was going to the shed, but I saw Benny, and he's never more than ten feet from Bear."

"What did you hear?" Bear asked.

"All of it, I think," Ace said. "I'm sorry. I won't say a word to anyone."

Two more secrets, and Ace felt like he might throw up.

"I'd really appreciate that," Duke said gruffly. "Bear." He tipped his hat and strode away, ignoring Benny's thumping tail and practically flying down the steps.

Ace watched him go, because holding the mighty Bear's gaze was out of the question.

"Not a word," Bear said. "To anyone. Got it, Ace?"

"Yes, sir," he said automatically, very much like the way he had to Bear's mother only a couple of days ago. "I won't say anything."

Bear looked out over the ranch too. "I do wish the past

could stay in the past sometimes." With that, he walked away too, bending down to stroke Benny's head just once before they went into the homestead together.

"Dear God," Ace practically moaned as he sagged against the porch railing, looking up as he petitioned the Lord. "How many secrets am I going to have to keep from my family?"

Chapter Eight

Cactus Glover sat at the tiny table in his tiny kitchen, a single bowl of soup in front of him. His skills included horseback riding, glaring, and making meals that fed exactly one.

He stared at the phone he'd propped up against the bag of croutons, wishing his glare could burn a hole in the device.

He swiped at it like a tiger clawing at his next meal. The phone clunked against the table, but at least Cactus wouldn't have to see the idiotic dating app he'd opened.

"You're not doing that." He stuck a bite of too-hot soup in his mouth and immediately regretted it. But it had to stay in or go out, and he wasn't going to spit into his food.

So it burned all the way down his throat and into his stomach, ruining any appetite he'd had in the first place.

He had been dating Violet Hamshire, but he'd had to break it off. It wasn't fair to keep seeing her when he felt absolutely nothing for her. In fact, that was Cactus's definition of torture.

"No, it's not," he said. "Your definition of torture is going to church every week and seeing Willa, and you do that willingly."

Dr. Thompson, his therapist, had been encouraging Cactus to do things in a completely different way than he'd ever done them before.

"If you normally put your pants on with your right leg first, try using your left. If you always load the dishwasher after every meal, see if you can let the dishes pile up before you touch them."

Stupid stuff, in Cactus's opinion. He'd tried to put his pants on by leading with his left leg, and he'd dang near hit his head on the corner of the dresser when he'd stumbled and fallen. As he lived alone, a head injury like that could prove fatal if no one found him in time.

As he got up and rinsed his hard work down the drain, Cactus stalled once again. Yes, he normally cleaned up after every meal. That way, when it came time to eat again, everything sat ready and waiting for him.

He set the dirty bowl in the sink, wondering what it would prove.

He looked out the window above the sink, disliking the time change that made darkness cover Texas an hour earlier than it normally did. He also disliked the way his brain told him that it wasn't only because he lived alone that it would take a while for someone to find him should he get injured.

He'd purposely kept everyone at arm's length for a very long time. In the past couple of years, he'd actually made some great progress. He'd started talking to more brothers and cousins, and he'd started to integrate himself back into the family. But he could feel himself sliding backward. Maybe he was running backward. He wasn't sure.

Cactus had a love-hate relationship with God, and he stood in his small house, grateful for it, for the ranch where he lived, and the land surrounding him. At the same time, he was angry—still—and he wanted the Lord to please, please direct his feet toward a path that would get him to happiness.

"I'm honestly not sure how much longer I can exist like this," he whispered. He reminded himself that he had found some closure surrounding his son and his ex-wife.

He'd even texted Allison this year, telling her she was welcome at Shiloh Ridge any time if she'd like to visit their son's grave. She'd replied that she appreciated the offer, and she might take him up on it sometime.

He'd wanted to ask her where she was living. He'd wanted to know if she'd found a way to move on. He'd wanted to find out if she'd found someone else to love, and started a new life, the way she'd said she would.

He thought of the last time he'd seen her, her tears streaming down her face, her pained, high-pitched voice telling him she was going to do her best to find peace and start again.

She'd encouraged him to do the same.

Cactus had hated her for a long time because of that. He did *not* understand how one could find peace after the death of their child. He couldn't fathom starting again. He hadn't *wanted* to start again. He wanted what he'd already had.

Someone knocked on his front door, and Cactus turned away from the window. He'd left his hate in the past, so he *had* made some progress.

"Comin'," he said so Sammy would know he'd heard her. Cactus invited very few people out to his cabin, and Sammy served as a very physical reminder of what Bear had that Cactus did not. At the same time, she'd lost someone very important to her too, and Cactus's soul had bonded with hers the first time he'd met her. So while she reminded him of all he'd lost, he loved her like an older brother and he'd do anything to make her happy.

He opened the door and found the pretty brunette standing on the porch with her son, Lincoln. "Evenin', Cactus," she said with a tired smile. "Link, tell 'im."

Cactus looked down at the child. "Tell me what?"

"So, Bishy said you were thinkin' about gettin' a dog."

"Can you talk like a normal person?" Sammy asked, and Cactus glanced at her. Had she not heard herself say "Evenin'," and "tell 'im"?

"Yes, ma'am," Lincoln said. He looked from her to Cactus. "Uncle Bishop was helping me walk Benny, and he said you wanted a dog. There's this boy in my class whose dog just had puppies, and they're going to be real big dogs." He looked up at Sammy, who nodded. "He said they were great Danes and mastiffs combined, and I told Uncle Bishop about them tonight, and he said you would want one." Link started to bounce on the balls of his feet. "Uncle Cactus, don't you want a big dog? He could keep you company out here, and you could train 'im to walk alongside your horse, and he would keep your feet warm in the winter."

Cactus grinned at the child. "Come in, boy," he said, and Lincoln stepped past him, still chattering.

Cactus met Sammy's eye and kept his smile in place. "Thank you for bringing him."

"You're not upset?"

Cactus shrugged, though he really did adore Lincoln. "Who can stay upset at Lincoln?"

Sammy entered the house and sat down on the couch, a groan coming from her mouth. "I can't wait until this baby comes."

"I'll bet," Cactus said as he settled onto the love seat. Lincoln climbed up next to him, snuggling in close, and Cactus put his arm around the boy. "Did you bring your book to read?"

"Yep."

Lincoln started to read, and Cactus looked at Sammy. "Still not going to find out if you're having a boy or a girl?"

She shook her head, a smile touching her lips. "You know how much Bear loves surprises."

Cactus laughed, because that was the opposite of the truth.

"I can't fit under the cars anymore, Charles." Sammy pushed herself to the edge of the couch. "I can't wait to fix up your hair."

"First," Cactus said, fixing her with a hard glare. "It's just a haircut. Nothing wild. Second, I'm sorry you can't work on your cars anymore."

She nodded, something sparking in her eyes. "It's okay."

"Yes, it is," Cactus said. "Because your baby is worth a

few months where you can't slide under a car and fiddle around with a wrench."

Their eyes met, and Cactus dropped his head in apology, though he probably didn't need to. He heard Lincoln read a word incorrectly, and he said, "That word is dynasty." He grinned at the boy's slip. "Not *die*-nasty."

He started to chuckle, the sound growing and morphing as he heard the mispronunciation in Lincoln's sweet voice over and over.

Sammy started to giggle too, and Lincoln stopped reading. "What?" he asked, pure innocence in his expression.

"Nothin', boy," Cactus said, squeezing him tight against his side. "Keep reading while your momma cuts my hair."

CACTUS SAT IN HIS TRUCK AND WATCHED PEOPLE WALK toward the chapel. A happy couple swung their toddler between them every time he ran forward and launched himself into the air.

A single mother hurried through the wind with her two kids. An elderly couple clasped hands and kept their heads bent, their attention on the ground as they walked.

Cactus sat and watched like this every week, but today, he realized how everyone was welcome here. They all came from different walks of life, and lived within a completely unique set of circumstances, but the Lord loved them all.

He wanted everyone to come to Him, including Cactus, who closed his eyes and somehow left part of himself in the driver's seat while the other part of him walked across the lot by himself.

A single cowboy, his head held high as he tucked one hand in one pocket and hoped no one was watching him.

He breathed in and opened his eyes. He made the solitary walk across the lot exactly as he'd imagined he would and up the steps.

He usually arrived pretty late to church, because he wanted to slip in without talking to anyone, and better yet, get out before everyone else.

Today, though, the choir hadn't even started to sing yet, and he entered the chapel to the sound of organ music only.

Today, he thought he might try sitting with his family. As if on cue, Sammy turned around, and Cactus lifted his hand. She raised her eyebrows, and he nodded.

She set about moving everyone down the row, causing a big fuss, which was exactly what Cactus didn't want.

He ran his hand over his trimmed beard and drew in a breath. Before he could take a single step, a woman said, "Good morning, Cactus."

He nearly tripped as he turned toward her and tried to go down the aisle at the same time. He managed to catch himself by grabbing onto the back of a pew, thankfully, because when he turned to the woman, he came face-to-face with Willa Knowlton.

He hadn't even seen her sitting in the back row. She stood now, her smile lovely and revealing straight, white teeth. She wore a beautiful dress the color of midnight, with silver sailboats dotting it. A pair of diamond studs twinkled in her ears, and he found her so put together without being flashy or overdone.

His heart leapt into the back of his throat, choking him. It quickly fell to his boots when she added, "I heard you've got a beautiful bass singing voice, Cactus." She nodded to someone as they passed by, and Cactus wished he could fold himself into a smaller package so everyone would stop staring at him. Oh, and she really needed to stop saying his name in her mesmerizing voice. He was never going to be able to fall asleep again, because he'd just lay there and re-imagine his name in her voice over and over again.

The choir stood to sing, the music switching from organ to piano and drums. Cactus looked up to the front, his eyes catching on both Bear and Sammy as they gaped at him.

Help me, he thought, praying with everything inside him that the Lord would send a savior to rescue him from this conversation. He had enough brothers and cousins to get the job done. The Lord just needed to inspire one to come get him and lead him to the family row.

"Do you want to sit by me?" Willa asked, and she stepped back into the pew, moving down to make room for him.

Cactus still hadn't even said hello, nor had he denied or confirmed that he had a "beautiful bass singing voice."

The choir started to sing, and some in the congregation began clapping. He looked at Willa, her expression open and dare he say...eager?

He didn't look back toward Sammy and Bear. His phone buzzed in his pocket and that would be one of them. Probably both. More buzzing, and Cactus had a horrible sinking feeling in his stomach that everyone in the whole family had now seen him.

He needed to sit down or go home.

He slid onto the pew with Willa, flashing her a smile. As the choir sang their opening number, he leaned over and said, "You're not leading the music today?"

She shook her head, her beautiful, dark, strawberry blonde hair swinging with the movement. Her hazel eyes met his, and her smile widened. "My brother found someone else. It was time for me to let someone else have a turn anyway."

"So you're not doing the Christmas program this year?"

She shook her head, and then nodded. Cactus squinted at her, and she gave a light laugh that was quiet enough not to disturb those around them. "Not for the church. But I'm leading a big community choir for the Christmas Festival this year."

"Oh, that's amazing," he said as the choir finished their number. He faced the front again, his hands tucked between his knees though he'd very much like to lean back in the pew and put his arm around Willa's shoulders. If he didn't do that, he'd certainly claim her hand in his before the pastor could even finish the announcements.

"I *hope* it'll be amazing," Willa said as her brother announced the hymn they'd sing together as a congregation.

Cactus didn't normally sing, but today, Willa had the book open to the right page and she moved it so it hovered between them.

He had no choice but to reach out and hold the half closest to him, and Willa leaned in closer. So close, Cactus caught the floral and whimsical scent of her perfume.

He closed his eyes and took a deeper breath, because she made him fire on all cylinders.

"Perhaps with you in the choir, it *will* be amazing," she whispered just as the song began.

She didn't start singing, and Cactus certainly didn't. Wouldn't.

He couldn't believe he'd fallen into this trap, and he wanted to flip the book up so it would close and neither of them could read the words.

At the same time, the horrible, sickening thought that he should open his mouth and sing also ran through his mind.

Chapter Nine

Willa Knowlton couldn't believe Cactus Glover had sat down beside her. She'd seen him come to church many times, and today he'd been earlier than usual. He didn't sit by his family, but he usually found a spot on the end of a bench near the back.

She'd seen him get up and leave in the middle of her sermon, and she'd watched him slip out the back door the moment the closing song started. She'd never seen him anywhere but at church, and she could admit to herself that she'd been looking.

He'd asked her out after they'd met at the tack and feed store, where he'd acted like he worked there. She'd never asked him why he'd done that, because she hadn't wanted to embarrass him.

Perhaps she hadn't wanted to embarrass herself for the assumption she'd made. She'd been touched by his kindness, and she thought about him every single day. When he'd called to ask her to dinner, she'd been shocked but also pleased.

Willa had also known she wasn't ready to begin a relationship with a man like Cactus Glover. He possessed wisdom in the navy recesses of his eyes, and while he put off an air that mimicked his name, she suspected he had more depth than anyone Willa had ever met before.

He'd experienced true pain and suffering, the same way she had.

She'd wanted to go to dinner with him, but the wounds in her life had still been weeping. When Patrick had called and said an old friend of his from the seminary had fallen and he needed someone to come help, Willa had jumped at the opportunity.

She'd already had her bags packed, in fact. She'd been five minutes away from throwing her suitcases in the back of a cab and flipping a coin at every intersection to decide which way to tell the driver to go.

Instead, her brother had picked her up the next day, and they'd made the six-hour drive to Three Rivers, Texas together with his girls. Patrick was exceptionally talented at getting people to trust him and talk to him, and while Willa knew this and had vowed not to tell him anything, six hours in a vehicle together was a long time.

And she'd been in so much pain.

Willa could breathe without a pinch in her lungs now, and she thanked the Lord that so much had been healed in the past six months. She thought that if Cactus asked her to dinner now, she'd say yes.

The man intrigued her, and not just because of his good looks and depth of spirit.

A new voice joined the chorus, and Willa closed her eyes to hear it better. She'd always been touched by music, and her momma had once said she could hear harmonies no one else could.

She didn't dare move too much for fear that Cactus would silence his beautiful voice. Rich, deep, and perfectly in-tune, the man had been blessed with an incredible voice. Pastor Summers had been right.

Willa smiled as she opened her eyes, joining her soprano voice to the hymn when the third verse started. Cactus sang with her, one of them high and one low, until the end of the song. He gently put pressure on the book, and she released it. He let it close easily, and he tucked it between the two of them on the bench.

She did glance at him then, and he leaned back against the pew, his eyes straight forward as he folded his arms. She felt the tension radiating from him, and she wanted to tell him to relax. At the same time, she would never tell another person to relax, as it sounded so condescending and cruel to her.

"I know what you did there," he whispered, his head inclining toward hers slightly.

"What did I do?" she asked, feeling like a sixteen-year-old again, sitting next to the cutest boy in school.

"You got me to sing so you could hear my voice."

"Guilty," she said with a smile.

"You're going to ask me to join the community choir."

"Most likely."

"I'm not going to do it," he said.

Willa didn't know what to say to that, so she focused on her brother's face behind the mic and tried to pick up where he was in the sermon. It was impossible with Cactus at her side. Her skin buzzed with an energy she hadn't experienced before, and all Willa could think about was how she could see him again.

When, and how. What they could do together. This was her first year in Three Rivers, but she'd heard several stories about the holiday festivities the town hosted. Everything from tree decorating contests, to opportunities to serve in the children's wing at the hospital, to putting together care packages for soldiers serving overseas. She'd even heard talk of a Wassail Weekend, and as a lover of hot apple cider, Willa was looking forward to marking that on her calendar.

The full list of activities and events would be published sometime this week, and Willa could already feel the Christmas cheer vibrating through the air.

Before she knew it, Cactus stood up, and Willa glanced at him, thinking him getting ready to make his escape.

But no, everyone else had stood too, because the sermon had ended and the closing song had begun. Embarrassment filled her as she quickly got to her feet, the ache in her knee smarting as she put her weight on it.

Cactus glanced at her, but he hadn't picked up the hymnal. Willa didn't either, because she knew this song by heart. She grinned at him and opened her mouth to sing. He didn't, but it didn't matter. She'd heard his voice, and it had been glorious and beautiful.

As the last verse came to a close, Willa felt her time with

Cactus rapidly ending too. She stopped singing and leaned toward him. "I heard the town kicks off Christmas with a tree-lighting...thing. Do you—?" She cut off as he swung his head toward her and looked at her fully.

Something stormed on his handsome face, and it ignited irritation inside her chest. She wasn't going to ask him to the tree lighting now. With him glaring at her like that, she wasn't going to talk to him ever again.

"What were you saying?" he asked as the song ended completely and the congregation started to enter the aisles.

"Nothing," she said, turning to pick up her purse. "Nothing at all."

"It sounded like you were going to ask me to the tree-lighting...thing." Something sparkled in those eyes, but Willa couldn't determine if it was dangerous or flirty before Cactus shuttered it away.

"I wasn't," she said.

"Good," he said. "Because I wouldn't go. I don't do stuff like that."

"Participate in your community events?" she fired at him, her eyebrows going up in a challenge. Her heart beat faster and faster, and it wasn't only because he turned fully toward her, completely blocking anyone from exiting the bench on his side.

"That's right," he said.

"Because you're spending time at the tack and feed store, posing as someone who helps people find rabbit feed."

His eyes blazed now, and it was definitely with an angry fire. "You asked me where the feed was, and I knew. I told you. I never *posed* as anything." He also didn't bother to keep his voice down, and a couple in the pew in front of them waiting to get to the aisle looked at the two of them. "In fact, Miss Knowlton, you're the one who assumed I worked there without asking."

"You could've said so," she said.

"Why would I? Is it not okay for me to be neighborly and helpful? The rabbits survived, I assume."

Willa lifted her shoulders a tad higher and shook her hair back over them. "Yes."

Cactus gave her a smile that could've been a smirk. "Did they eat better than you?"

Willa's frustration with him faded slightly, but he'd already ignited every cell in her body. "As a matter of fact, they didn't. My brother is single, you see, and it turns out that he doesn't really know what a vegetable is."

Cactus burst out laughing, and Willa glanced around again, almost embarrassed by the volume of it. At the same time, the gorgeous, deep laugh tickled something inside her too.

"Cactus?"

Willa looked past him to a man of equal height and breadth, and he definitely belonged in the same family as Cactus.

"Hello, Pastor Knowlton," he said.

"Hello," she said. "I'm not the pastor anymore, so you can just call me Willa." She put her placid smile on her face as Cactus looked at the other man. He nodded and raised his eyebrows, obviously communicating something to Cactus he didn't like.

Finally, he said, "I'm not introducing you to her. You

already know her, *and* she just told you her name." He looked at Willa, nodded once, the brim of his cowboy hat nearly concealing his face, and left the pew.

The man stood there with his pregnant wife, and he extended his hand toward Willa. "I'm Bear Glover, Cactus's older brother. My wife, Sammy. Our son, Lincoln."

"Of course," Willa said, shaking his hand and then Sammy's, smiling at Lincoln last. "Nice to meet y'all."

"Can I just ask you one thing?" Sammy asked, stepping partially in front of Bear. "How did you get him to sit down?"

"No, no," Bear said. "Baby, you should've asked her how she got him to sing."

"Two things, then," Sammy said, and Willa looked back and forth between the two of them. They simply looked at her, not an ounce of teasing in sight. They really wanted to know. Others in the Glover family crowded behind them too, men and a couple of women, their eyes just as anxious and just as eager to hear her answers.

"Move along," one of the women said. "Leave her alone." She shooed the group forward, but she stayed back, her eyes barely leaving Willa's as she watched her family leave. "The real question is how you got him to stay all the way to the end of the service."

"No," a man said as they came back into the chapel. "I want to know what you did to get him so riled up that he'd argue with you right here in church." He actually looked semi-gleeful about their argument.

Willa had no idea what to say, and she rarely found herself in such a position. Embarrassment filled her that they'd heard the argument, but she still felt like she couldn't walk away. They both looked at her, until finally the woman said, "I'm Arizona, Cactus's sister."

"Willa." She shook Arizona's hand while she said, "This is my cousin, Ace."

"And you're all Glovers?" Willa asked.

"That's right," Ace said with a smile. "It can get over-whelming, trust me. Sometimes I even forget how many of us there are."

"You do not," Arizona said as she swatted at Ace's shoulder. "There are twelve of us. Nine boys. Three girls, and we live up at Shiloh Ridge Ranch."

Willa had heard of it, only because she'd asked Stan Summers who Cactus Glover was. She felt like she deserved to know, as he'd given the man her phone number.

Ace looked at his phone. "I have to go, or I won't have a ride back to the ranch. Nice to meet you, Willa." He touched the brim of his cowboy hat and ducked out the back of the chapel.

Willa managed to step into the aisle, hoping to shake Arizona by going down the hall to Patrick's office. His girls would be there, waiting for her, and she'd take them back to her house until Patrick finished up here.

The woman followed her, though, saying, "Quick tip on Cactus. He only *pretends* to have a loud bark." She gave Willa a knowing smile and hurried out the front doors.

"What in the world does she think she knows?" Willa murmured to herself. She also didn't believe her, not even for a second. Cactus had a loud bark, period. He'd nearly shouted at her in the back row of the chapel, mere moments after the service had ended.

"Aunt Willa," Gigi called, and she turned away from the doors Arizona had gone through to receive her six-year-old niece. She smiled as she lifted the girl into her arms, ignoring the stitch of pain in her back that caused her to spasm.

"What's Mariah doing?" she asked. "Doesn't she know we have cookies to bake today?"

Gigi's face lit up. "Can we make those oatmeal ones with the white chocolate chips and the red raisins?"

Willa giggled and nodded. "Yes, baby. We can make those." She cast another look toward the doors before putting Gigi back on her feet so they could walk down the hall and find her sister.

After all, Willa needed a lot of cookies in order to figure out why she'd engaged in an argument with a man she barely knew. Not only that, but a man she'd been thinking about for months. A man she'd hoped would ask her out again.

She shook herself at yet another bad judgment call and started mentally going over the ingredients she'd need to make homemade Oreos in addition to the white chocolate cranberry cookies Gigi wanted.

Chapter Ten

Ranger Glover stood beside Oakley's shoulder, his hand gripping hers. Dr. Monroe stood and started to remove her gloves. "You're done, Oakley." She wore the news on her face, and Ranger bowed his head, the anguish streaming through him stretching toward infinity.

Dr. Monroe stepped on the pedal to open the garbage can and tossed her gloves inside while Oakley covered up her legs and sat up. Ranger moved to her side and looked at her. She already knew too.

"It's definitely another miscarriage." Dr. Monroe sat on her rolling stool and moved right into Oakley's knees. "I'm so sorry, Oakley." She actually reached up and brushed at her dark eyes. Ranger focused on the doctor's long, thick eyelashes, as well as her sleek, straight, nearly black hair. He couldn't look at his wife again.

"I think y'all should take a break." Dr. Monroe looked at Ranger. "I know you want a child, and there's nothing more I want too—except for your health and well-being, Oakley. You've had two miscarriages in what?" She glanced over at her nurse, though the other woman in the room gave no indication of anything. "Just under nine months. Your body needs time to heal."

Ranger's heart needed that time too, and he'd never felt anything as true or as deep as that. Beside him, Oakley nodded, her tears flowing down her face in a steady clip. She made no move to wipe them, and Dr. Monroe zipped over to the counter and picked up the tissue box. She extended it to Oakley, who took a couple and covered her whole face as she sobbed.

He could not stop this pain, and this level of helplessness actually ignited a fury inside him unlike any he'd felt before.

Dr. Monroe gave him a small smile he could not return. Her eyes were so wide and so full of concern, and she touched Oakley's knee. "I can give you something for the next couple of weeks. Rycor. It's an anti-depressant—a light one. It'll help you deal with the feelings you're having."

Oakley shook her head and laced her fingers in Ranger's. "I'll be okay," she said, squeezing his hand with what felt like every ounce of strength she had.

The doctor nodded, her concern never wavering. "Oakley, I want you to take a prenatal vitamin. I want you to come back in June, and we'll do an assessment of everything. We'll do blood work and check to make sure you're as healthy and as ready as possible to carry a baby. Okay?"

Oakley nodded, but to Ranger, June felt impossibly far away. It was over seven months away. "Then what?"

"Then, you two can try again." Dr. Monroe tried the

small smile on her, quickly sobering. "We know you can get pregnant. Instead of waiting to take a test from the supermarket, you'll come here. We'll do a blood test on the third day, and the fourth, and the fifth until we know if you're pregnant or not. Once you are, we'll start the progesterone treatments." She nodded to the nurse, who came forward and handed Oakley a couple of sheets of paper.

"They're perfectly fine for you and the baby," Dr. Monroe said. "It's a shot you get every week to make sure your body knows it's pregnant. What's happening, I think, is that the baby isn't producing enough progesterone, and that's a signal to your body that you're not pregnant. So it wants to menstruate as usual. The shots keep that pregnancy hormone high enough, until the baby is big enough to do that itself."

Oakley nodded, handing the pages to Ranger. He nearly fisted them, the white noise racing through his ears and blood deafening and crippling. "Then what?"

"Then, once you reach the second trimester, and your blood work shows that your body is producing the needed hormones itself, that's it. You carry that baby to full-term." She grinned as if such a thing could really be so simple. If it was, Ranger wouldn't be in the blasted room the size of a postage stamp, grieving the loss of his second chance at fatherhood.

His poor, lovely wife wouldn't be experiencing abdominal pain and losing blood so quickly she nearly passed out. She wouldn't be tired for weeks following this, and he wouldn't have to try to tell himself that everything would be okay.

Nothing was okay.

Dr. Monroe nodded and stood. She murmured something to her nurse, and she hugged Oakley tightly. "We're going to get it right next time," she said. "We know more now." She straightened and looked at Ranger. "Plenty of fluids and rest, both of you. If she's bleeding severely, you get her to the hospital."

"Yes, ma'am," Ranger said woodenly, not even recognizing his own voice. The doctor left, and he helped Oakley get dressed, leaving behind the soiled gown that only tied in the back. He walked right beside her back to the truck, and he stood inches behind her as she climbed in.

Oakley cried while Ranger choked the steering wheel. He'd promised Bear they'd pick up the pets from the groomer, and he had to leave her while he ran inside to get Benny and The General.

The cat really didn't like the groomer, and he wasn't shy about letting everyone know. The General didn't like much of anyone, especially Benny, Lincoln's dog, but Ranger held onto the leash in one hand and the cat carrier with the yowling cat in the other.

He got them both in the back seat, noting that Oakley simply stared out the window now. Blank from here until the horizon, and Ranger's hatred at this situation bloomed again.

"Ready?" he asked over The General's protests at being left in the cat carrier. Oakley simply nodded, her chest lifting every time she hiccuped.

Only a few blocks later, she twisted around and got The General out of his carrier. The cat wasn't what anyone would call a loving friend, but right now, he curled up on Oakley's lap in the front seat and settled right down. She stroked him absently while Ranger struggled to find something to say.

Benny put his paws up on the console between the two front seats, and Ranger said, "No, bud. Stay in the back."

He went, only to come forward again a few seconds later. He pressed his nose to Oakley's cheek, and she lifted her hand and cuddled his face against hers. Fresh tears came, and Ranger prayed to know what to say or what to do to help her.

Nothing came, and he wondered if that was the answer. There simply was nothing to be said or done to help her right now. Crying was okay, and he should let her carry on with that.

By the time they reached the turn-off for Shiloh Ridge, she'd calmed and wiped her face with a couple of napkins from the glove box. At the homestead, she drew a deep breath and opened her door.

Ranger met her and The General at the front of the truck with Benny, and they went straight in the front door of the homestead and up the steps, no discussion needed. He couldn't face anyone right now, and truth be told, he wasn't even sure he could face his wife.

He put coffee on in their wing of the house while she went down the hall to the master suite. Silence permeated everything, and Ranger stood in front of the huge window that looked out over the ranch from his second-floor living room.

Everything outside existed in shades of brown, white, and gray. Nothing seemed alive or thriving, and a deep, penetrating numbness overcame him. It wasn't until Benny nosed his hand that Ranger smelled the fresh coffee and turned away from the barren landscape.

He poured two cups of coffee and took long minutes to stir in cream and sugar before going down the hall to the bedroom. Oakley had curled herself into their bed, and he set their coffee on her nightstand. He leaned over and pressed a kiss to the corner of her eye.

She wept, and Ranger discarded his boots and his belt and climbed into bed behind her, wrapping her in his embrace and holding her tightly against his chest. He wasn't sure if the action was meant to comfort her or himself.

Ranger wanted to be a father desperately, and he felt the loss of another child like a whip across his soul. He pressed his eyes closed and prayed that the Lord would help him be strong for his wife. Ranger didn't have to deal with physical ailments on top of the crushing emotional blow, and he tightened his arms around her as he began to weep too.

He didn't tell her it would be okay. He didn't tell her they'd try again. Right now, Ranger needed to grieve, and he needed to find a way to do that with his wife and within the framework of his other responsibilities.

"Baby?" he finally whispered. "I'm going to ask Ward to take over Two Cents in Amarillo."

Oakley rolled toward him, her face only inches from his now. They existed together in this narrow space of time and with her so close, Ranger felt the weight of the world disappear. "What do you think of hiring someone to do some of what you do at Mack's?" he asked. "I think we need time, baby."

"Time for what?" She cradled his face in her hands, her eyes focused somewhere down by his mouth.

Ranger let his eyes drift closed, and the world further narrowed. Just her and him and the sound of their breathing. Just the light, feminine touch of her fingers along his jaw. Just the warmth of the two of them together.

"Time for us," he said, not sure how to explain it. "Time to grieve together. Time to talk about everything. Time to just be who we want to be." He opened his eyes again and looked into hers. "Just time."

She searched his face, finally giving him a small nod. "I'll talk to Vanessa today."

"Not today," Ranger whispered. "Today, we're just staying here."

Her face fell again, and her chin wobbled as her emotions overcame her once more. "I love you, Ranger Glover. Thank you for giving me time."

"When my father died," he said as she slid her hands down to his chest and then one around his back. "I didn't take any time. I had to process it all and keep going to work. I had to set the example for everyone. I had to be the strong one." His chest heaved now as fresh waves of pain rolled through him.

"I did the same thing when we lost our first baby. I can't do it again. I'm trying, baby, and I will be there for you when you need me, but I'm not going to pretend like I'm okay when I'm not, and I don't think anyone expects us to."

Oakley just nodded and reached up and stroked his face. He loved that comforting touch, and he kissed her gently. "I think we should tell the family." His nerves raged at him, but he plowed on. "They can help too. I believe in the power of prayer."

"I do too."

"My mother has special sway with the Lord," Ranger said with a smile through his anguish. "At least that's what she told us kids growing up." He laughed quietly, the sound only lasting for a moment or two. "We believed her too. When Ace didn't make it home one night from a dance, she got us all up and into the living room. We all knelt at the couch while she prayed for him and his safety and to know what to do to bring him home. I have no doubt she did that privately for all of us, all the time."

"What happened?" Oakley asked.

"She stood up and said, 'Okay. Ranger you go get the spotlights from the barn. You and Daddy will take the night truck and drive down to town. See if he's off the road or needs help.' She gave every one of us a job, and right in the middle of telling Etta she needed to go find Ace's backpack, she paused. She tilted her head to the left and she said, 'I need to call Carrie.' Then she walked over to the phone and with all of us standing there listening, even Daddy, she called someone she barely knew."

Ranger let that powerful feeling and the immense lesson he'd learned that day flow through him. He drew in a breath and pushed it all out. "I learned that God answers prayers that night. I learned that my mother did have a special conduit to Him. I learned that He loves me, and He loves her, and He loves Ace."

"Where was he?"

"Carrie Dawson had found Ace walking on the side of the

road, on the highway back toward town. She picked him up and took him to the gas station, where he filled up a can. He said he could walk back, and it was late. Carrie wouldn't let him, and she took him back to his truck and waited to make sure it would start. It wouldn't, and they had arrived at her house thirty seconds before Mother called. She was trying to get Ace to tell her our phone number so she could call and let us know where he was. He was a little panicked and hadn't been able to tell her yet. Daddy and I went to get him, and we didn't see his truck on the highway where Carrie said it had been. It wasn't there."

"Where was it?"

Ranger shivered now, the same way he had then. "We went the next day in the light, and we still couldn't find it. Ace insisted he'd parked it near Quail Creek Road. He even found his footprints and an oil stain from the old truck. We reported it stolen, and about two weeks later, we learned there had been a string of vehicle thefts late at night, when someone had been injured during the robbery. Mother sobbed and sobbed and she told us all that God had protected Ace that night because of our prayers and that Carrie Dawson, who was never out that late, had been sent to save him."

There were so many more lessons Ranger had learned through that experience, but he was suddenly so tired. He closed his eyes. "Let's go see Mother tomorrow, okay? Maybe she can pray for us and we'll find some relief for even an hour."

Oakley nestled into his chest and said, "I'd like that. Ranger, I don't want to tell anyone. I don't care if they know, but can someone else tell them? And can we ask them not to ask me about it? I don't—I'm not ready to talk about it."

"Of course," he said. "We'll tell Mother and she'll handle everything." He'd seen her do it before and she'd do so again. He and Oakley settled into silence, and he sent a prayer of gratitude heavenward for such an angel mother that he could rely on, even now.

Chapter Eleven

Holly Ann stood in front of the full-length mirror in her bedroom, the bright red and white assaulting her eyes. "This isn't right," she muttered to herself, trying to get the big Santa coat down around her hips.

She wore the bodysuit under the costume, the same as she had been for the past four years, and she'd never had a problem with the coat riding up like that. Feeling clownish, she stared into her own eyes, trying to find the solution.

Her father would be here in a few minutes, as she needed help getting the beard and hat ready this year. Since she'd been named the chairperson for the Christmas Festival, she'd be extremely busy and torn in a dozen different directions. She needed to be able to step into the role of Santa in less than five minutes and slip out of the suit, the wig, and the persona just as quickly.

Her family had been the Santa Claus in Three Rivers for four generations, and she was the first female Kris Kringle. A sense of pride filled her as she took in the baggy pants that would look spectacular once she tucked them into the over-sized black boots. The pieces themselves never really inspired her, but with the wide, black belt around her waist, the fluffy beard against her face, and the twinkle in her eye that came every time she sat on Santa's throne, Holly Ann did love playing the holiday hero that made children's wishes come true.

The role was important to her, because she felt like so many of her childhood prayers and wishes and dreams had not come true. Her mother hadn't returned after walking out on her and Bethany Rose, for example, and she'd never gotten her Telly Talksalot doll. The year Bethany Rose had opened an Easy Bake Oven had been the highlight of the holidays for Holly Ann, and she loved holding children on her lap—even while they screamed—and letting them whisper their deepest wishes in her ear.

In her time on the throne, Holly Ann had personally donated Christmas to a dozen families, sponsoring those she knew wouldn't have anything after their children had perched on her knee and admitted all they wanted was a new pair of shoes.

She'd made sure that tiny boy last year had gotten them. His sister had received a new dress too, and Holly Ann had bought every toy on their Santa Shops For Kids list. That program would not be getting cut this year, though Holly Ann knew she needed to pare down the list of activities in the Christmas Festival.

She thought about the free miniature golf night, and that could probably go. Three Rivers designed a ton of events for families and kids, and the miniature golf course didn't need to benefit from it. Families could take their children for sleigh rides in the downtown park or to write letters to Santa at the founder's fountain.

Holly Ann tilted her head as she settled the cheery Santa hat right above her eyebrows. Since she sported far darker features than her father, Holly Ann wore blue-colored contacts while playing Santa Claus, and getting those in and out would probably take the longest amount of time.

She finger-combed the hair she'd glued inside the elfish hat and played with the fold of it, pulling on the white puff ball to get it to lay right.

Finally satisfied, she picked up the belt and wrapped it around her waist. When it wouldn't go all the way to the hole she'd used last year, lightning struck her mind. She'd started a catering company this year, and she may or may not have put on a few pounds.

Her eyes widened in the mirror, and she quickly stripped everything off—the suit, the hat and wig, the bodysuit, and hurried into the bathroom.

"Thirteen pounds," she said, her voice mostly a gasp as she stared at the number on the scale. She looked up, but there was no mirror there. "You've gained thirteen pounds since last year. No wonder the suit doesn't fit."

Horrified and disappointed, Holly Ann stepped off the scale. She'd never cared much about her weight, and perhaps her clothes had been a tad too tight recently. She liked her curves, and she liked food.

But thirteen pounds?

She carefully stepped back into the body suit, wondering

if she could shave some padding out of it. After all, she now had more natural padding than before. The costume went over that, and she latched the belt one hole bigger.

Santa didn't need a waist, and the belt did help the coat sit better on her hips. She repositioned the hat and stepped into the enormous boots. She wouldn't be able to run anywhere in these, and she reminded herself that she'd need to be sure to schedule herself time to change and get to Santa's appointed appearance spots in plenty of time. The last thing she needed was to fall flat on her face because she was in a rush.

No one wanted to talk to Santa when he had a black eye, and she wouldn't be able to hide an injury the way she did her eye color.

With only the beard left, Holly Ann faced the mirror again. This was always the trickiest part, and it could take her twenty minutes to get the facial hair positioned correctly and glued in place. "You don't have that kind of time this year," she told her reflection. "You have to practice until you can do it in two minutes flat."

Before she could begin, her doorbell rang. Snickers jumped to his feet from his nap time position on the bed, barking as he ran to the edge of the mattress.

"Yes, you're ferocious," she said to him. "Come in!" she yelled, hoping her voice was loud enough for Daddy to hear.

She reached up under the Santa cap and looped the beard around her ears. "Maybe I can glue the beard to the hat too," she mused. Make the hair, hat, and beard all one piece. That could speed things up.

"Holly Ann?" a man called.

"In the bedroom," she called back, distracted by the stupid loop that wouldn't go up under the hair right on the left side. Yes, she definitely needed to make this a single piece. Then she could have everything arranged and correct before she even started getting dressed.

"It's Ace. You want me to come into the bedroom?"

Holly Ann's vision turned white. Her heartbeat raced. Her fingers turned numb. She dropped the beard.

Her reflection was that of a female-faced Santa Claus, and Ace Glover absolutely could not see her like this.

Gaining control of herself, she reached out and slapped the bedroom door closed even as footsteps came closer. "No!" she yelled a moment before the door slammed closed. "Sorry, I'll be right out."

She pressed her eyes closed and held very still as if that would get Ace to leave. What in the world was he doing here?

An alarm went off on her phone, forcing Holly Ann to turn and walk in the bulky boots to check what she needed to do. *Lunch with Ace* sat on the screen, and she groaned as she remembered that she'd agreed to go eat with his family up at the ranch today. They got together every Sabbath, and Holly Ann had been excited to attend today.

She sat heavily on the edge of her bed, her phone gripped in her hands. Could she cancel now? He was already here, and she'd already talked to him. What would she even say?

The doorbell rang again, and Holly Ann pressed her eyes closed. "Dear Lord, he's going to have to meet my father without me." She looked up at the ceiling. "Help him."

She felt bad praying when she'd skipped church, and she

vowed to get up on time next week. *Change and get out there*, her mind screamed at her.

She didn't move, because she needed Daddy's help with this Santa suit, and he was leaving town for the next week to teach at a police academy conference.

"Do you want me to get that?" Ace asked, his voice dangerously close to the door.

"Yes," Holly Ann called. "It's my dad. Will you send him back here for me? I'm not feeling very well, and I need to talk to him."

"Sure thing."

The doorbell rang again, and Holly Ann shook her head. "Jeez, Dad, give me two seconds." She could just see him standing on the porch, the first two digits of 911 already dialed, his thumb hovering over the second one. He was jumpy and paranoid, but also the best man Holly Ann knew. He'd do anything for her and Bethany Ann, and he believed in anything and everything Holly Ann had ever wanted to do or try.

He'd given her the funding to start Three Cakes, and she'd have him paid back in another four months, if business kept up as it currently was.

"Holly Ann?" Her father's knock came on the door, and then it started to open. He slipped inside, barely opening the door wide enough for him to enter. He wore a sharp look in his eyes, some of it edged with concern.

"What is Ace Glover doing here?" he hissed as he came closer.

"I forgot we were going to lunch with his family." Holly

Ann stood up. "So help me really fast, Daddy. Then I can go with him too."

"Help you really fast," Daddy said, shaking his head. "This is not something you rush, Holly Ann." He had a special way of making her three-syllable name into five.

"Daddy, I have to rush it this year." She met her father's eye in the mirror. "I just need help with the beard. I have to be able to get it on and in place quickly. What do you think I should do?"

He scanned her from the cap to the big, black boots, a smile taking over his features. He beamed at her. "I love this suit." He brushed something from her shoulder, and she let him have a moment.

Then she said, "Help me, Daddy," in a tone that had him squaring his shoulders and rolling them back as if he were about to enter a boxing ring for the fight of his life. "I think if you sew in the beard on one side, then all you'll have to do is put on the cap, pull the beard up and around, and secure it on the other side."

"Genius," she said. "Could I use a snap?"

Daddy stuck his finger up into her hat above her ear. "I think a button would be better. It'll give you some wiggle room and be easier to attach by yourself."

"I can't really sew," Holly Ann said, thinking of her younger sister. Bethany Ann could make the most complicated of Halloween outfits out of thread and fabric and feathers. The only problem was she didn't know about this Broadbent tradition either.

"Yes, you can," Daddy said. "It was one of the classes you took during that decade where you were trying to find your self." He didn't smile, but he didn't intend for his words to be cruel. They sort of stung Holly Ann, but she didn't show it.

She couldn't help her gypsy spirit, though she worked incredibly hard to subdue it. She did not want to be like her mother. She would not abandon her father and sister, despite her longing to see more of the world. To quell her need to constantly be doing something new, Holly Ann had tried dozens of different things, trying to find the one item that she could cling to and own.

She'd learned to paint with oils and watercolors. She'd taken several gardening classes, and for a while there, she thought she'd open her own landscaping company. That hadn't panned out, because Holly Ann didn't like working in blazing hot temperatures and having mud under her nails.

She'd worked for a theater company as an acting coach for a while, and she'd taken singing lessons. She'd taken one sewing class, but as that memory surged forward, so did the one where she hadn't been any good at making straight lines with a needle and thread.

"You'd do it by hand," Daddy said. "I know your mother taught you how to sew on buttons."

Holly Ann said nothing, but she was already planning how she could sew in the beard. "Okay," she finally said. "Help me mark it."

Together, they positioned the beard where it needed to go, making minute adjustments and ensuring it didn't catch on the collar of her coat, where it could get pulled off easily.

"Right here," Daddy said, looking at her in the mirror. "It's perfect. I'll pin it."

Holly Ann resisted the urge to tell him to hurry. Every

second they were in here together meant Ace was waiting out in her house somewhere. The reason she needed to provide changed with every breath, because what would he believe for why her father had come into her bedroom and not come out for fifteen minutes?

With the beard pinned, Holly Ann said, "Okay. You go out and entertain Ace for a few minutes while I change and get this put away."

"Entertain Ace?"

"Be nice to him, Daddy." Holly Ann reached down and pushed off one boot. "I like this man."

Daddy grunted, the sound morphing into muttered words she didn't catch as he left the bedroom. She didn't have time to worry about it right now. She put the boots in the corner and stripped all the clothes off. She hung them on the special, extra-large hangers and did the same with the bodysuit.

She removed the cap with the pinned beard last and set it on the shelf in her closet just-so. She'd have time to sew the beard tonight, after she returned from the ranch.

Since she'd forgotten Ace was coming, she hadn't chosen her outfit, and her mind raced with what she should wear to Sunday dinner with his entire family. At his generational ranch, where she'd only been once before.

In the end, she chose clothes she loved and felt comfortable in, and she double-checked to make sure the closet door was closed before she left her bedroom. As she hurried down the hall, her shoes in her hands, she heard Ace say, "...that would be my mother," and then he chuckled.

She burst into the living room, scanning to take in the

scene as quickly as possible. Ace sat on the couch, seemingly at ease in her house, one arm up on the back of the couch. Daddy perched on the piano bench facing Ace, his expression open and curious.

"Is that right?" he asked, clearly in awe. "Well, I'll be."

"You'll be what?" Holly Ann asked, causing her father to turn toward her and Ace to leap to his feet. Their eyes met, and Holly Ann stepped toward him. "I'm so sorry, Ace. I wasn't feeling well, and...I'm okay now." She leaned right into him, balancing herself with one hand on his shoulder and kissed his cheek. "I just need to let Snickers out and put on my shoes and...." She glanced around, completely out of her element.

"I'll take Snickers," Daddy said, bending to scoop up the little dog. "He likes me, and I need a friend today."

Holly Ann met her dad's eyes, regret and guilt combining into a dangerous cocktail inside her. "Sorry, Daddy."

"We don't have to go," Ace said.

"I want to." Holly Ann sat down and slipped on her shoes. "Should I follow you up or are you willing to drive me all the way back down here?"

"I'll drive you," he said, swallowing as he glanced at Daddy. "I saw they got your door off."

"They did." Holly Ann smiled as she rose to her feet. She took his hand, claiming him in front of her father. She'd tried to wander from Ace before. She feared she'd do it again. Looking at him, this kind, hard-working, handsome cowboy, she really didn't want to hurt him. At the same time, she couldn't tell him about the Santa suit, and what good, kind, loving relationship was built on a secret? What relationship would work with a woman who couldn't stick to any one thing? Whose attention skipped from thing to thing as easily as the wind changed direction?

She swallowed down the questions and fears, thanked Daddy for taking Snickers, and nodded Ace toward the exit.

Chapter Twelve

A ce turned away from the gaping garage in front of him, his truck already in reverse. "When did they say the new door will be in?" He honestly hadn't thought it would take a week to replace her garage door. At least she could drive her own car now.

"Tomorrow" she said, and he felt her smile fill the cab.

He looked at her, and she sure didn't seem sick. She'd put a thin coat over the pine green sweater she'd had on, the scooping neck something that had made Ace swallow hard. The navy blue coat had enormous buttons up the front, tapered in at the waist, and flared over her hips.

Ace could only think about kissing her. And then kissing her again while he put his hands on the belt around her waist. And then kissing her again as he slid his fingers through the silky, black ribbons of her hair.

He swallowed and shifted in his seat. He'd kissed Holly

Ann before, but it had been a while since they'd shared a really good kiss.

"Tell me what to expect up here today," she said.

That got Ace talking, and the nervousness scampering through him settled into a normal knot of nerves he could deal with. He told her about the people who clashed, and the stories about Judge and Mister sounded pretty ridiculous as he told a couple.

"Sometimes Bear and Ranger argue a little. Ward isn't all that happy with Ranger right now either." He glanced at her as they started down the South highway. "But we all get over things. We forgive each other, and we move on. If things get real bad, Bear and Ranger will call a family meeting."

"How often do you have family meetings?"

"Every so often," Ace said. "You were going to come to dinner after one last week. It wasn't about anything bad, though."

"But you just said he called a family meeting when things got bad."

"They're for discussions," Ace said, trying to figure out how to explain it. "So, we have twelve of us, right? I have eleven siblings or cousins, and we all work at the ranch. Everyone except the twins lives up there. Some of us—them—some people are getting married now, and they can't live with their brother with their new wife, right?" He glanced at her, wondering if she'd heard all of that stumbling. "So we're building new houses, and looking at some of our adjacent properties to make sure any Glover who wants to stay at Shiloh Ridge can actually do that."

"I see," she said. "It makes things less complicated when there's just two of you."

"That it does," he said with a smile. "Is that you saying you don't want a big family?" He didn't dare look at her, in case this conversation was a bit premature.

The weight of her gaze fell on the side of his face, but he gripped the steering wheel as if he was driving into the heart of a terrible storm.

"I don't know," she said.

"You don't know if you want a big family?"

"I don't know," she said, and her voice had turned quieter than normal.

Ace dared to look at her then. "It's okay if you don't."

"What if I don't want children at all?" She looked out the passenger window, and Ace didn't like that. A new distance started to open between them, and he desperately needed to claw it back.

"Hey, tell me what's going on in your head," he said.

Holly Ann crossed her legs, which was a real feat in the jeans she'd painted onto her skin. He catalogued the movement and focused on the road again.

"Only if you tell me something you've never told anyone."

"I have so many secrets," he said, a frown infecting his mood. "They're not all about me, though. Is that part of the deal?"

"Not necessarily."

"Okay," he said. When she didn't start, Ace blurted, "I saw my Aunt Lois out on a date with the fire chief. Like, they're dating. They were holding hands and everything, and she told me I couldn't tell anyone, and Bishop—that's her son and my cousin—is like, my best friend, and I'm dying inside."

He took a deep breath, and it cleansed his lungs as if he'd been holding dirty water in there for hours.

He sighed, physically feeling a weight leave his soul. "Wow, that felt great to say out loud to someone else." He glanced at her, suddenly afraid again. "You can't say anything to anyone."

"I won't," she promised, her smile glorious. "Wow, go Aunt Lois."

"Right?" Ace chuckled, relaxing even further. "You catered her birthday lunch. She's seventy-seven."

"She must've been lonely."

"Uncle Stone died fifteen years ago." Ace hadn't given it much thought, but yes, Aunt Lois was probably lonely. His mother at least had daily activities at the assisted living facility, with plenty of people her age, three meals a day, and a van that took them around to dozens of different places in Three Rivers.

"What about your dad?" Holly Ann asked.

Ace's skin prickled, and he cleared his throat. "Uh, Daddy died almost six years ago now."

"How did he die?"

"Prostate cancer," Ace said. "Same as Uncle Stone. See, there's another thing Bear called a family meeting about. He said both of our fathers had died from this disease, and we needed to be vigilant with our health. I'm only thirty-five, but I got screened this summer."

"That's smart," Holly Ann said.

Ace let her settle back into silence, and he struggled to

decide how far to push her as he made the turn from asphalt to gravel and started up to Shiloh Ridge.

"We own all of this," he said. "Both sides of the road. This is the old Kinder Ranch land. There's a house out there Bishop and Montana are going to work on. One of us will live there."

"Where will you live?"

"It's undecided right now." Ace hadn't been surprised at the meeting last week. He'd always known Ward would stay at Bull House. It had never been on Ace's radar before, because he hadn't been thinking wife and family before.

He was now. At least the wife part.

"We're almost there," he said. "Do you want to tell me your secret right now, or wait?" He looked over at her, and their eyes met. Hers reminded him of a deep, dark night with a full super-moon filling the blackness with silver light. With holiness and wonder, the kind that made a man pause and contemplate the nature of his existence and how he fit into this wide world.

"Can we wait?" she finally asked. "I haven't met your whole family before."

"Actually—"

"As your girlfriend," she clarified.

When Ace glanced back at her, she did look slightly pale. Maybe she was sick, or maybe the thought of meeting his entire loud, obnoxious, largely male family brought a pinch to her stomach the same way it did his.

He pulled up to True Blue and parked next to Bishop's truck. The scent of sweet barbecue sauce hung in the air, and he said, "Well, here we are."

Neither of them moved, and Ace stared at the beautiful barn door Bishop had made with his bare hands. The man had a real affinity for wood, and Ace wondered what talent he had that could be compared with Bishop's.

He couldn't think of one, and he jumped as someone knocked on his window. He looked left to find Preacher standing there, a big, goofy grin on his face.

"Idiot," Ace muttered under his breath, his heart still beating with lots of extra adrenaline.

He opened the door, Preacher's annoying laughter so much louder. "You should've seen your face."

"You should see yours after I rearrange it for you."

Preacher danced away from him, still chuckling, and went into the barn with Judge, who also grinned like a fool. No wonder Mister didn't like living with the two of them. They did like to play tricks and pranks on people, and Ace normally didn't mind. He also didn't normally have Holly Ann with him.

She met him at the front of the truck, her long, cool fingers sliding along his forearm and into his. They breathed together, and Ace said, "That was Preacher and Judge. They're my cousins."

They entered the barn too, and Ace knew they'd be some of the last to arrive. Sure enough, they were the very last to arrive, and Etta gave him a glare as she nodded to Ida. The microphone clicked on, and she said, "Okay, we're ready."

She welcomed everyone as if they'd have a program later and went over the food the same way she always did. At least she, Ida, and Bishop had made one of Ace's favorite meals—

gravy-covered pork chops, garlic mashed potatoes, and lemony green beans.

"Mother has an announcement, and then she'll say grace."

In the space between Etta handing Mother the mic, Ace hurried Holly Ann to a couple of seats next to Bishop and Montana, flashing his cousin a grateful smile.

"Thank you, Etta," Mother said. She stood at the front of the room, which semi-surprised Ace. She was a little older than Aunt Lois, and she had some mobility issues due to a knee replacement and then a hip replacement on the same side only a year later. She'd moved into the assisted living facility following the second surgery, claiming she didn't want to be a burden at the ranch, and she'd like to be in town anyway.

Ace was taking her home that afternoon when he took Holly, and he normally enjoyed talking with his mother.

Mother took a sharp breath, and Ace leaned forward. Something was wrong, and his pulse crashed through his veins and lodged in his throat.

"What's goin' on?" Bishop whispered, but Ace just shook his head.

"You might have noticed that Ranger and Oakley aren't here," Mother said, her voice steady though she looked nervous with wide eyes painted with seriousness. "They're taking some time to recover from the loss of their second baby." She paused as emotion rolled across her face. Ace tried to breathe and found he couldn't get a whole breath. Beside him, Bishop actually stood up.

"They do not want any questions right now. Things are quite raw for them, especially Oakley—" Mother's voice broke, and Ace knew she loved Oakley deeply. She continued anyway, her voice tight and pinched, coming from down deep in her chest. "They would appreciate your prayers and kindness. Let them bring up anything they want to talk about, and don't go walking on eggshells around them. They want to be treated normally, but with the knowledge of the pain they're currently dealing with."

Montana touched Bishop's arm, and he fell back into his seat. He lived with Ranger and Oakley in the homestead, and he'd been working with Ranger on his app for a while now.

Ace didn't know what to say. He wanted to fly down the road and straight to Ranger and just hug him. He wanted to take him a huge bag of peanut M&Ms—his favorite candy—and just sit with him until everything didn't hurt anymore.

Mother nodded, folded her arms, and began to pray. A measure of unrest had started to play through Ace, and it took him a moment to bow his head too.

He loved listening to his mother pray, as she had a soothing yet firm voice, and surely even the Lord wouldn't dare to disobey her.

She prayed for health and strength for everyone present, for the calming power of the Holy Ghost to comfort Oakley and Ranger, and for continued safety of Sammy and Bear's baby.

By the time she finished, his eyelashes had tears clinging to them, and he quickly wiped his face before he looked up. He wasn't the only one weeping, and for that, he was grateful.

No one moved the way they normally did, almost like the

reverence and spirit his mother had called down from heaven had glued them to their seats.

Ace looked around at everyone in the barn. All of his siblings—except Ranger—were there. Ida had Brady at her side. Arizona had brought her boyfriend, Duke, and Ace looked quickly away from them. Bear and Sammy and Lincoln sat with Ward, Cactus, and Mister.

Aunt Lois, Judge, and Preacher still had their heads bowed, and it wasn't until Etta stood up and said, "Come on, everyone. Let's eat," that anyone moved.

Bear stood first, reaching for Lincoln's hand. The two of them led the way, and Ace simply watched.

Holly Ann laced her arm through his and leaned into him. He ducked his head to the right as she whispered in his ear, "That was beautiful, Ace."

He nodded, because it was.

Her fingers tightened. "I'm not sure I belong here."

He turned further, dropping his head slightly to protect the two of them from everyone else. "What do you mean? Of course you do."

"You guys are so...connected. You have deep roots here."

"Yes," he said slowly. "You're connected to your father and your sister." He knew, because she'd texted him about her sister's birthday party in December already.

"This is my secret," she whispered. "I'm not sure I'm capable of growing roots."

He waited for her to say more. "You're going to have to explain that, sweetheart." His chest didn't like the sound of it though, and it had started caving in toward his heart, almost like it wanted to protect the vital organ from getting broken.

"I have a gypsy soul," she said, as serious as he'd ever heard her. "Like my mother."

"Holly Ann," he said gently. "That's not true."

"She left, because she didn't like being stuck in one place, with the same life day in and day out. I hate that too. I've had at least ten different careers. I'm always moving from one thing to the next."

"You've stayed in Three Rivers," he said. "For thirty-seven years. That's a lot of roots for not having any."

"I hate schedules and routines."

"That's different than not having roots." They stayed very close together, but not facing. Her body heat seeped into his, and he sure didn't want her to leave town. At the same time, she'd tried to leave *him* in her past a couple of times now. Maybe three. Was that part of her wandering heart? Would she ever be able to commit to him fully?

The turmoil inside him rotated slowly, picking up speed with each new question he thought of.

Holly Ann lifted her head, her hand slipping along his arm as she did. "Let's go eat," she said. "We can talk more about this later."

Ace nodded, because this lunch was somber enough already. He stood with her and kept her hand secured in his. His eyes met Ward's, and he headed over to his older brother. They grabbed onto one another, and Ace said, "Let's go see him tonight."

"I'll text him in a bit," Ward said. They separated, and he looked at Holly Ann.

"My brother, Ward," Ace said, taking her hand and bringing her to his side again. "Ward, you remember Holly Ann."

"Of course I do." Ward smiled at her, and Ace wondered why he hadn't been able to find someone to fall in love with. He was tall and strong and hardworking. He was loyal and true and just so *good*. Ace had looked up to him his whole life, and he couldn't imagine not having his brother for his hero.

Mother arrived back at the table, and she put her plate of food at her spot before turning to Ace and Holly Ann. "Introduce me to this lovely woman," she said, her smile warm and inviting.

"Momma," Ace said, his voice catching. "This is my Holly Ann."

Holly Ann's hand squeezed, and he squeezed back. "Holly Ann, my mother, Dawna."

Mother grinned at Holly Ann and opened her arms, making Ace tense. But Holly Ann released his hand, grinned, and stepped forward and into his mother's arms.

Chapter Thirteen

Holly Ann hadn't been hugged by a mother in years and years and years. Ace's mother possessed warmth and strength and she had no problem giving it to everyone around her.

Holly Ann found herself gripping the woman with something inside her she didn't know existed. The desire to have a maternal figure in her life. The desire to be a mother herself.

The idea terrified her, because she would not put a child through what she and Bethany Rose had gone through. She didn't trust herself to not do the exact same thing her mom had done when she woke up one day and realized how trapped she was. How suffocating the routine of making breakfast for the kids was. How unhappy she was with every moment of every day.

Those were the words of her mother, the explanations she'd given over the years for why she'd had to walk away.

She hadn't walked, though she claimed she'd been miserable for years before she'd finally found the courage to leave. In Holly Ann's opinion, she'd run.

She'd broken everything, and then she'd sprinted away from the scattered shards of three other lives.

Daddy had picked up as many as he could. Holly Ann had helped when she could. Bethany Rose hadn't started when there were big pieces to collect, but she'd been bringing tiny fragments back to the table for years now.

The three of them had made the new version of their family work, even as jagged and crooked as it had been.

Ace's mother stepped back but took hold of one of Holly Ann's hands. "Why don't you bring me some of those caramel brownies you made for Lois's birthday? They don't make many desserts at Nestled Oak."

"They do too, Mother," Ida said, arriving on the scene. She gave Holly Ann a knowing smile. "Sometimes Mother *only* eats desserts."

"That was a secret," Dawna shot her daughter a look and sat down. She looked at her plate, which held two desserts and a pork chop. "Well, perhaps I do like having dessert first."

Ace started to laugh, which gave Holly Ann permission to giggle too. She'd gladly make as many brownies as his mother wanted, and she leaned down and told her as much before going with Ace to get something to eat.

The mood lightened from there, and she enjoyed eating delicious food with Bishop and his girlfriend, Montana Martin, and Mister, who came and joined them about halfway through the meal.

Ace didn't act strangely after what she'd said, and he

didn't push her to say more about it in mixed company. She listened to him talk with Bishop and Montana about a shed they'd be working on that week, and she asked Mister about the ranch and what he did there.

He talked about cattle as if she knew the ins and outs of what it took to keep thirty thousand of them alive, and she nodded along as if she did. He seemed nice enough, and he definitely possessed those Glover genes that put him on a plane higher than the average man.

"Are you seeing anyone?" she asked, and Mister looked up at her in pure surprise.

"No," he said slowly, glancing at Ace.

Holly Ann smiled at him. "I happen to know someone you might like. I'm pretty sure she'd like you."

"Yeah?" he asked. "How do you know?"

"Well." She looked up to that dark brown cowboy hat and back to his wide shoulders. "You're good-looking. Don't tell me no one's ever told you that."

He just blinked at her, his eyes wide.

"You have a job," she added. "That's a big plus for women."

"A job?" he repeated.

A good one, if Holly Ann could judge by this barn. She'd been here before, and the place oozed money. She wasn't sure what the rest of the ranch looked like, but thirty thousand head of cattle felt huge to her, and the homestead they'd passed on the way to the barn could only be classified as a mansion.

"And you've been talking to me like a normal person for a while now." She gave him another encouraging smile. "Maybe you don't do blind dates, but I think Claudia would like you."

"How do you know Claudia?" Mister folded his arms, and he almost settled his expression into a glare. One wrong answer, and the blind date would be a no-go.

"She works at the art center downtown. I took a bunch of painting classes there. She's amazing with oils, but her real love is sculpture."

Mister gave nothing away, and he flicked his gaze to Ace. Holly Ann turned toward him too, finding his conversation with Bishop and Montana had wrapped up.

"What's goin' on here?" he asked, looking from her to Mister.

"I'm trying to set him up with Claudia Gray," she said with a big smile. "He's not so sure he wants to go out with a *gorgeous*, talented blonde woman with a master's degree in art history."

"Oh, well, it's the art history," Ace teased. "Mister has a short-term memory problem. He can't even remember what he did last week."

Mister smiled and shook his head at Ace. His eyes came back to Holly Ann's, and he sobered a little. "I've never been on a blind date."

"Really?" Holly Ann asked. "You clearly need more female interference in your life." She laughed and so did he.

Then he said, "Why not? Set it up."

Ace whooped, and Holly Ann felt the same joy in her soul. "Be sure to tell Claudia that he hasn't been out with anyone in a while and to be patient."

"Hey," Mister said.

"What?" Ace asked. "You haven't."

"Doesn't mean I don't know how to act on a date."

"Do you?" Ace asked. "First date, Mister. What would you do?"

Holly Ann sure did like listening to them go back and forth, neither of them giving a single inch though they both made good points.

Looking around, Holly Ann liked everything she saw. The close relationships she could feel and see. The well-kept buildings. The way they all stood up about the same time and helped to clean up.

They were a family, and the spirit of that couldn't be denied. Holly Ann stood and started helping to fold chairs and put them away, because she wanted to belong to these people as much as they belonged to each other.

She wasn't sure what that meant, or how she could do that without getting buried alive.

Chapter Fourteen

Bishop bent over and picked up the nail gun, passing it to Montana. She was easily the sexiest woman in the world, especially with that tool belt around her waist.

She handled power tools in such a way that had him lying awake at night, wishing she was right beside him in bed.

Soon, he told himself.

Today, they needed to frame this shed, and then he was driving down to Ida's tonight to start planning their Thanksgiving menu. They were meeting late this year, and his anxiety over the lack of a plan made him quiet and contemplative. That might've been from the news about Ranger and Oakley trying to have a child and not finding success yet.

He hadn't seen his cousin yet, though they lived together, but he had made breakfast for Oakley that morning. She hadn't been dressed for work, and she'd curled into the couch in the main room with Benny and The General after she ate a few bites of the ham and cheese omelet Bishop had made for her.

Montana had arrived a few minutes later, and she'd looked at the plate of half-eaten food, picked it up, and taken it to the couch with her. She'd asked Oakley if she could eat it, and then she'd proceeded to tell her about something Aurora had said in a text, and right before his eyes, Oakley had opened up. She chatted with Montana like nothing was wrong at all, and Montana had finished the conversation with, "I swear, I'm not going to survive until that girl graduates from high school."

She'd grinned at Oakley, leaned over to hug her, and she'd said, "We better get out there. I see Ace is already hovering around the foundation."

Bishop had gone with her, grabbing her hand and pressing her into the side of the homestead and kissing her. She'd giggled against his lips, and he couldn't explain when she'd asked him what that was for.

He didn't know how to say *for being normal with Oakley.* Or *for fitting right in with everyone already here at the ranch.* Or *don't worry about Aurora. She's a good girl.*

Montana didn't like it when he told her not to worry about Aurora. She was her mother, and according to Montana, mothers worried about their daughters.

Bishop looked at Ace, and he knew not all mothers were like Montana. His cousin had laid on Bishop's private couch in his little living room away from the rest of the homestead last night, lamenting several things Holly Ann had said about her "gypsy soul."

Bishop hadn't known how to help him either. He didn't

know how to even talk to Oakley, and he was pretty sure he'd be seven shades of awkward if he ever saw Ranger.

"How's it coming?"

Bishop jerked upright at the sound of Ranger's voice. "Good," he said, stepping over the floor studs quickly, nearly hopping from one to the next, until he stood next to his cousin on the dew-stained grass. It would likely snow soon. At the very least, a cold rain would make itself known in Three Rivers. Up in the hills, where Shiloh Ridge sat, they usually got more ice and snow than the town in the lower valley.

"We're framing today," Bishop said, glancing up at the sky. "It's supposed to storm tomorrow, so Montana and I will cover it all in the morning, and then we'll see where we are once that's all done."

Ranger walked around toward the front corner. Or what would be the front corner of the shed. "It'll fit the two ATVs?"

"It's the same specs that we went over," Bishop said, following him. His mind raced. What could he say to let Ranger know that he'd been thinking about him? That he'd spent extra time in his prayers just for him and Oakley? Did he just come out and say that?

Bishop usually didn't have such a block in his mouth.

"It'll fit two ATVs easy," Ace said, coming around the other way and meeting them. "Plus all those yardwork tools you think you're going to use." He grinned at his brother and stepped right into him. He hugged him tight, said something Bishop couldn't hear, and clapped Ranger on the back.

The embrace lasted several long seconds before they

parted, and Ranger turned back to Bishop. "I suppose you want to hug me too."

Bishop grinned and said, "Yeah, kinda."

Ranger opened his arms and said, "Get over here then."

Bishop did, feeling selfish and ridiculous as he took comfort from Ranger instead of the other way around. "I'm right there in the house," he said. "For anything."

"I know," Ranger said. He pulled back and held onto Bishop's face. "You're a good man, Bishop." He smiled though it definitely shone with pain. He stepped back and let his hands fall into his coat pockets. Bishop had shed his coat once he'd started nailing studs to cement. If he wasn't working though, he'd get cold soon enough.

"I asked Ward to take over the major updates with Two Cents," Ranger said, gazing at the load of lumber on the ground over by Ace. "I know you're really busy with all the construction on the ranch, and you guys are working on redesigns for Cactus, and all of that." He raised his eyes to Ace, and then back to Bishop. "I just need some time off. I'm going to work around the ranch like usual. Maybe not as much as usual, actually, but I just can't focus on the app right now."

Bishop nearly leapt toward him. "I can keep up with the day-to-day stuff," he said. "Ward can run the big updates, and I'll do the polls we have scheduled. We've already talked about those. I can manage the spam comments, and I can go through the server specs. I've seen you do it."

Ranger grinned, and he almost looked like the man Bishop had always known. He'd changed too, and Bishop supposed that every life experience a person had added a new layer to a them. Sometimes those things were physical, like scars or a limp similar to the one Aunt Dawna had from her surgeries.

But more often than not, a person carried emotional and spiritual wounds, scars, and limps that no one ever saw until they really knew that person.

"Thank you, Bishop," Ranger said. "I knew I could count on you and Ward." He looked back at Ace, and asked, "Can I steal you for a second?"

The two brothers walked off, and Bishop watched them go, suddenly feeling left out of something he had no right to even be in. He hated this part of himself, and he wished he could be content with himself, and with the people he loved.

"Bishop," Montana called, and the urgency in her voice had him spinning toward her. He didn't need to ask what the problem was. The nail gun had gone wild, spitting a new nail out every second.

He ran toward the cord as Montana tried to pull it tight enough to get it out of the generator he'd wheeled out here last night.

He grabbed the cord and yanked, and the nail gun powered down with one last nail being driven into the ground near Montana.

With his heartbeat sprinting, she danced across the floor studs again, asking, "You okay, love?"

"Yeah." She took a breath and tossed the now-smoking nail gun onto the grass. Their eyes met, and Bishop kept moving toward her, a smile filling the empty spaces in his soul. He laughed as he reached her and gathered her into his arms.

She wrapped her arms around his back, giving a little laugh too. "I know you guys like to repair and recycle and all of that, but we just need to replace that thing. It was possessed."

"Right?" He kept chuckling as he added, "It's been acting up for several months now."

"Good thing we were on the ground when that happened," she said. "Otherwise, we'd have been shooting nails all over Shiloh Ridge."

THE NEXT DAY, MONTANA BROUGHT HER DAUGHTER Aurora to the ranch. Oliver Walker came too, and Ace wasted no time in snagging them to help with the re-fencing project going on around Shiloh Ridge.

"We'll be back in time for lunch," Ace called over his shoulder.

"Make sure you bring Cactus," Montana yelled after them. Only Ollie answered her, and Bishop didn't miss that. The boy had been working hard to get back into Montana's good graces—and Aurora's—since the night they'd decorated the angel tree.

She turned and faced Bishop. "Thanks for letting me bring them up here today."

"Any time," he said. "Bear will always put a pair of hands to work. He took Link out to the corral this morning to reset a gate."

"Lincoln weighs about ten pounds," Montana said,

bending to pick up one of the tarps Bishop had ordered. "There's no way he can reset a gate."

"Yes, well, don't tell Bear that." Bishop grinned as he reached for a tarp too. They unbagged them and got to work covering the bare wood they'd put together yesterday. "How's the library coming?"

"Really good," she said. "It'll be done on time, and I think the entire City Council nearly fell out of their chairs when I gave them that update." She wore a sunny smile on her face, and Bishop loved this happy version of herself she'd become.

"And Cactus?"

She sent him a dark look among the sunshine. "Your brother is impossible. You know what he said last night? 'You choose.'" She shook her head. "If I wanted to choose, I'd have just made one design."

They threaded together the two tarps and reached for two more. "Cactus must be going through something," he said.

"I'll say," Montana said. "Who else would argue with a pastor right in the chapel? And the way he refused to introduce her to Bear?" She shook her head. "I don't get him. I know he likes her."

"Yeah." Bishop didn't know what thoughts ran through Cactus's head. He knew he sometimes reacted without thinking and then had to backtrack, make apologies, and try again. He was a lot like Bear in that regard. "Let's see what we can get out of him this afternoon. With Ollie and Aurora around, he might not bite off our heads."

"If you even say a word that sounds like Willa, he's going to walk out." She sighed and handed Bishop the end of the tarp. "Please don't say anything. I *need* him to choose a design, or I can't start ordering the stuff we need for his project. And you know what that means? It means we're behind on *our* house. The one we're fitting in around all the other projects going on around here."

Bishop didn't commit right away, and Montana sent a glare in his direction. He tried to dodge it, but he should've known such a thing was impossible. The woman's opinion mattered too much to him, and he didn't want to disappoint her.

"Bishop."

"All right, all right," he said with a grin. "I won't say anything to upset him." Cactus had not been back to church since the near-yelling match with Willa Knowlton, and Bishop had only seen him once—that same day at lunch.

He hadn't asked him to confirm for Thanksgiving, because he hadn't thought he needed to. As he and Montana covered their hard work from yesterday, Bishop thought he better text Cactus and make sure he was coming to dinner next week.

"Did you know Sammy and Oakley are going to get their nails done with Ida and Etta?" Bishop asked, trying to make his voice nonchalant.

Montana looked over to him, clear surprise in her eyes. "Yes," she said. "They invited me."

"You didn't want to go?"

She shrugged and bent to fold the tarp at the corner and set it in place with the weight. "I don't get the point of painting my nails. They just get all ragged the next day." She shrugged and looked toward the homestead. "I could just hang out."

"Yeah," Bishop said. "You could. If you don't want to, that's fine too."

"I don't know," she said with a sigh. "I'm not really into girly stuff like that, and then I wonder if there's something wrong with me, and then everything just...doesn't make sense. It's easier to say no." She bent and dug at the grass that had been nailed down, pulling out some of the metal that had been deposited there.

She straightened and kicked at the ground, and Bishop just watched. "It's okay. We had plans with Cactus, and I really do need him to pick a design."

Bishop nodded and reached for her. She came to his side, and with the framed shed covered, and today being a Saturday, he simply took Montana back to the house, where he started lunch and she sat on the couch.

Later, the front door opened and voices met his ears. Relief ran through him when he recognized Cactus's deep tone, and he grinned at his brother when he entered the kitchen.

Then he saw the mud.

"You guys," he said, glaring at the dirty floor and then the trio that had tracked in all the mud. "Come on. Some of us live here."

"Sorry, sir," Ollie said, kicking off his boots. He took his and Aurora's to the deck while Cactus took his sweet time removing his boots. Then Ollie took those too.

"He's not your slave," Bishop said darkly, unsure of why he was trying to provoke Cactus already.

"He's so eager though," Cactus said, watching Oliver drop the boots on the deck.

"Be nice to him." Bishop exchanged a glance with Aurora, who gave him a smile and rolled her eyes. At least Cactus's bark was much louder than his bite when it came to kids. "Lunch is ready." He turned and collected the pot of pasta from the stove. "Come on, Ollie. Time to eat."

Montana rose from the couch too, and Bishop said a prayer. "Okay," he said as Cactus picked up a plate and started putting the fettuccini Alfredo on it. "Two things, Cactus. First, you have to pick a design today, so Montana can order your supplies. Second, we need an update regarding Willa Knowlton."

Montana sucked in a breath and slapped him on the chest. "Bishop."

"Come *on*," Bishop said. "I haven't seen Cactus since that Sunday, and I know he's dying to tell me." He grinned at his brother, who hadn't looked up from the pot of pasta.

He finally did, moving out of the way so Aurora could get some food. She said, "Willa Knowlton is literally the first pastor who hasn't put me to sleep." She piled some noodles on her plate. "This looks great, Bishop. Thank you so much."

"Yes, thank you," Ollie said, smiling at Bishop. He was a great kid, and Bishop sure did like him. He nodded and watched Cactus, who hadn't looked away from Aurora.

"What do you like about her?" he asked her.

She glanced up and then back to the tray of garlic bread. "Willa?"

"Yes," Cactus practically growled.

She gazed evenly at him for a moment and then said, "I'll tell you if you tell me what *you* like so much about her."

"Ho ho!" Bishop said, his glee soaring toward the sky. "Nice one, Aurora."

Cactus rolled his eyes and moved over to the table. "Fine," he said. "I can do that."

"You go first," Aurora said, and Bishop needed to pack her in his pocket every time he went out to the Edge Cabin.

Cactus cleared his throat and took a bite of his lunch. By the time he finished chewing and swallowing, everyone had gotten a plate of food and joined him at the table.

"She's really pretty," he said. "Number one."

"You're not getting away with just that," Aurora said.

"I know." Cactus glared at her. "I don't know." He pushed his fettuccini noodles around on his plate but didn't take another bite. "Haven't you ever just met someone and there was this crackle? This attraction between the two of you that you think, 'I need to get to know this person. I think we could be good friends.'?" He looked around at everyone, and Bishop forced himself not to say anything. After all, Cactus rarely strung together so many words.

"That's how I felt when I met Willa. I asked her out, and she said no." He looked down then, making everyone stare at the top of this cowboy hat. "Then she asked me to sit by her at church, but it was really just to hear me sing, because she wants me to be in her blasted community choir. And I don't know. I felt kind of used? And kind of stupid? And then those things get me to angry pretty fast, and the next thing I know, I'm yelling at her in the chapel."

He sighed, and Bishop's heart tore and bled for him. He

glanced at Montana, who openly gaped at Cactus. Aurora did too, and it was Ollie who said, "I know what to do here."

Cactus looked up and over to the sixteen-year-old, bright hope on his face. "You do?"

Ollie looked around the table, as if someone else would chime in first. "Yeah," he said, sliding his gaze back to Cactus. "You show up at her house and you apologize." He leaned forward a little. "It's best not to go during a big family party though, especially if she has a lot of brothers or uncles or...overprotective cowboys at said party."

Bishop burst out laughing, as did everyone else at the table, including Cactus. He didn't look like he'd be driving down to Willa's any time soon—for one, he didn't own a vehicle to drive—but at least he wasn't wallowing behind his cowboy hat anymore.

Cactus stopped laughing first, and Bishop added his brother to his list of people to pray for morning, noon, and night.

Chapter Fifteen

A ce wasn't anywhere near hungry when he turned where the map program told him to. "I can smell the butter out here."

Holly Ann grinned at him, and Ace smiled on back. Something seethed beneath his skin, where he'd kept it since she'd told him she didn't know if she wanted children, and since she'd told him she didn't want to put down roots because of her gypsy soul.

He hadn't known how to bring up the topic again, though she'd said they could talk more about it, and Thanksgiving Day didn't seem like a good time.

He hadn't known how to tell her that she'd put down a pretty healthy root system by purchasing a home in Three Rivers and then starting a catering business that matched the town name—Three Cakes.

He hadn't known how to see her every day because of her

crazy meeting schedule and the two parties she'd catered this week. He'd been busier than usual around the ranch, as Ranger's workload had shifted somewhat to Ward, which meant that some things that Ward usually did had fallen to Ace.

He'd given up trying to drive to town every day, and he'd settled for calling Holly Ann late at night or sometimes in the morning.

He reached across the console and took Holly Ann's hand in his. "It's so good to see you."

She giggled and squeezed his hand. "You've said that already. A few times."

"Well, I must mean it a few times over," he said. "I shouldn't have eaten that extra pecan pie before we left."

"I told you it was a mistake," she said in a falsely chastising tone. "It'll be fine. Just eat a little bit here. I don't even think you have to eat. I just wanted you here."

"Yeah?"

"Yeah," she said. "You've met my dad, but not my sister and her husband, and I don't know. It feels...."

Ace bumped over the dirt road, a petite, charming farm-house coming into view. "Feels like what?" he asked.

Holly Ann didn't answer until he'd come to a complete stop next to a truck that had seen a lot of mud in the very recent past. "Ace," she said, staring at the door.

"You're kind of freaking me out," he admitted with an airy chuckle.

She turned toward him, and Ace honestly couldn't handle any more revelations in the cab of this truck. There wasn't enough *air* to breathe in here.

"I've never brought a boyfriend to meet my family."

Ace searched her face. "I don't believe that." He grinned at her, but she didn't smile back. "Holly Ann, you're gorgeous. I know you've dated. How could you not have brought anyone home to meet your family?"

"My sister's on the porch."

"Wait, wait." Ace glanced up to the porch. A woman stood against the pillar, a flowery apron tied around her waist. She had brown hair too, but it wasn't nearly as long as Holly Ann's, and she didn't wear the same type of understated, fashionable clothes that Holly Ann did.

For example, Bethany Rose wore a pair of jeans that had been rolled at the ankle, a pair of flip flops though it had been raining on and off all day, and a gray T-shirt under the apron.

He'd never seen Holly Ann wear a T-shirt. Literally, ever, even when he showed up at her house unannounced. Even when she was set to work in a hot kitchen for hours, prepping food for someone else's party.

Today, she wore a black, textured pair of slacks that flowed like water when she walked, along with a silky, ivory blouse with at least four strings of colored jewels around her neck that made the plain clothing look like a million bucks.

Her hair had been curled and fell in loose waves halfway down her back, and Ace wished with everything inside him that he'd somehow found a way to sneak her out of the back of the barn where they'd eaten their Thanksgiving lunch with his family to kiss her.

If he had, he'd still be there, doing that.

"Holly Ann," he said, clearing the image of kissing her from his mind. "Talk to me."

She tore her eyes from her sister. "I haven't brought anyone home to meet them," she said. "Because no one ever sticks around that long, because I don't let them. I don't have long relationships, Ace. I like to move around. It's the gypsy soul." She flashed a smile filled with pain that Ace wished he could erase.

"You *like* to move around? Or you *liked* to move around?"

She turned the sober, serious atmosphere in his truck coy and cute with a single shoulder shrug and the words, "You're making me want to abandon the gypsy lifestyle, Mister Glover." The pretty little smile on her face made Ace duck his head, a quick smile touching his mouth too.

"Come on," Holly Ann said, opening her door. "My sister is going to have a nervous breakdown if we don't get out of the truck right now."

"All right," Ace drawled, already back to thinking about kissing her. As long as Holly Ann started thinking about planting herself right next to him, he could eat a thousand Thanksgiving dinners in a single day.

Holly Ann giggled as she hurried up the steps to hug her sister. The two women stood on the porch and watched Ace mount the steps slower than Holly Ann.

"Bethany Rose," she said, linking her arm through her sister's. "This is Ace Glover, my hot cowboy boyfriend." She grinned at him with the wattage of the sun, and dang if Ace's blood didn't turn to lava.

"Ace, this is my baby sister, Bethany Rose."

"So great to meet you," Ace said, grinning and shaking

her hand. "I understand you have yourself a hot cowboy husband?" He looked from her to Holly Ann, his eyebrows raised.

Bethany Rose laughed and gestured for them to come into the house. "Yes, come meet Kevin. He needs to be rescued from Daddy, as he is in rare form today."

Holly Ann groaned. "You're kidding. I told him he had to be on his best behavior."

"He thinks stories from his time in Vietnam *is* his best behavior." Bethany Ann spoke in a dry voice and tossed a sarcastic look over her shoulder.

"Vietnam?" Ace asked. "He served in the military?"

"Before he joined the police academy and became a cop," Holly Ann said.

"Detective," her father said, joining the conversation from the mouth of the hall.

Holly Ann cried out and jumped away from her father, pressing one hand over her heart. "Daddy," she chastised. "You can't just sneak up on people." She glared at him, and then looked at Ace. "He does that a lot."

"I do not," her father said. "Good to see you again, Ace."

"Sir." He touched the brim of his hat and then shook the man's hand.

"Is Ace your real name?" her dad asked, cocking his head to the side.

"Daddy," Holly Ann warned, and Ace sensed something behind the two-syllable word.

"What?" he asked. "It's an innocent question." His frown was forever embedded between his eyes, probably from the decades of investigating he'd done.

"No, it means you couldn't find him in your little database, and you want to know his legal name." Holly Ann cocked her hip and put one hand on it, clearly challenging him. Ace looked from her to her father, who didn't deny anything about a database.

The scent of butter and rising bread filled the air, but he couldn't be distracted by food right now. Holly Ann's relationship with her father fascinated him, and he couldn't decide if they were close or if she simply put up with him because he was her dad.

Probably the first one. Knowing what he did about her, she'd probably stepped up to help her dad as much as possible after her mother had left. She'd have tried to shelter Bethany Ann from anything disappointing or harmful.

"My daddy," Holly Ann said. "Senator Broadbent. Daddy, this is Ace Glover."

"I'd like to know more about this database," Ace said, grinning at her dad. "You sit by me at dinner, Senator."

Her dad blinked at him, his eyebrows going up. He clearly wasn't expecting that reaction from Ace.

"He did a background check on you, Ace." Holly Ann turned her cocked head him toward him, plenty of attitude on her face.

Ace couldn't help laughing, and he took her into his arms easily. She wasn't as melty as she usually was, but after only a few seconds, she did trill out a giggle and put her hands around the back of his neck. "Why are you laughing about this?" she asked, grinning at him.

"A background check on me?" He shook his head. "It's

laughable, that's why." He looked past Holly Ann and to her father. "My real name is Andrew Carmichael Glover."

"Andrew," Holly Ann repeated. "That doesn't really fit, does it?"

"We all go by other things," he said. "Do you really think my mother named Ranger Ranger?" He shook his head. "Well, the girls use their real names. It's only us boys who don't."

"What's Bear's name?"

"Bartholomew."

Holly Ann made a face and shook her head. "No, he's Bear."

"And I'm Ace."

"Where does that come from?" she asked.

"Yes, that's a good question." Senator crowded in closer to him and Holly Ann. "Why don't you use your real name?"

"Family tradition, I guess," Ace said. "For me, I have deadly aim. Even when I was a tiny, little boy, I could hit a target with my daddy's gun. I could throw a three-point shot when I was eight years old. I've hit more holes in one than anyone in town. Felix doesn't let me play mini-golf anymore." He grinned at Senator and then Holly Ann. "At some point, my grandmother started calling me Ace, and it stuck. That's about how it works."

"What's Ranger's name?"

"Richard."

"So normal. Andrew. Richard." Holly Ann gazed at him, wonder and...dare he say love? radiating from her face.

"I was real sorry to hear about your dad," Senator said. "I knew him, and he was a good man."

Ace grew serious, his hunger to talk about his father always just out of sight. It had a funny way of overtaking him at odd times, like when all of his cousins had gotten letters from their dad earlier this year. He'd wanted a letter from his father so badly, and he'd actually been angry that he didn't have one.

"I'd love to hear some stories about him," Ace said. "I really do want you to sit by me at dinner."

"Here he is," Bethany Rose said, leading her husband into the house through the back door. "I found him hiding out in the stable."

"I wasn't hiding out," her husband said, but he did look relieved to see Ace and Holly Ann there.

"Kevin, this is Holly Ann's boyfriend, Ace."

"Nice to meet you." Ace shook the other cowboy's hand. "Do you run this place alone?"

"Yes," he said. "Well, me and Beth. We do the best we can."

"How many head do you have?"

"Only three hundred," Kevin said. "You?"

"A lot more than that." Ace grinned at him. "But we all live and work up there. Ten of us full-time on the ranch. Two more who run our outreach and school programs. Plus seven full-time cowboys that live on-site and work year-round for us. We hire day laborers too, during peak seasons." Ace realized he might sound like he was bragging. He swallowed and retreated to Holly Ann's side.

"I just was saying we can handle more cattle because we have more people. That's all. Bigger doesn't mean we're better."

"Shiloh Ridge Ranch is the wealthiest ranch north of San Antonio?" Senator asked, and Ace turned back to him. He read from his phone. "Though now that the Walkers have also landed in Three Rivers, in the Texas Panhandle, about an hour east of Amarillo, the Seven Sons Ranch may give Shiloh Ridge a run for its money. Literally."

He looked up, his eyes even wider.

"You don't need to keep reading," Ace said, though he'd never seen anything about Shiloh Ridge. He didn't do much reading at all, actually.

"Though it'll be difficult to catch up to four generations of caring for the land, raising cattle, and investing in local Texas businesses. It'll take the heart, hard work, and family spirit that makes Shiloh Ridge Ranch really worth its weight in gold. With an annual gross revenue of over one billion dollars, the ranch and all its holdings are estimated to be worth thirty-one billion dollars, while Seven Sons still relies heavily on the personal income of its owners."

Ace squeezed Holly Ann's hand, but she didn't move or speak.

"Daddy," Bethany Rose said, stepping over to her father and taking his phone away from him. "Enough. You're embarrassing Ace, and we want him to come back." She opened a drawer in the kitchen and added, "You're not getting this back until you leave."

She surveyed the group. "Now come on. Kevin fried up a perfect turkey and everything else is getting cold."

Thankfully, Senator strode into the kitchen, already asking for his phone back. The things that made others uncomfortable didn't seem to bother him at all.

Ace cleared his throat and gently pulled his hand away from Holly Ann's. That thawed her, and she finally turned and met his eye. "Thirty-one billion dollars?"

"That's ranch worth," Ace said quickly, though he had plenty of personal money. He didn't want to have this conversation right now. It felt inappropriate, just like sneaking out to the barn to kiss her would've been.

"Come eat," Bethany Rose barked.

Ace nodded toward the table so Holly Ann would move. "Let's just add it to the list of things you and I need to talk about."

THE FOLLOWING DAY, ACE WENT OUT ON THE RANCH IN the morning and helped Preacher and Judge feed the horses. He hauled in fresh straw for a row of stalls, and he made sure every equine got fresh water and a new measure of hay.

He listened to Judge and Preacher go back and forth about the tree lighting ceremony that day in swatches of conversation as they worked in and out of the building. Yesterday's bad weather had cleared up, and Ace had sent a text to Holly Ann that morning that her prayers must've worked, as she'd been anxious about the weather for the lighting event for a week.

She'd only replied with a smiley face, and he hadn't engaged again. It was the first big event of the Christmas Festival, which would run all the way through New Year's Eve with the concluding event being the Light Parade that went until twelve-oh-one next year.

He was tired already, and yet he'd volunteered to take tickets for the sleigh rides in the park. He'd signed up to sell concessions at the church-sponsored ice skating afternoon in a couple of weeks. He'd even put his name down for clean-up after tonight's tree lighting and the gingerbread bake-off next weekend.

Ace normally spent a lot of time volunteering during the Christmas Festival. His workload was lighter in December, January, and February, and he wanted to put his time and energy to a good cause.

So lost in thought, he didn't notice that Judge and Preacher had gone quiet. His footsteps stalled as he tilted his head to listen. A silent Judge and Preacher spelled trouble for him, though he knew most of the practical jokes originated with Judge.

Ace actually liked Preacher when he could get him alone. They had great conversations about their flight simulators and the rotational practices of the grass in the pastures where they fed their cattle.

Preacher was smart, and while he loved to play video games and have fun, it wasn't the same type of fun as Judge, who much preferred playing tricks on people.

Judge helped Cactus a lot over the years, so he wasn't a heartless man. Of course, if Ace listened to and believed everything Mister said about Judge, one would think so.

"Preacher?" he called, because he could sometimes be appealed to.

Ace had told himself many times that not everyone got along, even in the same family. He and Ward reminded each other that it wasn't their job to take sides between

Mister and Judge. They were both glad Mister had come to live with them, and they liked having him around. At the same time, Ace could work well with and talk with Judge too.

When Preacher didn't answer, Ace quickly finished up with the last horse in his row and went outside to get in his truck and get out to Cactus's. They were going down to the tree lighting together, and while they didn't need to leave for a while, Cactus had promised Ace a good meal and a story about Willa Knowlton.

Ward would be working at Ranger's today, updating all the backend systems on Two Cents, as well as pushing out the entire Christmas Festival schedule of events so people in Three Rivers could vote for their most-anticipated activities. They could also leave ratings on every event, and Holly Ann had asked Ranger if she could meet with him to get the data he collected in the app.

He'd declined, but quickly referred her to Bishop, who was going to be handling all the polls, data, reviews, and more.

Ace kept his eyes on the ground, as Judge sure did like to set up tripping traps and take videos of his unsuspecting victims. Ace wasn't going to be one of them today, that was for sure. His thoughts ran away from him, though, because he wished he could be as involved in Two Cents—and Ranger's life—as Ward and Bishop were.

He looked up, searching for his truck. It was gone. His adrenaline soared, making a white, rushing noise in his ears. Then he roared, "Judge! You get my truck out here right now!" He pulled out his phone and added, "I'm calling the cops and reporting a theft." He mock tapped on the screen and searched the surrounding area.

If he had to go traipsing around this ranch to find his truck...either Judge or Preacher would definitely die that night in their sleep.

"I'm serious," he called, still trying to find one of them. He cursed himself for leaving the keys in the truck, though he always did. The only time he didn't was when he went to town.

"I am seriously going to kill him."

"I'm serious," Judge said in tone filled with laugher. He exited from the barn next door and held up Ace's keys. He laughed as he came closer, and Ace swiped the keys from him.

"I don't get why you think pranks are funny," he said. "Why is making someone else nervous or having them feel stupid funny?"

Judge sobered then, his dark eyes searching Ace's. "I don't know."

"You're forty years old, Judge. It might be time to grow up." He lifted the keys and pressed the panic button. Sound and light poured out of the space between two of their stables, and a moment later, Preacher came running out of the same area.

"Turn it off!" he yelled.

Ace didn't turn it off, because in that moment, he didn't care if Preacher went deaf. Maybe that would teach him not to move someone's car without telling them.

He waited until he was nice and close to the truck—and about to go deaf himself—before he silenced the alarm. He didn't say good-bye to his cousins, and he barely enjoyed lunch and story time with Cactus.

They drove down to the town of Three Rivers together, both of them silent, lost in their own thoughts. The closer Ace got to the downtown park, the more congested traffic became.

"Aren't you going to park at the bank?" Cactus asked as Ace went by it.

"No," he said. "Holly Ann gave me a parking pass for the VIP lot."

"Oh, a perk." Cactus grinned at him. By the time they made it into the gated lot, Ace thought they might as well have parked at the bank and walked, the way they usually did. It would've taken less time.

They began to wander around the winter wonderland, taking in the fountains and light displays. The enormous Christmas tree stood at least thirty feet tall, and the scent of the pine needles filled the air.

The tree with its hundreds of ornaments seemed so forlorn with unlit lights.

"Dear Lord, this is not happening," Cactus said, and he turned to go between two food booths.

Ace went right after him, because he knew Cactus didn't want to be alone tonight. He'd said he didn't mind being a third wheel, but they hadn't found Holly Ann yet, and she should've arrived at the same time they had.

"What's not happening?" he asked once he'd found Cactus hiding behind the bright blue shack of a Mexican restaurant in town.

"Willa's here," he said. "Of course she'd be here. She loves festivals and stuff."

"I didn't see her," Ace said. "Besides, didn't you say a mere two hours ago that you hoped you'd run into her so you could apologize?"

Cactus fixed him with those dark blue eyes, but Ace didn't back down. "That's what you said."

"I know what I said."

"Then stop cowering back here like a fool and come talk to her."

"She had her nieces with her."

"Even better," Ace said. "That makes the conversation happen quickly, and you can say what you need to say, and be done."

Cactus nodded and peeled himself away from the booth. Ace led the way back into the horseshoe-shaped area where all the edibles were. His stomach growled at him, but he wanted to eat with Holly Ann tonight.

He practically shoved Cactus toward Willa, a beautiful redhead who had one hand secured in that of a little girl on each side of her. She stood in front of Wild Caribbean, which was a huge mistake in Ace's mind. Out of all the places to eat here, he'd choose the food mashup of Caribbean with Texas barbecue dead last.

He'd been worried about forcing Cactus to apologize tonight, but he watched as Cactus removed his hat and held it to his chest while he spoke to Willa.

He watched her smile and nod, say something to him in what was surely a kind voice, and then tilt her head to the side. She'd clearly asked him a question, and then she looked down at her nieces.

Ace loved people-watching, and he started making up the dialog that went with the body language. Cactus put his hat back on and bent down in front of the smallest girl. She laughed and shook her head, and Ace smiled at how easily Cactus could apologize and make things right.

Willa and the girls turned to get their food, and Cactus looked over to Ace, his eyes wide. He gestured to indicate he was going to stay with them, and Ace waved to him.

And to think he'd been worried about leaving Cactus out or alone tonight.

Now *he* was the one standing alone, and he looked around for Holly Ann once more. He didn't see her, and she was now officially forty-five minutes late.

She didn't show up in time for them to get anything to eat before the tree lighting, and in fact, Ace stood at the back of the crowd, alone, his eyes squinted upward at the ridiculously dark tree.

He normally loved the tree-lighting ceremony, but Ace didn't like doing much of anything alone. Certainly not this, when there were so many families here. So many couples, cuddled into one another to stay warm until the great behemoth of a tree would be lit.

"Here we go, folks," someone said, and while it was a woman, it wasn't Holly Ann. She'd apparently forgotten where she was supposed to be tonight.

Maybe she's just busy, he told himself. He knew she was, but she hadn't called or texted, and that annoyed him. Even the busiest person in the world could text if they were running late or couldn't make it.

The tree burst to life, with hundreds of brightly colored and lit bulbs. The crowd broke out into cheers and applause, and the woman speaking into the mic could barely be heard as she said, "Now, let's welcome our special guest of honor, all the way from the North Pole...Santa!"

The shrieking turned up a notch, and Ace suddenly wanted nothing more than to get out of there.

Chapter Sixteen

Holly Ann settled onto Santa's throne, ready for the next two hours of smiling and holding children on her lap. The tree-lighting had gone brilliantly, and the crowd this year had tipped over ten thousand, thanks to the amazing weather and the push notification that had gone out on Two Cents.

She couldn't believe how big of a difference that had made, but the tree-lighting, which was the kick-off event of the Christmas Festival, always brought in the most people. Last year, only seventy-eight hundred residents of Three Rivers had attended, and they'd added another twenty-five percent this year.

The only difference was the utilization of Two Cents to push out the schedule of events, create polls for upcoming activities, and leave feedback on specific functions after they happened. She'd even worked with Ward to include a spot where people could suggest future activities right inside the app.

They'd been using their website and social media pages for all of that over the years, but Two Cents was something seemingly every resident in town used on a daily basis, and since the Festival had no app, and no way to build one reasonably before things kicked off, Holly Ann had partnered with them.

She looked out into the crowd as the first child came toward her, her stomach tight at all the cowboy hats she saw. Plenty of black ones swam in her vision, but none of them were attached to the cowboy she wanted to see.

"This is Michael," the helper elf said, and Holly Ann bent to pick up the child. He was probably four or five years old, and he stared at her with wide eyes.

"What do you want for Christmas?" Holly Ann asked. His bright brown eyes grew excited, and he started to talk, his parents taking pictures on the other side of the red carpet that led to her throne.

She kept her smile in place and listened to the little boy. She pointed to the camera when it was time, and she smiled like she was having the time of her life.

Child after child went through the line, and Holly Ann *was* having the time of her life. When she'd learned her father got to dress up and play Santa for the town, she'd been surprised but thrilled. When she'd learned she got to do it too, she'd taken on the challenge wholeheartedly.

Santa Claus meant something to these kids—and their parents. He represented the magic and wonder of the season, the same way Jesus Christ did. They both provided gifts, though very different types, and Holly Ann loved thinking about her Savior and all He'd done for her that year every time she sat on the throne and held a child on her lap.

While the helper elf tried to convince a sobbing child that Holly Ann was safe, she looked out into the sea of people again. She saw someone who looked very much like Ace, and she immediately ducked her head, her heart pounding. When she remembered the blue contacts and that all of her hair was tucked away, she looked up again.

The man leaning against the fence wasn't Ace, but his cousin, Cactus Glover. He stood alone, and he watched the helper elf with the little girl, a small smile on his face. Someone must've said something to him, because he turned his head, and then walked away.

In that moment, Holly Ann's memory fired something at her. A text Ace had sent. *I'm getting Cactus and we'll be down in town for the tree lighting. We'll meet you at five and we can get dinner from the trucks or the court.*

She moaned audibly, though the little girl was no closer to coming over so it didn't matter. She'd completely forgotten she was going to come to the tree lighting with Ace. She'd thought she could grab dinner with him, make up an emergency, and get dressed in time to play Santa.

Turned out, there had been a real emergency earlier that day, and she'd forgotten all about her plans with Ace. Could she pull out her phone and text him quickly?

The helper elf looked extremely flustered, and she turned to the parents for help. Holly Ann took the opportunity to ease her phone out from under her leg—she couldn't just ignore texts for hours on end. She was the Christmas Festival director. If something huge happened while she was playing her role, she'd have to make something up to get out of there.

Ace had texted only once, and it didn't sound good.

Guess you're too busy to see me tonight. Call me when you get a minute.

She sighed and quickly tapped out, *I'm so sorry. Something came up. I'll be free hopefully about eight. Will you still be here?*

If Cactus was still here, surely Ace was too.

Yes, his response came back. *Just call me.*

Okay, she said, and then the helper elf said, "This is Ellie," and Holly shoved her phone away. She pushed against the urgency screaming at her to get out of there, get changed, and get to Ace.

When she finished, she stole into the private lounge on the second-floor mall offices, changed quickly and tucked everything for the Santa suit inside a garment bag. She hung that in the closet, put the boots beneath it, and slid the door closed. She locked it, and pushed the key into her pocket.

She took a few precious minutes to fluff up her hair, which tended to stick flatly to her head after being under the wig and Santa cap for so long, put on a thin sheen of lip gloss, and put a mint in her mouth.

Then she left the office, which was marked for Santa only, and hurried down the hall. She caught sight of Rachel still in the office, and she poked her head inside. "You're still here?"

The assistant director turned around and smiled. "Just going over tomorrow's volunteers for the sleigh rides and sending reminder texts." She tapped the stack of papers in front of her. "I'm leaving in five."

"Perfect," Holly Ann said, though she'd been in Rachel's shoes. She'd wanted to make the director's job as easy as possible, because they had to deal with the public on top of everything else. "Thanks, Rachel."

"Are you getting something to eat?" Rachel asked, clicking on the computer now. "The crew is going to The Lucky Irish together."

"No, I've got to go meet my boyfriend." Holly Ann put a smile on her face, though she'd love to go out with the group of people she'd been planning the festival with for the past few weeks. Before that even, as the Christmas Festival had a lot of people who came back year after year to keep planning and serving and putting on the best holiday festival they could.

"Bummer," Rachel said, and she tucked her sandy blonde hair behind her ear as she glanced up. "Have fun with Ace, though."

"Yeah." Holly Ann ducked out of the room and quickly went down the steps. Her phone chimed several times as she did, and she cursed the dead spot on the second floor. She ignored the texts, none of which were from Ace, and called him instead.

"Hey," she said breathlessly, probably thanks to those extra thirteen pounds. "I'm done and headed outside. Where can I find you?"

"I'm standin' next to The Watering Hole."

Clear across the plaza from Holly Ann. "Great," she chirped anyway. "I'm about five minutes away."

"Okay," he said, and Holly Ann wanted to apologize again.

"I'm sorry," she said, really panting now. "It has been a day."

"I understand." He sounded less than understanding though. Perhaps he was just disappointed. A person could be disappointed and understanding at the same time, right? Frustration filled Holly Ann at the burden of trying to balance all she had to do for the festival, her catering load, being Santa, *and* spending time with Ace.

This is why you wanted to break up with him.

But at the same time, she absolutely didn't want to break up with him.

"I just got busy, and when I saw Cactus, I remembered you two were coming."

"You saw Cactus?"

"Yeah," Holly Ann said. "I didn't see you, though, and then I got stuck talking to someone about the sleigh rides tomorrow." She made herself stop talking, because she didn't want to lie to him. She hadn't been stuck talking to Rachel about the sleigh rides, though she had spoken to someone about them.

"Who?" he asked.

"Just—I don't know. Someone."

"Okay," he said. "I'll see you in a minute." The call ended, and Holly Ann's heartbeat sprinted in her chest. She didn't like lying to him, and she knew that half-truths would only get half the job done.

Plenty of people loitered around The Watering Hole, because it was a great place to get a drink and mingle. Ace stood on the outskirts of any of that, not holding anything to drink, and glancing around with a dark look on his face.

Holly Ann rushed right into the storm and said, "There you are," moments before wrapping him in her arms. "I'm sorry," she whispered. "Please don't be mad at me."

His arms came around her slowly, but he did breathe in deeply, and she hoped she didn't smell too much like the inside of a polyester Santa suit. Or too sweaty, as that thing was hot, and the weather today had been beautiful.

"It's okay," he whispered. "You're here now." He touched his lips to her neck, sending a shiver of desire and pleasure down her arm.

She giggled and stepped back. "I'm starving. Have you eaten? I'll take you somewhere quiet for dinner." That meant nowhere around here, and Holly Ann knew just the place.

"I could eat," he said, which meant he had eaten dinner at some point.

She grinned at him and laced her fingers through his, still concerned she hadn't been forgiven when he didn't return her smile. "When *can't* you eat?"

"Hey, I had a hard time yesterday," he said. "If your sister didn't make the best mashed potatoes on the planet, I wouldn't have been so tempted."

She laughed at his defense, glad some of the flirtatious qualities had returned to his voice. When she led him away from The Watering Hole, he did wear a smile.

Thank you, she prayed. *Help me to be honest with him. I don't want to hurt him.*

She really didn't, but she couldn't find a way through this maze. She did know where to take him for dinner, though. "She'll be thrilled. Bethany Rose always compares herself to me when it comes to cooking."

"She did an amazing job yesterday," Ace said. He walked slowly with her, and Holly Ann took a moment to just enjoy the November night. The air had cooled, as it did in the winter in Three Rivers, and the stars had started to come out.

She pulled in a long breath and looked up at the moon. "I love the night sky," she said. "Once, right after I graduated, I thought maybe I'd like to be an astronomer. An astronaut. Something where I could study stars."

"Why didn't you?" he asked.

"First off, the amount of physics involved in a program like that is insane." She grinned up at the brightest pricks of light, knowing it was Venus. "Not sure you know, but me and physics don't get along. Or me and math." She laughed a little. "I'm more of a dreamer, but I didn't see any Stargazing While You Daydream 101 classes."

He chuckled with her, and Holly Ann finally felt forgiven. The mood between them returned to casual and easy and supercharged with chemistry, the way it usually was.

"So that didn't work out," she said. "I took a baking class, and I really liked that. I took a web design class, and I thought I liked that. The second one was super hard, though, and I don't even think I finished it."

Holly Ann had a long list of things she hadn't finished, but she kept those under her tongue for now. "Did you ever take any classes, Ace?"

"Sure," he said. "I have a degree in Agricultural Science from Texas A&M."

"You do? Like a whole degree?" She gaped at him. "I didn't know that."

"Yes, ma'am." He smiled at her fondly, a new edge in his eye. "I liked the aggro-tech classes a lot, and the horticulture. I also excelled at crops and soils. That's what I do on the ranch, Holly Ann. I manage all the agricultural needs. It includes all the crops we plant and harvest—I decide what, where, when, and then what to do with them. Sometimes we feed them to our own animals, and sometimes we sell our crops. I manage all the fields—the soil quality, the fertilization, the pest control, the rotation of it all."

He stopped speaking, but Holly Ann liked listening to him talk. "Go on," she encouraged.

"It's boring," he said quietly.

"It is not," she said. "I like listening to you talk about your ranch. You're so excited about it." She tried to give him a smile, but his had disappeared.

"Yeah, excited about soil pH and rotational ranching practices," he said, shaking his head. "That's so lame."

"It is not," she insisted. "I don't even know what horticulture is. It sounds like a horrible disease." She tried another smile, pleased when he finally cracked.

"It's basically gardening," he said. "Garden management."

"Do you guys have a big garden up there?"

"Oh, yeah," he said. "Ward and I do all of that, from the planting to the care to the harvesting. We set huge baskets out on the front porch of Bull House, and everyone comes and gets what they want."

"Bull House?"

"That's my house," he explained. "It's named after my dad." He swallowed, and Holly Ann catalogued the movement down his throat. She reached up and touched his neck there, and he froze.

"You miss your dad," she said quietly, stalling with him.

He nodded, his eyes blazing with emotion now. The lights from the nearby shops haloed him, making him bright in some places and completely covered in shadows in others.

"I have a secret," she whispered.

"Oh, I have so many," Ace whispered back.

"What's one of yours?"

"You go first."

Holly Ann could still hear the noise from back by The Watering Hole. She and Ace still walked along the stores in the outdoor mall. They weren't in private by any stretch of the imagination, yet she felt like only he existed in her world. Just the two of them, and she felt herself falling, falling, falling in love with him.

"I miss my mother sometimes," she said, her voice hoarse. "It makes no sense, because I'm so angry with her, and I don't even like her. But sometimes...sometimes I really miss her. The holidays are one of those times, and she always brought us to the tree lighting, and I don't know."

She sighed out the rest of her breath, her head spinning so fast.

Ace searched her face, probably trying to absorb everything she'd said. "It's okay to miss your mother."

"Is it, though? Would you miss someone who abandoned you, just walked out one day and tried to make it seem like she had no other choice?"

"I don't know how to answer that, Holly Ann."

She nodded and took a step, gently pulling on his hand. "Sorry," she murmured. "That's the secret."

"I want to revisit the roots one too," he said just as quietly. "We never did finish that."

Holly Ann looked across the parking lot, unsure about going back to that topic. She had promised him they would, but she still felt as unsettled about it now as she had then. "I don't know if I want kids," she said. "Because I don't want to wake up one day the way my mother did and leave them." She looked up at Ace. "I'm so much like her, Ace, and I know you don't think I am, but I am."

Tears filled her eyes, and she hated that she'd taken this night in this direction. She sniffled and looked away again. The horizon faded into darkness, and it was deep and all-encompassing, pulling at her soul to go explore what she could outside the borders of Three Rivers.

"I don't want to have a family and then feel trapped by them. I don't want to pretend I'm happy when I'm not. I don't—I will not—get to the point where I simply can't make it through another day as it is, so I snap, pack a bag, and leave everything behind for my own sanity."

Ace said nothing, and that only added to the unrest swirling in her soul. It also gave her plenty of space to keep talking. She tried to resist the temptation, but she couldn't, and as he guided her toward his pickup truck, she said, "That's why I like not having roots. It's why I've never taken anyone home to meet my family, and it's why I haven't had a boyfriend for longer than a few months."

"We've been out for longer than a few months," he said. "And I met your family."

"Now you know why I'm terrified," Holly Ann said, flashing a smile that nearly fell off her face.

"Hey," he said, pausing at the passenger door of the truck. "Hey, look at me, okay?"

Holly Ann tried not to, but Ace Glover possessed a huge gravitational pull over her heart and soul, and her eyes found his easily. He wore nothing but compassion in his gaze, and he cupped her face in both of his hands.

"You are an amazing woman, Holly Ann," he said, his voice filled with the same power and fervor she'd heard his mother pray with. "I like you so, *so* much." He swallowed, pushing his one hand through her hair and bringing it back to the side of her face, his fingers wrapping around her ear and the back of her neck.

"I know you're worried about doing the same things your mother did, but baby, can't you see that you won't? Can you see that you know how horrible it was for you and Bethany Rose, and because of that experience, you'll never do it?"

Holly Ann tried to find the lie in his face or his voice. She couldn't, so she said nothing.

"I just don't believe it," he said. "Once we know how something feels, and we know how devastating something is, we would never do it to another human being, let alone our own flesh and blood." He shook his head. "I just do not think A, that you could do that to someone, even without your personal experience, and B, that you'll do it to your husband and children."

She nodded, because his reasoning made sense. Her mind warped her thoughts sometimes, and she really disliked that. "What's your secret?"

His kind smile covered his face, and he adjusted his hands on the sides of her face. "I haven't kissed you in a while, and I'm dying a slow death with every passing hour where your lips aren't on mine."

Holly Ann giggled. "Well, I can't be responsible for a cowboy's death."

"Mm." Ace held her face right where he wanted it, and he kissed her. Holly Ann melted into his touch, into every powerful stroke of his mouth against hers, matching him and hopefully showing him how very much she liked him too.

Chapter Seventeen

❧

Willa sang to herself as she unloaded the dishwasher. It was one of her most hated chores, but she found if she sang her favorite aria, the two-minute job got done easily. She wasn't even sure why she couldn't put the clean dishes where they belonged without souring her mood, only that it sometimes irritated her so much that she hand-washed dishes instead of emptying the dishwasher so she could put the dirty dishes in it.

With that done, she opened a container of wet dog food and mixed in the joint supplement that smelled more like dirt than anything healthy. Abe came over from his normal spot on the couch, his nose working overtime.

He could bite at his front right joint day and night and refuse to get off the couch to go out in the morning, but the moment the wet dog food came out, he was as spry as a pup. She grinned down at him and sang the end of her aria.

Abe just grinned his doggy grin, his tongue hanging out

of his mouth. Willa knew he wouldn't live forever, as she'd adopted him from the shelter in Temple the day her divorce had been finalized. They didn't know how old Abe was, and they'd said she could rename him. She hadn't, because the springer spaniel's name fit him so well.

She put the bowl down on his food mat and held up her hand. Abe sat right away, his eyes trained on the food she'd prepared for him. "Abe," she said, and he moved his gaze to hers. Satisfied, she said, "Okay," and he streaked past her to the bowl.

Willa hummed as she finished getting ready, her thoughts on the tree lighting from a week ago. Cactus Glover had marched right up to her in front of Mariah and Gigi, and Willa's first thought had been to hide the girls behind her and deal with the cowboy with a firm hand.

She hadn't expected him to sweep his cowboy hat off his head and hold it against his heartbeat. Cactus had a head full of gorgeous, chestnut brown hair, and the most magical voice that said, "Willa, please forgive me. I'm so sorry for what happened in church."

He'd toed the ground and dropped those navy eyes down. Looking back at her, he'd added. "Please. I can't go another night thinking about my terrible behavior and how it hurt you."

Willa really admired someone who could stand up and admit they were wrong. She'd had to do it in the past, and such a thing was not easy. She'd been married to someone who had not been able to apologize, and she knew the weakness such a thing really demonstrated.

Cactus possessed amazing strength, and looking into his

eyes, she'd forgiven him instantly. "I forgive you," she'd said. "If—" She'd held up her hand. "If you'll forgive me as well. My behavior was inappropriate as well, and I said unkind things. I hope you don't think too badly of me, and I apologize too."

He'd nodded, his jaw jumping. With his cowboy hat back on, Willa could've swooned on the spot. His handsomeness was indescribable, and Willa hadn't been as attracted to a man as much as she was Cactus Glover. Ever.

Are you here alone? Would you like to have dinner with us?

She'd asked him those questions, and he'd said yes though he hadn't come alone. He'd cleared it with his cousin, and he'd spent the evening with her and her nieces. Willa had enjoyed herself immensely, and she'd been to a few other holiday activities over the past week.

She'd looked for Cactus as the Stories for Soldiers event on Monday evening, as well as the gingerbread house decorating contest. He hadn't attended either. She'd searched for him at church, but he'd stayed away for yet another week.

Last night, after stewing about him all afternoon while she visited with Patrick and his girls, she'd finally reached down deep into her well of courage, and she'd texted him. *What does it take to get you off that ranch? Food? Salty popcorn? A chocolate cake?*

He'd called, which Willa also really liked. It spoke of his maturity and character, and some of his first words after she'd answered were, "I really hate texting sometimes. I find it so much easier to call. Hope that's okay."

She'd assured him it was, and then she'd said, "I'd like to

see you again, Cactus. Would you have time to go to lunch with me tomorrow?"

"Are you askin' me on a date, Willa?" Cactus had asked, his bass voice gruff.

"Yes, sir," she'd said, actually lifting her chin while she sat in her car in her own driveway.

He'd remained silent for several long moments, each one accelerating Willa's heartbeat until she felt sure her chest would explode. Then he'd cleared his throat and said, "I can move some things around and make lunch work."

"The church is sponsoring ice skating this afternoon," she said. "And I heard there's a peppermint candy tasting at the community center tonight...."

"Do you want to go ice skating, or...?"

Willa laughed lightly, glancing over to the cane she'd use to walk into the house. She never used it in public, and a lot of walking was difficult for her. An afternoon and evening out with Cactus...she might have to use the cane or find reasons to sit down often.

"Ice skating is fine," she said, and the call ended.

Her nerves had cascaded through her as the day wore on, and the sea of memories she held back with a makeshift dike threatened to flood her and drag her under about every other minute.

She tilted her head as she threaded her second earring through the hole in her lobe, her fingers shaking slightly. This time, it wasn't because of the car accident she'd been in over a year ago, but actual nerves.

A glance at the clock told her Cactus would be here any

minute, and she needed to brush her teeth. Women still needed to brush their teeth before dates, right?

"Not with Cactus Glover," she muttered. She couldn't imagine kissing him that night, not on the first date. She wasn't counting the couple of hours they'd spent together at the tree lighting. That was just a coincidence that they'd been in the same place at the same time.

Her doorbell rang as she rinsed her mouth, and Abe started barking in his rusty voice. He wasn't very loud, but he ran into the bedroom, barked at her, and ran back toward the front door. Because her home was a modest one-bedroom in an old part of Three Rivers named Monkeytown, Abe could run back and forth from the front door to her bedroom in a few seconds.

Willa followed the dog into the small living room and glanced into her kitchen. The scent of toast and coffee still hung in the air, but she told herself it could've been something worse.

"Stop it," she said to the dog, reaching past him to open the door. His tail wagged aggressively, hitting her calves as he stepped into the doorway as if Cactus had come to see him and him alone.

"Hello there," Cactus said, looking at Abe and then up to Willa. "Can I?"

"Go ahead."

Cactus bent over, his smile real and glorious as he scrubbed Abe's jowls with both of his hands. "Look at you, dog." He tilted Abe's head slightly. "You're an old man, aren't you?" He chuckled. "Me too, bud. Me too."

He even groaned as he straightened, his smile fading as

he drank in Willa in front of him. She'd been soaking in his presence too, admiring the black jeans, black cowboy boots, and black cowboy hat. His leather jacket wasn't black, but brown, with a dark green shirt underneath. It had a plaid pattern on it in white and black, and he was the picture of cowboy perfection. If she wrapped him in a red bow, he'd be the source of all the merry in her Christmas.

"You look fantastic," he said, finally bringing his eyes back to hers.

"Thank you," Willa said, looking down at what she'd chosen to wear. Her jeans were the classic blue, and she'd put on a pair of leather boots with cream-colored fur along the tops. Along with a cream and pale purple sweater, she felt somewhat like a unicorn candy cane, and almost pretty enough to be on Cactus's arm. "You look great too."

She wanted to take the words back as soon as she said them. Everything between them felt wooden, robotic. She wanted the easy conversation they'd enjoyed at the tree lighting, and she wondered how to get it.

"Should we go?" he asked. "I looked up good lunch places that serve soup, and I found one I think you'll like."

"That was just a suggestion," she said, reaching for the jacket she'd laid over the back of her couch. "Go on, Abe. Back inside." The springer spaniel obeyed her, and she caught sight of his hopeful face as she closed the door behind her.

As she met Cactus's eyes again, she said, "We can go anywhere."

"Bowled Over has lots of stuff," he said. "Have you been there?"

"No." She took her time moving down the few steps to the narrow sidewalk, and she eyed his huge truck as she neared it. "I'm sure it'll be fine."

He followed her around to her door and opened it for her. Willa wasn't sure she could get in, and humiliation filled her. Her stomach turned, and the flood started. She tried to hold it back, but the memories kept coming at her.

"You okay?" Cactus asked, a gentleness to his tone Willa really liked. It had been a while since a man besides her brother had spoken to her with such kindness.

"Uh, I don't know if I can get in this truck." She turned around, fear filling her eyes. She was going to have to tell him something she hadn't planned on revealing today. Or for a long, long time. "I was in a car accident a while ago, and I sometimes need a cane if I've been walking for a while. Steep stairs are hard, and...." She turned and looked at the running board, trying to judge if she could lift her leg that high or not.

"I'm sorry, Willa," Cactus said. "I didn't know." He exhaled and turned back toward her house, but she didn't have a garage. "Do you have a car? We could just take it."

Another dose of humiliation filled her. "No, I don't have a car." No reason to have a car when she couldn't have a driver's license. "I think I can do it." She reached down and put her hand beneath her knee, lifting it up and putting her foot on the running board.

Cactus pressed in close behind her, and the heat from his body sent her hormones into overdrive. Willa once again felt like a sixteen-year-old with her first boyfriend, and Cactus put his hand on her hip. "There you go. I've got you."

She pushed off with her good leg and quickly put her foot on the running board. She grunted, thrilled she'd been able to do it. She put her bad leg inside the truck first, then lowered herself to the seat. Heat filled her face, but she turned toward Cactus anyway.

He wore sympathy on his face, and she hated that. He erased it when his eyes met hers, and he said, "Okay?"

She nodded, her voice suddenly on vacation. He backed up and closed the door. As he rounded the hood of the truck, she buckled her seatbelt, wondering how many more times she'd need to get in this truck. "You did it once," she whispered to herself. "You can do it again."

Cactus got behind the wheel and started the truck. "This isn't even my vehicle," he said. "I—" He cleared his throat. "This is the first time I've come to town by myself in...years."

"Years?"

He put the truck in reverse and backed out of her driveway. "Yes, years."

"But you know how to drive?"

"Sure," he said. "I remember how to drive. I just don't like coming to town, and I don't need to, so therefore, I don't need a car." He cut a glance at her, and questions streamed through Willa's mind. He probably had plenty of his own too, about her lack of a vehicle and the accident. There was plenty more too, and Willa wondered what in the world she was doing. If this date led to a second one, and then a third, and then she and Cactus started dating, she'd have to tell him so many things she'd stopped talking about.

She'd have to let the memories out. She'd have to relive the worst moments of her life.

Willa hadn't been on a first date in a very long time, but she knew how to talk to people, so she glanced at Cactus and asked, "Did you grow up here in Three Rivers?"

"Yes, ma'am," he said. "Right up on that ranch where I still live." A smile played with the corners of his mouth, and he glanced at her. "What about you?"

"I grew up in a tiny town in the Hill Country. I most recently lived in Temple before coming here with Patrick."

"You must be close to him."

"Yes," Willa said, smiling at the thought of her brother. "We're close and always have been."

"Just the two of you in your family?"

"Yes," she said. "He's a few years younger than me, and I've always been overprotective of him. He struggled growing up, you see, and other kids made fun of him."

"Kids can be cruel," Cactus said.

"That they can." Willa looked out the window, her thoughts sailing far away. She reeled them back in and cleared her throat. "You have how many siblings? Ten?"

"Only six," he said. "Dear Lord, if I had ten siblings...." He chuckled and shook his head. "I can barely tolerate the ones I've got."

"Is that so? I thought you guys seemed really close."

"Oh, we're close," he said. "Sometimes a little too close, for those of us who like our privacy."

"Ah, I see." She smiled, because she understood the need for privacy. "I swear there are more than seven of you." She thought of the two rows those Glovers took up. "There are at least ten."

"Those are my cousins," he said. "Seven kids in my family. Five in my uncle's family. There's twelve of us."

"Amazing," Willa said, grinning.

"What's amazing is that we haven't killed each other yet."

Willa laughed, and when Cactus joined his voice to hers, they made such a beautiful harmony together that Willa suddenly felt strong and like she'd done something amazing by asking Cactus to take her to lunch.

He pulled up to a restaurant on the far end of Main Street Willa had driven past with Patrick before. She didn't have the expendable income to eat out, so she'd never been to Bowled Over or much of anywhere else in Three Rivers.

"Stay there," he said, but it sounded very much like a command. "I'll come help you, okay?"

She nodded, though she wanted to see if she could get out of the truck by herself. She didn't want to stumble and fall, especially in front of the best-looking man in the known universe. When he opened her door, she turned sideways and said, "I want to try it."

"It's okay, Willa. I'll borrow a smaller car next time, but I don't want you to get hurt today."

She met his eyes, determination streaming through her. "I don't like feeling weak, Cactus. Can you please let me try?"

"Of course." He stepped back, but he didn't go very far. He kept one hand on the door, which he'd opened as far as it would go.

Willa wished he'd close his eyes, but she'd made a big deal about getting out, so she had to deal with him watching. She put one hand out on the armrest on the door, and the other on the side of the truck where the door met it.

She scooted forward, feeling every one of her extra twenty pounds, and put the foot of her bad leg on the running board. She slid out of the car, her good leg taking her full weight as she landed on the ground.

Her knee smarted at the bend in it, but she brought it quickly to the ground and steadied herself with her hand still on the armrest. Triumph filled her, and she looked up at Cactus. "Victory."

He looked down at her with something swimming in his eyes that sent a thrill through Willa's body.

Desire.

Cactus Glover was looking at her with pure desire in those gorgeous eyes, and she felt the same thing blitzing through her veins. She reached for his hand, and said, "Will you be my human cane today, Mister Glover?"

"Yes, ma'am," he said, his voice that same gruff one he'd used on the phone. "In fact, it would be my pleasure."

Chapter Eighteen

Cactus laughed again, probably for the fifth or sixth time since picking up Willa. He found her real and refreshing, with plenty of the feminine softness that called to his male side. He loved that she'd been vulnerable with him about her injury, but tough enough to try to get in and out of the truck herself.

He'd immediately run through other vehicles he could use when he came to pick her up, but there wasn't a single sedan in the Glover family. He'd already decided to go buy one before his next date with Willa, and he could ask Ace if he could keep it in the garage at Bull House.

Their late lunch at Bowled Over had been delicious, and their conversation had been as easy today as it had been at the tree lighting. Then, they'd had her nieces to distract them in any awkward silences, and today, Cactus had just powered through them.

He'd learned that Willa didn't like mushrooms or red onions on her salads, and that she liked a lot of cheese and croutons in her soup. He'd told her his favorite food—steak and eggs—and he'd learned that she'd eat a deep dish pepperoni pizza for every meal if she could.

She loved spending time with her nieces, and with Abe in her house, she was clearly a dog person. She checked every box on Cactus's list—well, she would have if he'd had one, which he didn't.

They finished lunch, and he helped her back into the truck again. The church was sponsoring a free afternoon at the ice skating rink, and while Cactus wasn't thrilled to be going, Willa had seemed excited about it.

Ace would be there selling concessions, and that was only part of why Cactus would rather go somewhere else. He and Willa obviously weren't going to be ice skating, and he suspected she actually *needed* to go for PR purposes for the church.

She'd go around and visit with everyone, and as her escort, he'd be required to do the same. Cactus couldn't think of anything worse, and he grew quiet the closer to the skating rink he drove.

They arrived, and Cactus waited while she took her time getting out of the truck again. He found her strength and determination incredibly admirable, and with that cute sweater and that auburn hair...she was easily the sexiest woman he'd met in a decade.

He swallowed back his desire for her, telling himself he'd been waiting a long time to feel like this about a woman, and he could wait a little longer to make sure he did things right. He didn't want to move too fast, and he didn't want to let his temper get the best of him again. He didn't want any of his harsher character flaws to come out today, or else he wouldn't be getting a second date.

He desperately wanted that second date, and this time, he would ask her.

She laced her arm through his, and they faced the building. Cactus couldn't get himself to take the first step, because he would never choose to come to a place like this. He would never willingly wade into a crowd of people, and he paused to think about what Dr. Thompson had told him again on Friday.

Do something outside your comfort zone every single day.

He'd reported that putting his pants on starting with a different leg had almost killed him, as had leaving a dirty dish in the sink. He'd done them, and he hadn't died. He hadn't liked it either, but he'd done it.

He honestly didn't think he could do this.

"Are you okay?" Willa asked.

Cactus shook his head, his eyes fixed on the door where a family entered. Mom, Dad, four kids. That right there was more people than he wanted to be around. Eating at a restaurant he could handle, because he had a private booth or table. He always asked for a booth if he could get one, but better was having Ace or Bishop bring him food from town.

Eating out with Willa was extremely far outside his comfort zone, and his mind buzzed at him to leave. He had to leave now.

Willa stepped in front of him, reaching up and guiding his face so that he was looking at her. "Cactus."

He blinked, the panic in his blood ebbing slightly.

"Talk to me."

"I don't do well in crowds," he said, his voice way down deep in his throat. He cleared out the emotion. "I don't want to go in there." He looked away from her, embarrassed. His body heated from head to toe, because maybe he wasn't ready to be dating.

That made no sense, because he'd been out with other women. He'd taken them to restaurants and then along the river, where a nice walking path existed. He'd even planned dinner and a movie, or a coffee date in a new park on the edge of the woods on the east side of town.

He realized as he stood there that he could enjoy those dates, because he'd planned them. He'd chosen things he could handle, and places where he knew there wouldn't be hundreds of people.

"Maybe we could, I don't know, go see a movie. Or we could go back to your house, and I'll make you the one kind of cookie I know how to bake. Or you could come with me to buy a car you can get in and out of."

Willa blinked at him, then she started laughing. He wasn't sure why, because nothing he'd said was a joke or even remotely funny. She sobered quickly, and asked, "You're going to go buy a car?"

"Well, I don't have one," he said. "And all my family owns are trucks."

She smiled and tucked her hair behind her ear, looking

down at the ground. She reached out and took one of his hands in hers. Cactus pulled in a breath, pure heat roaring through him. Fireworks popped through every cell in his body, and he wanted to hold this woman's hand for a long, long time.

"You're going to buy a car so we can go out again," she said, her gaze still down.

"That's the idea," he admitted.

Her phone rang, and Willa fished it out of her coat pocket. Her expression changed from calm and casual to pure panic in less than a second. "I have to take this," she said, spinning away from him before he could see who'd called.

She walked away from him smoothly, and he had to watch very closely for a limp at all. He didn't think she'd been faking getting in and out of the truck, though, and he still wanted to buy a car.

Willa froze several feet from him, and an alarm went off in his head. He stepped toward her in case she fell, and he'd just reached her when her legs gave out. "Whoa," he said, catching her and easing her onto the ground. He glanced around, looking for someone to help.

"Willa," he said, peering down at her. Tears ran down her face, which had turned the color of cement. "Talk to me, Willa." He picked up her phone, which she'd dropped. The line was still connected, and he put it to his ear. "Who is this?"

"Call her brother," the man said.

Cactus pulled the phone from his ear as the call ended, and Willa groaned. "Willa," he said. "I'm calling Patrick." He had no idea what had happened, and he quickly tapped and swiped on her phone to get to her brother's name.

His line rang, and he answered on the second ring. "Pastor," Cactus said. "It's Cactus Glover. Willa got a call and she needs your help."

"A call from who?"

"I don't know," he said, but Willa said, "Maurice Maxwell."

Cactus repeated the name to the pastor, and he said, "I'll be right there. Where are you?"

"In the parking lot at the skating rink," Cactus said.

Her brother arrived only sixty seconds later, by which time, Willa had come back to most of her senses, but she'd been crying so hard Cactus hadn't been able to get anything out of her. Together with Patrick, they helped Willa stand, and Cactus handed her brother her phone.

"Thank you," Patrick said, and he led Willa away, his head bent close to hers as they talked. She limped much more noticeably now, and Cactus watched his first date go up in flames and the possibility of a second disappear onto a distant horizon.

"Maurice Maxwell," he said to himself, determined to figure out who that was and why he'd made Willa breakdown.

CACTUS STOOD AT THE BACK OF TRUE BLUE AND WATCHED his family assemble for their weekly Sabbath luncheon. Part of him wanted to slip out the door he'd come in, text Bishop that he wouldn't be there, and make another solitary bowl of soup in his cabin out on the edge of the ranch.

Something kept him in place, though, and it was the beautiful redhead he'd been out with last week.

Six days ago, and Cactus had texted Willa a few times. He'd gone to church today, hoping to see her and talk to her. He wanted to find out if she was okay, number one. Number two, he wanted to find out when he could take her to dinner again.

Number three, he simply wanted to hear her voice.

She hadn't been at church, and he'd had to settle for cornering her brother and asking about her. Patrick Corning had said Willa was doing well, but she'd had to return to the Hill Country for a few weeks. When Cactus had pressed him for more details, he'd said, "I'm afraid I can't say more. Willa will have to choose what she'd like to tell you and what she doesn't."

Cactus had to accept that, because he didn't need to get into another yelling match with another pastor at the back of the chapel.

Willa kept him at his family party, because he wanted to be able to become the man that could walk into the skating rink and socialize with the townspeople as Willa clung to his arm. He couldn't be the cowboy hermit if he wanted to be with Willa, and now that he'd spent a couple of days with her for longer than five minutes, he wanted to be with her more than ever.

Arizona burst into the barn, practically dragging her boyfriend behind her. Cactus straightened, because he sensed something had happened.

"Everyone," Zona called, and she could have a loud voice when she wanted to. She was the youngest of seven kids, and the only girl with six loud, annoying, constantly-jostling-for-position brothers.

"Hey," she yelled again, and Bear stepped over to her and looked at her and then Duke. He turned to face the crowd, only about half of whom had heard or listened to Zona. Bear whistled through his teeth, and that got everyone to stop talking and face him.

He nodded at Zona and Duke and retreated back to the crowd.

Zona wore pure excitement on her face, and Cactus knew what was coming. "Duke and I are engaged!" she yelled, bouncing on the balls of her feet in excitement. The room held its breath for a moment, and then Sammy rushed at Zona, followed closely by Ida and Etta.

Cactus met Bear's eye for a moment, an unspoken conversation happening between them. As far as Cactus knew, only he and Bear knew what Duke had done eighteen years ago. He told himself that Daddy wasn't here anymore, and he wouldn't have objected anyway. He'd forgiven Duke and encouraged him to stay and make things right with his folks.

Instead, Duke had left his family ranch to try to find his own place in the world. He'd returned a little over a year ago, and he and Zona had been dating for months now.

Mother enveloped Zona in a hug and held her tight. She stepped over to Duke and embraced him too, and Cactus felt Zona's joy as tears streamed down her face after Mother's hug. It was an embrace of acceptance, and Cactus often felt like crying after a hug like that from Mother.

Zona looked at Bear, the pause between them filled with meaning. She sobbed as he enveloped her in his arms, and he held her for several long seconds as he whispered in her ear. She nodded against his chest, finally stepping back and wiping her face. They shared another look, and then Zona hugged Preacher.

Bear turned and made his way over to Cactus, who'd settled against the wall again. "You knew about this, didn't you?" Cactus asked.

"Duke came and asked me for my blessing last month," he said, turning to face the crowd again. "I told him he had to tell Zona what he'd done, and if she didn't break up with him, that was my blessing."

Cactus had never been more glad to be the second-oldest son. He couldn't shoulder the responsibility of being the oldest, but there was no one better for the job than Bear. "Smart," he said. "I wouldn't have thought of that. Heck, I probably would've thrown Duke back to his own ranch the first time he dared to step foot over here."

Bear lifted one shoulder in a casual shrug. "Daddy forgave him. I figured I had to as well."

"Just another reason you're better than me."

"Nah," Bear said. "You've forgiven him too. You just don't want to admit it."

"He stole a quarter of a million dollars from Daddy," Cactus said. "From *us*, Bear."

"It was almost two decades ago," Bear said quietly. "He returned almost all of it. He owned up to what he'd done."

Cactus nodded. "I suppose you're right. I'd like to be forgiven for the things I do wrong." He watched Duke shaking hands with all the cowboys in the room, his smile wide and permanently stuck to his face. "Was he repentant when you talked to him?"

"Enough," Bear said. "Look at her, Cactus. She loves him. How do we hold a grudge forever?"

"We don't," Cactus said. "Look at him, Bear. He loves her too." He watched Zona migrate back to Duke's side and look up at him, her eyes shining with the emotion she felt for him. "Who knew someone could tame Zona's attitude and get her to slow down enough to fall in love?" He chuckled, thrilled for his sister.

"Love is a remarkable thing," Bear said. "It makes a man do things he thought he never would."

Cactus tossed him a sharp look, because he'd borrowed Bear's truck to take Willa to lunch. He'd confided in Bear after the date had ended hours early, and he waited for the questions about her to come.

"Heard from Willa?" Bear asked.

Cactus shook his head, the unrest in his soul expanding to infect his chest and make breathing feel like a hitch behind his lungs instead of oxygen going where it should.

"She'll call you," Bear said. "Sammy and I are praying for her—and you."

"Thank you," Cactus murmured. He'd had a rough road between him and the Lord, but he hadn't ever stopped praying. The problem was, he hadn't even thought to pray for Willa.

He did now, just pausing right where he stood and closing

his eyes. *Help her*, he prayed. *She obviously got some terrible news last week, and she left Three Rivers. Comfort her and bless her and protect her and please, if there's any way at all, bring her back to me.*

His mind finally felt at peace, and he added a mental *Amen*, and opened his eyes. Now all he had to do was go congratulate the happy couple, so he pushed away from the wall and started across the hall to Zona and Duke.

Chapter Nineteen

A ce put a check-mark next to the name the woman had given him and passed the little boy a bag of supplies. "Take that on down the hall, buddy. Room twelve. They're gonna start in about ten minutes." He smiled at the little boy and his mother and looked to the next person in line.

The children's cookie decorating class was one of his favorite events, because he could work inside and he got to see the wonder and joy of children. He continued to work to get everyone checked in, constantly pushing away thoughts of Holly Ann.

She'd canceled with him for that night, and if it had been the first time, Ace wouldn't be as frustrated. But it wasn't the first time. In the past couple of weeks, since the tree lighting, they'd had five or six nights of plans, and Holly Ann had either broken their plans a few hours beforehand or during the date on all but one of them.

He told himself he couldn't be frustrated.

It isn't going to be Christmas all year, he thought as he took the clipboard over to the desk at the community center. When he'd prayed after Holly Ann had rushed off during their dessert to deal with an "eggnog emergency" and never returned, that was the message the Lord had given him.

It wasn't going to be Christmas all year. He needed to give Holly Ann the space she needed to be the Christmas Festival chairperson, and he couldn't be upset when she had a job to do. She'd *told* him as much over a month ago.

The holiday fair had started over the weekend, and after returning the clipboard, he went into the triple wide gymnasium that could be sectioned off by huge canvas drapes that lowered from the ceiling. Today, though, the dividers were all up to create one massive space where vendors of all kinds had set up for the fair.

Ace loved wandering up and down the aisles, looking at anything and everything. The sweets always took up the aisle against the north wall, and Ace always started there. Then he could purchase a box of the peppermint squares he loved and snack on them while he shopped.

His mother loved the peppermint squares too, so he bought an extra box and started his pilgrimage up and down the aisles. He didn't normally spend a lot of time in the boutique booths, or the ones with lots of wooden decorations. The only time he had was when he was trying to meet a new woman.

Since he wasn't looking for a girlfriend this year, he left the ladies to their shopping and he focused on finding a few gifts for his family members. He found the cutest bandanna for Benny that could be threaded right onto his collar. He bought a dark blue one with the words *best friends* embroidered on it.

He bought a tub of sno-dough for Lincoln, though Bear would likely fillet him alive for doing it. He could just hear the grizzly bellowing at the huge mess the dough made. Just watching the kids at the trough in front of the booth told Ace that Lincoln would love the moldable, flaky dough, but that it was definitely messy.

He found a pair of wool socks for Judge, who loved to wear them year-round, something Ace did not understand. He didn't have to understand it to give a gift though, and he shifted his bags as he stepped over to a booth selling pocketknives.

Every cowboy should have a knife with them at all times, and Ace had gotten his first pocketknife from his father at the age of eight. He'd sat with him on the back porch as his father taught him how to open it, how to clean it, how to keep it sharp.

He spent a long time in the booth, asking questions and picking through knife after knife. He wanted a really good knife for Ward, and a really good knife for Bear. When he'd finally picked out the two he wanted, the gentleman who'd been helping him for half an hour asked, "Would you like any engravings?"

"Engravings?"

The man pulled out a laminated sheet and showed him the options. "We can do any of these as symbols. Most people put them down on the bottom of the handle. We can do names up to nine letters as well, depending on the knife.

For either of those, you can do nine letters." He looked up at Ace with eager eyes.

"Is that a bear?" Ace asked, pointing to the brown bear in the top corner.

"Yes, sir."

"I want that on this blue knife," he said. "And I want to put the name Ward on the silver one."

The man started filling out a form, and Ace asked, "How long does the engraving take?"

"I'll take them into the back and do them right now," he said. "It'll be about thirty minutes." He looked up. "Can you stick around for that long?"

Though the noise in the room was starting to wear him down, Ace nodded. He had plenty of other things he could buy. The Glover family didn't do a lot of gifts, and none were required. But Ace liked to buy something for someone when he saw it and it reminded him of them, or he knew they'd love it. If nothing stood out, he didn't get them anything.

They did draw names each year for Christmas, and this year, he'd drawn Preacher. He'd gotten lucky, honestly. He knew exactly what Preacher wanted, but he wouldn't find it at the holiday fair.

No he needed to get over to the mall and Gaming Guru. Then, he could pick out the newest joystick for Preacher's flight simulator, or he could pick up the newest NBA basketball game for his video game machine. Preacher loved playing the sports games, and while Ace would rather fly, he'd been known to sit down with Preacher and shoot hoops.

He wandered up and down the aisles, picking up a cookbook for Ida, and a book titled *50 Types of Toast* for Montana.

He grinned about that for a good while, because he'd had some of her peanut butter bacon toast, and then an avocado scrambled egg toast that had blown his mind. Lincoln asked her every morning she was in the homestead for a different type of toast, and while they'd framed the shed, he'd overheard her brainstorming with Bishop for different types of toast she could make for Link.

He really wanted to find something for Ranger and Oakley, so he decided to stay at the fair for another few minutes, hopeful that there'd be a booth on the next aisle that would hold the perfect present for them.

He turned a corner and nearly collided with a woman. "Sorry," he said automatically, his multiple bags sloshing around as he stumbled away from her. "Etta?"

His sister's eyes met his, and recognition lit them. A man stepped to her side, "You okay, sweetheart?" He looked at her and then Ace, his dark eyes lit from something within.

"Yes," Etta said, straightening her purse on her shoulder. Ace raised his eyebrows when she simply stood there, silent. "This is my brother, Ace," she finally said, but she certainly wasn't happy about it. "Ace, this is Noah Johnson."

"Nice to meet you," Ace said, extending his hand toward Noah. He wore a smile now, and he kept one hand on Etta's back as he reached with the other to shake Ace's hand. He wore a classy, expensive cowboy hat and a dark brown shirt with black lines that ran up and down and across. He had a big belt buckle on his belt, which held up his dark-wash jeans. He wore clean cowboy boots that had never seen dust, and he was exactly the type of man Ace would pair with Etta.

"So are you two dating?" he asked.

"Ace," Etta hissed.

Noah looked at her, clear surprise in his eyes. They had a silent conversation, and Etta said, "Yes, we're dating." She softened as she spoke, her eyes migrating back to Noah as she smiled. When she looked at Ace again, she added, "I haven't told anyone else, Ace. Will you hold onto this for now, please?"

Hold onto this? He nearly rolled his eyes at Etta's formality, but he nodded anyway. "Sure," he said.

"Thank you," she said, and they continued down the aisle. Ace turned and watched them go, wondering how old Noah Johnson was. He was clearly older than Etta, probably by a lot of years, and Ace wished he'd asked.

"No, you don't," he muttered to himself. "It would just be one more secret you'd need to keep." He was so sick of secrets, and he wasn't sure how much longer he could keep the ones swirling in his mind.

ACE TURNED DOWN THE DIRT ROAD THAT LED BACK TO THE farmhouse where he'd eaten Thanksgiving dinner with Holly Ann's family. The moment he rounded the corner and the house came into view, his stomach sank to the bottom of his cowboy boots.

Holly Ann's car wasn't there, and if she wasn't there yet, there was no way she was coming.

He thought about turning around and leaving. After all, this wasn't his family, and this wasn't his sister's birthday. He wasn't part of this family—yet—and he wondered what could've possibly happened today that would keep Holly Ann from her sister's birthday.

After all, she only had one sister, and they were extremely important to each other.

Represent her.

The thought came into his mind, and it kept him moving toward the farmhouse. He parked beside her father's truck and got out without hesitating. Holly Ann should've been here twenty minutes ago, with the birthday cake.

As it was, Ace didn't have anything for Bethany Rose, and foolishness filled him with every step up to the porch. He dutifully rang the doorbell though, and Senator opened the door less than a breath later. "It is him," he called over his shoulder. He focused on Ace again, a smile filling his whole face. "Evening, Ace."

"Good evening, sir." He shook the man's hand. "Sorry Holly Ann's not here. She was supposed to meet me, but I don't see her car."

"Oh, she had to run to town for something. What was it?" He stepped back, his last question aimed at Bethany Rose.

"Their helper elf didn't show up." Bethany Rose came out of the kitchen and gave Ace a quick hug. "You're the most adorable man ever. You're going to win some major points with Holly Ann for coming anyway."

Ace smiled at her, thinking he'd like to cash in his points for a quiet evening at home with Holly Ann, just the two of them. No emergencies. No gingerbread. No elves.

"Is she going to be the elf?" Ace asked, thinking he'd very much like to see her in that costume.

"Who knows?" Bethany Ann asked. "She'll figure something out. She always does." She gestured for him to sit down. "We were just waiting for you. I wasn't sure if you were still going to come."

"Sorry I'm late," he said, thinking he'd had no indication that he shouldn't go to Bethany Rose's for dinner. Holly Ann hadn't texted him about the missing elf, and a familiar irritation struck like lightning right against his spine. "I had to help my mother with something tonight."

"It's fine, it's fine." She shooed him over to the table now, where her birthday dinner sat waiting.

"Did you make this yourself?" he asked.

"Heavens, no." She laughed as she set a stack of napkins on the table. Ace took in the spread, so he knew who'd made this food before Bethany Rose said, "Holly Ann made it and brought it over."

"Mm." He could see her hand in the delicate scalloped potatoes, and she was the only one he knew who made a cherry-glazed meatloaf. A tray held eight of them, each about as big as a double-deck of cards. His mouth watered, and when he looked at the broccoli and craisin salad, he really missed Holly Ann.

Still, he prayed with her family, and he ate, contributing to the conversation as much as he was able.

Afterward, he wished Bethany Rose happy birthday and left the ranch on the north side of town. As he still needed a gift for Preacher, he stopped at the outdoor mall, finding the parking lot full out to the road. He supposed he wasn't the only person who hadn't found all of their gifts yet, though two weeks remained until Christmas.

And a week after that, Holly Ann would be done with all the craziness. *Three weeks*, he told himself. He could hang on for three more weeks.

He stopped in at Gaming Guru, taking a moment to just bask in the glorious sight of computers, gaming consoles, controllers, earphones, gaming chairs, and more.

He hadn't played a lot this fall, but Preacher had become good friends with Duke, and they played with Beau Peterson out at Three Rivers Ranch too.

Ace needed to get back into the games with them, because he realized as he stood in the video game store that he missed playing. Specifically, he missed playing with Preacher.

"Can I help you find something?"

"Definitely," Ace said. "Show me what you've got as far as joysticks for flight simulators." Maybe he'd buy something for himself since he was here and all. "And I want to know the newest, best NBA game."

"That's going to be Hoops 2K20," he said, indicating the wall to the right. "We've been selling a lot of those, so if you want it, we can grab it now before we look at joysticks."

"Yes, please," Ace said.

Thirty minutes later, he left the store with the video game only, because a joystick was such a personal choice. Preacher would likely want to come pick his own, and Ace thought he'd look around a bit more for something small to add to the basketball game he'd bought.

He skipped all the clothing stores but paused at a kiosk selling chocolate-covered items, his curiosity piqued.

They had the normal suspects, like almonds and raisins,

but they also sold chocolate-covered strawberries, dried mango, bacon, and even cinnamon bears.

He wanted to try all of it, so he sampled a little bit of several items, grateful for the woman helping him. "I'll take that sampler box," he finally said, thinking Oakley would like it. She'd filled a cupboard in the kitchen at the homestead with chocolate, and at the very least, it would be fun for her to sample the items the way he had.

"And I'll take a whole bag of these cinnamon bears." He lifted the large package, because Preacher seemed to have taste buds made of rubber. He loved salsas and hot sauces—the hotter the better—and these cinnamon bears whispered Preacher's name to Ace.

He continued through the mall until he reached the main doors that led out onto the plaza. He went that way, because Santa would be out there tonight, and if Holly Ann was dealing with an elf issue, maybe he'd get to see her for a moment.

Since the tree lighting ceremony and the hot kiss next to his truck, Ace hadn't let the opportunity to kiss her pass without taking it. He created the opportunity if he had to, and even if she'd had to leave in the middle of their date, he made sure to kiss her before she did.

The truth was, he was falling fast for her now that he'd managed to keep her in his life for so long.

He stalled at another kiosk, this one right inside the main entrance. He started digging through the cell phone cases, trying to find one that screamed Preacher to him. His real name was Paul, and he did possess a lot of gospel knowledge, but that was only part of the reason he'd been nick-named Preacher.

He loved to lecture, and he'd been the state champion in debate in high school. He'd been Preacher before that though, because he'd always been the one to bring everyone together, the way a preacher did for church.

Ace found as he picked through the phone cases. Preacher had aligned himself with Judge, who seemed on the opposite end of the spectrum when it came to unifying the family. Ace didn't know all the details of everyone's life—and he didn't want to know.

Ace knew both Preacher and Judge meant well, though. He'd had a spat with Zona about their daddy's Corvette, which Preacher had parked in the garage at the Ranch House. Not everyone got along all the time, but Ace truly believed they all tried to make things right if they could.

He finally found a black case with a simple line design going across it, making a town skyline. It felt like Preacher to him, and he bought the case and added it to the bag with the cinnamon bears and the video game.

Outside, the line to see Santa wasn't very long, and Ace stepped past the people waiting and the little elf hut they had to go into to get to where Santa sat on his throne. He looked into the roped off workshop and found a woman wearing the elf costume walking back over to the camera.

It wasn't Holly Ann, so the crisis must have been handled.

"A while ago," he said out loud. Yet Holly Ann hadn't come to dinner, and she hadn't called or texted him.

"Hey, Ace," someone said, and he glanced toward Alta Barber.

"Oh, hey," he said, smiling. He accepted her quick hug and stepped back. "Getting all your shopping done?"

"I hope so," she said. "I can't come here again. Just the parking situation is going to put me into labor." She laughed and then added, "Wait. That's what I want. I'm going to come every single day." She gave him a smile and looked over to a juggler that had just started his routine on the plaza.

Ace watched him too, noting the outfit had changed from green, yellow, and purple to red, green, and white. He also didn't juggle bowling pins as he usually did but had switched to giant candy canes.

Everything in Three Rivers screamed Christmas during December, and Ace was actually getting tired of it. He just wanted a plain vanilla shake, no peppermint swirl. He didn't want to park on the street to find a gift for his cousin. He wanted his girlfriend to keep the plans they made, and he knew that was the root of all of his frustrations.

He pushed them away and focused on Alta again. She said, "Well, you have a good night, Ace. You waitin' for Holly Ann?"

"No," he said, frowning. "Why? Have you seen her?"

"No," Alta said. "I just assumed she'd be here if you were." She flashed him a quick smile and turned toward her husband. "See you later." She walked away, every step looking painful and slow.

Ace watched Santa hold a little girl on his lap, his smile brilliant as he tilted his head so he could get his ear closer to the child's mouth. Ace moved closer, something pulling him over to the ropes separating Santa from the people walking in and out of the mall.

Santa giggled, and the little girl slid from his lap.

In that moment, Ace realized that Santa had *giggled*—and it had sounded like Holly Ann. His eyes met Santa's, and there was no way it could be Holly Ann. She had dark eyes the color of nearly-black coffee, and Santa had blue eyes.

Santa looked away from him and at the next child coming his way, and Ace turned and walked away.

"Don't be stupid," he told himself. "Holly Ann is not playing Santa Claus."

Chapter Twenty

Holly Ann couldn't get out of her Santa suit fast enough. She couldn't believe that Bethany Rose had changed the date of her party, and that it had then fallen on a Tuesday evening. She dressed as Santa and did her job every Tuesday night, and she'd been so late getting to the mall that night.

She'd had to make Bethany Rose's birthday dinner and drive it out to the ranch. She'd been stressed and exhausted before her shift began, and she hadn't had a spare second or brain cell to text Ace.

Seeing him standing just on the other side of the ropes, watching her, had sent her nerves on fire. "He doesn't know it's you," she told herself. There was no way. She'd checked her appearance the moment she'd entered the private suite, and every hair sat in the exact right place. There was not a single dark hair showing, and her contacts had concealed her true eye color.

She'd laughed with the little girl on her lap though, and if Ace had heard that….

She pushed it out of her head and pulled out her phone to send him a text. *Sorry about tonight. Did you end up staying for dinner?*

Yep, he responded. Nothing else.

Holly Ann sighed and pushed her hair off her face and forehead. She pressed her eyes closed, and they burned as if someone had rubbed sand in them. She was so tired, and she had another full day tomorrow, what with the Christmas movie in the park, and then Wassail Weekend coming up in just three days.

She didn't know how many more times she could apologize. She didn't know how many more dates she could break or leave early. Some had been because of real crises surrounding the festival. Some had been because she needed to get over to the mall and wear the suit.

Hope you got your elf problem sorted out, he said.

I did, Holly Ann sent back.

Too bad you couldn't come back to the ranch for dinner.

Yeah, I got stuck over at the mall.

I'll bet. That place is insane.

Holly Ann relaxed a little bit at the texting, because it meant Ace wasn't too upset with her. Her father and sister had both texted her about how great Ace was. That he'd come to the party and stayed, that he was articulate and kind, easy to talk to, and in Daddy's case, "the best man you've ever dated."

"No pressure or anything," Holly Ann said to herself. She finally zipped up the suit and hung it in the closet. With that locked and the key in her pocket, she turned to leave the mall. Finally.

She didn't remember last year being quite so exhausting, but she hadn't been in charge of the entire festival *and* playing Santa Claus.

I went after dinner, Ace said in his next text. *Too bad I didn't run into you.*

That is too bad, she said. *We could've gotten ice cream or something.*

Did you get to eat at all?

Holly Ann had not eaten, and her stomach threatened to claw itself inside out. She leaned her head back, stretching the ache in her neck, and wondering what to do. She didn't want to lie to Ace, but she'd seen him twenty minutes ago, standing on the other side of the ropes. He could very likely still be at the mall.

If she told him she hadn't eaten, he might suggest they get together. While Holly Ann wanted to see Ace and make sure they were okay, she really just wanted to go home and go to bed.

He'll let you do that too, she thought, and because she was so tired and her brain so soft against any defenses she might have had against Ace, she tapped the phone icon to call him.

"Hey," he said, but she couldn't tell his mood with the single word.

"Hey," she said. "I didn't eat, but I'm so exhausted. Do you think this could be one of those nights where you meet me at my house with something delicious? I'll eat it, and we can talk for a minute, and then you'll stay with me until I fall asleep?"

"I'd like that," he said quietly.

"Where are you?" she asked, putting one hand on her back and leaning into it to stretch her hip.

"I just left the mall. How about you?"

"I'm finishing up with Rachel, and then I'll be on my way." She hated that she'd skirted her physical location, but she told herself it wasn't a lie. She left the private room and went down the hall. Rachel had an invoice for her to sign, which Holly Ann did while Ace said he'd stop and get fried chicken and be at her house in no less than twenty minutes.

She beat him there, glad she could pull into her garage now and close the door behind her. It was supposed to snow this weekend, and Holly Ann had contingency plans for the outdoor events at the apple cider mill should the weather ruin their planned wassail tastings, dried apple wreaths, and apple carving.

She let Snickers out to take care of his business, and she changed out of her clothes into her pajamas. Ace knocked on the door a few minutes later, and Holly Ann called for him to come in.

He did, bending down to kiss her forehead before continuing into the kitchen. He put her food on a plate and brought it to her, settling himself onto the couch beside her. She took the fried chicken and French fries from him with a grateful smile.

"Thank you, baby." She leaned toward him to kiss him, glad when he received the kiss well. He pushed his hands into her hair and deepened the kiss, and Holly Ann went with him, because she knew how very much he missed her.

She missed him too. Very much, and she really wanted

him to know she hated that life wasn't perfect. That schedules didn't always match up. That she had a secret she hadn't told him.

He pulled away and sighed as he leaned back against the couch.

"Long day?" she asked.

"Yes," he said. "You?"

"The longest yet." She picked up a piece of fried chicken and bit into it.

"I found out my sister is dating Noah Johnson," he said. "Another secret I can't keep to myself anymore. Since you're my secret keeper, I figured you'd be safe to tell.'

"Etta?" Holly Ann asked, plenty of surprise in her tone.

"Yep." He looked at her. "Why the surprise?"

"Noah Johnson is what? Forty-five years old?" She picked up a couple of fries and bit off half of each.

"Is he?" Ace asked. "I don't know. He did seem older than her. I saw them a couple of days ago at the holiday fair."

"That was just yesterday, baby." She smiled at him. "You're so tired you don't even know what day of the week it is."

He chuckled and closed his eyes. "Maybe it was yesterday."

"It was, because you texted me about the peppermint squares, and you went right after you finished checking in kids for the cookie decorating class."

"Mm hm." He sure seemed like he was going to be the one to fall asleep first, but Holly Ann didn't mind. She finished eating while Ace breathed in and out, in and out, and then she lay down so her head was in his lap.

One big, rough, warm hand started to stroke her hair, and Holly Ann sighed at the tender touch. She let her eyes drift closed too, and she asked, "Ace?"

"Hmm?"

"Have you ever been in love?"

His hand stuttered for a second, then evened out. "Once," he said. "I asked Jeanie Penship to marry me."

Holly Ann wanted to be shocked, but she honestly didn't have the energy. "Oh?"

"Yeah," he said. "She said no, though. I'd read the signs all wrong, and she actually wanted to break up."

"Wow."

"Yeah." He chuckled. "I don't know if I was in love with her. Maybe I was. Maybe I wasn't. I felt like a fool, but I started dating Windy Lyson only a month later. So maybe I wasn't." His voice trailed off, but he said again, "Maybe I wasn't," real quiet.

"Why would that mean you weren't?" she asked.

"I don't know," he said, his fingers getting caught in her hair. He gently worked them through and started again. "If I was really in love with her, and she rejected my proposal of marriage, shouldn't I have been utterly devastated? Heartbroken? Angry and then horribly sad? I didn't feel any of those things. I was embarrassed. That was it."

"Hmm."

"When Cactus's marriage ended, he retreated to the Edge Cabin. He's lived out there for over ten years, and it's only been the past couple of years that he's even gone to town."

"Everyone deals with loss differently," Holly Ann said.

She knew that much, as she'd seen Daddy and Bethany Rose's reactions to her mother's disappearance.

He didn't say anything else, and Holly Ann's mind turned soft as she drifted into blissful sleep.

"I don't actually like wassail," she said on Friday afternoon. She and Ace stood in front of a folding table at the apple cider mill. Mother Nature had blown in a cold wind, but there was no precipitation—yet.

"Blasphemy," Ace said with a grin. She had no idea when he'd left the other night. She'd awakened sometime in the middle of the night, and she had a pillow under her head and a blanket covering her body. The food he'd brought sat in her fridge, and Snickers had been asleep on her hip. All the lights were off, and the house was locked up tight.

Ace had been gone, and she hated that he had such a long drive back to Shiloh Ridge Ranch. She also missed the ranch, and she really wanted to get back up there.

She watched him try the spiced wassail and make a face. "Way too much clove," he said, tossing the sample cup into the garbage can under the table. The wind picked up as if in protest to what he'd said about the wassail, and Holly Ann hunkered down in the collar of her coat.

"Can I come to lunch at the ranch on Sunday?" she asked.

Ace looked at her, his eyebrows up. "Of course," he said. "You're welcome any day."

"Is that so?" She led him to the next table, where they had a cinnamon wassail.

"That's so, Miss Broadbent," Ace said in a proper Texas drawl that made her smile. He tipped back another tester of wassail and smacked his lips. "Yes, this one's good." He smiled at the two women setting out cups, and they moved on.

Holly Ann took in the magnificence of the Texas sky above the orchards and mill. A new tasting table had been set up along the walking path that went along one of the three rivers for which Three Rivers was named. In the summertime, the grass here shone like emeralds, and families brought picnic baskets and Frisbees.

For the Christmas Festival, a few vendors had brought in food carts, and she really wanted one of the savory waffles from Waffled Up. They'd been assigned the spot the farthest from the entrance to the tasting tables, because then people would walk all the way down to the end of the route, and have to walk all the way back.

Holly Ann had learned a thing or two over the years of serving on the festival committee.

"I just remembered that our family gift exchange is this Sunday," he said. "If you're okay sitting through that, you can definitely still come to lunch."

"It's this Sunday?" she asked. "There's still quite a bit of time until Christmas."

"Nine days," he said. "Not that I'm counting down until you'll be free from this." He grinned at her as they arrived at the next table, which boasted pumpkin wassail.

Holly Ann could admit she was ready for the Christmas Festival to be done. She even thought she'd take a break from it next year. Pass the baton, so to speak, and just go back to wearing the suit.

"This is a no," Ace said, dropping his cup in the trash. "And yes, we do our gift exchange early. Usually on a Sunday, because it doesn't interfere with other holiday things, or much ranch work. Then, on the actual day, we can relax, get together with each other or not, and basically have a nice, relaxing Christmas."

"I bet things will get harder and harder as your family gets bigger."

"Yes," he said. "We're already seeing that. Ranger and Oakley want to have their own traditions, and yeah." He didn't say anything more about that, and Holly Ann let the topic drop.

In her pocket, her alarm went off, and she quickly stopped the vibrating.

"What was that?" Ace asked anyway.

"Nothing," she said.

They walked to the next table, and he sampled the rum raisin wassail. "Nope," he said. After stepping away from that station, he added, "If you have to go, Holly Ann, it's fine."

"We've only been here for a little bit," she said, eyeing the waffle cart up ahead. "I want a waffle. Whoever it is can wait."

She thought of the children who would have to wait for her to arrive, and guilt pinched in her stomach.

"All right," he said, the words full of doubt.

She'd snoozed the alarm, so it went off again while she ordered her waffle. She pulled her phone out of her pocket to turn off the alarm, and quickly shoved it back into her pocket. Her heart thrashed against her ribs at the words that had just imprinted on the backs of her eyelids.

Santa time!

She'd put that reminder on the alarm, as if she didn't know where she was supposed to be from six to eight p.m. every Friday night.

She told herself that that note could mean anything. It didn't mean she had to go dress up like Santa and hold children on her lap. Ace probably hadn't even seen it.

They got their waffles, and Holly Ann ate hers quickly. She tipped up on her toes and kissed Ace, tasting his pulled pork and provolone cheese before saying, "I have to go. I'm so sorry."

"Go," he said, lifting his waffle grilled cheese sandwich back to his mouth. "I'll call you later."

She gazed at him—this gorgeous, kind, good-hearted, amazing cowboy—for an extra-long moment. What would life be like with *him* as a husband? Could she be a wife and mother if *Ace* was the one at her side?

She turned away from him and from the thoughts, hurrying to her car now. After all, she had to transform herself from Holly Ann into Santa and put on a show for the waiting children at the mall.

The whole way there, she fantasized about what her life would be like at Shiloh Ridge Ranch. She dreamt of a big house with a whole wall of windows looking out over the valley where the town sat, and little boys with the same deep eyes that Ace had, and plenty of dark hair like her. Sometimes he'd take them out to work with him, giving her a break, and she'd make cupcake towers for their birthdays.

Everyone was so happy, and they all loved one another. There would be no sneaking off to play Santa Claus, because there'd be no secrets between them.

"If that's the life you want," Holly Ann said to herself. "Why can't you tell him about the suit right now?"

He'd have to find out sooner or later. Why not sooner?

Chapter Twenty-One

Ace sat on the bench at Cider Mill Park, the last of his toasty waffle sandwich long gone. Holly Ann was long gone too, and Ace looked up into the sky as the thunder rolled through the clouds.

He should get up and get under some type of shelter. His mind felt encased in cement, and every thought moved in slow-motion. The first drops of rain fell before he stood, and while others ran for the barn, Ace just walked.

He eventually made it to his truck and got behind the wheel. Cold water had soaked his shoulders and his cowboy hat, so he took that off and tossed it onto the seat next to him.

Santa time!

The note in Holly Ann's alarm made no sense.

The fact that it was her alarm buzzing and not Rachel or some other assistant calling to tell her about an emergency made no sense.

He heard Santa's giggle from the other night, and he closed his eyes, trying to see Holly Ann wearing a Santa Claus costume.

"It makes no sense," he said, opening his eyes. He started his truck and got out of the dirt parking lot at the cider mill. He had to drive all the way across town to get to the highway leading south, and then he had thirty more minutes to get home.

He didn't want to go back up to Shiloh Ridge. He didn't want to be alone with his thoughts.

He needed to know where Holly Ann had gone, and why.

Without a decision, Ace kept driving. He finally pulled over and tapped a couple of buttons on his screen to connect a call.

"Ace," Bishop said. "What's goin' on?"

"Do you have a minute?" Ace asked, watching the rain drive down on his windshield. Every other second, the wipers cleared it away with a *squelch-squelch* sound.

"Yep."

Ace didn't know how to start. He thought of Bishop's mother holding the fire chief's hand. He thought of Duke asking for Bear's blessing to marry Arizona, and Bear's response about something that had happened almost twenty years ago.

He thought about Etta dating Noah Johnson, and Ida asking Ward to walk her down the aisle, not Ranger.

He thought about Holly Ann potentially being Santa Claus.

"Ace?"

"Yeah," he said. "Sorry, I—it's nothing."

"It's obviously not nothing."

"It's Holly Ann," he said. "What if she...what if you found out Montana had been keeping a secret from you? A big secret?"

"Oh, boy." Bishop exhaled heavily. "I don't know, Ace. Secrets are hard, and I obviously don't know what's going on."

"I don't either," Ace said. "That's the problem."

"Have you asked Holly Ann?"

"No."

"I'm no expert," Bishop said. "But it seems to me that if you want to know something, you should ask her."

"Yeah." Ace's truck shook as a gust of wind blasted into it. He suddenly did want to return to Bull House, make another sandwich, and hide behind a computer screen. He could waste hours with his flight simulator, and he wouldn't have to talk to anyone.

"Bishop, what if it's a secret that isn't hurting anyone?"

"Well." Bishop paused for a few seconds, and Ace appreciated that his cousin didn't jump to tell him exactly what to do. "Does it really matter if no one is getting hurt?"

"I'm just tired of secrets," Ace said, reaching up and pressing his hand to his eyes. "I'm carrying so many secrets, and this just feels like one too many."

"Go slow and think," Bishop said. "You sometimes jump before you need to, and I know you really like this woman. Don't do anything without thinking it through first."

"I'll try," Ace said, because Bishop was right. He did sometimes react instead of taking time to think and ask questions and then make an informed decision.

"Hey, call me again if you need to," Bishop said. "I'll talk you off the ledge."

"Who are we talkin' off the edge?" Ward asked in the background, and Bishop said, "Ace."

"Oh, you've got Ace? Tell 'im we need eggs for dinner tomorrow night. Is he on his way back?" Halfway through the sentence, Bishop put the call on speaker, and Ace could hear Ward just fine.

"I can get eggs," he said. "What else? I'm not coming to town tomorrow."

"We need more coffee creamer," Ward said. "And paper plates."

"Got it." Ace thanked Bishop again and ended the call, trying not to be jealous that Bishop and Ward had gathered to work together on Two Cents. He didn't have to be involved in everything and yet, with all the secrets he currently held for other people, he felt like they'd placed a huge burden on him.

He turned around and headed back to the supermarket. Ward texted a few times on the way there, and when Ace pulled up, he had quite the list of groceries to get for tomorrow night's dinner at Bull House.

Ward apologized, saying he thought Ida would be engaged by then, and he wanted to make it a special dinner for her and Brady. Ace responded to say it was fine, and he pushed a cart around to get the items Ward had requested.

He'd gone grocery shopping so many times before that he didn't have to think to find anything. That gave his mind plenty of room to revolve around Holly Ann, and he decided to do what Bishop had advised.

He needed to ask her. Just flat-out. Ask her.

After drawing a deep breath, he called Holly Ann right there in the produce section. She answered with a, "Hey, babe. I have maybe thirty seconds."

"Oh, sorry," he said, his voice definitely more wooden than normal. Maybe she'd been too distracted to notice. "Listen, just really quick, you're coming on Sunday for lunch, right?"

"Yep."

"Okay," he said. "How are things over there? Anything I can do to help?"

"No," she said. "Rachel just needed some help with moving things indoors due to the storm. How did things go at the cider mill?"

"Good," Ace said. "They were moving the tables inside when I left."

"Okay," she said. "Sorry, Ace. I have to go so I can help Rachel get everything labeled for tomorrow's Nutcracker class."

"Sure." Ace couldn't bring himself to ask her if she was Santa Claus right now. "I'll talk to you later."

"Bye," she said, and the call ended.

Ace finished his shopping, and he decided to stop by the mall. If he could just get positive proof that she was Santa, then he could ask her and see what she said. Bishop's question ran through his mind: *Is the secret hurting anyone?*

No, it really wasn't.

It was the lying Ace didn't like. It made him question everything else Holly Ann had told him, including the stories about her mother and father, the way she said she felt about him. Just everything.

He pulled up to the mall amidst a drizzle. Glad the rain had tapered, he zipped up his jacket and hurried into the mall. He walked past all the stores to the main hub, where Santa's throne had been moved indoors. The fountain bubbled nearby, and the ropes separating the jolly old elf from the public barely left enough room for two people to pass.

Ace didn't stand anywhere that would call attention to himself, and he took a minute to get himself a cup of coffee. The hot liquid helped calm his mind and give him focus. He sat at a tiny round table in view of Santa Claus and watched him...her...someone lift child after child onto their lap.

He could see the shape of Holly Ann's smile on Santa's face, but was he imagining it because he wanted her to be Santa?

Did he *want* to find out she was lying to him?

"Why would anyone want that?" he muttered to himself.

He caught sight of Rachel Bloom, Holly Ann's assistant, walking by, her phone at her ear and a fresh cup of coffee in her hand. Swiftly, before he could lose sight of her in the bulging crowd at the mall, Ace got to his feet and followed Rachel.

She stopped talking on the phone after only a few seconds, and she turned down a hall that led to the restrooms. He hurried to the corner just in time to see her going through a door about halfway down the hall.

He jogged after her, catching the door before it slammed closed. He wasn't sure if it would lock or not, and he had a question to ask. Instead of staying in the shadows now, he called, "Rachel?"

Her footsteps came back down the steps and stood at the top of the staircase. "Ace," she said.

"Hey." He smiled at her and took a couple of steps forward.

"If you're looking for Holly Ann, I don't know where she is." Her heels clicked as she came down the steps, the sounds echoing in the stairwell.

Alarms wailed in his head. "Oh, I—"

"She was here, and then she was just gone. She's been doing that for the whole festival. Normally, it's fine, but we're dealing with a truck that won't arrive in time for the craft class tomorrow, and a high wind advisory that impacts all of our outdoor events for the next two days." Rachel arrived at the bottom of the steps, her blonde hair falling over her shoulders as she looked at him with displeasure in her eyes. "Do you know where she is?"

I have to go so I can help Rachel get everything labeled for tomorrow's Nutcracker class.

"Sorry, I don't," he said, and that was the absolute truth. He did not want to believe that Holly Ann had lied to him.

And for what?

Santa Claus?

If she was willing to lie for something so insignificant, what else would she lie about?

Rachel narrowed her eyes at him. "She hasn't been sneaking off with you, has she? She disappears every Friday and Saturday night. Saturday right after lunch. Every Tuesday."

Ace held up both hands as if in surrender. "I've hardly seen her during the festival, I swear."

Rachel nodded and then shook her head. "Fine. If you see her, tell her we have a real problem with the nutcrackers tomorrow."

"I will."

Rachel turned and went back upstairs, and Ace practically ran the other way. He dropped the rest of his coffee in the trash can and walked past Santa's spot again, staring at Santa, desperate to see dark hair among the white.

It was impossible to tell if the person in the red suit was Holly Ann or not. He retraced his steps and went behind the throne and around to where the parents queued up with their children. There, posted on the podium where the helper elf took the children's names, was the hours Santa would be available.

Tuesday, Friday, and Saturday evenings, along with a couple of hours right after lunchtime on Saturday.

A cold feeling filled Ace's chest, and he got out of the mall before he stomped right up to Santa Claus and accused him of being Holly Ann...and of lying to him.

Bishop would've been so proud.

He woke with dark eyes in his mind, and he sat up straight. "Holly Ann has dark brown eyes. Santa has blue eyes."

It wasn't her. It couldn't be her.

He worked in the stables that morning, and he texted

Holly Ann fifteen minutes after Santa should've been sitting on his throne, listening to children tell him what they wanted for Christmas.

She responded immediately with, *I can be there a little after eight.*

He looked up from his phone, standing on the side of the barn to protect himself from the wind. "A little after eight?" There was no way she could be at Shiloh Ridge Ranch to participate in their family dinner a little after eight, not when Santa was supposed to be in his workshop until eight and then the changing and then the drive....

"Unless 'a little after eight' means almost nine."

Okay, he sent to her. *See you then. I'll save you some pie.*

She sent him a smiley face, and Ace returned to Bull House to help Ward get the place cleaned up and get the food in the oven in time for their family dinner.

Mister caught Ace's eye, and he waved to him. He always cleared out during the family dinners, and Ace wasn't sure why. Both he and Ward had told him he could stay, but he didn't want to "intrude" on their core family traditions.

Ida and Brady arrived first, and she immediately stole Ward from the kitchen. Etta walked in next, and only two minutes later Ranger and Oakley entered the kitchen hand-in-hand.

"Ward," Ace called, and he and Ida returned.

"Something smells amazing," Ranger said, looking at the countertop. "You guys made pie?"

"It's the holidays," Ward said, grinning. "There should be pie every single day in December, don't you think?"

Everyone agreed, and Ace grinned around at his family.

He didn't have a significant other there, and neither did Ward or Etta. He caught her eye, and she lifted her right eyebrow. He simply nodded, because her secret was safe with him.

It wasn't hurting anyone that she wanted to keep her new relationship with Noah Johnson to herself for a little while. The Glovers could be a lot to handle, and he hadn't brought Holly Ann to the ranch for a while.

They all knew he was dating her, though.

Doesn't matter, he told himself as dinner got underway. Etta could tell people when she was ready.

He'd barely finished eating his pizza when his phone chimed. A text from Holly Ann: *I'm here, but I'm not exactly sure where your house is.*

"Holly Ann is here," he said. "I'll be right back."

"You invited Holly Ann?" Etta asked.

Ace didn't answer as he jogged toward the front door and outside. She was here before eight, and there was no way she could be Santa on that throne and at his house.

Outside, he strode down the sidewalk and onto the dirt road. "You turn right at the homestead," he said. "And just come down that road past it. There's a shed, and then you'll see me. I'm in the road."

"Okay," she said.

"Did you get everything done tonight?" he asked.

"Enough," she said with a sigh. "I'm just tired of it all. I wasn't this tired last year."

"I'll bet," he said, his heart booming in his chest. "Do you see me?" He lifted his hand above his head.

"Yep," she said. "I just pull in anywhere?"

"We have a driveway. Pull in beside Etta's gray SUV."

Holly Ann did, and the outdoor flood lights switched on with the movement. He met her at the car, smiling for all he was worth. He didn't have to ask her about Santa Claus now.

"Well, someone's happy tonight," she said as she emerged from the car.

"Yeah." Ace took her into his arms, enjoying the giggle and squeal that came from her mouth as he swung her around. When he set her down, they'd traded positions, and he faced the back of the car while she faced the house.

He leaned down and kissed her, the cool night suddenly steaming hot. He felt something switch inside him, and he slowed the kiss so she would know it wasn't just that he liked her.

He was in love with her.

"I brought some leftover cookies from our meeting this afternoon," she said as he dripped kisses from her mouth down to her collarbone.

"Mm."

"And I think we have an audience," she whispered.

That got Ace to mind his manners, and he straightened and looked behind him. The curtains in the window definitely fluttered, and he hadn't left the front door open.

He chuckled as Holly Ann giggled again, and he said, "I'll get the cookies."

"They're right there on the back seat."

She moved out of the way, and Ace opened the back door and ducked into the car to reach across to the other side of the seat. He'd just grabbed the tray of frosted sugar cookies when he caught sight of the bottle of contact solution.

He sucked in a breath and dropped the cookies. After picking up the bottle from the passenger-side floor in the back seat, another package fell down.

Ace frowned at it and picked it up too, his back starting to pinch.

"Ace?" Holly Ann called.

He stared at the box of colored contact lenses. Blue colored contact lenses.

Chapter Twenty-Two

Ward laughed at something Ranger had said. It was so good to see his brother start to emerge from the shell of a man he'd been the past couple of months. The more Ward thought about it, the more he realized Ranger had been distant and different for a lot longer than just two months. Maybe six or seven now.

He wasn't sure, because time at the ranch was fluid. It moved by, and Ward didn't keep track of it.

He was going to have to start doing a better job of that, though, if he wanted to be foreman. He'd been talking to Ranger and Bear about it for a few weeks now, and they were planning to make the announcement to the family in the New Year.

Ward's chest puffed up at the thought, and he worked to stuff back the pride. He wasn't better than anyone else out here at Shiloh Ridge. Just willing to do the work. Willing to admit he didn't have anything else going on in his life.

Willing to release control of some things in order to have loose control over a lot more responsibilities.

Brady Burton reached for another biscuit, saying, "Ward, my sister wanted me to ask you something."

The entire table hushed, and Ward looked around, feeling very much like they'd all been talking about him behind his back. He put a bite of pizza in his mouth and looked at Ranger, dozens of questions getting hurled at his older brother.

"Don't look at me," Ranger said. "I've been out of the loop for weeks now."

Ward switched his gaze to Brady, wishing the man's face wasn't blurry from only ten feet away. Ward really needed to swallow his pride and go get glasses. "Your sister?"

"Yeah. Her name's Edith."

"Yeah, and she's what? Five years younger than you?" Ward shook his head, unable to glance down to Mother. She'd encourage him to go out with anyone, even someone a decade younger than him. He may need glasses, but he could see what was happening here. "And didn't she go out with Bishop?"

"No," Brady said quickly. "Not my younger sister—and she never did go out with Bishop. He met Montana first."

"Mm." Ward looked down at his plate, his chest vibrating. He'd been out with a few women this year, but nothing serious. He didn't perpetuate a relationship if it wasn't going to be serious, and when one did get to that point and then didn't work out, Ward needed a long time to recover.

He honestly couldn't handle starting the journey again.

Dating and women were exhausting. "I think I'm good," he said, looking up.

"Come on, Ward," Etta said, looking from Mother to Ward. "Hear him out." She nodded at Brady. Ida watched Ward but said nothing, and he wished they'd taken the few minutes they'd had before everyone else had showed up to talk about this.

"Did you know?" he asked. He sure didn't appreciate being ganged up on.

"She's really great," Ida said. "Older than you, Ward." She cut a look at Brady, her bright eyes telling him to drop it now. Why, he didn't know. Maybe they'd just talk about it later, when everyone wasn't listening.

Instant regret filled Ward. He'd do anything for his sisters, especially Ida, and he sighed. "What's her name?" He didn't mean to sound so disgusted, but he couldn't pull the words back now.

"Cora," Brady said. "You know, now that I think about it, I don't know."

"What don't you know?" he asked.

"She's kinda...crazy."

"She is not," Ida said as Mother said, "I'm sure she's not crazy."

"Brady. She is not." Ida looked at Ward, an earnest look on her face. "She's been through some hard things. That's all."

"Yeah?" Ward asked, looking back and forth between the two of them. "What kind of hard things?"

When Brady wouldn't say, and Ida stayed quiet, Ward said again, "I think I'm good." He didn't need more crazy in his life. It was all he could do to keep some semblance of joy in his life, keep up with his work, and help Ranger with Two Cents. He already didn't get down to see Mother as often as he should, and guilt gutted Ward just by looking at her. On top of all of that, Ace had gone quiet the past week or so, and Ward hated that he didn't know every single detail of his brother's relationship with Holly Ann.

Speak of the devil, the couple walked into the kitchen, and Ace looked like he was about to be sick. He covered it with a smile and introduced Holly Ann around again, though they'd all met her before.

She got some food, and Ace took his spot down at the end of the table by her. The conversation picked up again, and Ward kept one ear on it, throwing something in when he had to, while watching Ace.

His brother didn't say much, but Holly Ann participated as if everything was fine. He perked up near the end of the meal when Ida brought out the pecan brownies, and Ward thought maybe he'd just needed a minute to acclimate to having his girlfriend at the family party.

It was new for them—Ace had been taking things with Holly Ann one step farther every single day—and perhaps he'd just needed some time to settle into the idea that they were now a serious couple.

Real serious.

Ward couldn't remember the last woman he'd brought home. Probably Angela, five years ago. He kept everyone he dated on the down-low for at least the first two months. Sometimes longer. Sometimes he just needed to commit to taking things from casual to kissing, and once he did that, he really had to like the woman.

"Brady and I have some news," Ida said, holding the pan of brownies away from everyone's greedy hands. She beamed at her boyfriend, who was about to become her fiancé. She put the treats down and held out her left hand. "He asked me to marry him, and I said yes!"

Etta shrieked, and both Holly Ann and Oakley swarmed Ida. They all laughed and hugged, and Ward had enough good sense to get the heck out of the way.

He stood back by Ranger and Ace, the three of them watching the women in their lives. "It's amazing how excited they get about being engaged," Ward said. "I don't get it. Is it that exciting, Range?"

"I mean, it's exciting," Ranger said. "I think I was just more relieved than anything. That alone makes you kind of excited, but it's because she didn't say no, not because you're going to get married."

Ace laughed, and Ward wasn't sure why. He cast his brother a look, but Ace just shook his head. "Look at Brady. The poor man needs to be saved from himself."

Ward waved at him to come join them, but before the cop could take a single step, Etta grabbed onto him and hugged him, still jumping up and down a little. The shocked look on Brady's face set Ward laughing, and that got Ace and Ranger laughing too.

Ida met his eye, and that sobered him right up. In fact, he nearly choked, and when she laced her arm through Brady's and approached her brothers, Ward stepped on away from Ranger and Ace.

Ranger grinned at the two of them, and he stepped into both of them and wrapped his arms around them pair of them simultaneously. "Congrats, you two. I can't wait to walk you down the aisle, Ida."

Ward pulled in a breath, his eyes widening. He met Ida's round eyes, and then Ace's. Ace nodded at Ranger's back, as if to say, *Go on now. Correct him.*

Ward shook his head just once. He couldn't take that from Ranger.

"Actually," Brady said. "We—"

"Actually," Ida said over him. "We're still trying to decide if we're going to have a really traditional wedding or not." She stepped back from Ranger and scanned everyone in front of her, her gaze skipping right past Ward.

"When's the date?" Mother asked, and Ida stepped into her and held her tight.

"We haven't picked a date yet," Ida said. "I thought you could help me with that, Mother."

"Of course, dear." She released Ida and hugged Brady. "I suppose you have busy times, right, Officer?"

"Yes, ma'am," Brady said.

"You'll live in town, I'm assuming," Mother said, smiling.

"Yes," Ida said. "We both have a house, and we haven't decided which one we'll keep, or if we'll get a new one entirely." She gave a light laugh where Ward heard all the trepidation and all the uncertainty. "We basically haven't decided hardly anything yet."

She gazed down at the ring, her face full of love. When she looked at Brady, she wore the same expression. Ida hugged Ace, and then she turned to Ward.

He gave her the nicest smile he could muster, but his heart beat inside a box that was entirely too small. He still managed to open his arms, and she embraced him. "I'm sorry," she whispered. "We should've talked to him privately, previous to announcing anything."

"Not your fault," Ward whispered.

Ida pulled back, but she stayed close to Ward, searching his face. "I'm sorry about bringing up Brady's sister."

Ward shook his head. "It's fine."

"I do think you should get out there again, Ward."

"I've tried, Ida."

She nodded, as she was never one to push him into conversations he didn't want to have. She'd never pressed him at all. She loved him and accepted him for who he was and what he did, and he'd never had to be anyone but himself with his sister.

She'd rescued him from one of his lowest lows, and he'd helped her in some of her most dire situations too. He really wanted to be the one to walk her down the aisle, but he couldn't take that privilege from Ranger, not when the man was in such a precarious emotional state.

"Ward," Mother said, and Ward stepped further from Ida.

"Yes, Mother?"

"Come help me with these brownies." She gave him a look that said she knew everything, and Ward's throat tightened.

He nodded, and said, "Yes, Mother," and left Ida to keep celebrating with the rest of his siblings.

Chapter Twenty-Three

Preacher Glover sat on the couch in the living room at the homestead, the evening sunlight golden and gorgeous as it glinted around the room. The sense of family and acceptance here made him squirm, because he didn't deserve to be accepted here.

His unhappiness became so apparent when surrounded by so much joy, and he simply wasn't comfortable inside his own skin, or inside his own family.

He hadn't felt like this until the past couple of years, and he'd placed the worst of his anger and frustration at himself on Arizona. Judge had placed it on Mister.

Guilt streamed through him, and he reminded himself he had a plan for how to fix the rift between him and his sister. The bridge between him and Mister was still intact, though it could use some improvements too. He glanced across the room to Mister, and he certainly didn't look happy either.

Mister barely looked up from his phone when he was

with the family, and Preacher often thought about him living in those cabins up by Zona and Mother by himself. No one else lived nearby, and Preacher wondered what the quiet would sound like up the hill, with no TV and no one else in the house.

Preacher needed to find out. He needed to get away from Judge, who was so loud all the time, in every way, so he could figure out who he was.

His phone buzzed in his palm, and he glanced at it since the meal hadn't started yet. He fully expected Mother to start walking around with the basket, so he better get a message off to Mindi if he didn't want to leave her hanging.

She'd said: *When will you be back in town?*

A smile touched his mouth, because it felt good to be wanted. A quick glance around the room, and he didn't see a single person who actually wanted him here. If he slipped out the side door, who would even notice?

Bishop was always wrapped up in what Bear, Ranger, and Cactus thought of him. He worked a lot with them, and he'd been so young when Daddy died. Preacher had never minded Bishop's close relationship with Bear, but it did remind him that he didn't have anything like that.

Arizona had tormented him growing up, and Preacher had taken his dislike of her into adulthood, and he wished he could root out those memories and start fresh. She wasn't the same person she'd been twenty years ago, and kids did stupid things. He wasn't perfect, that was for sure.

Another glance at Mister proved that. He and Judge had gotten in an argument months ago, and Mister had stormed out. He'd yelled that he never wanted to talk to Judge again, and as far as Preacher knew, they hadn't spoken. He'd tried to reach out to Mister, and they talked enough to get their jobs done around the ranch. But Preacher wanted to be friends with Mister again. Real friends.

Short of driving up to the cabin and knocking on the door, Preacher didn't know what else to do. They all managed to congregate in the same space, but there were enough people to keep the oil and water apart, and Preacher played his part by staying away from Zona.

Until tonight, he thought, his stomach buzzing with wasps.

"All right," Bishop said, and Preacher quickly typed out a message to Mindi.

I don't know. Why? You got something in mind?

She always had something in mind, and Preacher knew what it was. Her on-again, off-again boyfriend had probably done something stupid, and Mindi would want Preacher to show up in his best clothes, his arm cocked so she could hang on him, and she'd kiss him as much as he wanted.

He hadn't minded the fake relationship—until his feelings had started to turn real. He'd backed off then, but every time Mindi texted and said she needed help, he showered, shaved, and showed up. He let the pretty blonde hang on him, and giggle in his ear, and kiss him as if they were real serious.

Then, he might not hear from her for a while, or she might call the next day. Their longest stint had lasted about a month, and that was when Preacher had realized he actually liked Mindi for real.

Might be fun to go caroling on Monday night.

Preacher frowned at his phone. Caroling wasn't his idea

of a good time. Heck, going down to Three Rivers during the holiday season wasn't his idea of a fun time. Dealing with the flashing lights for three months out of the year was enough to push Preacher to the brink of insanity, but he couldn't ask Judge to back off on the light show he did every year. He really wanted to win this year, and he'd brought out thirty percent more lights.

Thirty percent more flashing meant thirty percent less sleep for Preacher. He also didn't have the heart to tell Judge he was never going to win the light show. The townspeople voted for the winner, and nobody drove all the way out to Shiloh Ridge to see his light show. He got less votes, because they got less traffic. Plain and simple.

"Judge is gonna say the prayer," Bishop said, and Preacher realized he'd missed the overview of the food for that day. He didn't care, because he could look at the spread on the fifteen-foot counter and see what he could eat.

He tucked his phone underneath his leg and swiped his cowboy hat off his head. He closed his eyes and held his hat to his chest as Judge said a prayer over the food. He waited to feel something warm and spiritual.

The zing in his chest came when Judge said, "Bless us all this Christmas season to remember our Lord and Savior, Jesus Christ," but other than that, he felt like his heart was made of stone.

"Amen," he said along with everyone else. Noise and chatter broke out instantly afterward, and Preacher stood up and turned around. The family had expanded in the past couple of years, and Preacher did love having Sammy, Oakley, and Montana in the homestead. He loved Lincoln and that blasted black and white cat that tried to give him attitude, though he was the newcomer.

Everyone loved Benny, Preacher included, and tonight, Ace had brought Holly Ann to the family gift exchange and dinner. They'd do the gifts after dinner, and Preacher wished he could stop time and then turn it backward.

He couldn't, though, so it marched forward as they ate sweet and sour meatballs, buttery sticky rice, and plenty of gourmet vegetables. He loved the roasted veg with stuffing on top, and then a creamy, herby sauce covering it all.

His mother sure did know how to get her sons to eat vegetables. He sat beside Judge and Ace, the two people on the ranch he got along with best. Holly Ann sat beside Ace, and she chatted with Judge about the horses here on the ranch, and he asked her about catering dinners once a week.

"I don't really do that," Holly Ann said. "Dinner for you and Preacher? Once a week?"

"Sure," he said, looking from Preacher to Holly Ann. "Why not?"

"Sounds like you need a wife," Holly Ann teased, and Preacher sure did like her. Ace laughed, but it was too loud and didn't quite fit in the conversation. Preacher looked at him in surprise, and Judge scowled at both of them.

"I'm going to put the ice cream in the machine," Etta yelled above the noise. "Let's do the presents, and then we'll have dessert."

People got up from the long table that could seat them all, and Preacher joined them. Always just going with the flow. Moving with the stream. Doing what everyone else did.

For once, he wanted to jump ship. Swim upstream. Take a sharp left, and see if anyone noticed at all.

Everyone noticed when Cactus left the family parties. Everyone noticed when Bear had a bad day. Everyone paid attention to Ranger and his well-being, because everyone loved Cactus, Bear, and Ranger.

No one even *thought* about Preacher, and he hated feeling insignificant.

It's not true, he told himself. Just a couple of months ago, Bishop had given a presentation just before they'd decorated the angel tree. He'd mentioned that Shiloh Ridge would most likely move toward having foremen, so Bear and Ranger wouldn't have to shoulder so much of the work.

Preacher's name had been mentioned as a possible foreman. He'd felt important then. He'd felt seen. In a family as large as his, that was huge, and he hated that it was so important to him. At the same time, Judge had counseled him not to ignore those feelings. It was okay to want to be important.

He took a seat on a different couch this time, after retrieving his gift from the front steps. He'd drawn Arizona's name this year, and he really wanted to make amends with her. His pulse throbbed in his throat as everyone finally found a place to sit in the huge living room. Having a room with enough seats was a blessing and a miracle, and Preacher did admire Bear for planning ahead and creating a place where they could all gather.

Bishop and Montana had finished True Blue earlier this year too, and the old barn his father and uncle had built provided a beautiful place for the Glover family to gather too.

"Okay," Bear said. "Let's get started. First, I wanted everyone to know that Ida and Brady got engaged this weekend." He grinned at the couple, and Ida beamed around at everyone. Preacher clapped along with everyone else, his smile genuine for the first time that evening. He did love his cousin Ida, as she took care of everyone, for almost every family meal, and Brady Burton was a good man and a good cop.

"Any other announcements?" Bear asked, and his gaze lingered on Ace and then Cactus. Neither of them said a word, and Preacher wondered what they'd say.

Surely it was too soon for Ace and Holly Ann to be engaged, and Cactus? The man barely left the ranch. How could he have any sort of announcement?

"All right," Bear said. "We'll have another family meeting the first week of January, for our annual ranch news. I'll send a text for the date and time of that, if you'll all send me times and dates that do *not* work for you. Okay?"

Several people murmured their assent, and then Bear reached into a jar that Mother held. He pulled out a slip of paper, and said, "Mister."

Mister smiled and got up, his silver-wrapped package in his hands. "I got Etta." He handed her the gift, both of them grinning.

She stood up and gave him a hug. "Thank you, Mister." She ripped the paper off the package to reveal a blue, flowery box of English tea.

"It's from England," Mister said. "I may or may not have raided your pantry to see which brand you like. I ordered it online."

Etta stared at the box and then lifted her eyes to Mister. "I love this tea. They don't make it for the US market anymore."

Mister pushed his cowboy hat forward, but he'd always been very, very good at giving gifts. Preacher swallowed, because everyone would be watching when he opened his gift, and then when Zona opened hers.

He thought of a line from the letter his father had written to him before he'd died.

Paul, we started calling you Preacher because of your gospel knowledge and the fact that you loved to tell everyone how to get along. Keep doing that, Preacher. They'll need it, and you'll be the uniting factor in the family.

He'd literally scoffed when he'd read that paragraph, but it would not leave him alone. The words nagged at him, tugged at his conscience, whispered that he wasn't doing what Daddy thought he should in every quiet moment in Preacher's life.

He had loved studying the gospel, and he'd even gone to the seminary for a year before returning to the ranch when Daddy fell seriously ill. He'd never gone back, and he didn't miss it. He could study the gospel and think about religious things without having to stand up in front of a congregation and preach.

He didn't want to do that anyway.

He wouldn't know how to tell people to hold on when God went silent on them. He hadn't been able to, and while he loved reading the scriptures and learning more about the life of the Savior, he often felt alone in this world.

"I got Preacher," someone said, and he pulled himself

from his thoughts. He looked up at Ace as his cousin brought over a red-and-white striped bag. Tons of billowy white paper ballooned out the top, and Preacher stood and took the bag from Ace. "You're going to love this," he said with a smile. He grabbed onto Preacher and clapped him on the back, and Preacher did feel close to Ace.

"I can't wait," Preacher said. He pulled the paper out of the top of the bag, finally finding a slim box, a wrapped case that felt suspiciously like a video game, and a bag of candy. He removed them and held them up. "Chocolate covered cinnamon bears."

He grinned at Ace, his mouth already watering. He loved hot candy, and nothing better than cinnamon bears.

"I *love* those," Sammy said, looking from Preacher to Ace. "Where did you get those?"

"There's a kiosk in the mall." He took his seat over by the window again, and he didn't seem very happy tonight either. Preacher had worked with him in the stables and played plenty of basketball with him enough to know, and he noted that Ace didn't reach for Holly Ann's hand.

The box held a new phone case, with a simple design that spoke to Preacher's crisp side. "Thank you, Ace." He unboxed the case and removed his current one, replacing it with the new one. He held it up. "It's like Three Rivers."

"It *is* Three Rivers," Ace said. "From your front porch. The town skyline."

Preacher grinned at the case, seeing the view in his mind's eye. He'd stood on the front porch probably hundreds of times and gazed down the hill toward the town of Three

Rivers. It was one of the only times he felt true peace and the pure love of God.

He hadn't done it for a while, and he really needed to. He needed some direction in his life, and he needed it from On High.

He ripped the paper from the case, and it was a video game. Hoops 2K20, and he grinned from ear to ear. "Thank you, Ace. We should play tonight." He lifted the game up as Ace nodded, his smile back on his face though his arms lay folded across his chest.

Preacher tucked all of his gifts back into the bag, swallowed, and bent to pick up his gift. "I got Arizona."

The room inhaled together, and it felt like everyone held their breath. Preacher was holding his as he crossed the room to where Zona sat on the hearth with her fiancé, Duke. She released his hand and stood up, her eyes searching Preacher's.

His mouth felt like someone had wiped it out with cotton. The box had been wrapped in gold paper with a metallic snowman print, with a red bow tied around it. He paused a couple of feet from her.

"I know we haven't always gotten along real well," he said, his voice low and scratchy and barely able to leave his throat. "I'm real sorry about that, and I'd really like to make things right and move forward."

"Me too," Zona said, reaching to take the gift as Preacher extended it toward her.

He took her into a hug and held her tight, saying, "I'm sorry, Zona. For whatever I've done that has hurt you." He knew one of the biggest things he'd done, and he hoped this gift would make it right.

"I'm sorry too, Preacher. You're a good man, and I'm the one to blame for everything."

Preacher pressed his eyes closed, wishing that meant no one else could see him. He finally cleared his throat and stepped back, ducked his head, and hurried back to his spot. Behind him, Zona tore the paper on the package, and while Bear patted his shoulder, and Bishop grinned at him, and Ranger nodded his approval, his heart pounded.

"Preacher," Zona gasped, looking up at him with wide eyes. "You didn't."

"You've wanted it your whole life," he said.

"What is it?" someone asked, and Duke and Ward, the two people closest to her craned their necks to see into the box.

The box itself was a decoy, and Zona lifted out the pair of car keys he'd carefully slid onto a brand-new keychain. She held them up, and Mister said, "Holy cow," right before Bear said, "Oh, my word."

"What is it?" Sammy asked.

"Yeah," Oakley said. "Some of us don't get it."

Zona rose to her feet, still staring at the keys. "They're the keys to Daddy's Corvette."

Every eye flew to Preacher. He held very still and noticed his pulse had completely quieted. "I kept it because I could," he said. "Just because I didn't want you to have it. It was stupid and cruel, and I apologize. It's yours. Daddy would've wanted you to have it." He almost made it through the speech, but his voice broke on the last word.

Zona burst into tears, and she rushed him. He didn't have time to stand up before she threw herself into his arms, and Preacher finally felt like he'd removed all the barriers between him and his sister, and they'd finally arrived in a place where they could both heal from past wounds.

Chapter Twenty-Four

Holly Ann had never experienced anything as beautiful and spiritual as the Glover family gift exchange. They stood to receive their gift. They hugged one another. They gave simple gifts and elaborate gifts. They genuinely seemed to love one another, though they were definitely *human* too.

They were imperfect. They had a past she didn't know about but really wanted to. She didn't get a gift, and she didn't give one, but she didn't need either. She laced her arm through Ace's and leaned her head against his bicep, glad when he squeezed her right against his body.

Once the last gift had been opened, Etta got up and said, "The ice cream is ready. There's pecan pie, triple-chocolate brownies, or apple crisp to go with it."

Ida joined her in the kitchen, and they started serving everyone in the family. Holly Ann watched as the oldest members of the family got their desserts first, and she sure did like watching Bishop take care of his mother, and Ward take care of his. With that done, they returned to the island to get their own sweets.

"What would you like, sweetheart?" Ace asked as he stood up.

"Apple crisp, please." She smiled at him as he walked away, and she looked around the living room. Most people had vacated it, but Holly Ann was content to stay right where she was. She wanted to attend many more Sunday evening dinners here at the homestead. She wanted to eat with Ace and his core family at the house next door.

She wanted to find out where Ace would live on this ranch, because she needed a vision of what her life at Shiloh Ridge Ranch would look like. She watched Ace talk and laugh with one of his cousins, and she smiled at Ward when he sat next to her with a bowl of brownies and ice cream.

"How's the festival going?" he asked.

"Good," she said, crossing her legs. "Good enough, at least."

"You sound a little unconvincing."

"It's a lot of work," she admitted. "I'm happy to do it, and I've been working with the festival in some capacity for years. I'm just...."

"Tired?" Ward supplied.

She nodded, looking back over to Ace. "What would Ace's girlfriend get him for Christmas?"

Ward glanced over to his brother too and took another bite of brownie. After he ate it, he said, "Ace is a pretty simple man, Holly Ann. He likes what all men like: good food, good company, and someone with a good heart."

She hoped she was good company for him, and she knew she could make good food. She felt good at heart, but she knew the suit she wore was coming between her and Ace. She wasn't sure how, only that she hated sneaking away from him, and she hated the half-truths she'd told him over the past few weeks.

He brought her a bowl of apple crisp with ice cream, caramel sauce swirled over all of it. "Oh, wow," she said, staring at the golden topping and the soft ice cream.

"Etta's a genius with crisps," Ace said. He turned back to the counter to get his own dessert, but after he got it, he didn't come sit by her again. Holly Ann watched as he stood next to Cactus in the kitchen, their conversation obviously very rousing.

He laughed a couple of times, and Holly Ann wondered what she was supposed to do. She suddenly felt like she existed behind a piece of thick plastic wrap. She was here in the house, and she could see and hear everyone else. But she was on the other side of the film, the other side of the barrier of trust, and it seemed as though no one wanted to be the first to admit she was there.

She finished her apple crisp, Ward's statement about being tired beyond true. Tomorrow was the beginning of another week—the last one of the festival—and Holly Ann had plenty to keep her busy.

She stood up and took her empty bowl into the kitchen, pressing against the plastic wrap. It bulged with her, but it didn't break.

Holly Ann touched Ace's arm, and said, "I'm going to go."

He put his half-eaten dessert on the table. "All right. I'll walk you out."

The fact that he didn't protest and ask her to stay didn't settle Holly Ann's nerves. She smiled at his sisters and even hugged them good-bye. His mother did the same, and Holly Ann pressed her eyes closed as she hugged Dawna Glover.

"Thank you for the cookies, dear."

"Of course." Holly Ann smiled at her and went with Ace toward the front door. Outside, the air bit at her face and hands, but she didn't put her coat on. Her steps slowed as she reached the edge of the porch, and she looked out into the night sky.

"It's so dark up here," she said. "You can see the whole galaxy."

"Sometimes," Ace said, going down the steps quickly. Holly Ann followed at a slower clip, wondering what had flipped inside of Ace, and when.

He waited at the bottom of the steps, and Holly Ann stepped to his side. "What did I do?" she asked, still taking in the vast infinity of the sky spreading before her. It was inky and oily, with drops of silver and gold for stars and planets. If she squinted, the lights blurred, almost like wet paint on a canvas as it blended together.

Ace didn't answer, and Holly Ann's irritation grew. She really shouldn't have important conversations while frustrated and tired, so she stepped toward her car. "I had a lovely time," she said. "Thank you for inviting me. You have a very special family."

His boots didn't crunch over the gravel behind her, and Holly Ann hated walking away from him.

Then don't, she thought, and she paused.

She turned around and met his eye. "Talk to me, Ace."

"Talk to you?"

"Yes."

Ace looked away, the moonlight shining silver on half his face. His eyes couldn't be seen because of the shadow from his cowboy hat. He looked back at her, his face still half-light and half-dark.

"I'm tired of secrets," he said, taking a step toward her.

She swallowed, because she still had some of those. "Me too."

"Are you?" he challenged.

"Yes."

"I can't hold any more secrets," he said. "I just need to know that we don't have any secrets between us." He gestured between the two of them, pacing closer. "Me and you. No secrets."

She swallowed, unable to hold his powerful gaze.

"Holly Ann," he said, doing that thing where he dragged out her name into more syllables than it had. "Are you...Santa Claus?"

Horror struck her right behind the heart. That organ thrashed like a fish out of water, like a hose with a rush of water coming from the end of it, like a balloon that had been blown up and then released.

"You are, aren't you?"

She couldn't see any way out of telling him now, and she realized she *wanted* to tell him. She'd been wanting to tell him for a while now. "Yes," she said, her voice scratching her throat. "I wanted to tell you, Ace. I did. It's just this family thing, and literally no one in town knows, and I...wanted to tell you."

"But you didn't," he said. "You lied to me instead."

"I—"

"Don't lie to me again," he said. "I know you weren't helping Rachel label anything last night. I ran into her, and she was pretty frustrated that you 'kept disappearing' right when she needed you. Every Tuesday, Friday, and Saturday night."

Holly Ann couldn't breathe, and she couldn't swallow. Everything inside her pulled tight, stitching in all the wrong ways, and she couldn't move as bound as she felt.

"I wanted to break up," she said. "To avoid this."

Ace stilled, and he'd come close enough that she could see under his cowboy hat now. Anger sparked in his eyes, but the real emotion there was betrayal. "Guess what, Holly Ann?" he asked. "You can have what you want." He fell back a step, then another. "Have a good night." He reached up and touched the brim of his cowboy hat, and then turned around and strode toward the porch.

"Wait," she called, pure instinct taking over. "I get what I want? What's that?"

"We're breaking up," he called over his shoulder. He took the steps two at a time and hit the porch at a near run. He practically yanked off the door of the homestead and went inside without looking back.

The rectangle of cheery, yellow light reminded Holly Ann of the atmosphere inside, and it called to her soul with a power she didn't understand.

We're breaking up.

"Just like that?" she whispered. "He didn't even let me explain." Numb, she got behind the wheel of her car and backed out of the space. On the way under the arch signaling her arrival at Shiloh Ridge Ranch, she said, "What is there to explain, Holly Ann? You lied to him, and you kept secrets from him."

Ace valued honesty, and he hated secrets.

"Stupid," she said, her voice breaking. Her heart did the same thing, and pure agony radiated through her whole body. This was why she didn't let anyone in as far as he'd gotten. This was why she didn't bring men home to meet her family.

This was why she didn't allow herself to fall in love and put down roots.

When she reached the highway, instead of turning left to get back to Three Rivers, she turned right. And just drove.

Chapter Twenty-Five

A ce stood under the arch in the homestead, the expansive kitchen to his left and in front of him, and the living room to his right. His chest rose and fell violently, and he really didn't want to be here with all of these people.

His eyes met Etta's first, and he was so far out of his head that he didn't hear the words she said.

"I have an announcement," he yelled, and that got most people to quiet down. "Lots of 'em, actually." He took a big breath, because there simply wasn't enough oxygen to be had. His mind buzzed, and everything around him vibrated.

"I am so sick of secrets. Family secrets and relationship secrets, and all kinds of blasted secrets."

"Ace," someone said, but he didn't care who.

"Aunt Lois is dating the fire chief. I saw them out on a date, and I wanted to tell you, Bishop. Bear. I really did." He met his aunt's eyes, and she wore shock on her face. "I don't know why you don't just tell your kids, Aunt Lois. I think it's great, and sweet, and it was super clear to me that Donald Parker really likes you."

He looked around the room again. "I don't get why we don't just tell each other stuff. Like, Cactus bought a car so he could go to town and see Willa without having to borrow a truck. It's parked in the garage at Bull House, as if no one will see him come and go from the ranch. He also goes to therapy most Fridays. We drive down together, and it's amazing. I love spending time with him and talking to him, and I just don't get why it has to be a secret."

Cactus simply stared at him, and Ace's chest shook slightly.

"Mister is living with me and Ward. He's not up at that cabin, all alone. So everyone can stop feeling sorry for him." He nodded at Mister, who just folded his arms. "Holly Ann was going to set him up with someone, but she's been too busy to do it."

He wasn't sure why he'd said that last bit. That wasn't a secret.

"Etta's dating Noah Johnson. I don't know how much older he is than her, but he's older, and they're cute together. He looked like he cared a lot about her, and I'm not sure why she didn't want anyone to know."

"Ace," she said, her voice full of chastisement.

"Sorry, Etta," he said. "I am. I'm sorry that I know Duke did something to Uncle Stone almost twenty years ago. I don't know what it was, praise the Lord, but I'm glad it didn't come between him and Zona."

He breathed in and out. "I hate secrets, and I hate that we walk on all these eggshells around each other."

He saw Ward stand up and start toward him, and Ace seized onto the thought of his brother.

"Ace," Ward said in a loud voice. "Enough."

"No," Ace said. "No, it's not enough. Why can't you and Ida just tell Ranger that she wants you to walk her down the aisle? It's nothing against him. He knows you two have a special friendship and always have. She deserves the wedding she wants, and you want to give that to her. He will too."

Ranger stood as well, confusion on his face.

"Mother," Ward said, and Ace actually laughed.

"You're going to tattle on me to Mother?" He shook his head and kept chuckling. "It's fine. Whatever. I'm just so sick of all the secrets. I'm tired of holding them, and I'm tired of the half-lies we tell each other and ourselves to make them okay. They're *not* okay."

His composure broke, and everything in his face grew hot.

"Come on," Ward growled as he reached Ace. He grabbed onto his arm and yanked him around.

"Let go of me." Ace wrenched his arm away from his brother, but he kept walking with him toward the still-open front door.

"You've got to stop this," Ward said, gesturing for him to go first. "These are not your things to tell."

"I don't care," Ace said, stomping out of the house. "Secrets are going to be the death of this family, and I'm not going to be the one to watch it go down in flames!" He strode to the top of the steps and kept going.

Ward followed him, as did a second set of footsteps. Ace didn't even know where he was going. He just had to get out of here. Get off this ranch. Get away from everyone who expected something from him. Get away from the perfect agony threatening to rip him apart one seam at a time.

Chapter Twenty-Six

Bear held very still after Ace, Ward, and Ranger had left. It was his house, and he should say something, but he honestly didn't know what.

Everyone else seemed to be encased in the same shock he was, and he finally managed to look at his mother. Her eyes met his, and he didn't even have to ask if what Ace had said was true or not.

It was. She *was* dating Donald Parker, the fire chief.

For some reason he couldn't name, his chest caved in on itself. Perhaps because he couldn't imagine Mother with anyone but Daddy. Or maybe because Bear hadn't realized how lonely Mother was. So lonely to the point that she'd wanted to start dating again.

He moved through the crowd until he stood in front of her. "I love you, Mother," he said, and he took her into a tight embrace that he hoped told her that she could date whoever she wanted, and he'd support it. He hoped it would convey his apologies for not realizing or knowing how lonely she was.

The spell that had held them all captive broke, and Ida said, "You're dating Noah Johnson?" while Judge asked, "What happened with Duke and Daddy almost twenty years ago?" and someone else said, "Mister isn't up at that cabin all alone. Praise the Lord."

Chaos ensued, and Bear stepped to Mother's side as Bishop came to stand in front of her. He grinned at her. "I knew you were sweet on the fire chief, Momma."

"Oh, you." She swatted at his chest, and they laughed together.

Oakley stood with Brady and Ida, saying something about how Ranger would've understood, and that Ace was right.

Duke said nothing, and Zona stood with her hand in his, clearly protective of him. Cactus sat very still at the table, and Bear knew it was because he hadn't used the new car he'd bought weeks ago to be able to take Willa Knowlton on dates, because she'd left town suddenly and hadn't returned yet.

Bear stood in the midst of all the talking, and he thought Ace had a point.

Secrets could be the death of a family, or a relationship, and he didn't want that to happen in his family.

Daddy had told him in his letter that he had a champion heart that could bring people together, and he felt like there was nothing this family needed more than that.

"All right," he said, raising his voice. He lifted both of his arms above his head too. "Quiet down, everyone. Quiet." He whistled through his teeth, and that shrill sound got most people to stop talking.

Mister finished his sentence and it echoed in the new silence. "...for a couple of nights is all." He looked around, clearly unhappy his secret had been shared. Bear hadn't even known he was living at Bull House, and while he didn't much care where Mister lived, it would've been nice to know he wasn't up in the top cabins all alone.

If he'd known Mister was in the hands of Ward and Ace, he wouldn't have worried as much. He wouldn't have had to spend so long on his knees in behalf of his brother. At the same time, perhaps all the times he'd prayed for Mister had led him to Bull House and the care of cousins who loved him and wanted him around.

"I'd like to have a family prayer," he said. "Aunt Dawna, will you say it?"

She nodded, though she looked a tiny bit afraid. Bear put one hand on Sammy's shoulder at the table, and one on his mother's. He closed his eyes and listened as Aunt Dawna said, "Dear Lord, we beseech thee for an outpouring of Thy spirit for any and all in this room. We ask the same blessing on Ace, Ranger, and Ward, who are not with us but that we hope will return soon. All should be welcome here, and we ask Thee to please soften our hearts so that all members of this family feel like they belong here, that they are important to the success of this ranch and to each other, and that we can have hearts that have an infinite capacity to love.

"We're grateful for those new additions to our family. For

Duke Rhinehart, and Montana Martin and her daughter, Aurora, for Oakley and The General, for Holly Ann Broadbent, and for dear Sammy and Lincoln. Please help them to forgive us for being so loud and so big and so secretive. Bless us all to trust each other more and keep less secrets and simply to be and do better. Amen."

"Amen," Bear whispered, opening his eyes to the same room and the same people who'd been there before. Something had changed though, and it sure seemed like perhaps they could all move forward together, united as a family.

In the resulting silence, it wasn't hard to hear the front door open. Three pairs of footsteps entered, and Ranger filled the archway that led into the foyer first. Then Ward.

Finally, Ace stepped between them, his eyes already on the floor. "I'm sorry," he said. "I sort of went crazy, and I apologize to anyone whose secret I told. It was not my place to do so, though I would appreciate it if no one asks me to keep a secret from any other member of this family in the future. I obviously can't do it, so it won't be safe with me anyway."

Bear grinned, because Ace was right. With his outburst, he'd just proven he was a terrible secret-keeper. He grinned, because it took strength and guts to come back to a crowd and apologize. He grinned, because Ward and Ranger were, and when they started laughing, Bear joined in.

"SO THEY BROKE UP?" BEAR ASKED SAMMY A COUPLE OF mornings later.

"Yes," Sammy said from her side of the bed.

Bear sat down and reached to pull on his boots. "That's too bad. I thought they were real good together." No wonder Ace had gone crazy the other night. He'd just learned a secret Holly Ann had been keeping from him, and they'd broken up mere moments before he'd stormed inside the homestead and blown open several landmines in the Glover family.

Cactus had retreated to the Edge Cabin, and no one had heard from him or seen him since. Duke and Zona had left the party really fast after the family prayer, and Bear didn't blame them one bit. If they ever came back, he'd be surprised.

Mother had told everyone remaining that she and Donald Parker had been seeing each other for four months. Four. *Months.* Bear still experienced a stupor of thought every time he tried to imagine his mother sneaking off the ranch to go out with her secret boyfriend.

Ward, Ranger, and Ida had worked things out, as had Mister. So those two revelations hadn't been too damaging, thank goodness. Neither had Etta's new relationship. She'd claimed she was taking things slow and introducing someone to a family as large as the Glovers took time. Bear could see that side of things easily, and he didn't fault her for keeping her new boyfriend in the shadows for a bit.

"They are really good together," Sammy said. "They'll get back together."

"Will they?"

"Of course." Sammy looked over at him. She'd stopped going into the shop early in the morning, and Bear liked that she had more relaxing days, especially since she was only nine weeks away from her due date now. "Haven't you seen them look at each other, Bear? They're in love. It'll work out."

"Will it?"

"We did," she said. "Ranger and Oakley did. Ace and Holly Ann will too."

"I wonder what her secret was, though," Bear said. "If it's a really big one, maybe Ace won't be able to get past it." Bear stood up and walked around to her side of the bed. "Love you, sweetheart. Are you going in today at all?"

"No," she said. "The shop's closed until the New Year." She looked up from her tablet and received his kiss. "We're still okay to give my guys their pay, though, right? And holiday bonuses?"

"Yep." Bear pressed his cheek to hers. "I can help you with the payroll when I get back."

"I can do stuff, Bear."

"I know," he said, falling back a step. "I just don't want you to have to." He crossed the room to the door. "I'm taking Link and Benny out to the pastures with me. Go back to sleep if you want."

"Okay," she said. "Be safe."

Bear left the bedroom, collected Lincoln and Benny from the couch in the living room, and together they all went downstairs. Bishop scrambled eggs at the stove, and they ate together while Lincoln told them all about some new video game that was coming out in a couple of months.

"Come on, bud," Bear said after he'd finished eating.

"We're rotating the herd this morning. Gotta take out some new salt licks, and make sure their water isn't frozen."

Lincoln skipped alongside him as if such chores were made of gold. Bear loved the boy's enthusiasm, and he considered driving out to Cactus's just to see how he was doing.

An hour later, Bear had just gotten back in the truck when his phone rang. He tapped on the screen to connect the call through the Bluetooth, and he held his hands up to the vents, which blew warm air onto his cold skin.

"Bear?"

"What's up, Jeremiah?" Jeremiah Walker owned Seven Sons Ranch, only about fifteen minutes from Shiloh Ridge. They attended ranch owners meetings together in town, and they'd worked together on a couple of collaborative agriculture projects.

Bear knew all the Walkers, and he liked them all. Sammy did some work for them from time to time, and they'd even attended their mother's parties after the completion of her law degree.

"I just got off the phone with Pete." Jeremiah sounded tired already, and winter ranching had a way of doing that to a man. "Squire's father died."

Bear's heart fell all the way to the floor in less time than a person could blink. "Oh, no." His thoughts flew to Squire Ackerman, another ranch owner, this time of a ranch much farther north than Shiloh Ridge. He'd known Squire for two decades, and he was a good man. A good father, and a dedicated son.

"How's Heidi?" Bear asked, thinking of Frank Ackerman's wife. She owned and operated the best bakery in town, and Bear couldn't imagine how it must feel to lose a spouse. His mother could, though, and Bear swallowed again as he thought of how lonely she must've been in the early days following Daddy's death.

How lonely she still was.

"Pete didn't say. The bakery is closed today. Ivory had gone to get something, and she said there's a big yellow sign on the door that says they'll be fulfilling holiday orders only, and that they'll then be closed through the New Year."

Bear shook his head, his thoughts scattering with the emotion. "This is too bad," he said.

"The funeral is on Friday," Jeremiah said. "Whit and I will be there."

"I'm sure I can be there too," Bear said. Squire had done a lot for Bear and Shiloh Ridge, and he liked to think he'd done a lot for Squire and Three Rivers Ranch. "I'll talk to Sammy, but I don't see why she wouldn't be able to come."

"Sounds good," Jeremiah said. "I'm gonna call Britt. I'm thinking maybe a few of us can go out to Three Rivers and see Squire. Just to show support."

"Have you talked to Wade?" Bear asked.

"Not yet."

"I'll call him," Bear said, as he had one more thing to talk to the man about. *No more secrets*, he thought as Jeremiah agreed and then the call ended. It was time for Bear to make sure both Wade and Duke knew there were no hard feelings between their two ranches. Zero. None. What's done was done.

Especially Duke, and he was going to be part of their extended family very soon, and Bear didn't want Zona to stop coming around because she was uncomfortable about what might be said about her or what questions she might get asked.

Chapter Twenty-Seven

❧

Squire Ackerman felt like he was drowning. He watched his wife, Kelly, help their daughter with something on her dress. They spoke, and Kelly smiled softly at Libby before drawing her into a hug.

Libby was a sweet girl who'd loved her grandfather dearly. She was the only granddaughter, and Squire's father had spoiled her relentlessly. If anyone was going to miss his dad more than him, it would be Libby.

Yet he couldn't get himself to leave the mouth of the hallway and go comfort her. He couldn't get his voice to work, or his mind to think, or his feet to move.

"Baby," Kelly said, somehow appearing in front of him. "Your tie's not even on right." She began fixing it, and Squire stood there, his heart beating and his eyes blinking, but only because he didn't have to tell his body to do those things.

Kelly finished and smoothed down his collar. "Squire,"

she said sharply, and he blinked his attention to her. "You have to be present today. You'll be upset if you're not."

"I'm present," he managed to say.

"No, you're not," she said as the back door opened and Finn walked in with the younger boys. "Look at me."

Squire moved his eyes back to hers. She'd been by his side for almost fifteen years now. They had three children together, and a family of four kids. He counted Finn as his, though his biological dad wouldn't give permission for Squire to adopt the boy. He never came around, and he never called, and he never sent gifts. In all ways except the legal one, Finn was Squire's son.

He loved him with the strength of the sun, and as he came toward Squire, life returned to him one shade at a time. Breath rushed at him, and Squire sucked in a breath.

"There you are," Kelly said, and Squire reached out and took her hand in his, squeezing it tightly.

"Dad," Finn said. "Uncle Pete and Aunt Chelsea just left."

Squire nodded and drew his sons into his side. He pulled Kelly and Libby toward him, and the six of them stood together, his arms trying to get around all of them though they couldn't quite reach.

"We're going to be okay," he whispered. "We're going to miss Granddaddy, but he's with the Lord now, and we'll be all right."

Libby sniffled, as did the two younger boys, Michael and Samuel.

"Sam, you make sure you get the program for our memory box," Kelly said. "Mikey, you need to sit by Rich to help keep him quiet during the service. He likes you best, and I put those gummy worms in your bag."

"Yes, Mama," Mike said.

"Libby, you're going to stay right by Grandma," Kelly continued. "And Squire, you're going to make sure you don't zone out."

"Yes, ma'am," Squire said, giving her a small smile. He loved her with everything he had, and he looked at Finn. "What's his job?"

"His job is to make sure I don't break down." Kelly's face scrunched with emotion, and she reached for Finn. They hugged, and then she said, "All right. We need to go so we're not late."

Everything took time out at Three Rivers Ranch. Their land sat forty-five minutes from the town of Three Rivers, and Squire had worked through many, many problems on the drive to or from the ranch. He'd had meaningful talks with his children, his wife, and his mother and father.

He'd learned to love the drive, even if it didn't provide the framework for an important conversation or a problem-solving session. The drive could remind him of the beauty of God's earth. It sometimes gave him the peace and quiet he couldn't find at the homestead as the children grew in their opinions and bodies. It sometimes just allowed him time to think, remember who he was, and refocus his attention where it needed to be.

He closed his eyes and thanked God for his blessings, of which he had many. He was able to employ dozens of people here at the ranch. He lived across the street from his best friend and his sister. He housed an equine therapy unit for

Pete, a boarding stable for Tad Jorgenson, and a training facility for Brynn Greene, all operations that helped countless people here in Texas and around the world.

As Kelly led the children out to the garage and the big family truck they drove to town when they went all together, Squire thought through the huge operation he was responsible for here. To think he hadn't wanted it once. To think he'd walked away for years while he earned his veterinary degree.

"Everything we have here is because of Granddaddy," he told the kids as he buckled his seat belt. "He worked this ranch so well, and he built the house we live in."

"By himself?" Sam asked, and Squire smiled at him in the rearview mirror.

"He had help, but he did a lot of it by himself." He backed out of the garage and got the truck going in the right direction down the dirt lane. They weren't the only ones leaving the ranch this morning, as the seventeen cowboys that lived and worked here at the ranch had all known his father. Everyone loved Daddy, even though he could be rough around the edges in the beginning.

The drive today happened quickly despite the distance. Everyone in the car stayed silent, and once Squire parked at the church, he felt like he could breathe. The sight of the stained glass windows against the bright white exterior brought him comfort, and he put his arm around Finn's shoulders.

"You okay?"

"Yeah." Finn nodded. "I just...what should I do with the Christmas present I got for Granddaddy?"

Squire swallowed, glancing at Kelly as she joined him. She hugged herself, and Squire started toward the church. "I think we should have a present-opening with Grandma," he said. "I'll talk to her about it."

Kelly looked at him and slipped one hand through his arm. He led his family into the church and went down the hall toward the room where they'd hold the viewing. People had already started to queue up, and Squire stopped to talk to a couple of friends from the tack and feed store.

Kelly got distracted by her cousin Crystal, and it took several long minutes for the whole family to make it into the room. The viewing wouldn't start for another ten minutes, and Squire ran his hand along the bottom half of the casket and gazed at his father's peaceful face.

Chelsea, his sister, pressed in close behind him, and Squire ducked his head as she leaned hers against his bicep. He didn't have to say anything, and Chelsea didn't either. She'd never imagined that she'd return to Three Rivers, and living at the ranch? She would've rather died. But she'd fallen in love with Pete, Squire's best friend from the Army, and they'd made an amazing life right across the street, with their four boys and all the horses at the equine therapy unit they owned and ran.

"I'm going to miss him," Chelsea said. "He used to bring the boys doughnut holes from the bakery and tell them they were grandpa kisses."

Squire smiled at the tender memory. "He loved the grandkids."

"There's Mom." Chelsea turned away from him, and Squire watched her cross the room to their mother. He'd seen her since Dad's death, of course, but today was different. Today, she was going to bury the man she'd loved for almost fifty years.

His chest tightened, and he didn't know how to breathe through that tension. Libby said, "Daddy, will you hold my hand?" and he looked down at his daughter. Everything suddenly made sense, and Squire smiled down at her.

"Of course, baby." He took her hand in his and turned away from the casket. "Let's go give Grandma a hug."

The viewing started the moment he arrived at his mother's side, and the long line of friends and family started. He shook hands and stuck right beside his mom to make sure she didn't get overwhelmed. When she needed a drink, he went to get it. When she didn't want to talk to someone anymore, he invented a reason he needed her for a moment.

He caught sight of Kelly's parents, and he left Libby with her grandmother to go stand with them for a few minutes. Kelly got taken by a few friends she worked out with when the weather was good, and Squire left Finn with his maternal grandparents when he saw Bear Glover and his wife walk in.

"Bear," Squire said, suddenly so relieved to see him. The man had already come to Three Rivers with a massive gift basket full of chocolate-covered pretzels, oatmeal cookies, and homemade bread. When Squire had asked where he'd gotten such a thing when the bakery was closed, Bear had said, "Holly Ann Broadbent." He'd pointed to the wrapping around the bread. "She owns Three Cakes."

He'd come with Jeremiah Walker, Britt Bellamore, Gavin Redd, and Wade Rhinehart. They'd only stayed for a few minutes, but it had meant the world to Squire to have his friends from the ranch owner's association be thinking about him.

"Heya, Squire." Bear opened his arms and folded Squire right inside them. He was a huge man, with plenty of charisma and power, and right now, Squire sure did need to know that life went on without his father.

Bear's father had died years ago, and all Squire had to do was look at him to know that yes, life went on. And it could be a good life.

He wanted to know how to make it through this day, and when Bear released him, Squire asked, "How do I survive this day?"

Bear looked over to the casket and back to Squire. "You let it hurt, Squire." He clapped him on the shoulder as he moved forward. "You have to let it hurt."

Squire nodded, the advice similar to but slightly different from what Kelly had told him. *Don't zone out.*

Let it hurt.

Losing his father *did* hurt. He'd gone to him so often for advice and direction, and now he wouldn't be able to.

A steady stream of cowboys followed Bear, and Squire's spirits cheered with each one. He shook hands with Ranger and his wife, Oakley, and he pulled Bishop into a hug and laughed lightly with him.

"Where are you burying him?" Bishop wanted to know.

"Right here in the church cemetery," Squire said.

"Ah, so a bit of a drive when you want to talk to him." Bishop gave him a sad smile. "I bet my daddy wishes he didn't rest only a few hundred yards from where I live. I'm sure he's sick of listening to me ask him what to do." He chuckled and moved forward with his fiancée's hand secured in his.

Squire marveled at the thought of talking to his father in the cemetery, and the idea made perfect sense. Yes, he'd have to drive a little bit to do it, but that was okay. He was already formulating their first chat.

Jeremiah Walker stepped into the room, and Squire gave him a big hug too. He somehow felt like he was comforting Jeremiah, not the other way around, and he liked that. "You remember my wife, Whitney," Jeremiah said.

"Of course." Squire hugged her too. All the Walkers had come, and Squire basked in the warmth of their friendship.

When it was finally time for the funeral to start, Squire kept one hand in Kelly's and one in his mother's. Libby held Mom's other hand, and they walked down the hall after the casket to the chapel.

The moment Squire sat down, a clear sense of comfort came over him. He looked up to the colorful glass and admired the bright light shining down onto the floor up on the dais.

Daddy was okay.

Squire would be okay too.

Chapter Twenty-Eight

Holly Ann closed her eyes and pressed her palms against them. Bright white lights popped in her vision, but she gained great relief from the pressure. She needed to go to bed, but she had a luncheon tomorrow, and her timeframe to get the food set up and leave the venue so she could do her last shift as Santa Claus at the mall was very slim.

Not only that, but her clients had ordered frozen desserts, and she had to get the ice cream in the freezer tonight or she wouldn't have it for the luncheon. So she kept whisking and flavoring. She cleaned her ice cream machine and churned the next flavor. She scraped it into molds and used a rubber spatula to smooth it all out.

Molds got pressed together and set on sheet trays. Those went in her deep freezer in the garage, and she got busy with the next task.

Her hands stayed busy, but her mind strayed down the

highway and up into the hills. She sucked in a breath and held it while she slid new sticks into the last ice cream bar mold.

She'd ruined everything with Ace with a few half-truths and a red Santa suit. She wanted to explain everything to him, but when she'd called on Monday, he hadn't answered. He'd texted a minute later with, *I just need some time to myself.*

Holly Ann knew then that she'd really hurt him. Ace *hated* being by himself, and he never took too much time to dwell on anything. She hadn't known how to press him though, and in the end, she'd respected his wishes and left him alone.

It had only been five days, but this week had been one of the longest of her life. Without him to text, she felt adrift. Knowing she wouldn't see him that day made every hour eternal.

She sniffled as she finished the last ice cream bars, pressed the molds together, and put them in the freezer. She cleaned up her kitchen methodically, making sure everything went back where it was supposed to so she could find the ingredients and utensils easily next time, and then she went to bed.

As tired as she was, Holly Ann laid in bed, her eyes closed and sleep eluding her. "Just make it to New Year's," she whispered. If she could make it nine more days, she'd be done with the Christmas Festival. Then maybe she'd know what to do about Ace.

HOLLY ANN SMILED AT THE SOFT, WHITE LIGHT emanating from Daddy's tree. He'd once again met her on the front step, taking the laundry basket of gifts from her with a "My goodness, Holly Ann. What is all of this?"

"Santa's arrived," she'd said, her voice as perky as she could make it.

She had no children who she could spoil, which was why she'd sponsored four families full of children this year through the Santa Shops For Kids program. Bethany Rose and Kevin didn't have children yet. It would be four adults for Christmas Eve dinner and gifts, and Holly Ann missed the loud, vibrant atmosphere of Shiloh Ridge Ranch.

Her emotions wobbled on the edge of a cliff. One wrong thought would push them over the edge, and she'd burst into a sob that would break her heart all over again. Her stomach trembled with the effort it took to keep her smile on her face as Bethany Rose finished spreading her gifts under the tree.

"Girls," Daddy said, and Holly Ann tore her eyes from the tree. He sat in his recliner, the same one he'd been relaxing in for the past two decades. She and Bethany Rose had tried to purchase him a new one for Father's Day, and he'd vehemently opposed them.

Holly Ann had given up trying to change her father, and she tried to just embrace him for who he was now, security cameras and old, plaid recliners and all.

Bethany Rose sat on the couch next to Holly Ann and sank into Kevin's side. "Merry Christmas, everyone," she said with a happy, chirping voice.

"Merry Christmas," Holly Ann said. "Daddy, what were you going to say?"

He hadn't wished them a Merry Christmas, and it took him several long seconds to pull his gaze from the crackling flames in the fireplace. "Girls, I'm going to sell the house."

Holly Ann opened her mouth to say something, but nothing came out.

"Why?" Bethany Ann asked.

Holly Ann knew why. Daddy was seventy-four years old, and yard work wasn't as easy as it used to be. He prided himself on taking care of things, and she'd never known him to pay for an oil change or to service the swamp cooler. Year after year, he was the one on the roof, flushing out the tubes and setting everything right.

He trimmed the trees, and he built bookcases. He fixed holes in the sheetrock, and he'd finished their entire back porch into a screened-in area, complete with new windows, proper supports, and automatic blinds.

"It's time," he said simply. "I'm looking at a smaller house in a planned community, where they have people to shovel the snow and mow the lawns. Or I'm thinking about one of those new condos on the northeast side of town."

"You'd be closer to us," Bethany Ann said. "In fact, why don't you just come live with us?" She straightened and looked at Kevin. "We have that big farmhouse, and he could be on the main level."

Holly Ann tucked her hair behind her ear and slid a glance at Bethany Rose's husband. Kevin was a saint, that was for sure, but he didn't want his father-in-law living with him.

"Beth, baby," he said. "Your daddy doesn't want to come

live on a noisy ranch. I think the whole point is for him to have a place to relax."

"Don't get a condo then, Daddy," Holly Ann said. "Go with the planned community. Is it that one over by Wilde and Organic?"

"Yep, that's the one." He looked from Holly Ann to Bethany Rose. "I know this house is where you grew up. I just can't take care of it anymore, and I have this feeling like the Lord needs it for someone else. A young family like we were once, who wants a big yard with lots of room for their kids and dogs to run around in." He smiled fondly, and Holly Ann's memories streamed through her head too.

"It's okay, Daddy," Holly Ann said. "We'll be okay coming to a different house for holidays." She nudged Bethany Rose's knee, and her sister looked at her with wide eyes. "I'm a little worried about one thing, though," she said.

"What's that?" Daddy asked.

"Will they let you put up your own security cameras on the exterior of the house in that planned community?" She cocked her head and grinned at him. "They have rules about that kind of stuff, you know."

Bethany Rose burst out laughing, and Daddy rolled his eyes.

"How will you know when we've arrived?" Holly Ann asked, trying hard not to giggle. She lost the battle and laughed, glad when Daddy joined in with the rest of them.

"All right," he said, heaving himself out of the recliner when the timer on the oven went off. "Come eat. We'll do presents after dinner, just like we always do."

Holly Ann got to her feet and pulled her sister to her

feet. "Come on, Bethy." She drew her into a hug. "You don't want Daddy at the ranch. Can you imagine?" They giggled together, and Holly Ann whispered, "Besides, aren't you and Kevin trying for a baby?"

"Yes," she whispered back. "It's just not going very well."

Holly Ann increased her grip on her sister. "I'm so sorry, sweetie."

Bethany Rose held her tight too, and Holly Ann pressed her eyes closed, a prayer streaming through her mind for her sister and her husband. When they parted, their eyes met, and Holly Ann simply nodded.

"Where's Ace?" Bethany Rose asked. "I thought he'd be here. Christmas Eve and all, with you two being so serious."

Holly Ann yanked on the chain holding her emotions in place. "Uh, yeah. He broke up with me."

"What?" Bethany Rose screeched, and that brought Kevin's and Daddy's attention to them from the kitchen.

Holly Ann waved at Bethany Rose to get her to be quiet, but she either didn't see or didn't care. "Why did he break up with you? You two are so cute together, and he—I just know he loves you. He came to my birthday dinner alone, for crying out loud." She stared at Holly with wide eyes filled with shock.

Holly Ann looked at Daddy, pleading with him to help her. She hadn't told him about the break-up either, but surely he would connect all the dots as to why Ace had broken up with her. He was a brilliant detective, after all.

But he said nothing. He stood in the kitchen with a serving spatula in his hand, his face full of surprise too. Kevin seemed to know when to stay out of things, and he simply took a seat at the dining room table.

Holly Ann couldn't hold back a hurricane, and her eyes filled with tears. Her chest tightened as if someone had put it in a vice, and everything felt so twisted. Her life made no sense without Ace Glover in it.

"I just needed to get through the Christmas Festival," she said as the tears fell down her face. Bethany Rose rushed at her and held her tight again, and a few moments later, Daddy arrived on the scene. "I was just too busy and didn't have time for him."

"Holly Ann," he said, his voice firm but full of compassion and kindness. "He knew about the Christmas Festival."

Translation: *There has to be something more.*

She hiccuped, which sent a sharp pain through her ribs and into her spine. She wanted to be alone, but if she was, this storm would howl for a while. She hated the cramped, hot feeling that came with crying, but she couldn't stop herself.

"He's smart," she said, her voice pinched and pitched toward the rafters. "He figured some stuff out and knew I'd been lying to him."

Daddy pulled in a breath, but Bethany Rose stepped back, frowns for miles on her face. "Lying to him? About what?" She looked toward Daddy, who had his eyes trained on the ground. She retreated further. "Something's going on that I don't know about."

Holly Ann's panic reared again. Bethany Rose hated being left out of things, and the three of them didn't keep secrets. They confided in one another, and they'd been close for decades.

This was going to devastate her too.

Holly Ann couldn't bring herself to say anything to her sister, just like she hadn't to Ace. Everything scrambled in her head, and she sank onto the loveseat she'd been about to pass on her way to dinner.

She put her head in her hands and commanded herself to *think*.

When problems arose during the festival, she stopped and brainstormed solutions. She and Rachel and the rest of the team found ways to fix the issues, by all of them coming together for a common purpose: put on the best festival Three Rivers had ever seen.

They'd done it.

Well, almost.

There was still one more event—the New Year's Eve parade, but everything was set for it. There were no more craft classes, and no more tastings. No more contests, and no more free movie nights or ice skating afternoons.

No more Santa visits.

"Daddy," Holly Ann said as she lifted her head. "Ace knows. Bethany Rose deserves to know."

"Did he tell anyone?"

Holly Ann shrugged. "I have no idea. We broke up a week ago." She thought of Ace, and his good heart. His kind, hardworking spirit. She thought of his quick smile, and his acceptance of her schedule, her desires, her life. Just her. He accepted *her*.

"I doubt he told anyone," she said quietly. "He's not that

kind of man." He wasn't vindictive or revengeful. He was hurt, and he felt betrayed. She'd seen that in his eyes seven days ago.

How do I erase that from his soul? she wondered. *How?*

She rose to her feet, her mind clear and the solution forward obvious. "Bethany Rose," she said. She wiped her face and squared her shoulders. She stood taller than her sister and weighed at least forty pounds more. "Daddy's been—"

"Holly Ann," Daddy said sharply.

She met his eye with a glare of her own. "The truth is how this family stays strong," she said evenly. She gestured to Kevin. "Come sit down for another minute, okay? Then we can eat."

Her tiredness almost overcame her, but Holly Ann could do this. Then she'd eat candied ham and plenty of bread, mashed potatoes, and pie. Everything would feel good again, and she'd sleep in her childhood bedroom for one more Christmas Eve.

Kevin joined Bethany Ann on the couch, and Holly Ann stepped over to her father's side. He still didn't look happy, but he didn't try to stop her again.

"Bethany Rose," she said. "Daddy's been playing Santa for the Christmas Festival here in town for forty-seven years."

Her sister's eyes flew to their father. "What?"

"Remember how we used to be so confused when he'd just disappear? He said there were cases, but there weren't. He'd tell Mom that he had to run to the station, but then he'd be gone all evening." She cut a look at Daddy out of the corner of her eye. "He was dressing up as Santa and going to the mall."

Bethany Rose looked half-confused and half-scared.

"Well, he passed the torch to me four years ago," she said. "The Broadbents have been playing Santa for generations here in this town, and it was my turn. But no one knows who Santa is, right? It's always been a hugely guarded town and festival secret, and Daddy swore me to secrecy. It's even become *part of* the festival—guess who Santa is." She swallowed and centered her thoughts again.

"I haven't told anyone—not you, my favorite person on the planet—and not Ace." Fresh tears threatened to burn down her face again, but she managed to keep them from doing so. "He found out anyway, because I guess that's what happens when you spend a lot of time together with someone, and you tell them things you've never told anyone, and you open doors in your life you've never opened before."

Holly Ann wished the ground would open up and swallow her whole. It would be far less painful than standing there, talking about Ace and the relationship she'd allowed herself to have with him. It would be far less horrifying than watching Bethany Rose's betrayal roll across her face.

"We should've told you," Holly Ann said. "Both of you. I'm so sorry." She pressed her palms together, forcing her mind to quiet again. "There. That's it." She looked at Daddy. "Unless you have something to say?"

He looked torn for a moment, and then he sighed. "I was taught that the secret of Santa Claus should be kept no matter what." He moved his eyes from Holly Ann to Bethany Rose and Kevin on the couch. They'd clasped hands, so at least she wouldn't be dealing with this alone. Kevin actually smiled, like this was no big deal.

Holly Ann realized something then—this was no big deal. This was a children's fantasy, and while she didn't want to break any hearts by telling them Santa wasn't real, she certainly didn't have to suffer with one of her own.

"But I can see that times change," Daddy said. "As long as we can keep the secret within our own family, I think we'll be okay."

Silence filled the house for several long moments. Then Bethany Rose asked, "So I shouldn't guess that Holly Ann is Santa on the Two Cents app?"

Another beat of silence passed, and then all four of them burst out laughing. It rang through Holly Ann's ears, and filled her chest, and lifted her soul. She shook her head and wiped her face again. She'd need to get down the hall to the bathroom to make sure she didn't have black streaks across her face.

"No," she said. "Don't say it's me in that poll." She'd asked Ward to put the poll on the Two Cents app, and it was really fun for her to see the results coming in, especially because they updated hourly.

Not a single person had suspected it was her—except for Ace.

Ace. You need to go talk to Ace.

"Listen," she said. "Can we get this show on the road? I have someone else I need to go talk to tonight."

Chapter Twenty-Nine

A ce lay on the couch in the living room at Bull House, something on the television in front of him. He was skipping dinner with the family, which was saying something, because it was Sunday *and* Christmas Eve.

Bishop, Mister, and Ward had been decorating True Blue for a week, transforming the barn into Country Christmas Central, with poinsettias, pine wreaths, and pounds of garland. Bright tinsel caught his eye when he went out to work on the ranch in the mornings, and Ace had watched the florist deliver huge displays of festive flowers for the centerpieces.

Sammy's parents had come, and Montana's extended family, including her daughter's boyfriend and his family. Ace knew Tripp and Ivory Walker, and he didn't mind that their numbers kept swelling and swelling.

He normally loved being around people.

This year, Bear had asked Pastor Summers if they could host anyone who didn't have family, and the numbers had grown again. When Ace had come inside the house a half an hour ago, he'd seen the pastor arrive with his wife.

A sigh came out of his mouth, and his eyes drifted to the clock on the cable box. Dinner would start in fifteen minutes. No one would know he wasn't going to come yet.

He closed his eyes, because it was late. They always had a late dinner on Christmas Eve, so anyone who wanted to attend the light parade could do so. Oakley had driven her race cars in the parade last year, and she'd been such a big hit that they'd asked her to do so again.

Not they, he thought. *Holly Ann.*

He couldn't get her out of his head, and he didn't even want her to go. He wanted her to come to dinner tonight, and he wondered if he called her.... "Would she come?" he asked out loud, wishing he had a dog or a horse to answer him. He'd even take The General, the snobby cat that lived next door.

His phone rang, and he knew it would be Bishop before he even lifted it to check. Sure enough, his cousin's name sat on the screen. Ace swiped on the call and said, "Yeah?" hoping that was neutral enough to mask his feelings.

"Hey, can you stop by the homestead and grab something for me?"

Ace sat up, a sigh coming from his mouth. How could he say he wasn't coming? And if he did just grab the item and take it to True Blue, he wouldn't be able to leave. He knew that. The party-like atmosphere and scent of delicious food would be too tempting for him.

Everyone at the ranch knew he'd broken up with Holly Ann. Only Ward had spoken to him about it. In fact, only a few people were currently speaking to him at all. Though he'd apologized to everyone, he knew he'd hurt Zona and Duke, and he hadn't been able to get Cactus to respond to a call or a text.

Mister didn't seem angry, but he didn't say much to Ace, and Etta had stayed after the party to lecture Ace for telling everyone about Noah. *The family is huge*, she'd said. *It wasn't that big of a deal. I wasn't keeping him secret, for crying out loud. We were going out in public. Just because I didn't tell you lot the moment we went out doesn't make it a crime.*

Ace knew that. He did.

Ranger, Ward, and Ida had forgiven him, but things had changed between him and Ward. They'd been confidants before, and now Ace knew his older brother wouldn't tell him anything sensitive or important.

He hated that, and he needed to sit down with Ward and clear things up.

He'd gone up to the Top Cottage to apologize to Aunt Lois, and she alone had forgiven him easily. She'd hugged him tightly and told him he was a good man.

He didn't feel like a good man. He felt like he'd betrayed all the people he cared about most. Misery swam through him, and he simply wanted to disappear. Get in his truck and go somewhere else for a little while.

Why can't you? he asked himself as Bishop asked him if he was still there.

"Yeah," Ace said with a sigh. "What do you need?"

"I left all the music sitting on the table in the foyer. Could you just grab it real quick?"

"Sure." Ace got to his feet and padded over to the front door. "I just have to pull on my boots."

Thankfully, someone distracted Bishop, and he said, "Okay, gotta go." The call ended, and Ace set his phone on the back of the couch as he collected his boots. Bishop should've asked why he'd taken his boots off when dinner started so soon. He should've asked why Ace wasn't already down at True Blue. He should've asked why he'd sighed so many times.

The fact was, Bishop was busy with something else. Everyone was, and Ace had lost his anchor in the Glover family. He'd lost Ranger to Oakley and that new, core family. He'd lost Ward by spilling his secret. He'd lost Bishop to the events, to Montana, to True Blue itself.

He'd lost Cactus, and everything in his body tightened. He couldn't lose Cactus—how did he fix things with Cactus?

He'd lost Mister, and he'd lost the trust of his sisters.

He'd caused a problem with Zona and Duke, which caused problems for Bear, and guilt combined sharply with regret, stabbing through him. It entered his heart, which bled and wept for all he'd done to his family.

Worst of all, he'd lost Holly Ann.

Ace spiraled, because he'd lost everything, and he simply didn't know how to make it all right. Sometimes an apology wasn't enough. Behavior couldn't be undone. Words couldn't be unsaid. Feelings couldn't be ironed flat and forgotten just because he said, "I'm sorry."

Even if he was sorry. Truly, deeply sorry.

He pulled on his boots, but instead of grabbing his jacket and going, he went down the hall to his bedroom. He got out a backpack and put a few changes of fresh clothes inside. He went across the hall to grab a few toiletries, and with a bag packed, he collected his leather jacket, keys, and wallet before heading out.

The CDs and Bishop's iPod sat where he'd said they'd be, and Ace arrived at True Blue a few minute later. Others were still arriving too. Judge and Preacher directed them where to park, but Ace took a spot way down the lane so he could get out quickly.

He wasn't going to stay. He told himself that with every step he took. He joined the flow of people entering the barn, their exclamations of how beautiful it was warranted. True Blue had truly been decked out for the holidays, and the scent of cinnamon and pine combined with the savory smells of good food.

Bishop, Ida, and Etta had been working for days for this meal, and Ace regretted that he'd miss it. He swept the huge ballroom in the barn, looking for Cactus. If he was there, Ace didn't see him, but the place teemed with people, many of them wearing cowboy hats.

He found Bishop in the kitchen, and his cousin's face lit up at the sight of him. "Ace." He hugged him quickly and took the items. "You're a life-saver." He hurried out of the kitchen, and Ace looked at his sisters.

"Merry Christmas, Ace," Ida said with a beautiful smile. She continued to mix the salad in the bowl in front of her.

"Why do you look like you've swallowed lemons?" Etta asked, frowning at him as she brushed butter over the tops of a sheet tray of golden rolls. "It's *Christmas*, Ace. Cheer up."

"I'm sorry," he said, wishing they could hear and feel the depth of it.

Maybe they did, because they both stopped working. The twins exchanged a glance with each other, and then simultaneously looked back at Ace.

"Honey, you have nothing to be sorry for." Ida left her salad and came toward Ace. "You actually *helped* me and Brady. I didn't know how to tell Ranger, and Ward wasn't about to." She put a tentative smile on her face, but Ace didn't feel any better.

"He doesn't talk to me the same," he said, looking away. "Ward, I mean."

"He will," Etta said gently. "He's just trying to work out some things."

"See? And I don't even know what things." Ace shook his head. "It's fine. I made the bed, and now I have to figure out how to lie in it." His father had said that a lot. *You make the bed you sleep in, son. If you don't like it, get up and remake it.*

He didn't know how, and he just needed some time and space. He'd asked Holly Ann for that, and she'd been real great about giving it to him. She hadn't tried to call or text again, and since he hadn't gone to town, he hadn't seen her for a week.

"Listen," he said just as Ida put her hand on his forearm. He flinched away from her, and she withdrew her hand. "Sorry."

"Go on," Etta said, pressing in on his other side.

He looked at the twins, just a couple of years younger

than him. He may not have the same friendship with Ida that Ward did, but Ace had always gotten along with everyone in his family. He was the middle child of five, and he liked to think he could bring the two older boys together with the two younger twin girls. *He* kept them all together.

Except now, he'd blown them apart.

He took them into his arms now though, one on each side. "I love you guys," he whispered. "I'm leaving for a little bit."

"Leaving?" Ida asked, fear in her voice. "Ace, no. You don't need to leave." She stepped back, concern in her wide wyes. "Where will you even go?"

Etta looked at him with surprise and a little bit of fear too, waiting for his answer.

"Just somewhere else," he said, dropping his head so he didn't have to see their faces past his cowboy hat. "I won't ask you to keep it a secret or anything. I don't know when I'll be back."

Music began to play through the speaker system, festive holiday music with a light beat and plenty of familiarity.

"Where are you going?" Etta pressed.

"I haven't decided," he said. "I have a phone. I'll keep you informed." He turned to leave just as Bishop came bustling back into the kitchen.

"Okay," his cousin said, pure joy radiating from him. "That's done. Almost everyone is here. Pastor Summers says he's waiting for a few more people. Should we start loading the buffet?"

He didn't seem to notice that anything was wrong, and why should he? Bishop possessed a sunny, optimistic personality that drew everyone to him effortlessly. It was Ace who'd pushed everyone into a corner they didn't want to be in.

He paused next to his cousin anyway. "Is Cactus here?"

Bishop sobered and finally seemed to clue in to the thundercloud hovering just inches above Ace's head. He swallowed and shook his head. "I haven't seen him yet."

Yet.

That meant he wasn't coming.

Ace nodded. "I'll call him."

"I already tried," Bishop said. "No answer."

Pure guilt filled Ace. Anger quickly followed, and it was directed at himself *and* Cactus. The man could be so stubborn sometimes. He nodded and left the kitchen.

Just then, an uproar filled True Blue, and people began crowding around someone. Ace took the opportunity to skirt around the back of the hall, using the arrival to escape without having to talk to anyone else in the family.

But it was Willa Knowlton who'd entered the barn, and Ace's eyes widened. She'd left town weeks earlier, right in the middle of a date with Cactus, and he hadn't heard from her since.

She looked around the room while accepting hugs and hellos, and Ace knew she was looking for him. She'd come tonight just to see him.

Ace pulled out his phone as he slipped out the front door of the barn and back into the night. He pressed into the shadows of the barn and stilled to avoid Judge and Preacher, who were walking in.

"...love Christmas," Judge said happily.

"Yeah," Preacher said, but it didn't sound like he agreed

all that much. "You go ahead. I think I left my phone in the truck."

Judge went inside, but Preacher didn't. He turned and retreated a few steps until he stood outside the cheery light spilling from the entrance of the barn. He sighed, and Ace knew the frustration it carried. Knew it deeply. Felt it in his very soul.

"What am I doing here?" Preacher asked, his face tipped up to the night sky. Clouds swirled through it, catching the moonlight and trapping it as they moved in the atmospheric winds. "Why don't I fit in this family? Why did You send me to them?"

Another sigh fell from his mouth, and he pulled his phone from his pocket. He hadn't left it in the truck, and Ace had never realized how unhappy Preacher was. Sure, he was a little quieter than Judge. He let Judge lead in every way, but Ace hadn't noticed him being upset about that.

He lifted his phone to his ear and said, "Hey, Mister."

Mister? Ace hadn't realized the two of them were that close. Of course, it was Judge that Mister had a problem with, and well, Preacher and Judge were a pair. They always had been.

Ace didn't want to stand here and listen to this. It was simply another secret he didn't want to know.

He stepped out of the shadows and made his footsteps heavy as he approached Preacher, who turned around to see who was coming. Relief filled his face at the sight of Ace, and he said, "I don't want to, though."

Ace nodded to him and stopped next to him. "I'm leaving

town for a little bit," he said. "Do you want to come with me?"

Preacher's eyes widened, and he said, "I have to go, Mister." He hung up and lowered the phone. "You're leaving town?"

"Yes."

"Where are you going?"

"I have no idea." He looked at Preacher, and so much was said between them. "I have money, and I'm sure I can find a hotel somewhere. It's not rocket science." Just because no one left the ranch didn't mean it couldn't be done.

In fact, it was time for someone to do it.

Even when Cactus ran, he didn't run off the land. Everyone knew where to find him, because he *wanted* them to find him.

Ace didn't want anyone to find him for a while. He needed to find himself.

"I'm leaving right now," Ace said. 'I have a bag in my truck. If you want to come, you're welcome. I can take you home and wait while you pack some clothes or whatever."

Without hesitation, Preacher said, "Let's go."

Ace started toward his truck, and once they were both inside, he said, "I don't want to talk. I don't want a bunch of questions. Okay?"

"Ditto," Preacher said, not even looking at him.

Ace drove down the road to the side lane that led around the hill to the house where Preacher and Judge lived. Preacher got out and ran inside, and Ace tapped to get a call connected to Cactus.

The line rang and rang, and frustration filled and filled

Ace's lungs. After the voicemail message had barked out, "It's Cactus. I probably won't listen to this, because I didn't answer your call for a reason. But whatever. Leave a message if you want," Ace sighed and shook his head.

"Cactus," he said. "You need to get over to True Blue. Willa Knowlton showed up, and it was obvious to anyone with eyes that she was looking for you. I'm not there, so don't worry. I'm not going to say anything again, and you won't have to see me." He sighed, because he hated this contention. He wasn't sure how Bear had dealt with his grizzly attitude, hurting people, and then apologizing all these years. It was horrible, and Ace hated it.

"Just get over there, okay? You and Willa will be good together, and she's back in town. Okay, bye. Merry Christmas."

He ended the call and leaned back against the head rest, a sigh coming from his mouth. He let his eyes drift closed, wondering if he should go south or north once he reached the highway. He'd ask Preacher and let him decide.

The door opened, startling him, and Preacher tossed a bag in the back seat before climbing in the front. The overhead light went off after he closed is door, and Ace asked, "Ready?"

"Yep."

He backed out of the driveway and made his way through the darkness to the main road. Down the hill he went, and when he reached the highway, he looked left and then right. "Which way do you want to go?"

"Texas is south," Preacher said. "The rest of the world is north."

He looked at Ace, and with the lights on the dashboard and a hint of moonlight in the cab, he could see Preacher's face just fine. "North," they said together, and Ace flipped on his blinker.

Then he made the turn and drove away from Shiloh Ridge Ranch.

Chapter Thirty

Cactus glared at his phone. If it rang one more time....

"Put it on silent then," he told himself. He knew how to disconnect from everyone. He knew how to go silent. He'd only gone part of the way this time, and he couldn't figure out why.

He sighed as he reached for his jacket and pulled it on. He left through the back door, leaving his phone on the kitchen counter, and walked through the night to the tree that guarded his son's grave.

He kept a chair there, and he sat heavily in it. "I feel like I've taken ten steps backward," he said. "Willa still won't answer me. I have that blasted car for no reason. And everyone keeps calling."

He wanted them to call. It meant he hadn't been forgotten, and he actually appreciated hearing his phone ring and chime. No one had come out to the Edge Cabin except for Bear, and Cactus hadn't even let him inside.

Then, when Lincoln and Benny had shown up, Cactus had relented. He couldn't say no to Lincoln, and that blasted black and white dog had stolen his heart too.

Bishop had called and texted every day. Cactus would answer texts, but he didn't want to talk. "I do and I don't," he said to the night, to the trees, to the sky, to the Lord. "I don't understand, Lord. Why do I run like this? How do I figure out how to stay?"

You have stayed.

The thought filled him, though it barely belonged to him. He let it wash through his mind and fill his soul as he examined it.

He supposed he had stayed. He could've packed a few bags, loaded everything into his brand-new sedan, and left the ranch. He'd never done that. Even in his worst times, even when he had nothing here, even when the very sight of this ranch made him furious and then miserable, he'd stayed.

He may have removed himself emotionally from the family, but he'd stayed on the land. He maybe have removed himself spiritually from the Lord, but he'd stayed in the fold. He went to church. He prayed. He believed in God; he just wasn't sure God believed in him.

No one had said anything to Cactus after Ace's tirade last week. "That's because they don't care," he murmured. "They don't care that you bought a car so you could take Willa on a date. They don't care that you go to therapy. Heck, most of them knew that anyway."

That part was at least true. He'd told Bear, Ranger, and Ward about the therapy a long time ago. Judge knew too, because Cactus had told him he didn't need to burden him anymore. Ace and Bishop knew, because they refused to retreat very far when Cactus pushed everyone away.

Who cared if Zona, Ida, and Etta knew?

He let the breeze track across his face, and he enjoyed the dark silence for a few minutes, letting his thoughts settle. Eventually, the jacket wasn't warm enough, and Cactus hurried back inside.

His phone rang as he opened the back door, but he'd found a place of peace, and he picked up the device. Ace's name sat there, and Cactus should answer it. The man had been suffering for a week now.

He tapped on the screen, but he was just one microsecond too late, and the call went to voicemail. He sighed and checked the other call from earlier. Bishop. Of course. It was Christmas Eve, and the barn wore its best face for the holidays.

Cactus didn't want to miss the meal with his family, but he didn't know how to come back. "You just go walk in," he told himself. "You've done it before."

His phone bleeped, and he dialed his voicemail.

"Cactus," Ace said. "You need to get over to True Blue. Willa Knowlton showed up, and it was obvious to anyone with eyes that she was looking for you. I'm not there, so don't worry. I'm not going to say anything again, and you won't have to see me."

Cactus's heart leapt, and he didn't think Ace would lie to him.

"Willa's back? And she's at the barn?" He needed to get to the barn as fast as possible. He looked down at his clothes, and he wasn't sure he could go like this. He couldn't remember when he'd washed these jeans, and didn't Christmas Eve call for slacks? Maybe an ugly sweater?

What would Willa be wearing?

Ace continued with, "Just get over there, okay? You and Willa will be good together, and she's back in town. Okay, bye. Merry Christmas."

"Merry Christmas," Cactus said to the message, and then he tapped the one to return the message sender's call.

"Cactus," Ace said, surprise heavy in his voice. "You called me back."

"I did," he said. "Listen, first, I'm not upset with you."

Ace said nothing, and Cactus didn't expect him to. "About Willa...."

"You're on speaker with Preacher."

Cactus cleared his throat. "Okay," he said. "Was Willa dressed up? Are people wearing jeans and stuff?" He expected Ace to laugh, but he didn't. Of course he wouldn't. Ace didn't make fun of Cactus about things that were important to him.

"I didn't notice, honestly," Ace said. "She was sort of surrounded by people."

Of course she was. Everyone loved Willa, and Bear had offered the barn and their Christmas Eve meal to the pastor and congregation for anyone who didn't have family in town for the holidays.

"I'm sure whatever you're wearing is fine," Ace said. "She won't care, Cactus. It's not about what you have on. It's about *you*."

Cactus swallowed, because *he* was what was lacking. "Okay," he said. "Listen, thanks for calling to tell me."

"Of course. I thought you'd want to know."

"I do."

"Don't think too hard about it," Ace said. "Get on Matador, and go."

"I'm going to show up smelling like horse," Cactus grumbled.

Ace chuckled then, but Cactus should've bought a truck when he'd bought that car. Then he could've driven to True Blue and wowed Willa with his masculine cologne.

Ace said something about needing to go, and Cactus let him end the call. He hurried into his bedroom and changed into a fresh pair of jeans and a clean red and white plaid shirt from his closet. He put the leather jacket back on, then took it off to spray on a bit of cologne.

He could walk, but it would take thirty minutes, or he could ride Matador and get there in ten. He opted for the horse, praying the whole ride to True Blue that his fresh clothes and cologne would cover up any horsey smell he might pick up.

After looping the reins over the post behind the barn, and removing the saddle on Matador, he hurried through the back door. Noise met his ears instantly, and Cactus nearly turned right back around. He didn't like crowds, and sometimes he couldn't even tolerate his own family.

He paused in the back of the room and scanned the large hall in front of him. Definitely fifty or sixty people, and he told himself he went to church with at least that many people. More, even.

He saw Bear and Sammy standing near the pastor, both of them nodding at something Pastor Summers said. Bishop,

Ida, and Etta bustled around the buffet, setting out bowls and trays of food.

Dinner hadn't started yet, and Cactus wondered if he could just slip into the room. He spotted Mother, and she'd brought Donald Parker to their Christmas Eve dinner. He gaped at her, the joy on her face the most wonderful thing he'd ever seen.

The first couple of steps in her direction were the hardest, but after that, he moved easily. He hadn't seen Willa yet, but he wanted to speak to his mother first anyway. She saw him coming from a dozen paces away, and she rose to her feet.

Her smile flitted easily across her face, and she held out one hand toward him. He took it when he reached her and said, "Mother," before he leaned in and kissed her cheek quickly.

"Cactus," she said, stepping to his side and facing the fire chief. "This is Donald Parker. Don, my second son, Charles. We call him Cactus."

"Real nice to meet you," Donald said, and Cactus shook his hand.

"You too," he said, smiling in a way that felt very real to him. He met Mother's eyes again. "Have you seen Willa?"

Mother inclined her head to her right, where the rest of the barn lay, and Cactus turned, expecting to have to search for the woman who'd been plaguing him since the very moment he'd met her.

She stood maybe ten feet from him, a nervous look on her face. She wore a pair of black pants and a festive blouse in white with colored holiday lights strung across it. Her hair fell over her shoulders in pretty auburn waves, and she tried a smile on her face.

Cactus returned it and released his mother's hand, his pulse positively pounding through his whole body. He took a step toward her just as a child ran up to her. She turned her attention to the boy, who was maybe ten or eleven, and he signed to her with his hands.

Surprise bolted through Cactus when she spoke back to him, saying the words out loud as she made the signs. "Save me a spot, Mitchell." She glanced at Cactus. "Two spots." She smiled at the child, and he turned and ran off again, leaving Willa to watch him and then turn back to Cactus.

He'd closed more distance between them, and he slowed the closer he got. He stepped to her side and easily slid his hand right into hers. She sucked in a breath and looked down at their twined fingers. "I thought you'd be so angry," she whispered.

He heard her even among all of the chatter in the barn, along with the music piping through the speakers.

"Not angry," he said. "Confused, sure. Frustrated you didn't call back, yes. But honestly, Willa, I'm just glad you're back."

"I got a new phone," she said. "I didn't have any numbers in it."

"A new phone, huh?" he asked. "I'm real interested in hearing all about it. Would you be available to go to dinner with me sometime soon?"

Willa's hand in his tightened, and she tugged him slightly closer to her. "You might want to wait to ask me out," she said.

"Why?"

"Until you're sure you want to truly go out with me."

"Willa," he said. "Of course—"

"I have to tell you something." Her eyes widened. "It's going to change everything." She swallowed and Cactus felt her anxiety as if it were his. She indicated something across the room, and Cactus looked out across the hall.

"That little boy," she said. "The one who just came up to me? See him?"

Cactus saw him standing next to Willa's brother, his back to him and Willa. "Yes," he said. "I see him."

"He's my son."

The bottom fell out of Cactus's stomach, and numbness flowed through him. She gently slipped her fingers away from his, and he let her, because he couldn't do much more than breathe and blink.

"Your son?" he asked.

"His name's Mitchell. He's ten years old, and he was born with congenital hearing loss."

Cactus looked back at her and found her beaming with love for her son. He had no idea what to say, so he just looked back to the little boy.

A ten-year-old boy.

Cactus should have one of those too.

"I told him to save me two seats, but if you'd rather sit with your family, I understand." She took a step away from him as if she'd leave him standing there alone. "And if you'd rather not go out, I *completely* understand that too. Really, Cactus. No hard feelings, and no explanations needed." She moved again.

"Willa," he said, and she turned back to him. "Can I have your new number?"

Another smile touched her lips. "Sure." She gave it to him, and he typed it into his phone. He looked up again, his heart thrashing now.

He moved toward her, stuffing his phone in his back pocket in one step, and taking her hand in the next. "How will you introduce me to your son?" he asked as they started the walk toward the table very near the front of the room.

He was aware of everyone's eyes on him and Willa as they walked, but he didn't care. Not one bit. Let them look. Let them all talk.

"I think we'll go with friends for now," Willa said, glancing up at him. "How's that?"

"That's fine," Cactus said. "For now." He leaned closer and slowed his step. His hand tightened around hers. "You tell me when you're available for dinner, lunch, breakfast, whatever, and I'll be there."

Willa nodded and swallowed, and Cactus felt sure she knew he wanted to be more than friends. A lot more.

Patrick signed something to Mitchell, and he turned around as they approached.

"Mitch," Willa said, removing her hand from Cactus's so she could talk to her son. "I want you to meet my friend, Cactus." She indicated him, and Cactus raised his hand in a wave. It probably meant something else in sign language, but he had no idea what.

Mitchell smiled and stuck out his hand, and Cactus shook it. The boy had dark brown eyes that hadn't come from Willa, but his hair color mirrored hers. A deep, dark blonde with plenty of red in there. His hair had been cut recently, as everything was trimmed up nice and neat, and he wore a pair of jeans and a long-sleeved shirt in red and white.

He signed something to his mother, and Willa giggled.

"What did he say?" Cactus asked. He'd need to learn sign language quickly if he wanted this boy and his mother in his life.

"He said the two of you match." She reached out and flipped open his jacket a little bit more. "Red and white, like candy canes." She beamed at her son, and moved her hands again. "Did you save us two spots?"

Mitch turned and showed them to her, and she took the one next to him, and Cactus took the one next to her. It felt strange to be at a table without any other Glovers, but also a bit magical at the same time.

"Cactus," a little girl said to his right, and he turned toward Gigi.

"Heya, Gigi," he said, smiling at the little blonde girl.

"Do you believe in Santa Claus?" she asked, her six-year-old face open and unassuming.

"I sure do," he said proudly and without hesitation. Willa's hand landed on his knee under the table, and a jolt of electricity flowed through him. "In fact, Santa's brought me some pretty amazing gifts over the years."

Her eyes widened and she stared at him. "Like what?" she asked.

"Well," he said, covering Willa's hand on his leg with one of his. "This one year, he brought me a brand-new horse...."

Chapter Thirty-One

olly Ann pulled up to the barn where she'd catered
Lois Glover's birthday party. The drive had taken no
time at all, because she'd been so nervous. She hoped there
would be plenty of people here, and perhaps she could
simply text Ace that she'd like to see him if at all possible,
and could he please come out?

By the number of cars and trucks parked in front of the
barn and down the road, having a crowd wouldn't be an issue.

Finding Ace could be though, and Holly Ann decided to
get out of her car and walk inside the barn. If she texted, he
might ignore her or not see it.

"If he ignores you, that's a pretty big sign, isn't it?" Her
footsteps slowed, and she had no idea what to do. Text first
and see if he responded? Go inside and refuse to give him
more time? Refuse to let him break up with her, the way he'd
done a couple of months ago to her?

Before she could make a decision and choose a direction,

the massive barn door slid open and people started spilling out into the night. Not wanting to be caught standing there, Holly Ann quickly ducked back to her car, sliding behind the wheel and closing the door so she sat bathed in darkness.

From her parallel parking position along the side of the road, she could see everyone as they left the barn and flowed toward their vehicles. The stream evened and slowed, and finally, the Glovers started to come outside.

She saw Ranger and Oakley leave first, then Arizona and Duke. Ward came out with his mother and Mister, and the three of them got in the same truck and rumbled away. Cactus and Willa Knowlton exited with a child, as well as Bear, Sammy, Lincoln, and Sammy's parents.

Lois herself came out with Donald Parker, and Montana Martin with her family. Judge exited alone, and Holly Ann found that odd. He usually stuck with Preacher and even Ace, but neither of them came outside.

Hers was now one of the last cars in the lot, and Judge saw it. She wanted to duck down, but when he made a beeline for her, she couldn't. She'd been spotted. She rolled down her window and he leaned over. "He's not here."

"Ace?"

"Yeah." Judge didn't sound too happy about it either. "He and Preacher left."

"Oh, okay," she said, reaching up to grip the wheel. "Do you think it's too late to go to Bull House and see him?" She'd come all this way, and she wasn't sure she'd be able to work up her bravery to do it again.

"No," Judge said. "I mean, they're not here on the ranch at all. They didn't come to dinner. They left."

Holly Ann couldn't read his expression, and she must've looked stunned or confused, both feelings running through her, because Judge opened the door and sat in the passenger seat.

She could see him then, and he definitely wasn't happy.

"They left the ranch?"

"Mm."

"When will they be back?" Maybe they'd just run to town for a few groceries before Christmas Day, when all the stores would be closed. "I could wait a little while."

"No one knows when they'll be back. Heck, Ace and Preacher don't know when they'll be back."

"You're not making any sense," Holly Ann said.

Judge turned toward her, his dark eyes firing dangerously. "Ace and Preacher packed a bag and left town. They're gone."

Holly Ann understood that. Her mouth widened. She was the one who didn't want to put down roots. She was the one who would pack a bag and leave town if things got too hard. She had the gypsy soul—not Ace.

None of what Judge had said added up to anything remotely close to what Ace would do.

"Why?" she asked.

"Who knows?" Judge asked. "Ace has been miserable since the night you guys broke up. He came back in the house and said so much stuff."

Her heart beat against the back of her tongue. "What kind of stuff?" she managed to ask.

"Everything," Judge said. "All these secrets about all these different people in the family."

Holly Ann couldn't breathe. Her mouth felt sticky and stale.

"He apologized, but once a secret's been said, it's really hard to take that back."

She could only nod, though Judge wasn't looking at her.

"Anyway, it's been a little…delicate around her for a few days, and I guess he maybe didn't want to keep tiptoeing around. I don't know." He sighed as if Ace leaving town for a few days placed a great burden on him personally.

"Do you…." Holly Ann trailed off, her idea starting to take shape, but she needed a little more time to formulate it.

"Do I what?" Judge asked.

"Do you think you could keep an eye out and let me know when he returns?"

Judge looked at her fully then, his eyes wide. "Why? What are you going to do?"

"I'm going to apologize too, and I'm going to pray he'll take me back."

Judge studied her for another moment, then two, then ten. Finally, he said, "All right. I'll get everyone on-board, and the moment any of us sees him, we'll text you."

Relief rushed through her, and she said, "Great. Thanks, Judge."

He nodded and got out of her car. He didn't look back as he crossed the road to his truck, and Holly Ann didn't stay any longer, because Ace wasn't even here.

"How could he not be here?" she asked herself as she drove back down the hill in the pitch black night, only the moon and her headlights for guidance. As she headed home, she prayed for direction too.

Nothing came, and she fell asleep on Christmas Eve with tears on her pillow and Snickers curled into her side.

———

HOLLY ANN SUFFERED THROUGH HER SECOND-WORST Christmas of her life. The first had been the very first one after her mother had left Three Rivers, and just she, Bethany Rose, and Daddy had been present for their traditional Christmas brunch, which came right after all the presents had been opened.

She didn't have any presents to open, and her family had gotten together last night for their holiday meal.

She made her own French toast, sausage links, and plenty of whipped cream and strawberries. She ate alone, feeding bits of fruit, meat, and bread to Snickers.

She skipped the after-Christmas sales in the mall stores, boutiques, and online.

By December twenty-seventh, she'd started to grow angry. She checked her phone every other minute, it seemed, just to make sure no one from the Glover family had texted. The only person who did message her was Bethany Rose, and she'd taken to asking about Ace every single day.

She wasn't helping, and Holly Ann had the very real desire to pack her own bag and skip town.

The next day, she met with her committee that had been by her side every step of the way for the Christmas Festival. They had a ton to go over and finalize for the last event they'd be responsible for—the New Year's Eve light parade.

To make things easier and to push them all through one

more event, Holly Ann had stayed up late last night making buttermilk bars. She laid them out on the table in the meeting room on the second floor at the mall, along with napkins and cups. She brought in the milk and juice she'd bought that morning, and she smiled as the crew started to arrive.

"Help yourself," she said, gesturing to the spread on the table. "We have a lot to go over." She exhaled as she gathered her hair into a makeshift ponytail and secured it with an elastic from the middle of the table.

People chatted and ate, and Holly Ann moved to the front of the room to fiddle with the projector for her presentation. Ten minutes later, Rachel signaled to her from the end of the long table, and Holly Ann raised her hand to get everyone's attention.

"All right," she said, really laying on her Texan accent. "Let's settle down and get started." She tapped on her laptop track pad. "The light parade is being narrated by Kimberly and Aaron Jacobs this year."

She let the bomb drop, and a moment of silence passed while everyone absorbed the picture of the celebrity man-and-wife team who wrote and recorded the best country music in the country.

"What?" Jim yelled from two feet away.

"You're kidding," someone else said.

"Holly Ann, how did you get the Jacobs?"

She basked in the wonder and shock and delight coming from the committee. She gestured for them to keep telling her how amazing she was, laughing as the praise continued.

Once they'd mostly quieted down, Holly Ann indicated Rachel.

"Rachel's sister knows Kimberly, and she somehow got them to come. So it wasn't me at all." She grinned at Rachel, who she hoped would be the chairperson for the Christmas Festival next year.

At the same time, Holly Ann knew the City Council usually had the same person do it for several years before passing the torch to the next person. Holly Ann had been working with Craig Manchester for five years with him as the chairperson, and while she hadn't signed anything committing her to continuing her service for the festival, it was implied.

She did draw a salary from it, and she'd needed it this year, because if she dedicated over two months of her time to the festival, she couldn't build her catering as much.

The vision of Ace's handsome face floated through her mind, and she didn't think their relationship would survive another Christmas Festival with her as the chairperson. Their relationship hadn't survived this festival.

In fact, they had no relationship right now.

Frustration filled her, and she clicked to get to the next slide. It took a couple extra seconds to focus on what she needed to say next, and then she said, "We've got three new balloons this year, thanks to a generous donation from the Texas Rancher's Association. They'll lead the parade, along with the three we've already got."

She tapped and showed two of the new balloons that had arrived yesterday. "The first is a horse, which seems fitting. The second is a cactus, which I don't really understand, but it's really cute in the dark. Bright green, with pink lights for the blossoms."

Another tap, and the last balloon came up. "This one is a little boy with a dog. It's actually an extra-large balloon, so it's really expensive and beautiful." She gazed at the picture of the lit balloon, a smile filling her soul.

She continued through the slides, highlighting the big entries and why they were important. About halfway through, she wiped her brow of the thin sheen of sweat there and pulled off her sweatshirt.

Rachel took over for a few minutes to detail the mayor's car, which would drive down the parade route right in the middle of the shindig, and Holly Ann draped her sweatshirt over the back of her empty chair and took a drink from her water bottle.

She breathed, hating that giving a twenty-minute presentation about entrants in the light parade made her sweat. Perhaps that was the doughnut she'd consumed this morning, or the two she'd eaten moments before bed last night.

Rachel finished her presentation about the mayor and his Southern belle wife, and Holly Ann took her place at the front of the room again. She went through another slide, knowing she needed to wrap it up quickly. The buttermilk bars on the table weren't the only glazed things in the room, and a few seats away, Christina actually nodded off for a moment.

"Okay, so let's skip ahead to refreshments." She'd been planning a hot chocolate bar for the entire town for the past month, and she knew she could get some good business from it.

Before she could say anything, though, her phone rang on the table in front of her. Ward's name sat on it, and everything inside her body stopped. Her heart. Her mind. Her breathing.

Only the shrill, old-fashioned ring penetrated her awareness, and she leapt toward the device. "Ward," she said, realizing she still stood in front of her whole committee.

"Ace is back," he said. "He's currently in the shower. I just got home for lunch, and he was here."

"Thank you," Holly Ann said, her mind racing now. She hung up and started for the exit. "I'm so sorry," she called over her shoulder. "I have to go. Rachel?" She didn't even wait for her second-in-command to confirm before she broke into a jog and left the conference room.

Her name got called behind her, but she couldn't slow down.

Ace had returned.

The late December air nipped at her bare arms as she left the mall, and it wasn't any warmer in her car, as the day had been clouded and windy since dawn. She drove to Shiloh Ridge Ranch as fast as she could, not even glancing down at her speedometer. She wasn't sure what she'd say when she got there, and she wished she'd had the foresight to grab her sweatshirt. Or her jacket.

Or a buttermilk bar.

She groaned. "Ace would've loved those buttermilk bars," she said. As it was, she had nothing. No speech prepared. No peace offering. She hadn't even put on makeup that morning and she currently had office supplies holding back her hair.

She reached up and pulled the elastic from her hair, using

the rearview mirror to check the state of it. Horrendous. Her hair hung in dark, limp strings, and honestly, it would be better back in the ponytail.

After coming to a stop in front of Bull House, she grabbed the rubber band again and scraped her hair back into its ponytail. She got out of her car and looked down at her clothes. Plain blue jeans and a pale pink tank top that held a stain from the apple juice she'd dripped on it at some time in the past.

Nothing felt right about this outfit, and Holly Ann's heart zipped through her whole body. It wasn't a pounding beat or a fluttering beat. It felt like a buzz, like it was thumping so fast that it created a steady stream of noise.

She wiped her hands down her jeans, noting the multiple cars in front of the house. She wasn't the only one excited Ace was back. She felt like she might throw up, and she steadied herself against the hood of the car.

Because of her father, Holly Ann could see the slightest flutter of curtains in a window, and someone was definitely standing there, watching. The buzz in her veins increased to a chainsaw-like hum, and she told herself to take a step.

Just one step. If she could just get started, she could get through this. She could finish it.

Focusing on the front door, which had been painted a bright red since the last time she'd been here, Holly Ann gathered her courage. "Super festive," she muttered to herself, and that red door increased her bravery.

She took the first step.

Before she knew it, she'd arrived on the porch, and she'd raised her hand to knock. The door opened a moment later, and Ida stood there. "Holly Ann," she said, stepping right into her and hugging her as if they were old friends.

Holly Ann held onto Ace's sister and drew from her strength. Behind her, the foyer expanded into the living room, and then the kitchen and dining room at the back of the large house.

All of Ace's siblings were there, as were Cactus and Bishop. Ward had obviously called them all, and obviously before her.

She couldn't see Ward, though, and Ace himself wasn't in the room either.

"Ward's been stalling him," Ida explained as she stepped back and turned to face the other Glovers too. "Until you got here."

Holly Ann looked at her, shock flowing through her veins. "Why?"

Ida hooked her arm through Holly Ann's. "This is what we do, Holly Ann. We're loud, and messy, and we say things that hurt each other. We do things wrong, and we try to fix them. We're in each other's business all the time —like *all* the time—and I guess Ward wanted to make sure you knew that's what you really wanted when you say you want Ace."

Holly Ann had no idea what to say, because there were a lot of Glovers up here at this ranch. They were loud, and messy, and they loved each other with big hearts. They weren't perfect, but Holly Ann certainly wasn't either. Her father had security cameras on his own driveway so he'd know the moment Holly Ann pulled in, for crying out loud. If she wanted two seconds to herself before she went in to deal with her own loud, messy family, she better take them before she pulled in the driveway.

"I've had someone in my business my whole life," she said. "Two people, actually."

"There are a lot more than two of us here," Ida said, passing her to Etta, who also hugged her. How they could just drop everything to be here in the middle of the day astounded her. She and Ace hadn't talked about too many serious things yet, though they had mentioned children in the past, as well as where Ace would live up here on the ranch. Oh, and all of Ace's money.

They also all wore concern on their faces, and Holly Ann's anxiety fired on all cylinders. "What's going on?" she asked, glancing around. She hated towering above the twins, and she stepped closer to Bishop.

"Ace left the ranch," he said.

"Yeah," Holly Ann said. "That's what Judge told me."

Ranger rose to his feet from the dining room table, his eyes serious and his chin down, his cowboy hat concealing his face. He looked up, and he said, "He's never left the ranch before."

"Ever?"

"Ever."

Holly Ann looked around, unsure of what this all meant. But it felt serious. "Because of me?"

"Because he stood in the homestead and raged out all of our secrets," Ranger said. "And he was embarrassed and needed some time to himself."

"We don't get much of that around here," Cactus said. "That's for sure."

Holly Ann's vision turned white. *Raged out all of our secrets.* Had he told them that she dressed up as Santa Claus?

Looking around at all of the people in the living room and kitchen, she couldn't tell if they knew or not.

Before she could flee, voices came down the hall, and one struck her right inside her heart. She loved that voice. She loved the man who owned it. She loved him more than dressing like Santa and holding children on her lap.

"...just saying I'm hungry, and you're driving me crazy already. I'm thinking of going back to New Orleans just to get away—" He cut off as he entered the kitchen. He scanned the area, his eyes skipping over Holly Ann completely and returning to Ward. "You called everyone? But you couldn't call for pizza? Why is there no pizza here, Ward?"

"I didn't have time," Ward said crisply. "There were a lot of calls to make."

Ace gestured to the room again. "Clearly."

Holly Ann pressed her hands together, thinking maybe she could simply get lost in the crowd. Ace was not in a good mood, and she didn't think he'd appreciate her being there.

"I got something better than pizza," Ward said. "If you'd take two seconds to look."

Holly Ann felt every eye zero in on her, but she couldn't look anywhere but at Ace. He turned to face the room again, a dark storm raging across his handsome features. He didn't have his cowboy hat on, and his dark hair was damp as it fell across his forehead. She wanted to brush it away and kiss him, but he hadn't even seen her yet.

He wore a pair of black jeans and a faded gray T-shirt

with the words *Don't Mess With Texas* across the front in what had probably been black lettering at some time in the past.

His eyes met hers, and everything cleared from his face.

"Finally," someone nearby Holly Ann muttered, but she didn't know who. It didn't matter who. The world had narrowed to just the two of them, and Holly Ann stepped forward. One step, then two.

Before she knew it, she arrived in front of Ace and ran her fingers up the sides of his face. "Hey," she said, the words of her heart streaming through her now. "I know you said you wanted time and space, and I'm fine to give you more if you need them. Wait." She smiled at him, a light giggle coming from her mouth.

"No, I'm not. I'm not fine to let you break up with me. I don't want to break up. You drove to my house once and refused to let me put us on pause. This is me doing the same thing."

He hadn't shaved in several days, and his facial hair was soft beneath her fingertips. She looked at his mouth, quickly pulling her gaze away and clearing her throat. "I love you, Ace Glover," she said. "I love you more than my caramel chocolate brownies. I love you more than Three Cakes. I love you more than Sa—Christmas." Tears filled her eyes as she searched his face, trying to read the emotions in his expression.

"I won't keep any more secrets from you," she whispered. "Please forgive me. Let me explain a little more. Sit with me and stay with me, and please don't give up on us."

Holly Ann closed her eyes and leaned her forehead against his. "Please."

A few moments of silence passed, and then Ace whispered, "Well, that was pretty dang perfect, and anything I say now is going to sound lame."

Holly Ann giggled, the sound bursting from her with an airy beginning. "All you have to do is say yes, that you'll forgive me, and then I can kiss you."

"Mm." His arms came around her, and that was as good as a yes for Holly Ann. Her body warmed, notwithstanding the audience they had, and she swayed with him. "I don't think that's going to happen. *I'm* going to kiss *you*, Holly Ann."

"So that's a yes?"

Instead of answering verbally, Ace leaned down and kissed her. A round of applause and loud cheering filled Bull House, complete with an ear-splitting whistle that came from only a couple of feet away.

Holly Ann broke the kiss, laughing but also flinching away from Ranger and that whistle. She cuddled into Ace's chest as he laughed too. Then he swatted Ward in the chest and told him he should've warned him. Ward just grinned at him with the widest smile Holly Ann had ever seen on the man's face.

She stepped away from Ace and into Ward's arms. "Oh," he said.

"Thank you," she said right in his ear. "I had no plan, and...thank you."

"You're enough, Holly Ann. He doesn't need anything else."

Holly Ann settled flat on her feet again. "Actually, I think I heard the man say he was hungry."

Behind her, someone knocked—more like pounded—and she turned toward the front door. A moment later, Bear entered carrying no less than six pizza boxes. "Pizza's here," he called, and Holly Ann turned back to Ward, her eyes wide.

"I made a *lot* of calls," he said, grinning.

He hugged Ace too, and then went to get plates out of the cupboard as Bear spread food across the countertop.

Holly Ann stepped back to Ace's side and put her hand in his. She looked at him, and while they still had a lot to talk about, she figured he should get some food in him first.

Chapter Thirty-Two

Ace loved his family with the power of gravity. He ate almost half of the frosted cinnamon pizza Bear had brought, and he didn't feel bad about it like he had in the past.

He'd been gone for only five days, but it felt like a lot longer than that. He and Preacher had enjoyed themselves in New Orleans, and he'd miss the beignets, that was for sure.

He glanced over at Holly Ann. She could most likely make beignets for him every day of the week, and he couldn't wait to be alone with her. He had so much more to say, including the three words she'd said to him several times. He wanted to listen to her explanations, and he wanted to run his hands through her silky hair while he kissed her without his entire family watching.

They needed more time to talk, to work out the finer details of how they'd merge their lives, and to make sure they had the same goals moving forward.

When most of the boxes were empty, Ace stood up. "Thanks for the pizza, Bear," he said, picking up Holly Ann's paper plate too. He took them both to the garbage can and moved back over to her. Leaning down, he put his mouth right against her ear and said, "I'm getting my jacket and my boots. Wanna go for a walk with me?"

She tilted her head, exposing more of her neck, and his pulse pounded through his whole body. "I sort of ran out of a meeting without my jacket or sweatshirt."

"I'll get you something." With that, he hurried away from the fray in the kitchen, only slightly worried about leaving Holly Ann there with them. She'd obviously integrated into the Glovers at some point, and Ace sure did like that.

He pulled on a clean pair of cowboy boots, grabbed a hat from his closet, and pulled a hooded sweatshirt from a hanger. Back in the kitchen, Holly Ann had stood, and he handed her the hoodie. He collected his jacket from the front closet, and he stepped out of the house amidst a couple of jeers and a few catcalls.

With the door closed, he finally found the silence he loved about Shiloh Ridge Ranch. A sigh pulled through his whole body and exhaled out of his mouth. He looked at Holly Ann, who'd zipped up his hoodie and tucked her hands in the front of it.

He put his arm around her shoulders, and she curled into his chest. "First," he said. "Before we even go, I have to say something."

"Okay." Her arms around his back felt so good. So much better than anything he'd experienced before, and they'd shared some pretty passionate kisses. This felt like her hanging onto him, claiming him, and he sure did enjoy the feeling of belonging and acceptance that came with her touch.

"I love you, Holly Ann," he said, the words filling him with joy as they left his mouth. "I've loved you for a long time, it feels like, and I apologize for breaking up with you prematurely."

She tipped her head up to meet his eyes, hers wide with surprise. He kissed her, this time without anyone watching and with the kind of passion and precision he wanted to. She kissed him back, those glorious hands sliding up his arms to his shoulders and then back to his face.

"I love you," he whispered, pulling away for a moment to get the words out. He kissed her again, his fingers working the rubber band out of her hair so he could rake his fingers through it.

"I love you," he said again as he broke that kiss and moved his lips across her jaw and down her neck. She sighed into his touch, and heat filled Ace's head. With some difficulty, he gained control of himself and pulled away.

He felt like his face steamed in the winter air, and he cleared his throat as he took the first steps toward the edge of the porch.

"Where did you go?" she asked.

"New Orleans," he said. "Neither Preacher nor I had ever been, and we figured...." He shrugged. "It was pretty fun. We took a cemetery tour. We slept as late as we wanted. We ate all this delicious food."

Holly Ann remained silent, and Ace supposed she needed

a little explanation. "After I found out about your—found out you—"

"That I'm Santa Claus," she said.

Ace looked at her. "Yes. That."

"I'm going to explain about that."

He nodded and led them down the stairs to the sidewalk. "After I found out about that, I sort of went ballistic. I had all these secrets inside me, and I couldn't handle one more. I couldn't handle lying to anyone, because I knew how awful it was to be lied to."

"I'm so sorry," she said.

"I've already forgiven you," he said gently, walking with her past his sister's SUV. "I went back into the party and I told everyone's secrets."

"Ace."

"I know," he said miserably. Thankfully, it only lasted for a few moments, because he'd made his peace with what he'd done. He'd apologized, and he'd been forgiven by those he'd hurt. "I didn't tell yours, by the way. I can practically feel you wanting to know."

She visibly and emotionally relaxed, and Ace looked out over the ranch. Clouds hung low in the sky today, and he liked a melancholy day at Shiloh Ridge as much as a blue-sky-sunny day.

"Thank you, Ace."

"Tell me about it," he said.

"The Broadbents have been playing Santa here in Three Rivers for four generations," she began, and Ace listened as she talked about her father wearing the suit for so long. She told him it was her turn, and the secrecy of it had been so ingrained in her that she hadn't even told Bethany Rose.

"I bet that didn't go over well," Ace said.

"It was difficult," Holly Ann admitted. "So we're redoing how we keep the secret. Spouses and children can know."

"I don't suppose that extends to cousins and siblings of in-laws."

"No," she said with a wide smile. "I don't suppose it does." She paused next to the big, red hay barn. "I've never been on a tour of this ranch."

Her meaning clear, Ace grinned at her and pointed to the barn. "We keep hay in there. There's a big old loft just filled with the stuff. When I was a boy, I'd sneak up there in the afternoons when I was supposed to be watering horses, and I'd sleep. Daddy made us all get up at four-thirty to get chores done before school, and by three o'clock in the afternoon, I was wiped out."

"I'll bet," she said, grinning at him. "I stayed up until twelve-thirty last night making buttermilk bars for my meeting today."

"Mm, buttermilk bars," he said. "You're always bragging about those, but I've yet to taste one."

"I think there will be time," she said.

"Can you make beignets?" he asked.

She laughed, the sound filling his soul and the sky above. He wished he could collect it and listen to it later, after she'd left the ranch.

As she quieted, he said, "So, sweetheart, where do we go from here?"

"I don't know," she said slowly.

"Bishop and Montana are getting married in April," Ace said.

Holly Ann whipped her attention to him, and Ace knew April was out of the question for her.

"Okay," he said chuckling at the surprise in her pretty eyes. "April is out for us."

They stepped beyond the barn, and Ace's beloved fields spread before them. "Oh, wow," Holly Ann said.

"This is my playground," he said. "When Bear doesn't need me to look at a tractor or a combine, I'm out here." He paused on the edge of a hay field and looked over their land. "Cactus lives out there about a thirty-minute walk."

"Where are all the cows?" she asked.

Ace pointed north and south. "Both ends right now. We drive them up into the hills to the west in the summertime, and we keep them in the grass pastures on the ranch for a few months in the winter, for birthing season and to tag 'em, round 'em up for selling, all of that."

"Do you work with the cattle?"

"Tons," he said. "I manage all of the pastures, and work closely with Ward for the rotational ranching method we do here. If our beef are exclusively grass-fed, we can sell them for more."

"Fascinating." She gazed out across the fields and land. "Where would we live, Ace?" she asked.

"Once Arizona gets married," he said. "And Aunt Lois moves into the homestead after Bishop does, the Top Cottage will be open. It's a cozy little cottage—only three bedrooms. Two baths. It has a brand-new roof though, because it got ripped off in the tornadoes that came through town a couple of years ago."

He looked south, where the Top Cottage sat up the road past True Blue, which he couldn't see. "So we could live there. Bishop's also planning to build more houses for people who need them. He and Montana are working on theirs right now, so I'm not sure about the timeline."

Ace thought of Cactus, and he had a complete remodel and expansion happening too. Then Ace remembered how much money he had in this bank account, and he could hire a company to come build him a house. He just needed approval from the family on the location.

"You wouldn't want to live in town?"

Ace looked at Holly Ann. "I...I have not actually considered that, honestly."

"I'm okay with living up here," she said breezily. "It's beautiful here."

He turned her south, and they walked along a footpath that would take them over to the chicken coops, calving stalls, and the long rows of stables.

After several steps, Ace asked, "What about kids, love?" He glanced at her and continued with, "I saw you with those kids on your lap at the mall. I know you were behind the beard and the hat and the colored contacts, but I *saw* you."

She nodded, but she didn't commit to anything.

"This land has a way of pulling you in," he said quietly. "Even though I enjoyed New Orleans, I couldn't wait to get back here. There's nowhere like Texas, and nowhere like the Panhandle, and absolutely nowhere like Shiloh Ridge Ranch." He took a deep breath and felt himself settle back into who he truly was. "It tugs you under gently, until your roots are long and deep, and you absolutely belong here."

"I can feel it already," she murmured.

"You'd be a wonderful mother," he said. "It's not a deal-breaker for me either way, Holly Ann. I'd love kids with your beautiful eyes, and my love of the land, and your skill in the kitchen."

She grinned at him. "You know kids are their own people too, right? They're not just copies of their parents."

"Yeah," he said with a sigh, still thinking of a little girl that looked like her. "I know."

"There's just one more thing I need to know about," Holly Ann said. "And that's how much money you make working in your beloved fields."

"Oh." Ace looked up at the clouds as a clap of thunder filled the sky. "The thing is…the ranch is really profitable. We do all these investments—and have for years—and have a family motto of reuse, repair, and recycle. We don't spend money we don't need to, and we save and invest. So." He cleared his throat. "I've got money. The ranch has money."

"Sounds like a lot."

"Why do you think that?"

"You won't say how much."

Ace approached the corner of the first stable. He paused and took her into his arms. "Does it matter to you?"

"Not particularly," she said. "I'm just trying to get a picture of our life together." She put her hands on the collar of his jacket and straightened it. "And to be perfectly trans-parent, I am in love with you, but I'd love some time for the two of us to date and get to know each other better without any secrets, any half-truths, and absolutely no trace of Christmas."

"That sounds like heaven," he whispered.

"What about an autumn wedding?" she asked.

"Is that a proposal?" he teased.

"Heavens, no." She laughed and got them moving along the path again. "You're doing that, Andrew. Don't you think for a moment you can pass that off to me."

Ace laughed at the use of his real name and the way she'd squeezed his hand a little tighter at the end of the sentence. "I'll think of something amazing," he said, pulling her into his side. "Long engagement or short?"

"I think you'll know when it's time," she said. "I want it to be a surprise."

"You got it." He had no idea how to propose to a woman like Holly Ann. He'd asked another woman to marry him in the past, but he'd literally asked her over dinner in a restaurant. He wanted this proposal to be something. To *mean* something.

You have time, he told himself.

"I know you're busy with the light parade," he said. "But how about we plan a fun date on New Year's Day?"

"Sure," she said. "What did you have in mind?"

"Honestly?"

"Yes, cowboy. Honestly." She bumped him with her hip. "We're not keeping secrets or telling half-truths to each other. Not again." She met his eye, hers filled with seriousness. "Right, Ace? Promise me we're not."

"We're not," he promised. "I was thinking we should go try some beignets together. Then you'll know exactly what I like, and you can start working on recreating them."

"You want to go to New Orleans on New Year's Day?"

"Sure," he said. "I know Marcy Walker has an airstrip, and I happen to have enough money to find a charter plane."

Holly Ann stopped walking and stared at him, her mouth dropping open. "You do?"

"I do," he said, grinning at her. "A chartered flight to New Orleans is basically a drop in the bucket for a cowboy billionaire."

Chapter Thirty-Three

Holly Ann stepped out of the fitting room, her dress stuck to her body like a second skin. At least Montana had chosen a good color for her bridesmaids' dresses, and the periwinkle fabric brought out the highlights in her hair. She could just see the color palate for her makeup, and she'd talk to Montana about it as they lunched.

She'd become close with Montana over the past couple of months, because Ace and Bishop were close as cousins. Everyone at Shiloh Ridge had been welcoming and kind—those she spoke with at least. There were some that Ace didn't seem to interact with as much, which meant she didn't either.

She didn't know Judge very well, and Arizona had practically disappeared as she planned her own wedding for the beginning of June. She'd be moving off the ranch, and her mother would be moving into the homestead in only three weeks, after Bishop and Montana tied the knot.

"Holly Ann," Sammy breathed. She wasn't trying on dresses today, because she was a week from her due date and wouldn't be wearing a periwinkle dress in the same size that she was now. She had a fitting in a month, and Shelley at Your Forever I-Do had promised she'd have Sammy's dress ready for the wedding.

"You look amazing." Sammy got to her feet and slid her hand down Holly Ann's side and hip. "How'd you get that on so fast?"

No one else had come out yet, and Holly Ann twisted and turned to see herself in the four-way mirror. "I'm really good at changing," she said, thinking of her ritual with the Santa suit. "This dress does amazing things for my chest."

"That's the new bra," her attendant said.

"Yes," Holly Ann said. "I need three of those."

"I'll see if we have them." Myra smiled at her and smoothed the wide strap into place on her back.

"I'm serious," Holly Ann said as Myra walked away. "If you have three in my size, I'll take them." She admired her curvy form in the mirror, and soon enough, Oakley joined her.

"Oakley," Sammy said, her voice full of air again. "How gorgeous are you?"

"Not as gorgeous as you." Oakley grinned at Sammy and reached one hand out. "Can I?"

"Of course."

Oakley put her hand lightly on Sammy's pregnant belly, and Holly Ann knew in that moment she wanted to be a mother. She wanted to carry a life inside her, and she wanted to experience the wonder of bringing a baby into the world.

She concealed her small smile and turned toward Aurora as the teen emerged from the dressing room. All the women exclaimed over her, including Holly Ann, who said, "Look how grown up you look, Rory. Wow."

"Ollie's not going to be able to contain himself."

"Oakley," Montana chastised.

"Sorry," Oakley said.

Sammy's eyes filled with tears as she stroked her hand down Aurora's hair. "You're beautiful."

"How are we feeling about the fittings, ladies?" Shelley asked, her clipboard in hand.

"Mine's too long in the body," Oakley said, lifting up a fistful of fabric. Shelley made a note while Oakley's attendant pulled things up and measured for exact inches and half-inches.

"Aurora needs a bit more up top," her attendant said, literally grabbing a handful of fabric that bunched around the teen's chest.

"We can put in a tuck," Shelley said, stepping over to the girl. "Or we can put in a breast enhancer, or we can put her in a molded cup bralette."

"Breast enhancer?" Montana and Aurora said at the same time, but their tones existed on opposite ends of the spectrum. Montana actually wore a horrified look on her face, while Aurora looked beyond hopeful.

"What does that entail?" Montana asked.

"We put in a couple of silicon inserts into the bralette." She glanced at Kris, the attendant. "We could do both. The bralette, and the inserts." She turned her attention back to

Aurora and pulled the fabric out. "It would be maybe a single size. There's not much extra room here."

She looked at Montana. "So we could tuck the fabric and alter the dress to the smaller size. Or we can leave the dress, and bring the extra size in the form of inserts and an undergarment."

"Mom," Aurora said, a clear note of pleading in her voice.

"How much is the bralette and the inserts?" she asked.

"I'll pay for them," Holly Ann said, regretting it the moment the sentence left her mouth. "I mean…if it's okay with your mom, Aurora. I'll pay for them." She met Montana's eyes in one of the mirrors, a silent apology passing from Holly Ann to her.

"Money's not really an issue, Montana," Oakley muttered. "If she wants them, let her have them."

"It's your wedding," Sammy said when Montana continued to hesitate.

"Oh, all right," Montana finally said. "Put her in the bralette and let's see what it looks like."

Aurora moved back into the dressing room, and Shelley turned her attention to Holly Ann. She grinned at her and made a single mark on her clipboard. "You look amazing in that dress." She scanned her from head to toe and back. "You should come model for us."

"Really?" Holly Ann asked. "You want plus-sized models?"

"Always," Shelley said. "This needs nothing, in my opinion. Where's Myra?"

"Right here," the woman said as she bustled up. "We had three of those bras, Holly Ann."

"Perfect," she said, smiling at her attendant.

"Myra, adjustments?" Shelley asked, and Myra scanned Holly Ann too.

"Nothing. This fits her like a glove. We should get her to come model for us. I know Henry's coming next Friday." She looked from Holly Ann to Shelley. "She could wear the new Alice Bunson, and it would look amazing with her coloring." Myra fingered Holly Ann's hair and looked at Shelley hopefully.

"I agree. Do we have the AB in her size?"

"Yes," Myra said.

Shelley turned her attention to Holly Ann. "Do you have an extra minute? We could put you in it now and make any alterations before next week. If you can come on Friday, that is."

Holly Ann would clear her schedule of anything to be there next Friday modeling some designer dress on her size-fourteen frame. "I can be here," she said.

"Great," Shelley said, and Myra hurried off to get the Alice Bunson gown.

HOURS LATER, HOLLY ANN CARRIED HER NEW ALICE Bunson wedding dress into her house and down the hall to her bedroom. She loved spending time with her friends, trying on dresses and going to lunch. They'd split up an hour ago, and she'd returned to Your Forever I-Do to purchase the dress she'd tried on earlier that day.

She'd have to take it back tomorrow to get a few minor alterations completed before the shoot next week, but she'd wanted to show it to Bethany Rose. Her sister should be here any minute, and Holly Ann kicked off her shoes and hung the dress in her closet, right next to the Santa suit that was tucked away in a nearly identical black garment bag.

Her phone chimed and the doorbell rang at the same time. Snickers barked and scampered down the hall.

"Oh, it's just me, you silly thing," Bethany Rose said.

"He needs to go out," Holly Ann called.

"All right," her sister called, and her footsteps went away from the hall leading to Holly Ann's bedroom. She stepped out of her jeans and shed her blouse, adjusted her new, amazing bra, and unzipped the bag holding her dress.

She took it off the hanger and eased into it, turning her back toward the doorway, so when her sister entered, she wouldn't be able to see the full beauty of the dress.

Bethany Rose's footsteps came closer, and then they stopped. "Holly Ann."

"Come help me with the zipper in the back." Holly Ann gathered her hair over her shoulder so Bethany Rose could access the zipper.

Her fingers held a chill as she lightly touched Holly Ann's back. "This is a wedding dress, Hols."

"I'm aware."

"I thought you weren't getting married until, and I quote, 'at least October.'"

"I'm not."

"It's not even March yet."

"I'm aware."

"Okay, you're annoying me." Bethany Rose finished with the dress, and Holly Ann put her hair back over her shoulder.

She pressed back into her sister, nudging her back until Holly Ann could see the full length of herself in the dress in the mirror.

A sense of wonder and stillness held her in place as she gazed at the dress.

"I see why you bought it," Bethany Rose finally said.

"Right?" Holly Ann asked. "It'll be perfect in October, or July, or April."

"When is Ace going to ask?"

"I don't know." Holly Ann smiled at herself in the mirror. "I told him I wanted it to be a surprise, *and* that I wanted time to date and fall even more in love with him."

"Yeah, that's why he took you to New Orleans and back in a single day and then flew in hot dogs from New York City just because you said you wanted to try one."

Holly Ann giggled with her sister. "He's something else," she said. "He didn't try this hard all of last year."

"He's not trying hard," Bethany Rose said. "He loves you, and now that he doesn't have to hide it, he's going to show you."

"I don't need him to show me," Holly Ann said. "I can feel it. He says it. I know it."

Bethany Rose rested her chin on Holly Ann's shoulder. "Daddy said he got an offer on the house today."

"Oh." Holly Ann wasn't sure why her mood had dampened. She'd known for a while that Daddy would sell the house and leave it.

"It's a good offer, he said, and he's going to take it."

Holly Ann nodded, and she drew in a deep breath as her doorbell rang again. She looked toward the open door, as did

Bethany Ann. Snickers yowled out a series of barks, all twenty pounds of him racing toward the front door.

"Holly Ann," Ace's voice came down the hall. "It's just me."

"Oh, my word," she hissed. "Get the door. He can't see this dress!"

Bethany Rose hurried over to the door and said, "I'll stall him. Can you—?"

"No, I can't get the zipper." Panic reared up inside Holly Ann, and Bethany slammed the door, shock on her face when she turned back. "What is he doing here?"

"He visits his mother on Thursdays," Holly Ann said. "He stops by in the evenings. I just forgot." This scenario seemed so familiar to one from a few months ago that Holly Ann had to giggle as her sister unzipped her wedding gown.

"Okay, you get out of this, and hurry up, because I'm not good with making stuff up about why you can't come out."

"Just tell him I'm changing. It's the truth," Holly Ann said, and Bethany Rose slipped out the door through the smallest opening possible.

She quickly pushed the dress off her hips and hung it back on the hanger. She zipped up the bag and pushed it against the one holding her Santa suit. She nudged the closet door closed and put her clothes back on. After taking a moment to fix her hair and press her lips together, she left the bedroom, glancing over her shoulder at the secret in the closet.

In the living room, Ace stood with Snickers in his arms while Bethany Rose stood in front of the fridge, both doors wide open.

"Hey, baby," she drawled, stepping over to her boyfriend and her dog.

"There you are." He grinned at her and kissed her quickly. "How was the shopping and the lunch?"

"Amazing," she said.

"Are we not going out?" he asked, nodding toward Bethany Rose.

"We are," she said. "Unless you want me to heat up some of that sausage and potato casserole from the Keller anniversary...."

"I have a special reservation tonight," Ace said with a bright glint in his eyes.

"You do?"

"Holly Ann," he said, his voice a bit frustrated. "It's your birthday this weekend."

"Yeah," she said. "On *Sunday*. Not today."

"We're celebrating all weekend," he said. "Starting today."

"I didn't know Thursday was part of the weekend."

"Well, now you do." He grinned at her and set Snickers on the floor. "It's right here in town."

"Great," she said. "I have that private dinner tomorrow night."

"Oh, I've heard about that," Ace said with a smile. "What did Cactus decide on for the main course?"

"He is impossible," Holly Ann said. "I told him he wasn't great at making decisions, and he just chuckled and asked me if I thought no one had told him that before." She rolled her eyes. "I mentioned it to Montana, and she nearly lost her mind. I guess he hadn't picked the plans for his house yet."

"So what are you making?"

"I want to do the spice-rubbed pork loin, so that's what I'm going to do. He said to surprise him, and I think that probably will."

"When you finish at his house, will you bring me the leftovers?" He took her into his arms, and she sure did enjoy the strength in his biceps and the ease with which he teased her and then kissed her.

"I'm still here," Bethany Rose said, and Holly Ann broke the kiss by ducking her head. She stepped away from Ace to walk her sister to the door, and they had an entire conversation with a single look.

"Call me later," Bethany Rose said.

"I will." Holly Ann waved to her sister and turned back to Ace, who stood there watching them.

"What am I missing?"

Holly Ann took a couple of slow, teasing steps toward him. "I may or may not have bought a dress today."

"Oh? I thought Montana was paying for the bridesmaids' dresses."

"It's a wedding dress," Holly Ann said, reaching him and tiptoeing her fingers up the front of his jacket.

His eyebrows went up farther, but he didn't ask another question.

"It's all-season, so I'm still in no hurry."

"Mm." He reached up and pushed his cowboy hat forward. "Do I get to see the dress?"

"No way, cowboy," she said. "That's bad luck."

He nodded, the hint of a smile barely showing beneath the brim of his cowboy hat. "All right. Should we go?"

"Yep." She turned back to the coat closet by the front

door and took out her jacket. Ace stepped over to her and helped her put it on, and she grabbed his lapels and drew him in for a kiss.

SUNDAY MORNING, HOLLY ANN WOKE, AND IN THAT FEW moments before she had to face the world as a thirty-eight-year-old, she felt a sense of peace and pure contentment. She loved the softness of the morning before the busyness of the day began, and she felt it a special gift from God that she could start each day this way.

She got up and picked up her phone, holding it as she stretched toward the wall to her left, then over to her right.

She already had texts, and she grinned at the one that had come in at twelve-oh-one. From Ace: *I better be the first one to wish you happy birthday. I set an alarm to send this text. I love you, and I hope this year is the best one for you yet.*

She smiled at her device and sent him a heart emoji.

Her phone rang in the next moment, and she swiped on the call from the sweetest boyfriend on the planet. "Hey, baby."

"Just reminding you that I'm bringing breakfast," he said. "I'm almost there."

Holly Ann scoffed even as warmth ran through her. "Reminding a person of something indicates that you've told them before."

"Yes, well, I suppose I'm just bringing you breakfast then, and I wanted to make sure you weren't walking around the house in your wedding dress or anything."

She laughed and said, "I just got up. I think I'm going to shower, but you can come in and get started."

"Will do."

Holly Ann did just what she said, and she dressed in her red and white polka dot dress for church. Just because it was her birthday didn't mean she and Ace wouldn't go hear a sermon. Besides, it was Willa's turn to preach, and Holly Ann really liked her talks.

When she walked out into the kitchen, the scent of maple syrup and sausage filled the air, and Ace's presence in the house reminded her of how much she loved him. He wore a white shirt, no tie yet, black slacks, and an apron over his clothes.

His cowboy hat sat on the end of the counter, his tie draped over it. So he was planning to go to church too.

She took in the tray of French toast on the counter, as well as the pan full of sausage links.

"Wow," she said. "Did you make this?"

He chuckled and shook his head. "No." He opened the microwave and took out a glass measuring cup of syrup. "This is the second time I've heated syrup. The first time it boiled all over. Then it was like, chunky, and your microwave was full of it." He peered inside the appliance. "I think I cleaned it all up."

Holly Ann giggled, and she shook her head. "You're really impossible in the kitchen."

"I've told you that a bunch of times," he said, grinning as he came around her island. "Have I told you today that I love you?"

"Yes," she said. "As a matter of fact. At twelve-oh-one this morning."

He shook his head, chuckling again as he took her into his arms. "I love you, Holly Ann."

"I love you too, Ace."

Instead of kissing her, he stepped over to the counter and picked up his tie and cowboy hat. He draped his tie around his neck and settled his hat onto his head. "Let's eat before this gets too much colder."

He put a plate in front of her. "I asked Ida what to do because you were in the shower, and she said to put the French toast in the oven. I didn't dare do that, because the last time I turned on an oven, I filled the house with smoke." He shrugged and gave her a coy smile. "So."

He moved around the counter and paused. "Oh, what's this?" He put his hand flat on the surface, and Holly Ann looked down to see a black velvet box sitting there.

She gasped, and somehow that removed all the air from her lungs. "Andrew," she said, her voice twice as high as normal.

He picked it up. "Maybe I should open it?" His eyes sparkled with pure delight, and he looked down at the box. He cracked it open and turned it toward her. He dropped to both knees and held up the box with the diamond ring in it. "Holly Ann Broadbent. I'm really bad in the kitchen. I sometimes say too much. I get excited over soils and crops and cattle. But I love you, and I will do everything in my power to make you happy every day of your life. Will you marry me?"

Holly Ann's eyes filled with tears and she clasped her

hands together in front of her, the sight of the man she loved holding up a diamond the best thing she'd ever seen. "yes," she whispered.

"I didn't quite hear you."

"Yes," she said louder. "Yes, yes, a million times yes." She got down on the floor with him, as she was so tall, and took his face in her hands again. She kissed him, this man who loved her and whom she loved.

He pulled away a few seconds later and slipped the ring on her finger. Their eyes met again, and they said, "I love you," together before she reached out to tuck his tie under his collar. She proceeded to knot it, her fingers working the silk into place.

"There," she said, looking at him.

Ace growled, his desire for her shining in his eyes and a grin curving his lips. Then he touched his mouth to hers again, and kissing her fiancé brought more joy to Holly Ann than she'd ever felt before.

She couldn't wait to marry Ace Glover, and she pulled away and asked, "Do we have to wait until October to get married?"

"You tell me when you want to say I-do, sweetheart, and I'll be there."

Read on for the first couple of chapters of the next book in the Shiloh Ridge Ranch in Three Rivers series, **THE HARMONY OF HOLLY**.

Sneak Peek! The Harmony of Holly
Chapter One:

C actus Glover put on his left blinker and turned into a cul-de-sac. The teenagers in the back seat had fallen silent a couple of minutes ago, and he wasn't sure what to make of that. He couldn't believe he'd allowed Aurora Martin and Oliver Walker to come along on this little expedition in the first place.

He glanced over at Lincoln, who sat in the front seat. The boy pointed up ahead. "It's that one on the left. The blue house."

"All right." Cactus pulled into the driveway of the appointed house, which stood two stories tall and could easily fit three of his houses inside. His brother, Bishop, and his fiancée, Montana, had started construction on the Edge Cabin. It would be another few months at least until the expansion and remodel finished, but Cactus had made peace with the dust.

Sort of. As much peace as Cactus could make with

anything, he'd made it with the constant film of dirt in his house.

He worked all the time, so at least he didn't have to be home with the hammering, sawing, and loud music Bishop liked to play while working on a project.

Their birthing season at Shiloh Ridge had extended into March this year, and Cactus frowned just thinking about it.

"You're still gonna get the dog, right?" Lincoln asked.

"Yes," Cactus said.

"We're just sittin' here," Link said.

"We're waitin' for Grandmother," Cactus said. He caught movement in his rearview mirror. A black truck eased in front of the blue house, kissing the curb as Cactus had taken the driveway. "There she is. Everyone out."

He opened his door and got out of the sedan he'd bought so he could take Willa Knowlton to dinner. Aurora and Ollie got out on his side, and the teens immediately locked hands again. He swallowed back the pinch in his chest, as well as his annoyance, and stepped down the driveway.

"Donald," he said, reaching to shake his mother's boyfriend's hand. "Mother." He gave her a quick kiss on the cheek, noting they reached for each other too. He turned away, telling himself that he'd see Willa soon. Hopefully.

He exhaled out and faced the white front door. "All right. Let's go check out these dogs." He reached for Lincoln so he'd have someone's hand to hold, even if it was a nine-year-old's. He also told himself he was thrilled his mother had found someone to spend good time with. Donald made her laugh and smile in a way Cactus hadn't seen for a while, and he'd spent so much time observing everyone in the Glover family, he felt like he would know.

"Jace says they're so cute," Link said, trying to dance ahead of Cactus. "Are you gonna get the gray one or the black one?" He looked up at Cactus, pure wonder in his wide eyes.

Cactus loved the boy with his whole heart, and he smiled at him. "I'm not sure yet," he said. "I want to see 'em both again."

"But we're taking them home today, right?" Link asked. "And you said I could sleep over, remember, Cactus? So I can help with the puppy."

"I remember," Cactus said, trying to keep the dryness out of his voice. Lincoln had asked him about fifty times if he could sleep over to help Cactus with his new puppy, as if he couldn't do it himself. Cactus had had a few dogs over the years, and he knew what to do with a pup, but he'd told Lincoln that of course he needed the boy's help.

Cactus was almost forty-four years old, and if he didn't have to take the dog out in the middle of the night, he was all for that.

Besides, Sammy and Bear—Lincoln's parents—were expecting their baby any day now, and Cactus had agreed to be in charge of the boy. He could feed a child and make sure he got his homework done. Lincoln loved to come out to the Edge and read to Cactus anyway, and he came almost every day as it was. Driving him to school would be the only thing Cactus wasn't currently doing that he'd have to add to his plate.

That task got him to town, and he'd asked Willa if she might be able to go to breakfast next week.

Since Christmas Eve, when he'd gotten his cousin's message and hurried to the barn because Willa was there, they'd been out a few times. Her schedule had changed, as she'd picked up her sermons again, and she'd taken a long-term substitute teaching job at the high school, leading all three choirs there.

Cactus had heard the woman sing, and she could take that position permanently and take the music department into the stratosphere. She possessed the voice of an angel, and her soprano voice melded well with his deep, bass tone.

He didn't always get to sit next to her in church, but when he did, he sure did like it. She let him hold her hand—at least until she had to sign to Mitchell. Her son.

Since she'd regained custody of him, Willa had grown exponentially busier. Cactus still had cattle to monitor, and then branding sat right around the corner. Then he'd spearhead the breeding at Shiloh Ridge, and after that, he'd have to administer all the antibiotics for the year before they drove their cattle out into the nearby hills and wilderness.

If Mother Nature kept the rain to a minimum, summer was actually his easiest time. He worked a lot once birthing season started, and from about November to May, he seriously wondered why he loved maintaining a healthy herd so much.

He reached the front door first, and he rang the doorbell. It warbled on the other side of the door, and more than one dog began to bark. He looked down at Link. "I'm not takin' one if they yap all the time." That was the last thing he needed.

"We can train 'im up real good," Link said. "Benny doesn't bark, because Bear trained him not to."

"Yes, well, I'm not Bear." Cactus had been living in his older brother's shadow forever, and he normally didn't mind. Bear wasn't perfect by any stretch of the imagination, but there were very few people or beasts who dared to defy him.

Cactus put on a spiny skin and barked out mean things to protect himself and keep others away, but he really had a heart of marshmallow. If he got a puppy and it wanted to bark, well, he'd probably let it.

The front door opened, and a little boy Lincoln's age stood there. He looked up at Cactus with wide, round eyes, and then he looked at Lincoln. "Heya, Link."

"Hi, Jace." Link let go of Cactus's hand and went inside the house. "Can we see the puppies? My uncle says he's not real sure which one he wants."

"Come in," Jace said. He turned and walked away, Link skipping along with him. Cactus stepped inside, everyone he'd brought with him filing in after him.

A woman wearing an apron over her clothes stepped out of the kitchen, drying her hands on a towel. She grinned at the crowd. "Hello, come in. You're here to see the puppies?"

"Cactus Glover," he said, reaching to shake her hand.

"Emily Butler. Come in."

"My mother," Cactus said. "Her boyfriend, Donald Parker." He let them shake hands, and then he introduced Aurora and Ollie.

"How many dogs are you thinking of getting?" Emily asked, tucking her short brown hair behind her ear.

"I'm considering one," Donald said. "I'm going to retire soon, and I need something to fill my time."

That was news to Cactus, but he said nothing.

"I honestly don't know," he said to Emily. "The kids are just along for the fun this afternoon."

"We've got three boys and two girls left," she said. "The multi-colored ones are taken, but we've got solid black and solid gray." She led them past the kitchen and into the back of the house, which was one big living room connected to the dining room.

A low fence kept the puppies in the living room, but they all crowded over by it, as Jace and Link already stood there, reaching in to pat them as they cooed at the pups.

"Come on, Cactus," Link said over his shoulder. "Come look at this one."

Cactus joined the boy at his side, and he had a gray puppy licking his hand. "He's so cute, Cactus. I like the gray ones better. You can see their faces."

"You sure can," Cactus said. He twisted back to Emily. "Can I pick them up?"

"Go ahead. Handle them. Get in there with them. We want you to pick the one you like best." She smiled and turned to Aurora as the girl asked her something.

Cactus bent and picked up the gray puppy. The animal was a beast already, easily weighing twenty pounds. The dog licked his face, and Cactus chuckled. Yes, this dog was cute. Cactus could easily see him coming to live out on the Edge, and he scrubbed the dog's back, his skin wrinkling up the way a mastiff's did.

"Look at this one," Link said, grunting. Cactus caught him trying to heft a black puppy up and over the gate, and thankfully, Donald stepped in and took the dog from Link's skinny arms.

"I think I like the black ones," he said to Lincoln, crouching down so Lincoln could get all the puppy's love without having to hold the animal. "You don't like them?"

"I like 'em," Link said, looking from the dog to Donald. "I just think you can see the eyes better on the gray ones."

"That's probably true." Donald cuddled the puppy and then lifted it over the gate again. He stepped inside and started interacting with all the puppies, but the one in Cactus's arms had settled right down. He rested his head against his chest, right above his heartbeat, and Cactus knew he'd be taking this dog home with him.

He stroked the canine, a perfect calmness filling him. He probably should've heeded Dr. Thompson's advice about getting a dog months ago, but he hadn't believed something as simple as a puppy could rid him of the anxiety and anger he'd carried for so long.

One of the pups kept barking, and Cactus would never pick him. Donald passed him by too, and Cactus turned to Mother. "What do you think?"

"I think that puppy has you wrapped around his paw already." She smiled at Cactus and patted his shoulder. "You're just going to get one?"

"I don't know." He slid the dog he held into his mother's arms and joined Donald in the pen. Several of the puppies came up to him, and Emily told him the ones with collars had already been claimed.

He wanted a dog that liked people, not the one that shied away from him and stayed in the corner. He didn't want one that was too aggressive, like the one who'd jumped up on him. Or one too vocal, like the one still crying at Donald's feet.

There were plenty of other choices, and he bent to pick up a black pup without a collar. This one went right for his face too, and he turned his head. He thought he'd like a pair, and he had the money. Two dogs weren't really more work than one, especially if he was taking them at the same time. He'd be going out anyway. He'd be feeding them anyway. He'd be leash training anyway.

"I like this one too," he said to Emily.

"That's Rosa," she said. "The gray one is Louis. You can name them whatever you want, of course. But you've got a black girl and a gray boy."

"I want them both," he said.

"And I want this one," Donald said, that black pup back in his arms.

Emily grinned at them and said, "Let me get the paperwork printed. You guys are ready to take them today?"

"Yes, yes, yes!" Link said, jumping up and down. Mother laughed and drew him away from his friend to pat the calm, gray dog she held. Cactus stepped out of the pen with the black dog, and he handed it to Ollie so he could sign paperwork and pay for his new puppies.

Back in the car, Aurora giggled in the back seat as the puppies kept climbing all over her and Ollie.

"You two okay back there?" he asked.

"Yes, sir," Ollie said, laughing with Aurora. "I'm going to ask my dad about getting a dog. These are *so* cute."

Cactus said nothing, but he hoped Tripp Walker wouldn't be too upset. If someone didn't have a dog, there was usually a reason why.

His phone rang, and Ranger's name came up on the screen. Cactus reached out and tapped the phone icon to connect the call, giving the car a moment to allow the sound to come through the speakers. "Hey, Range."

"Sammy and Bear just left the ranch. Her contractions are four and a half minutes apart, though they're not lasting a full minute. They want you and Link there."

Cactus's pulse went nuts, and he pulled to the side of the road, trying to think. "Okay," he said. "Do you need me to call anyone?"

"I'm putting it on the family text right now," Ranger said. "I just called you, because you have Link."

"Right." He started nodding, the landscape beyond the windshield blurring. He got thrown back almost twelve years, to the birth of his own son. This panic felt so familiar, and he pushed against it so he could think clearly.

"Ollie, can I drop you and Aurora at her place? Or yours?"

"Either," Ollie said.

"My mom will probably go to the hospital," Aurora said. "Should I just go with you?"

"If you want," Cactus said. "Oliver?"

"I can call my dad," he said. "But I'm sure I can come along."

"We have two puppies," Cactus said, his mind whirring.

Who could he call for help? He didn't have time to get back up to Shiloh Ridge and back to the hospital. Maybe he did. He didn't know how long it would take for Sammy to deliver.

Allison had been in labor for hours, and maybe he did have time to get to the Edge Cabin and back. He didn't want to leave the pups alone in the house. He could only imagine the nightmare he'd come home to.

He picked up his phone and tapped a couple of times. The line rang, and he started praying that Willa would answer.

"Cactus," she said, her voice bright and cheery. "I got your text. I just needed to look at the sub schedule first, but then Mitch wanted to make banana pancakes." She laughed lightly, and Cactus grinned at the sound of it.

"I have a favor to ask," he asked.

"Go for it."

"I just picked up two puppies, and Ranger just called to say Sammy went into labor. I've got Lincoln with me, and we need to get over to the hospital...." He let the sentence hang there.

"You want me to babysit your puppies," she said, her voice slightly less enthused now.

"That I do," he said, sighing. "It's fine. We could be hours at the hospital. I can take them to the ranch." He could leave them in the barn with the horses.

"You don't have time for that," she said. "I can take them, Cactus."

"You sure?"

"Of course." She sounded sure then. "We're just at home."

"I'll be there really soon," he said. "I'm only a few minutes away." Cactus eased back onto the road and made the next left turn. Only five minutes later, he turned into Willa's driveway.

She rose from the front porch, and Cactus couldn't help staring for a moment. She wore jeans and a red collared blouse with white polka dots on it. Her son stood too, and Lincoln said, "I wish I could play with Mitch." He looked at Cactus. "Do I have to come to the hospital?"

"Yes," Cactus said firmly. "Your mother is having the baby, Link. You can play with Mitch another day." He got out of the car and opened the back door.

Oliver got out with one puppy in his arms, and he handed it to Cactus. "I'll get the other one."

Cactus took the gray pup toward Willa, whose gorgeous hair called to him. He needed to touch it and slide his fingers through it as he kissed her. The past ten weeks had been a bit maddening to him, but he'd coached himself to be patient. Willa had several new things in her life right now, and she was juggling a lot.

"Look how adorable," Willa said, her smile bright and her eyes locked on Cactus's.

"I'm sure you're talking about the puppy," Cactus said with a grin.

"Maybe." Willa stepped right up to him and pressed her lips to his cheek, the wiggling dog between them.

Cactus's mind blanked, and had it not been for Oliver, he probably would've stayed staring at Willa, her touch burning through his face and down into his neck.

"You could probably put them in the back yard," he said, and that got Cactus to thaw.

"Yeah," he said. "They'll be fine back there."

"I know what to do with a puppy," Willa said, taking the black puppy from Oliver. "You can give that one to Mitch." She turned, and Mitchell stood right behind her.

Cactus swallowed, because he hadn't spent a lot of time with Mitchell. He was a year older than Lincoln, so they weren't in the same grade, though Bear had told him to take him to Willa's so the two boys could play together.

That'll give you a chance to see her, Bear had said.

Cactus had suggested it once, but Willa had said Mitch had not had a good day at school, and he'd never brought it up again. She hadn't either, and he wasn't sure what to do with that information.

He'd been learning and practicing sign language, and he shifted the puppy to his left arm so he could say hello.

Mitch's face burst into a grin, and he signed back.

Cactus could sign *dog* and he spelled out the name he'd chosen for this one. *T-a-n-k*. He raised his eyebrows, and Mitchell signed something that Cactus didn't get all of. He needed real, live practice, and he told himself he wasn't going to let Willa put so much distance between them for much longer.

He cocked his head and signed for Mitch to slow down. *I'm new and don't know everything.*

Mitch slowed down, and Cactus got the gist of the question. He shrugged and signed, *I don't know. I thought I'd only get one dog, but I got two. It's a girl. How about you think of a name for me, and when I get back, we'll talk about it?*

Mitchell's face lit up, and he reached for the gray puppy. He vocalized something, but since he'd been born deaf, he didn't know the sounds he made, and Cactus couldn't understand what he'd said.

He watched the boy head back toward the front porch, and his eyes lifted to Willa's. She stood at the bottom of the steps, a shocked look on her face.

"What?" he asked.

"You just signed with Mitch," she said.

Cactus pulled in a breath, but he didn't know what to say. So he just shrugged again. He signed, *I've learned a little. Call you later?*

She nodded, and Cactus turned away from her before he closed the distance between them and told her he'd go to any end of the earth to be with her, and that of course that included learning sign language so he could converse with her son.

Sneak Peek! The Harmony of Holly
Chapter Two:

W illa Knowlton watched her son take two dogs inside her house. That alone should've set her every nerve on fire, as those canines weren't potty trained at all, and her home had plenty of carpet to get ruined.

Not only that, but she didn't own the home, and her landlords had a way of popping by at the most inopportune times. In that moment, she remembered that dogs weren't allowed here, and that was why she'd homed Abe, her springer spaniel, with Patrick for the time being.

She'd had to move from the one-bedroom where Abe could live with her to this two-bedroom rental so Mitch would have a bedroom, and giving up a dog to gain a son had been well worth it.

Mitch giggled from inside the house, and Willa absolutely loved the sound of it. She'd missed her son terribly, and there had been countless nights where she'd laid awake, praying with everything she had that she'd see Mitchell again in this lifetime.

The Lord had answered her prayers, and she couldn't believe all that had happened in the past three months.

She turned back to the road as Cactus revved the engine and drove away. Her heart jumped over a couple of beats, reminding her of the sexy cowboy she'd seen signing to her son.

"Signing," she said, her voice quiet to her own ears. She'd shown up at the Glover family ranch on Christmas Eve, a ten-year-old child in tow, and Cactus had taken it all in stride.

"Right." She scoffed as she went up the steps and into the house. She needed to corral these puppies in the kitchen so if any accidents happened, she could easily wipe them up. She also needed to find a way to cage her thoughts about Cactus Glover.

She didn't think for a moment that he'd taken her reappearance in town with a deaf child in stride. The man held everything so tight—*so tight*—and he'd probably been lying awake at night too.

"Let's keep them in here," she said as she signed to Mitch. He sat on the floor as the puppies played with him and each other. He caught the end of her sign, and she repeated it so he'd bring the pups into the kitchen.

"You could also take them outside," she said. "The back yard is fenced."

I'll do that, Mitch said, and he pulled open the sliding door that led down four steps to the yard. Early March had brought more sunshine to the Texas Panhandle, but Willa still pulled on her jacket before she joined her son outside.

The sun wouldn't reach back here until afternoon, and Willa sat in the rocking chair on the small deck and pulled up her sermon on her phone. Pastor Summers had just talked to her and Patrick, and he'd be announcing his retirement in the next month or two.

She and her brother had been preaching on a regular schedule for about nine months now. She'd taken a break over the holidays, but she couldn't wait to share the responsibilities with only Patrick. Right now, she stood behind the mic about once a month, and she'd gone back to leading the choir.

It had been plenty because of her long-term substitute job, but that would end in another five weeks.

Willa read what her thoughts had been this week, as she never really taught from a script. She made notes all week about what came to her mind, what struck her, things that had happened, and somehow a message came from all of that.

She had another twenty-four hours to make it all come together, and she typed in a couple of things about being available to help a friend in need.

Out in the yard, one of the puppies yipped, and Willa glanced up to find Mitch rolling in the grass as the dog leapt over him. "He needs a dog," she said aloud to herself. That was one thing she loved about having a deaf child—she didn't have to censor the way she talked out loud to herself, something she'd done since childhood.

His birthday would come before summer, and she opened

a new note and started a list of things she might be able to give to him. She wasn't sure she could handle a puppy, but the animal shelter had to have adult dogs that needed a good home. She'd heard of some deaf people getting a hearing dog, and Willa wondered if such a thing was out of her reach.

Mitch had never been anything but a cheerful, happy child. Even when she'd woken up at the scene of the accident, with pain and panic pouring through her, she'd found Mitchell charming the EMTs who'd arrived while she'd been passed out.

She toed herself back and forth, using her good right leg, because teaching all day, every day, had really put a strain on her injured body. She front-loaded with painkillers at breakfast, and she took them when Patrick picked her up every afternoon too.

Her phone chimed, and she swiped on the message that popped up at the top of the screen. Martha Webster, her landlord, had said, *We have the doorbell light now. Can we come install it tomorrow?*

Sure, Willa responded. She didn't anticipate Mitch being home alone very often, but he could easily answer the door when someone came over. The child was very astute, and he responded well to vibration too. His alarm clock vibrated and flashed, and he never tried to stay in bed when he should be up and getting ready for school.

She knew that would all change in a few years when he hit his teens, and Willa couldn't wait. She'd missed enough of his life, and she didn't care if it was hard, easy, or in-between. She wanted to be there.

Her phone rang this time, and Willa grinned at Cactus's

name. His picture came up too, and it showed a long-haired cowboy she'd never seen before. The Cactus she knew had trim, neat hair and plenty of life in his deep, dark blue eyes.

She'd have to tell him he needed to update his profile picture, but right now, she just swiped up to connect the call. "Hey, stranger," she said, wondering if that counted as flirting or not.

He chuckled. "Would you believe me if I said I may have dropped my wallet at your place?"

She got to her feet and signaled to Mitch. He sat up and she signed quickly that she needed to run out front for a minute. "Stay here," she said as she signed.

"I can go look." Inside the house, she glanced at their breakfast dishes, deciding to ignore them for the day. "You were only here for a minute."

"It's not in my pocket," he said. "It's the only place I can think it would be. I paid for the puppies, and we got in the car. My cousin called about five minutes later, and I came to your house."

Willa reached the front door and went back outside. She held onto the railing as she went down the steps, a soft grunt coming from her mouth.

"How are you feeling?" Cactus asked.

"I'm a little tired," she admitted. "Teaching is hard work, and I'm on my feet all day long."

"I'll bet it is hard," he said. "You need one of those soaker tubs that athletes use."

She laughed, because such a thing was laughable. "Right," she said with a hint of sarcasm. "This house is bigger than my other one, but it's still only one bathroom. Surprisingly, it doesn't have a soaker tub."

Cactus chuckled too. "Listen, if it looks like Sammy isn't going to have this baby any time soon, I'll come get the dogs."

"Okay." Willa walked down the sidewalk, and sure enough, a brown leather wallet sat in the grass. "Your wallet is here."

"Perfect," he said, a measure of relief in his voice. "I'll come grab that from you at some point too."

"All right." Willa found she didn't want him to go. "How's Sammy doing?"

"They're not even here yet," he said with a sigh. "I should've just taken the dogs up to the ranch."

"It's fine," Willa said. "I'm happy to help, Cactus." She didn't mention that she technically couldn't have dogs here. And technically, she didn't. They weren't her dogs, and surely she could have friends come visit who owned dogs. "You should see Mitch. He's in heaven."

"He can come see them anytime," Cactus said. "Or I'll bring them down to him."

Willa made her way back to the steps with his wallet in hand. She sat down, groaning as she did. "You're learning to sign?"

"Yes, ma'am."

"How?"

"Believe it or not, I have the Internet up at the ranch." His voice held plenty of teasing, and Willa sure did like the sound of his voice in her ear. "How did you learn?"

Willa exhaled and remembered the day she'd learned Mitchell was deaf. "I took a class. A lot of classes."

"When did you find out Mitch was deaf?"

"When he was about three months old," she said. "I immediately started learning sign language, and as he grew and got older, I was able to teach him."

"That's amazing," he said. "You know what? I'm going to leave Link here with Aurora and Ollie and come get my wallet and dogs. Sammy's not going to have the baby in the next hour."

"Probably not," Willa said. "Most births take a little longer than that."

"Especially first babies," he said, and Willa heard something in his voice. Something that said he knew what he was talking about.

Before she could ask, he said, "I'm on my way, and I think I'm gonna stop at Meat, Pray, Eat. Do you guys want hamburgers for lunch?"

"Is the sky blue?" she asked with a laugh. "Anything without mushrooms for me," she said. "Mitch likes cheese and bacon on his. Nothing else."

"Nothing? No mayo? Ketchup?"

"Ketchup," she said.

"I'll be back in a few minutes." Cactus exuded confidence, and Willa did like that. She held her phone in her lap, the wallet on the step beside her, and waited for him to return. She didn't live that far from the hospital, but she decided to return to the back yard and Mitch. He didn't usually call if he needed help, though he did have working vocal cords. That was why listening to him laugh brought her such joy.

He still ran in the back yard, letting the puppies gallop after him, a smile on all of their faces. That made Willa smile, and the wattage of that only increased when she heard Cactus call, "Willa?"

"On the back porch," she called back to him, and a few moments later, she heard his footsteps. The sliding screen door screeched as it opened, and she looked over to him. Her pulse started acting erratically, and a man hadn't affected her like this for many, many years.

"Hey," he said gently, and she watched him lace so many things back where he wanted them. She wanted to unravel them one string at a time, and she wondered how hard she'd have to pull. What secrets she'd have to tell. What ghosts he had in his closets.

"Here's your wallet," she said with a smile.

He came closer and took it from her. "Thank you." He looked out to Mitch and the dogs. "Oh, he loves them."

"He really does," Willa said.

"Has he had a dog before?" Cactus asked, barely glancing at her again.

"No," she said.

"You had a dog. Abe. Where is he?" He turned toward her fully, curiosity in his expression.

"This rental doesn't allow pets," she said. "Patrick has Abe."

"Oh."

"You can sit if you want," she said, noticing the paper bags of food. "Or should we go inside?"

"Let's go inside," he said, nodding out to the yard. "How do you get his attention?"

"Stand at the top of the steps there and raise your hand. Wave a little. He'll see you."

Cactus moved over to the top of the steps leading from the deck to the yard and did what she said. Mitch did notice Cactus and came racing toward him. Cactus chuckled as the boy flew up the steps and into Cactus's arms.

He might be prickly with his siblings and cousins, but he was nothing but a softie when it came to kids. Just the fact that he'd had Lincoln, as well as Aurora and her boyfriend, with him to pick out his puppies spoke of that.

They'd probably asked if they could come, and he didn't have the heart to tell them no. Watching him laugh with her son as he held him made Willa's heart pinch. She realized what she'd been missing all this time, and she pressed her eyes closed and said a quick prayer that she and Cactus could find their way through the maze in front of them to a happy ending.

He looked her way, and Willa knew then that she'd have to go backward in order to move forward—and that she'd have to bring Cactus with her.

"Come on, boy," he said, looking right at Mitch. "I brought you a hamburger." He put the boy down and led him inside the house, whistling for the puppies to follow him.

And of course they did.

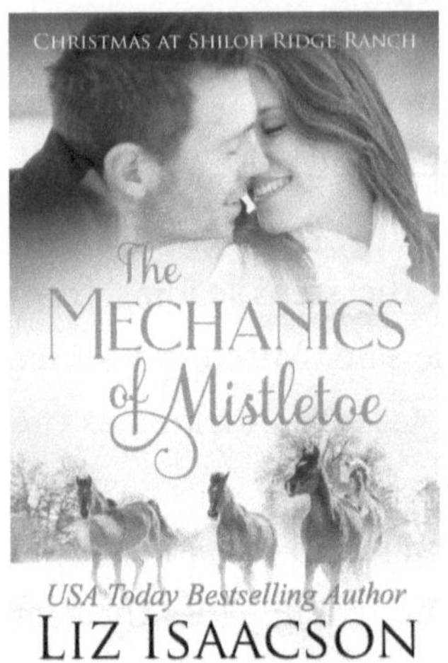

The Mechanics of Mistletoe (Book 1): Bear Glover can be a grizzly or a teddy, and he's always thought he'd be just fine working his generational family ranch and going back to the ancient homestead alone. But his crush on Samantha Benton won't go away. She's a genius with a wrench on Bear's tractors...and his heart. Can he tame his wild side and get the girl, or will he be left broken-hearted this Christmas season?

The Horsepower of the Holiday (Book 2): Ranger Glover has worked at Shiloh Ridge Ranch his entire life. The cowboys do everything from horseback there, but when he goes to town to trade in some trucks, somehow Oakley Hatch persuades him to take some ATVs back to the ranch. (Bear is NOT happy.)

She's a former race car driver who's got Ranger all revved up... Can he remember who he is and get Oakley to slow down enough to fall in love, or will there simply be too much horsepower in the holiday this year for a real relationship?

The Construction of Cheer (Book 3): Bishop Glover is the youngest brother, and he usually keeps his head down and gets the job done. When Montana Martin shows up at Shiloh Ridge Ranch looking for work, he finds himself inventing construction projects that need doing just to keep her coming around. (Again, Bear is NOT happy.) She wants to build her own construction firm, but she ends up carving a place for herself inside Bishop's heart. Can he convince her *he's* all she needs this Christmas season, or will her cheer rest solely on the success of her business?

The Secret of Santa (Book 4): He's a fun-loving cowboy with a heart of gold. She's the woman who keeps putting him on hold. Can Ace and Holly Ann make a relationship work this Christmas?

The Harmony of Holly (Book 5): He's as prickly as his name, but the new woman in town has caught his eye. Can Cactus shelve his temper and shed his cowboy hermit skin fast enough to make a relationship with Willa work?

The Chemistry of Christmas (Book 6): He's the black sheep of the family, and she's a chemist who understands formulas, not emotions. Can Preacher and Charlie take their quirks and turn them into a strong relationship this Christmas?

The Delivery of Decor (Book 7): When he falls, he falls hard and deep. She literally drives away from every relationship she's ever had. Can Ward somehow get Dot to stay this Christmas?

The Networking of the Nativity (Book 8): He's had a crush on her for years. She doesn't want to date until her daughter is out of the house. Will June take a change on Judge when the success of his Christmas light display depends on her networking abilities?

The Wrangling of the Wreath (Book 9): He's been so busy trying to find Miss Right. She's been right in front of him the whole time. This Christmas, can Mister and Libby take their relationship out of the best friend zone?

Rhett's Make-Believe Marriage (Book 1): She needs a husband to be credible as a matchmaker. He wants to help a neighbor. Will their fake marriage take them out of the friend zone?

Tripp's Trivial Tie (Book 2): She needs a husband to keep her son. He's wanted to take their relationship to the next level, but she's always pushing him away. Will their trivial tie take them all the way to happily-ever-after?

Liam's Invented I-Do (Book 3): She's desperate to save her ranch. He wants to help her any way he can. Will their invented I-Do open doors that have previously been closed and lead to a happily-ever-after for both of them?

Jeremiah's Bogus Bride (Book 4): He wants to prove to his brothers that he's not broken. She just wants him. Will a fake marriage heal him or push her further away?

Wyatt's Pretend Pledge (Book 5): To get her inheritance, she needs a husband. He's wanted to fly with her for ages. Can their pretend pledge turn into something real?

Skyler's Wanna-Be Wife (Book 6): She needs a new last name to stay in school. He's willing to help a fellow student. Can this wanna-be wife show the playboy that some things should be taken seriously?

Micah's Mock Matrimony (Book 7): They were just actors auditioning for a play. The marriage was just for the audition – until a clerical error results in a legal marriage. Can these two ex-lovers negotiate this new ground between them and achieve new roles in each other's lives?

Her Cowboy Billionaire Birthday Wish (Book 1): All the maid at Whiskey Mountain Lodge wants for her birthday is a handsome cowboy billionaire. And Colton can make that wish come true—if only he hadn't escaped to Coral Canyon after being left at the altar...

Her Cowboy Billionaire Butler (Book 2): She broke up with him to date another man...who broke her heart. He's a former CEO with nothing to do who can't get her out of his head. Can Wes and Bree find a way toward happily-ever-after at Whiskey Mountain Lodge?

Her Cowboy Billionaire Best Friend's Brother (Book 3): She's best friends with the single dad cowboy's brother and has watched two friends find love with the sexy new cowboys in town. When Gray Hammond comes to Whiskey Mountain Lodge with his son, will Elise finally get her own happily-ever-after with one of the Hammond brothers?

Her Cowboy Billionaire Beast (Book 4): A cowboy billionaire beast, his new manager, and the Christmas traditions that soften his heart and bring them together.

Her Cowboy Billionaire Bad Boy (Book 5): A cowboy billionaire cop who's a stickler for rules, the woman he pulls over when he's not even on duty, and the personal mandates he has to break to keep her in his life...

Her Cowboy Billionaire Best Friend (Book 1): Graham Whittaker returns to Coral Canyon a few days after Christmas—after the death of his father. He takes over the energy company his dad built from the ground up and buys a high-end lodge to live in—only a mile from the home of his once-best friend, Laney McAllister. They were best friends once, but Laney's always entertained feelings for him, and spending so much time with him while they make Christmas memories puts her heart in danger of getting broken again...

Her Cowboy Billionaire Boss (Book 2): Since the death of his wife a few years ago, Eli Whittaker has been running from one job to another, unable to find somewhere for him and his son to settle. Meg Palmer is Stockton's nanny, and she comes with her boss, Eli, to the lodge, her long-time crush on the man no different in Wyoming than it was on the beach. When she confesses her feelings for him and gets nothing in return, she's crushed, embarrassed, and unsure if she can stay in Coral Canyon for Christmas. Then Eli starts to show some feelings for her too...

Her Cowboy Billionaire Boyfriend (Book 3): Andrew Whittaker is the public face for the Whittaker Brothers' family energy company, and with his older brother's robot about to be announced, he needs a press secretary to help him get everything ready and tour the state to make the announcements. When he's hit by a protest sign being carried by the company's biggest opponent, Rebecca Collings, he learns with a few clicks that she has the background they need. He offers her the job of press secretary when she thought she was going to be arrested, and not only because the spark between them in so hot Andrew can't see straight.

Can Becca and Andrew work together and keep their relationship a secret? Or will hearts break in this classic romance retelling reminiscent of *Two Weeks Notice*?

Her Cowboy Billionaire Bodyguard (Book 4): Beau Whittaker has watched his brothers find love one by one, but every attempt he's made has ended in disaster. Lily Everett has been in the spotlight since childhood and has half a dozen platinum records with her two sisters. She's taking a break from the brutal music industry and hiding out in Wyoming while her ex-husband continues to cause trouble for her. When she hears of Beau Whittaker and what he offers his clients, she wants to meet him. Beau is instantly attracted to Lily, but he tried a relationship with his last client that left a scar that still hasn't healed...

Can Lily use the spirit of Christmas to discover what matters most? Will Beau open his heart to the possibility of love with someone so different from him?

Her Cowboy Billionaire Bull Rider (Book 5): Todd Christopherson has just retired from the professional rodeo circuit and returned to his hometown of Coral Canyon. Problem is, he's got no family there anymore, no land, and no job. Not that he needs a job--he's got plenty of money from his illustrious career riding bulls.

Then Todd gets thrown during a routine horseback ride up the canyon, and his only support as he recovers physically is the beautiful Violet Everett. She's no nurse, but she does the best she can for the handsome cowboy. **Will she lose her heart to the billionaire bull rider? Can Todd trust that God led him to Coral Canyon...and Vi?**

Her Cowboy Billionaire Bachelor (Book 6): Rose Everett isn't sure what to do with her life now that her country music career is on hold. After all, with both of her sisters in Coral Canyon, and one about to have a baby, they're not making albums anymore.

Liam Murphy has been working for Doctors Without Borders, but he's back in the US now, and looking to start a new clinic in Coral Canyon, where he spent his summers.

When Rose wins a date with Liam in a bachelor auction, their relationship blooms and grows quickly. **Can Liam and Rose find a solution to their problems that doesn't involve one of them leaving Coral Canyon with a broken heart?**

Her Cowboy Billionaire Blind Date (Book 7): Her sons want her to be happy, but she's too old to be set up on a blind date...isn't she?

Amanda Whittaker has been looking for a second chance at love since the death of her husband several years ago. Finley Barber is a cowboy in every sense of the word. Born and raised on a racehorse farm in Kentucky, he's since moved to Dog Valley and started his own breeding stable for champion horses. He hasn't dated in years, and everything about Amanda makes him nervous.

Will Amanda take the leap of faith required to be with Finn? Or will he become just another boyfriend who doesn't make the cut?

Her Cowboy Billionaire Best Man (Book 8): When Celia Abbott-Armstrong runs into a gorgeous cowboy at her best friend's wedding, she decides she's ready to start dating again.

But the cowboy is Zach Zuckerman, and the Zuckermans and Abbotts have been at war for generations.

Can Zach and Celia find a way to reconcile their family's differences so they can have a future together?

Second Chance Ranch: A Three Rivers Ranch Romance (Book 1): After his deployment, injured and discharged Major Squire Ackerman returns to Three Rivers Ranch, wanting to forgive Kelly for ignoring him a decade ago. He'd like to provide the stable life she needs, but with old wounds opening and a ranch on the brink of financial collapse, it will take patience and faith to make their second chance possible.

Third Time's the Charm: A Three Rivers Ranch Romance (Book 2): First Lieutenant Peter Marshall has a truckload of debt and no way to provide for a family, but Chelsea helps him see past all the obstacles, all the scars. With so many unknowns, can Pete and Chelsea develop the love, acceptance, and faith needed to find their happily ever after?

Fourth and Long: A Three Rivers Ranch Romance (Book 3): Commander Brett Murphy goes to Three Rivers Ranch to find some rest and relaxation with his Army buddies. Having his ex-wife show up with a seven-year-old she claims is his son is anything but the R&R he craves. Kate needs to make amends, and Brett needs to find forgiveness, but are they too late to find their happily ever after?

Fifth Generation Cowboy: A Three Rivers Ranch Romance (Book 4): Tom Lovell has watched his friends find their true happiness on Three Rivers Ranch, but everywhere he looks, he only sees friends. Rose Reyes has been bringing her daughter out to the ranch for equine therapy for months, but it doesn't seem to be working. Her challenges with Mari are just as frustrating as ever. Could Tom be exactly what Rose needs? Can he remove his friendship blinders and find love with someone who's been right in front of him all this time?

Sixth Street Love Affair: A Three Rivers Ranch Romance (Book 5): After losing his wife a few years back, Garth Ahlstrom thinks he's ready for a second chance at love. But Juliette Thompson has a secret that could destroy their budding relationship. Can they find the strength, patience, and faith to make things work?

The Seventh Sergeant: A Three Rivers Ranch Romance (Book 6): Life has finally started to settle down for Sergeant Reese Sanders after his devastating injury overseas. Discharged from the Army and now with a good job at Courage Reins, he's finally found happiness—until a horrific fall puts him right back where he was years ago: Injured and depressed.

Carly Watters, Reese's new veteran care coordinator, dislikes small towns almost as much as she loathes cowboys. But she finds herself faced with both when she gets assigned to Reese's case. Do they have the humility and faith to make their relationship more than professional?

Eight Second Ride: A Three Rivers Ranch Romance (Book 7): Ethan Greene loves his work at Three Rivers Ranch, but he can't seem to find the right woman to settle down with. When sassy yet vulnerable Brynn Bowman shows up at the ranch to recruit him back to the rodeo circuit, he takes a different approach with the barrel racing champion. His patience and newfound faith pay off when a friendship--and more--starts with Brynn. But she wants out of the rodeo circuit right when Ethan wants to rejoin. Can they find the path God wants them to take and still stay together?

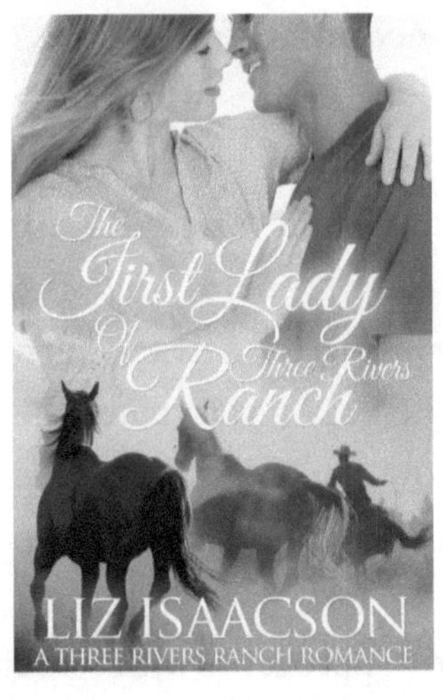

The First Lady of Three Rivers Ranch: A Three Rivers Ranch Romance (Book 8): Heidi Duffin has been dreaming about opening her own bakery since she was thirteen years old. She scrimped and saved for years to afford baking and pastry school in San Francisco. And now she only has one year left before she's a certified pastry chef. Frank Ackerman's father has recently retired, and he's taken over the largest cattle ranch in the Texas Panhandle. A horseman through and through, he's also nearing thirty-one and looking for someone to bring love and joy to a homestead that's been dominated by men for a decade. But when he convinces Heidi to come clean the cowboy cabins, she changes all that. But the siren's call of a bakery is still loud in Heidi's ears, even if she's also seeing a future with Frank. Can she rely on her faith in ways she's never had to before or will their relationship end when summer does?

Christmas in Three Rivers: A Three Rivers Ranch Romance (Book 9): Isn't Christmas the best time to fall in love? The cowboys of Three Rivers Ranch think so. Join four of them as they journey toward their path to happily ever after in four, all-new novellas in the Amazon #1 Bestselling Three Rivers Ranch Romance series.

THE NINTH INNING: The Christmas season has never felt like such a burden to boutique owner Andrea Larsen. But with Mama gone and the holidays upon her, Andy finds herself wishing she hadn't been so quick to judge her former boyfriend, cowboy Lawrence Collins. Well, Lawrence hasn't forgotten about Andy either, and he devises a plan to get her out to the ranch so they can reconnect. Do they have the faith and humility to patch things up and start a new relationship?

TEN DAYS IN TOWN: Sandy Keller is tired of the dating scene in Three Rivers. Though she owns the pancake house, she's looking for a fresh start, which means an escape from the town where she grew up. When her older brother's best friend, Tad Jorgensen, comes to town for the holidays, it is a balm to his weary soul. A helicopter tour guide who experienced a near-death experience, he's looking to start over too--but in Three Rivers. Can Sandy and Tad navigate their troubles to find the path God wants them to take--and discover true love--in only ten days?

ELEVEN YEAR REUNION: Pastry chef extraordinaire, Grace Lewis has moved to Three Rivers to help Heidi Ackerman open a bakery in Three Rivers. Grace relishes the idea of starting over in a town where no one knows about her failed cupcakery. She doesn't expect to run into her old high school boyfriend, Jonathan Carver. A carpenter working at Three Rivers Ranch, Jon's in town against his will. But with Grace now on the scene, Jon's thinking life in Three Rivers is suddenly looking up. But with her focus on baking and his disdain for small towns, can they make their eleven year reunion stick?

THE TWELFTH TOWN: Newscaster Taryn Tucker has had enough of life on-screen. She's bounced from town to town before arriving in Three Rivers, completely alone and completely anonymous--just the way she now likes it. She takes a job cleaning at Three Rivers Ranch, hoping for a chance to figure out who she is and where God wants her. When she meets happy-go-lucky cowhand Kenny Stockton, she doesn't expect sparks to fly. Kenny's always been "the best friend" for his female friends, but the pull between him and Taryn can't be denied. Will they have the courage and faith necessary to make their opposite worlds mesh?

Lucky Number Thirteen: A Three Rivers Ranch Romance (Book 10): Tanner Wolf, a rodeo champion ten times over, is excited to be riding in Three Rivers for the first time since he left his philandering ways and found religion. Seeing his old friends Ethan and Brynn is therapuetic--until a terrible accident lands him in the hospital. With his rodeo career over, Tanner thinks maybe he'll stay in town--and it's not just because his nurse, Summer Hamblin, is the prettiest woman he's ever met. But Summer's the queen of first dates, and as she looks for a way to make a relationship with the transient rodeo star work Summer's not sure she has the fortitude to go on a second date. Can they find love among the tragedy?

The Curse of February Fourteenth: A Three Rivers Ranch Romance (Book 11): Cal Hodgkins, cowboy veterinarian at Bowman's Breeds, isn't planning to meet anyone at the masked dance in small-town Three Rivers. He just wants to get his bachelor friends off his back and sit on the sidelines to drink his punch. But when he sees a woman dressed in gorgeous butterfly wings and cowgirl boots with blue stitching, he's smitten. Too bad she runs away from the dance before he can get her name, leaving only her boot behind...

Fifteen Minutes of Fame: A Three Rivers Ranch Romance (Book 12): Navy Richards is thirty-five years of tired—tired of dating the same men, working a demanding job, and getting her heart broken over and over again. Her aunt has always spoken highly of the matchmaker in Three Rivers, Texas, so she takes a six-month sabbatical from her high-stress job as a pediatric nurse, hops on a bus, and meets with the matchmaker. Then she meets Gavin Redd. He's handsome, he's hardworking, and he's a cowboy. But is he an Aquarius too? Navy's not making a move until she knows for sure...

Sixteen Steps to Fall in Love: A Three Rivers Ranch Romance (Book 13): A chance encounter at a dog park sheds new light on the tall, talented Boone that Nicole can't ignore. As they get to know each other better and start to dig into each other's past, Nicole is the one who wants to run. This time from her growing admiration and attachment to Boone. From her aging parents. From herself.

But Boone feels the attraction between them too, and he decides he's tired of running and ready to make Three Rivers his permanent home. **Can Boone and Nicole use their faith to overcome their differences and find a happily-ever-after together?**

The Sleigh on Seventeenth Street: A Three Rivers Ranch Romance (Book 14): A cowboy with skills as an electrician tries a relationship with a down-on-her luck plumber. Can Dylan and Camila make water and electricity play nicely together this Christmas season? Or will they get shocked as they try to make their relationship work?

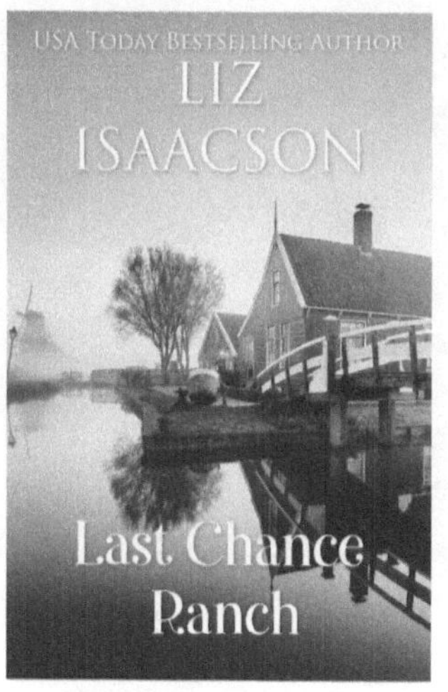

Last Chance Ranch (Book 1):
A cowgirl down on her luck hires a man who's good with horses and under the hood of a car. Can Hudson fine tune Scarlett's heart as they work together? Or will things backfire and make everything worse at Last Chance Ranch?

Last Chance Cowboy (Book 2): A billionaire cowboy without a home meets a woman who secretly makes food videos to pay her debts...Can Carson and Adele do more than fight in the kitchens at Last Chance Ranch?

Last Chance Wedding (Book 3): A female carpenter needs a husband just for a few days... Can Jeri and Sawyer navigate the minefield of a pretend marriage before their feelings become real?

Last Chance Reunion (Book 4): An Army cowboy, the woman he dated years ago, and their last chance at Last Chance Ranch... Can Dave and Sissy put aside hurt feelings and make their second chance romance work?

Last Chance Lake (Book 5): A former dairy farmer and the marketing director on the ranch have to work together to make the cow cuddling program a success. But can Karla let Cache into her life? Or will she keep all her secrets from him – and keep *him* a secret too?

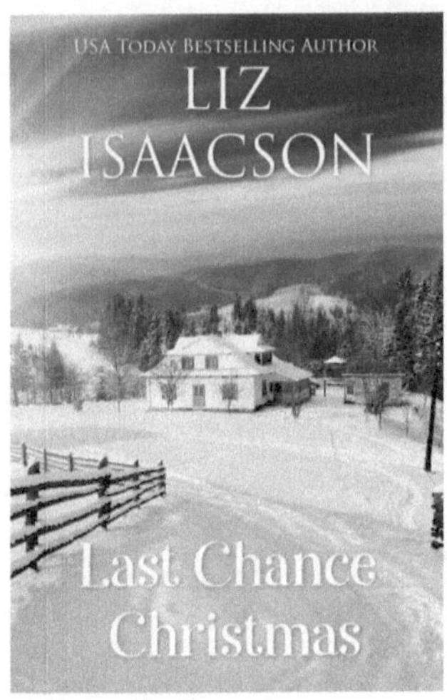

Last Chance Christmas (Book 6): She's tired of having her heart broken by cowboys. He waited too long to ask her out. Can Lance fix things quickly, or will Amber leave Last Chance Ranch before he can tell her how he feels?

Her Billionaire Cowboy (Book 1): Tucker Jenkins has had enough of tall buildings, traffic, and has traded in his technology firm in New York City for Steeple Ridge Horse Farm in rural Vermont. Missy Marino has worked at the farm since she was a teen, and she's always dreamed of owning it. But her ex-husband left her with a truckload of debt, making her fantasies of owning the farm unfulfilled. Tucker didn't come to the country to find a new wife, but he supposes a woman could help him start over in Steeple Ridge. Will Tucker and Missy be able to navigate the shaky ground between them to find a new beginning?

Her Restless Cowboy: A Butters Brothers Novel, Steeple Ridge Romance (Book 2): Ben Buttars is the youngest of the four Buttars brothers who come to Steeple Ridge Farm, and he finally feels like he's landed somewhere he can make a life for himself. Reagan Cantwell is a decade older than Ben and the recreational direction for the town of Island Park. Though Ben is young, he knows what he wants—and that's Rae. Can she figure out how to put what matters most in her life—family and faith—above her job before she loses Ben?

Her Faithful Cowboy: A Butters Brothers Novel, Steeple Ridge Romance (Book 3): Sam Buttars has spent the last decade making sure he and his brothers stay together. They've been at Steeple Ridge for a while now, but with the youngest married and happy, the siren's call to return to his parents' farm in Wyoming is loud in Sam's ears. He'd just go if it weren't for beautiful Bonnie Sherman, who roped his heart the first time he saw her. Do Sam and Bonnie have the faith to find comfort in each other instead of in the people who've already passed?

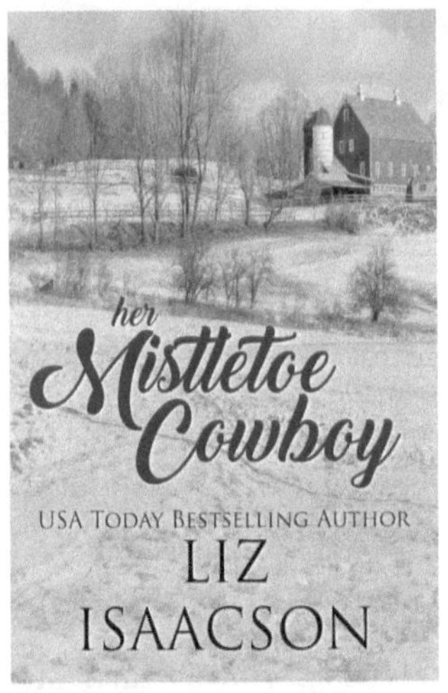 **Her Mistletoe Cowboy: A Butters Brothers Novel, Steeple Ridge Romance (Book 4):** Logan Buttars has always been good-natured and happy-go-lucky. After watching two of his brothers settle down, he recognizes a void in his life he didn't know about. Veterinarian Layla Guyman has appreciated Logan's friendship and easy way with animals when he comes into the clinic to get the service dogs. But with his future at Steeple Ridge in the balance, she's not sure a relationship with him is worth the risk. Can she rely on her faith and employ patience to tame Logan's wild heart?

Her Patient Cowboy: A Butters Brothers Novel, Steeple Ridge Romance (Book 5): Darren Buttars is cool, collected, and quiet—and utterly devastated when his girlfriend of nine months, Farrah Irvine, breaks up with him because he wanted her to ride her horse in a parade. But Farrah doesn't ride anymore, a fact she made very clear to Darren. She returned to her childhood home with so much baggage, she doesn't know where to start with the unpacking. Darren's the only Buttars brother who isn't married, and he wants to make Island Park his permanent home—with Farrah. Can they find their way through the heartache to achieve a happily-ever-after together?

Craving the Cowboy (Book 1): Dwayne Carver is set to inherit his family's ranch in the heart of Texas Hill Country, and in order to keep up with his ranch duties and fulfill his dreams of owning a horse farm, he hires top trainer Felicity Lightburne. They get along great, and she can envision herself on this new farm—at least until her mother falls ill and she has to return to help her. Can Dwayne and Felicity work through their differences to find their happily-ever-after?

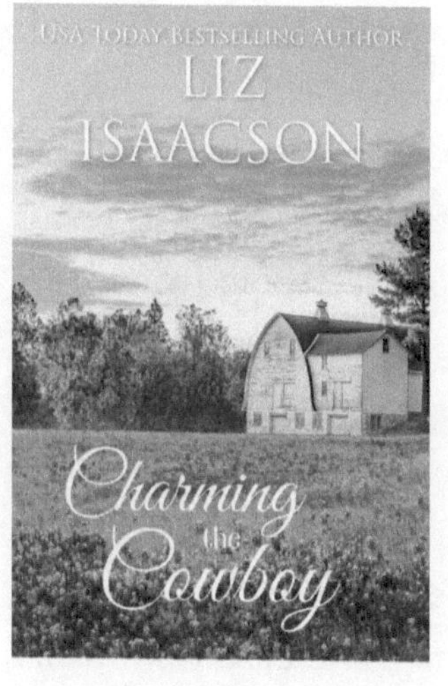

Charming the Cowboy (Book 2): Third grade teacher Heather Carver has had her eye on Levi Rhodes for a couple of years now, but he seems to be blind to her attempts to charm him. When she breaks her arm while on his horse ranch, Heather infiltrates Levi's life in ways he's never thought of, and his strict anti-female stance slips. Will Heather heal his emotional scars and he care for her physical ones so they can have a real relationship?

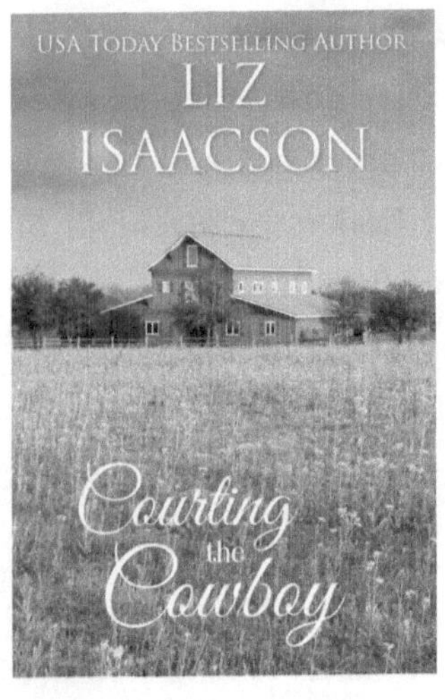

Courting the Cowboy (Book 3): Frustrated with the cowboy-only dating scene in Grape Seed Falls, May Sotheby joins Texas-Faithful.com, hoping to find her soul mate without having to relocate--or deal with cowboy hats and boots. She has no idea that Kurt Pemberton, foreman at Grape Seed Ranch, is the man she starts communicating with... Will May be able to follow her heart and get Kurt to forgive her so they can be together?

Claiming the Cowboy, Royal Brothers Book 1 (Grape Seed Falls Romance Book 4): Unwilling to be tied down, farrier Robin Cook has managed to pack her entire life into a two-hundred-and-eighty square-foot house, and that includes her Yorkie. Cowboy and co-foreman, Shane Royal has had his heart set on Robin for three years, even though she flat-out turned him down the last time he asked her to dinner. But she's back at Grape Seed Ranch for five weeks as she works her horseshoeing magic, and he's still interested, despite a bitter life lesson that left a bad taste for marriage in his mouth.

Robin's interested in him too. But can she find room for Shane in her tiny house--and can he take a chance on her with his tired heart?

Catching the Cowboy, Royal Brothers Book 2 (Grape Seed Falls Romance Book 5): Dylan Royal is good at two things: whistling and caring for cattle. When his cows are being attacked by an unknown wild animal, he calls Texas Parks & Wildlife for help. He wasn't expecting a beautiful mammologist to show up, all flirty and fun and everything Dylan didn't know he wanted in his life.

Hazel Brewster has gone on more first dates than anyone in Grape Seed Falls, and she thinks maybe Dylan deserves a second... Can they find their way through wild animals, huge life changes, and their emotional pasts to find their forever future?

Cheering the Cowboy, Royal Brothers Book 3 (Grape Seed Falls Romance Book 6): Austin Royal loves his life on his new ranch with his brothers. But he doesn't love that Shayleigh Hatch came with the property, nor that he has to take the blame for the fact that he now owns her childhood ranch. They rarely have a conversation that doesn't leave him furious and frustrated--and yet he's still attracted to Shay in a strange, new way.

Shay inexplicably likes him too, which utterly confuses and angers her. As they work to make this Christmas the best the Triple Towers Ranch has ever seen, can they also navigate through their rocky relationship to smoother waters?

The Redesigned Ranch (Book 1): Jace Lovell only has one thing left after his fiancé abandons him at the altar: his job at Horseshoe Home Ranch. Belle Edmunds is back in Gold Valley and she's desperate to build a portfolio that she can use to start her own firm in Montana. Jace isn't anywhere near forgiving his fiancé, and he's not sure he's ready for a new relationship with someone as fiery and beautiful as Belle. Can she employ her patience while he figures out how to forgive so they can find their own brand of happily-ever-after?

The Snowstorm in Gold Valley (Book 2): Professional snowboarder Sterling Maughan has sequestered himself in his family's cabin in the exclusive mountain community above Gold Valley, Montana after a devastating fall that ended his career. Norah Watson cleans Sterling's cabin and the more time they spend together, the more Sterling is interested in all things Norah. As his body heals, so does his faith. Will Norah be able to trust Sterling so they can have a chance at true love?

The Cabin on Bear Mountain (Book 3): Landon Edmunds has been a cowboy his whole life. An accident five years ago ended his successful rodeo career, and now he's looking to start a horse ranch--and he's looking outside of Montana. Which would be great if God hadn't brought Megan Palmer back to Gold Valley right when Landon is looking to leave.

Megan and Landon work together well, and as sparks fly, she's sure God brought her back to Gold Valley so she could find her happily ever after. Through serious discussion and prayer, can Landon and Megan find their future together?

Be sure to check out the spinoff series, the Brush Creek Brides romances after you read FALLING FOR HIS BEST FRIEND. Start with A WEDDING FOR THE WIDOWER.

The Cowboy at the Creek (Book 4): Twelve years ago, Owen Carr left Gold Valley—and his long-time girlfriend—in favor of a country music career in Nashville. Married and divorced, Natalie teaches ballet at the dance studio in Gold Valley, but she never auditioned for the professional company the way she dreamed of doing. With Owen back, she realizes all the opportunities she missed out on when he left all those years ago—including a future with him. Can they mend broken bridges in order to have a second chance at love?

The Wedding in the Winter (Book 5): Caleb Chamberlain has spent the last five years recovering from a horrible breakup, his alcoholism that stemmed from it, and the car accident that left him hospitalized. He's finally on the right track in his life—until Holly Gray, his twin brother's ex-fiance mistakes him for Nathan. Holly's back in Gold Valley to get the required veterinarian hours to apply for her graduate program. When the herd at Horseshoe Home comes down with pneumonia, Caleb and Holly are forced to work together in close quarters. Holly's over Nathan, but she hasn't forgiven him—or the woman she believes broke up their relationship. Can Caleb and Holly navigate such a rough past to find their happily-ever-after?

The Long Way Home (Book 6): Ty Barker has been dancing through the last thirty years of his life--and he's suddenly realized he's alone. River Lee Whitely is back in Gold Valley with her two little girls after a divorce that's left deep scars. She has a job at Silver Creek that requires her to be able to ride a horse, and she nearly tramples Ty at her first lesson. That's just fine by him, because River Lee is the girl Ty has never gotten over. Ty realizes River Lee needs time to settle into her new job, her new home, her new life as a single parent, but going slow has never been his style. But for River Lee, can Ty take the necessary steps to keep her in his life?

Christmas at the Ranch (Book 7): Archer Bailey has already lost one job to Emersyn Enders, so he deliberately doesn't tell her about the cowhand job up at Horseshoe Home Ranch. Emery's temporary job is ending, but her obligations to her physically disabled sister aren't. As Archer and Emery work together, its clear that the sparks flying between them aren't all from their friendly competition over a job. Will Emery and Archer be able to navigate the ranch, their close quarters, and their individual circumstances to find love this holiday season?

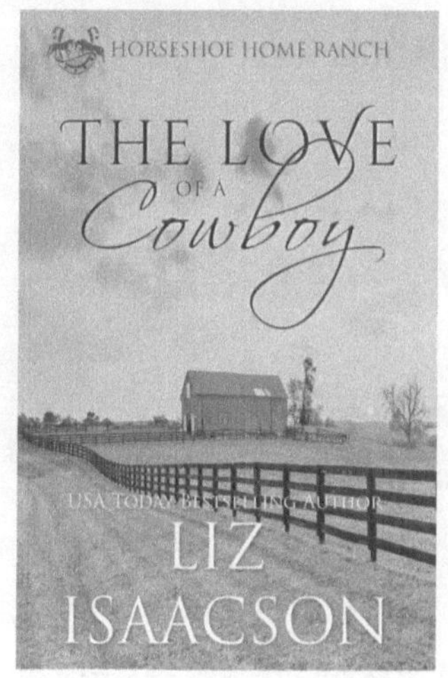

The Love of a Cowboy (Book 8): Cowboy Elliott Hawthorne has just lost his best friend and cabin mate to the worst thing imaginable—marriage. When his brother calls about an accident with their father, Elliott rushes down to Gold Valley from the ranch only to be met with the most beautiful woman he's ever seen. His father's new physical therapist, London Marsh, likes the handsome face and gentle spirit she sees in Elliott too. Can Elliott and London navigate difficult family situations to find a happily-ever-after?

Brush Creek Cowboy: Brush Creek Cowboys Romance (Book 1): Former rodeo champion and cowboy Walker Thompson trains horses at Brush Creek Horse Ranch, where he lives a simple life in his cabin with his ten-year-old son. A widower of six years, he's worked with Tess Wagner, a widow who came to Brush Creek to escape the turmoil of her life to give her seven-year-old son a slower pace of life. But Tess's breast cancer is back...

Walker will have to decide if he'd rather spend even a short time with Tess than not have her in his life at all. Tess wants to feel God's love and power, but can she discover and accept God's will in order to find her happy ending?

The Cowboy's Challenge: Brush Creek Brides Romance (Book 2): Cowboy and professional roper Justin Jackman has found solitude at Brush Creek Horse Ranch, preferring his time with the animals he trains over dating. With two failed engagements in his past, he's not really inter-ested in getting his heart stomped on again. But when flirty and fun Renee Martin picks him up at a church ice cream bar--on a bet, no less--he finds himself more than just a little interested. His Gen-X attitudes are attractive to her; her Millennial behaviors drive him nuts. Can Justin look past their differences and take a chance on another engagement?

A Cowboy Proposal: Brush Creek Brides Romance (Book 3): Ted Caldwell has been a retired bronc rider for years, and he thought he was perfectly happy training horses to buck at Brush Creek Ranch. He was wrong. When he meets April Nox, who comes to the ranch to hide her pregnancy from all her friends back in Jackson Hole, Ted realizes he has a huge family-shaped hole in his life. April is embarrassed, heartbroken, and trying to find her extinguished faith. She's never ridden a horse and wants nothing to do with a cowboy ever again. Can Ted and April create a family of happiness and love from a tragedy?

A New Family for the Cowboy: Brush Creek Brides Romance (Book 4): Blake Gibbons oversees all the agriculture at Brush Creek Horse Ranch, sometimes moonlighting as a general contractor. When he meets Erin Shields, new in town, at her aunt's bakery, he's instantly smitten. Erin moved to Brush Creek after a divorce that left her penniless, homeless, and a single mother of three children under age eight. She's nowhere near ready to start dating again, but the longer Blake hangs around the bakery, the more she starts to like him. Can Blake and Erin find a way to blend their lifestyles and become a family?

The Cowboy and the Champion: Brush Creek Brides Romance (Book 5): Emmett Graves has always had a positive outlook on life. He adores training horses to become barrel racing champions during the day and cuddling with his cat at night. Fresh off her professional rodeo retirement, Molly Brady comes to Brush Creek Horse Ranch as Emmett's protege. He's not thrilled, and she's allergic to cats. Oh, and she'd like to stay cowboy-free, thank you very much. But Emmett's about as cowboy as they come.... Can Emmett and Molly work together without falling in love?

Schooled by the Cowboy: Brush Creek Brides Romance (Book 6): Grant Ford spends his days training cattle—when he's not camped out at the elementary school hoping to catch a glimpse of his ex-girlfriend. When principal Shannon Sharpe confronts him and asks him to stay away from the school, the spark between them is instant and hot. Shan-

non's expecting a transfer very soon, but she also needs a summer outdoor coordinator—and Grant fits the bill. Just because he's handsome and everything Shannon's ever wanted in a cowboy husband means nothing. Will Grant and Shannon be able to survive the summer or will the Utah heat be too much for them to handle?

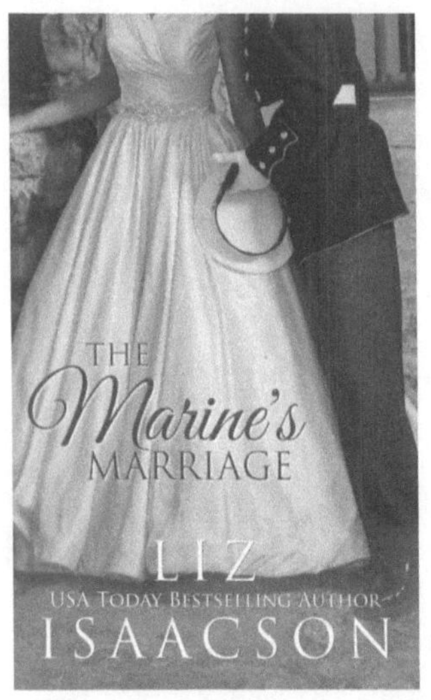

The Marine's Marriage: A Fuller Family Novel - Brush Creek Brides Romance (Book 1): Tate Benson can't believe he's come to Nowhere, Utah, to fix up a house that hasn't been inhabited in years. But he has. Because he's retired from the Marines and looking to start a life as a police officer in small-town Brush Creek. Wren Fuller has her hands full most days running her family's company. When Tate calls and demands a maid for that morning, she decides to have the calls forwarded to her cell and go help him out. She didn't know he was moving in next door, and she's completely unprepared for his handsomeness, his kind heart, and his wounded soul.Can Tate and Wren weather a relationship when they're also next-door neighbors?

The Firefighter's Fiancé: A Fuller Family Novel - Brush Creek Brides Romance (Book 2): Cora Wesley comes to Brush Creek, hoping to get some in-the-wild firefighting training as she prepares to put in her application to be a hotshot. When she meets Brennan Fuller, the spark between them is hot and instant. As they get to know each other, her deadline is  constantly looming over them, and Brennan starts to wonder if he can break ranks in the family business. He's okay mowing lawns and hanging out with his brothers, but he dreams of being able to go to college and become a landscape architect, but he's just not sure it can be done. Will Cora and Brennan be able to endure their trials to find true love?

The Trooper's Treasure: A Fuller Family Novel - Brush Creek Brides Romance (Book 3): Dawn Fuller has made some mistakes in her life, and she's not proud of the way McDermott Boyd found her off the road one day last year. She's spent a hard year wrestling with her choices and trying to fix them, glad for McDermott's acceptance and friendship. He lost his wife years ago, done his best with his daughter, and now he's ready to move on. Can McDermott help Dawn find a way past her former mistakes and down a path that leads to love, family, and happiness?

The Detective's Date: A Fuller Family Novel - Brush Creek Brides Romance (Book 4): Dahlia Reid is one of the best detectives Brush Creek and the surrounding towns has ever had. She's given up on the idea of marriage—and pleasing her mother—and has dedicated herself fully to her job. Which is great, since one of the most perplexing cases of her career

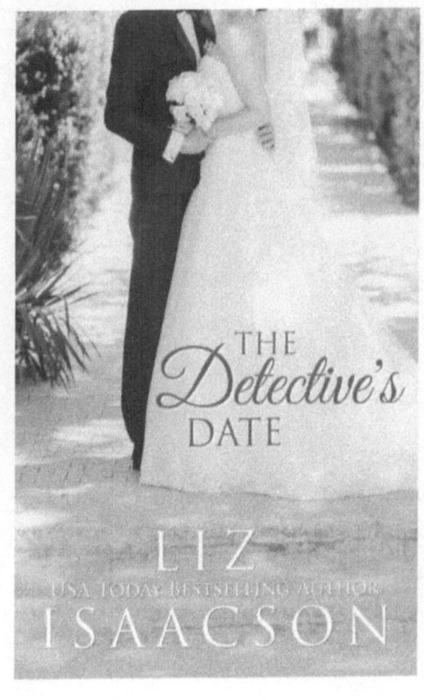

has come to town. Kyler Fuller thinks he's finally ready to move past the woman who ghosted him years ago. He's cut his hair, and he's ready to start dating. Too bad every woman he's been out with is about as interesting as a lamppost—until Dahlia. He finds her beautiful, her quick wit a breath of fresh air, and her intelligence sexy. Can Kyler and Dahlia use their faith to find a way through the obstacles threatening to keep them apart?

The Paramedic's Partner: A Fuller Family Novel - Brush Creek Brides Romance (Book 5): Jazzy Fuller has always been overshadowed by her prettier, more popular twin, Fabiana. Fabi meets paramedic Max Robinson at the park and sets a date with him only to come down with the flu. So she convinces Jazzy to cut her hair and take her place on the date. And the spark between Jazzy and Max is hot and instant...if only he knew she wasn't her sister, Fabi.

Max drives the ambulance for the town of Brush Creek with is partner Ed Moon, and neither of them have been all that lucky in love. Until Max suggests to who he thinks is Fabi that they should double with Ed and Jazzy. They do, and Fabi is smitten with the steady, strong Ed Moon. As each twin falls further and further in love with their respective paramedic, it becomes obvious they'll need to come clean about the switcheroo sooner rather than later...or risk losing their hearts.

The Chief's Catch: A Fuller Family Novel - Brush Creek Brides Romance (Book 6): Berlin Fuller has struck out with the dating scene in Brush Creek more times than she cares to admit. When she makes a deal with her friends that they can choose the next man she goes out with, she didn't dream they'd pick surly Cole Fairbanks, the new Chief of Police.

His friends call him the Beast and challenge him to complete ten dates that summer or give up his bonus check. When Berlin approaches him, stuttering about the deal with her friends and claiming they don't actually have to go out, he's intrigued. As the summer passes, Cole finds himself burning both ends of the candle to keep up with his job and his new relationship. When he unleashes the Beast one time too many, Berlin will have to decide if she can tame him or if she should walk away.

About Liz

Liz Isaacson writes inspirational romance, usually set in Texas, or Montana, or anywhere else horses and cowboys exist. She lives in Utah, where she writes full-time, drives her daughter to her acting classes, and eats a lot of peanut butter M&Ms while writing. Find her on her website at lizisaacson.com.